CW01573337

Death in The Slushpile

Blake Detective Series, Volume 5

Jon Mason

Published by Jon Mason, 2024.

This is a work of fiction. Similarities to real people, plac
are entirely coincidental.

DEATH IN THE SLUSHPILE

First edition. September 1, 2024.

Copyright © 2024 Jon Mason.

ISBN: 978-1916757110

Written by Jon Mason.

Table of Contents

Death in the Slushpile | Blake | One....1
Two....4
Three....10
Green | Four....15
Five....21
Blake | Six....25
Seven....27
Green | Eight....34
Nine....46
Ten....48
Eleven....56
Twelve....64
Blake | Thirteen....71
Green | Fourteen....77
Blake | Fifteen....89
Green / Blake | Sixteen....93
Seventeen....97
Eighteen....103
Nineteen....105
Twenty....108
Twenty One....110
Twenty-Two....113
Beck | Twenty-Three....116
Twenty-Four....119
Twenty-Five....123
Twenty-Six....136
Blake | Twenty-Seven....138
Green | Twenty-Eight....142
Blake | Twenty-Nine....148
Thirty....152
Thirty-One....159

Green | Thirty-Two 160
Blake | Thirty-Three 162
Green/Beck | Thirty-Four 165
Thirty-Five 168
Thirty-Six 180
Blake | Thirty-Seven 182
Green | Thirty-Eight 188
Thirty Nine 194
Forty 197
Forty-One 202
Forty-Two 209
Blake | Forty-Three 211
Beck | Forty-Four 214
Forty-Five 221
Forty-Six 225
Forty-Seven 227
Blake | Forty-Eight 229
Forty-Nine 230
Beck/Blake | Fifty 236
Blake | Fifty-One 237
Beck | Fifty-Two 248
Fifty-Three 253
Fifty-Four 261
Blake | Fifty-Five 269
Beck | Fifty-Six 271
Blake | Fifty-Seven 278
Beck | Fifty-Eight 282
Blake | Fifty-Nine 288
Beck/Blake | Sixty 290
Sixty-One 293
Sixty-Two 319
Sixty-Three 323
Sixty-Four 326

Also by Jon Mason

Blake Detective Series
Dance With the Devil
The Blooding of Brian Blake
Nemesis
Counting The Dead
Death in The Slushpile

Watch for more at www.jonmasonbooks.com.

Sixty-Five 327
Beck | Sixty-Six 344
Blake | Sixty-Seven 348
Sixty-Eight 352
Sixty-Nine 355
Seventy 359
Seventy-One 364
Bibliography 366

To my mother who instilled in me her love of literature

Death in the Slushpile

Blake

One

It was good to start the day with a murder. It concentrated the mind.

A quick glance at the map. Next left would take me down to the river. The recently commissioned Emley Moor TV mast replacing the one that collapsed, on the horizon. Wainhouse Tower to the right.

The track was badly rutted; no doubt by the demolition crew's equipment. The gearbox protested as I dropped into second. This bucket of a Mk1 Cortina was ready for the knacker's yard. As I rounded the bend the mill came into view. Bleak and depressing. A horrible place to die. Ignition off I peered out at the rain. It was like sitting inside a kettledrum with transparent sides. Raincoat collar up. 'Why is it always bloody raining?' I muttered as I picked my way through the debris, not wanting to slip and twist an ankle. The sooner this eyesore was down the better. Until then there was work to be done.

Twenty yards ahead, Sergeant Joshua Maston, nearly got his time in. Five ten. Overweight. World-weary. If this was as bad as I'd been told Maston would be glad to be out of the way. John Carter, early turn for 6 beat, was on the door. 'Morning Brian,' he grinned. 'You're bright and early.'

I wrinkled my nose. 'Yeah. Got the early call. Should've been on at ten. Just getting ready to take the wife to her mother's for some shopping.'

'Sounds like rescuing the perishing to me,' quipped Maston.

I laughed. 'Who found the body, Sarge?'

'Old Joe, Joe Carver. Night-watchman,' he pointed out the elderly male sprawled in an armchair in the building's foyer. 'Says it wasn't there when he checked earlier. He's pissed. Stinks of whisky. A half-bottle of the Co-op's finest in his pocket. Or what's left. I'll lay odds he didn't buy it.'

Joe Carver was a regular. Didn't stop drinking 'til he fell over. Probably wouldn't remember a thing when he sobered up. 'I'll have a chat later. Who's been in?'

'Just the three. Me, Carter and Joe.'

I nodded. 'Fine. As soon as the others start to arrive will you put someone up where my car is. Last thing we need are rubberneckers and the Press tramping all over the shop. And keep a record of who they are and the time. No warrant card. No entry.'

Maston turned to the unfortunate PC. 'Got that?'

Carter looked out at the rain, grimaced and nodded. 'Yes, Sarge.'

Satisfied that was under control. 'Which room?' I said.

'That one,' Maston hung back pointing at the door in front. 'You don't mind if ...?'

He didn't want to go in. It *was* bad. I smiled. 'No, that's all right, Sarge.'

Two

They referred to it as a room. A void would have been more accurate. Almost a hundred yards long by fifty wide. A fifteen-foot ceiling. High in the far wall a half dozen dead industrial extractor fans, blades like mechanical ghosts rotating silently in the wind. In the far right-hand corner double push-bar fire doors. By the right wall a semi-collapsed guard-rail to protect the unwary from stepping into oblivion. A dead Victorian weaving shed, devoid of all machines, furniture or almost anything else for that matter. A pair of sack wheels adjacent to the window on the left. Although it was pouring down outside there were no footprints anywhere near the body. Thirty yards away the object of my attendance. Time for objectivity not emotion: Male. Naked. Tall. Powerful. Sitting upright, taped into a Windsor armchair.

No sign of shoes, clothing or personal effects. Duct tape pinioning wrists and elbows to the arm rests. Legs over the wrists and taped, exposing where his genitals should have been. Ankles and torso taped. Tape round the head covering the eyes. No visible head wounds. Reddening and what appeared to be a puncture wound in the right deltoid. Tape dangling from his right cheek. Between his legs was a bloody mess. The blood had overflowed from the seat into a congealing pool around the chair legs. *Just how long ago had this happened?* A series of small cuts in his right forearm. Four had been bleeding. The higher up the forearm the less blood. The fifth just plasma. *A test for heart death*? *Somewhat excessive*. A stab wound between the ninth and tenth ribs. Left of the victim's sternum. A trickle of blood. A *coup de grace*? *Overkill?* Someone had taken their time.

The door behind me opened. Footsteps echoing. If they'd gotten passed Maston I didn't need to look. 'Stand where you are, please.' My voice rang round the empty space. The footsteps stopped. The *pièce de résistance,* the missing penis and testicles were sown neatly into his mouth resting across his chin. Blood had dripped down his chest. That was a sickener. The question was - prior to heart death or not? One for the pathologist. My guess was prior. This was personal. More to the point it was the second identical killing in the last ten days. I took a further minute to crouch and scrutinise the floor immediately surrounding the chair and check his feet. They were clean. His hands indicated he was not a manual worker.

I stood and turned to find DS Creighton, Inspector Nicholson, formerly a sergeant on the Wainwright team, and Detective Inspector Tristram Priestly, my new boss. Noted for being abrupt. Observing. 'Good morning, sir,' I said to DS Creighton. 'Sorry ...'

He looked grim. 'Don't apologise, Blake,' he said. 'Your observations?'

I nodded. 'The night watchman claims that the body wasn't here when he did his rounds earlier. He's pissed. Probably hasn't a clue when he did check before finding the body just after seven.'

'I've already spoken with him,' said DS Creighton. 'I agree. At the moment he doesn't know what day it is. An in-depth interview will have to wait. Carry on.'

I nodded. 'Sir. Whoever did this the planning was meticulous. They took their time. The victim was alive when he arrived. It was dry. Other than mine there is no trace of any footprints, muddy or otherwise. His feet are clean. He is over six feet tall and well-muscled. What looks like a puncture wound in his right deltoid. Perhaps injected with something to incapacitate him. Otherwise, why not fight back before he was taped into the chair? Did he undress voluntarily? If so, why? Where are his clothes and possessions? It doesn't appear likely it was a tryst gone wrong. And the stab wound. Finally, where did the chair and the sack-wheels come from?

I waited for a few seconds. There were no comments. 'I understand this is remarkably similar to the earlier murder: The chair. Naked. Eyes taped. Perhaps a couple of years older than me. The manner in which he's been trussed. The mutilation. The stitching of his genitals is neat; almost as if they were taking pride in what they were doing. Almost ritualised. Stitching through flesh is quite difficult. But one thing I didn't notice on the first report was anything like these,' I pointed out the cuts on the forearm. They stepped forward to look. 'There are five. Four showing that they had been bleeding and just one which hadn't .. And what's the link between the two victims.'

The ensuing silence was broken by Detective Inspector Priestly. 'The link, Blake,' he said with emphasis, 'They were murdered by the same person or persons. I'd heard you were big on ideas. I have to say that some of yours are exotic if not quixotic. To be appointed to CID with two and a half years' service is remarkable. Your report and exam result from your CID course were impressive. But you will find that the work of the detective is hard. Nose to the grindstone. Not acting on exotic hunches. You've a great deal to learn. Leave the planning and analysis to those with the experience, understood?'

He wasn't having a go at me *per se*, just letting me know in front of the area detective superintendent that the freedom I had under Mr Valentine's tutelage was ended.

Graeme Valentine, now Superintendent at Holmfirth, had been a detective constable, my father's friend and subordinate in March 1950. Present when my father had been murdered. He was unable to prevent the knife attack but arrested the assailant, cradling my father's head, watching his eyes as the light faded. He had been the divisional DCI when Sergeant McGill and I unearthed Sally Dunster's body in March 1964. The start of the Wainwright case (*Counting the Dead*) and had seconded me to the team. I owed him a great deal.

I was now under Detective Inspector Priestley's supervision. That question had never been in doubt. What could I say? 'Yes sir. I understand.' Inspector Nicholson was gazing round the room and the Superintendent holding back a smile.

'I'm sure Blake will have taken your words to heart, Mr Priestly. However, I think some of his observations have merit. We can discuss those along with everything else later.' The Superintendent turned to Inspector Nicholson. 'Will you ensure that we don't have anyone gathering outside. And have a search made for extraneous tyre tracks and footprints, always assuming this rain hasn't washed them out. We'll have a full search made in due course. Contractors are to be kept out of the way. The only people in this room are the pathologist, forensic and the photographer.'

He acknowledged and left.

'Blake, you will supervise here. Ensure the photographer doesn't make excuses and leave early.' I nodded. I knew what he meant. Some of the photographers were apt to be squeamish. 'Once the pathologist and forensic have completed you will accompany the body to the mortuary. Complete the sudden death report then liaise with the coroner's officer. You will attend the postmortem.'

I acknowledged and stood back whilst DS Creighton and DI Priestly carried out their own examination and left.

They hadn't been gone five minutes when the photographer arrived, traipsing mud and dripping water. He took one look at the victim. 'Bloody hell, I'll bet that hurt,' he said and laughed. 'You're DC Blake?'

I nodded. There would be no trouble with this one.

'John Dixon. Right, what do you want?'

I walked him round the scene. Pointed out the salient shots and stood back. It amazed me that with all the improvements in camera technology the police insisted on still using the old cameras complete with plates. I asked him. Why?

'Fair question,' he replied. 'But no matter what they've got on the market at the moment you can't get the definition when you blow them up. In a case like this you never know what the investigating officer will want enlarging. Or indeed, the Defence. If we produce an image that isn't pin-sharp it may throw the entire case. An open goal for the defence.'

I couldn't argue with that. He was good. Within twenty minutes he was gone.

Three

08:30. Detective Inspector Priestly returned accompanied by the pathologist. Professor Snodgrass stood inside the doorway taking in the scene, including me. 'We've met before,' His voice deep and sonorous. He held his hand up as I was about to answer. 'No, don't tell me ... Blake,' he said at length. 'You're in the CID now?' I agreed. 'Good. It was a young woman ... Sally Dunster.' I agreed again. He nodded smiled and indicated the victim. 'Tell me what you see.'

I went through my little presentation again. Professor Snodgrass looked on and nodded. 'How old do you think he is?' he said.

'A bit difficult with his eyes being taped. As a rough guess I would suggest late twenties.'

He didn't comment. 'And what do you make of these?' He indicated the cuts on the victim's right forearm.

Thanks Professor. 'Not sure.'

'Guess,' he said. 'Something you can do. But I can't.'

'My gut reaction was a cardiac countdown.'

'If it stops bleeding, he's dead?' said the detective inspector.

'Yes, sir.'

'But Professor,' said the detective inspector. 'Wouldn't that be obvious from the chest wound and the blood loss?'

He threw it straight back at me. 'It's a novel suggestion. Want to try and answer it?'

I took that as a compliment. Although how the inspector would react, I didn't know. 'Sir, you can't get muscular development like the victim has without a strong heart. So, unless something had been administered that affects the heart rate he would have a natural fight-flight response. Including rapid heart rate. The murderer wouldn't have objected to being seen because the victim would be dead. But taping the eyes and I suggest from that tape adhering to his cheek which appears to have been over his mouth, the victim is in isolation. He can hear but not see and probably can't speak or shout. We'll probably never know what was said, if anything, but at some point, the murderer grabs him by the genitals, pulls, slices him off, lock, stock and barrel.'

I was on the end of a pointed look from the inspector. 'Blake, are you qualified to make these comments about the heart etc?'

'Yes sir. My degree is in exercise physiology and anatomy; sports science.'

Another look followed by a grudging. 'Very well, carry on.'

'The loss of blood would be exacerbated by a corresponding increase in heart rate. The effect of gravity would continue to draw down blood from below the heart.

The cuts to the forearm would stop bleeding when the heart stopped. The chest wound would guarantee death. However, it might have been postmortem.'

'But that's ...' We never found out what the DI was about to say. He went pale. His eyes rolled as he slumped against me. I lowered him to the floor, slackened his tie and undid his top shirt button. There was a rapid carotid pulse. A film of sweat on his forehead.

The Professor checked the DI's pulse against his watch. 'You can never tell who will be affected,' he said. 'Even experienced detectives. I think he's just fainted. Leave him here, he can't fall any further. Check on him in a minute or so.'

'Can you give me an idea when death occurred, Professor?'

'Rigor isn't established yet,' he said moving the victim's hands and feet. 'Within the last six hours. I'll try to be more accurate after I've carried out the PM.'

I glanced at my watch. A mortified DI came round a few seconds later. 'You went a little dizzy, sir,' I said as I helped him to his feet.

'Anybody come in?' He looked embarrassed.

'No one, sir.'

He nodded. 'Thanks.'

'Has this ever happened before, Mr Priestly?' the Professor sounded concerned.

'Never.'

'Well, it's probably nothing. Just one of those things. However, my advice would be to have a quiet word with your GP. Tell him who sent you, if you like,' he added with a touch of black humour. 'Better safe than sorry.' The inspector nodded. We watched as he fastened his shirt, straightened his tie and went for a walk around the void.

'One thing Professor. How soon can I remove our victim from his prison?'

He bit his lip. 'Forensic are en route?'

'Yes, Professor.'

'Be guided by what they say.' I nodded. 'As soon as possible, the poor man's suffered enough. At least we can give him a degree of dignity.' I nodded again. 'You're providing continuity for the body?'

'I am, Professor.'

'Very well. I will do the PM at LGI, ten a.m. tomorrow.' He had a quiet word with the inspector and they left together. He didn't look well.

Two minutes later Inspector Nicholson returned with one Dr Jack Hawkins forensic biologist. I greeted him with a grin. 'Hi Jack, how's tricks?'

He returned my grin. 'As I live and breathe, Detective Constable Blake. I haven't seen you for what? All of six months. Since the Wainwright trial. People will be starting to talk.' We shook hands. 'I heard about your appendix. That was tough luck.' I had to agree. Since my attachment to the Forensic Science Lab two years before, we had dogged each other's footsteps albeit in a friendly manner.

He turned to the inspector. 'Mr Nicholson, every time Brian and I meet there are multiple bodies. Can't you do something with him. Like, have him transferred?'

'Sorry Doc,' he replied with as serious a face as he could manage. 'He's much too valuable.'

'Ah well, it was worth a try,' he smiled and winked before turning to the victim. 'Poor bastard,' I heard him mutter. 'Whose wife have you been screwing?' A couple of minutes later he removed two large sheets of plastic from his kit and opened them side-by-side behind the victim. He gave us a pair of surgical gloves each. Between us, avoiding the blood, we carried the chair and contents placing it on the left-hand sheet. Tape severed we lifted the occupant from his prison and laid him on the second sheet as the undertakers arrived.

The chair, securely wrapped in plastic, had already left for the Forensic Science Lab at Harrogate. I was to follow the body to the LGI mortuary when Jack stopped me to confirm details of the PM. We would meet again in the morning.

I had a quick chat with Inspector Nicholson, principally concerning Detective Inspector Priestly. He was overseeing the search of the demolition site.

Safely deposited at LGI I left our victim in the hands of the Coroner's Officer.

Green

Four

Lewis Green's mind was occupied with the initial negotiations between Global Films and his agents, Friedricksons, re Marchant's latest best seller, *The Unsilent Grave.* Yanked out of his reverie by that demanding demonic tool of communication, answered by Margaret, Margaret Kelly, his resident major-domo without whom the office would disappear beneath a tsunami of paper.

'Knock, knock.' Margaret bumped the half-open door with her ample backside, early mail in one hand his coffee in the other. 'Lewis, that call was from Joan. She's had a puncture, waiting for the AA. And the answer to your next question is,' she smiled. 'How long is a piece of string?'

'Thanks, Margaret,' he replied. Joan Grey, secretary, fiancée and none-live-in-lover. Over the moon when he proposed but now would neither name the day nor move in. And they say that men won't make a commitment. Since Carol - the woman with the most beautiful blue eyes. The French couture. The woman who had not been wearing her wedding ring when they first met and, had given him the *small gift* of a Rolex. There had been no other woman with whom he had formed an attachment, lasting or otherwise; except Joan.

'Anything special?' he glanced at the watch. Its dedication impressed on his brain:

I will always remember

C.

He could *never* forget.

Had it not been for the promise ...

'Just the one,' she said as she dropped the mail in his in-tray. 'It's on top.'

The stack of identical large envelopes drew a sigh. They meant only one thing. Today's consignment of unsolicited query letters, manuscripts and synopses from would-be authors. All of them hopeful. Some of them deluded. Most destined for disappointment. There was a saying that everyone had a book inside them. He had his doubts. Many of them should never have seen the light of day. If he had £5 for every submission that crossed his desk that promised: Would be the next million best seller. Would make him rich. Was better science fiction than Wyndham and Heinlein. More competent than Hemingway or Steinbeck. Made Tolkien look stupid. Better thrillers than Christie or Fleming, he would be wealthy indeed. No! No, you can't trash internationally acclaimed authors and expect to be welcomed with open arms. However, life as a literary agent was not to break dreams but to sift and riddle the alluvium of the Slushpile, seeking those rare nuggets. You never knew. The question was: Would today be different? Nevertheless, no matter how fretful the senders were waiting for the reply they would go to the bottom of the pile. He was also under contract to Finsbury Templeton Books to deal with submissions sent directly to them, and, like it or not they came first. Personal submissions had their own special place – The Slushpile.

Margaret's *special* he saved until last. He drained the cup of now cold coffee.

A single tri-fold sheet of cream wove. A single line of italic text across the centre:

Be sure your sins have found you out!

In most cases it might have been a simple prank. Innocuous. Not in this case. The same bitter taste from the early hours of that fateful day never far below the surface. The memories awoke. The note almost slipped from his fingers.

He was the second child of third generation wine importers of Bristol: Clive and Patricia Beck. His given name was Martin. But for his sins he had changed his name to *Lewis Green*. He could never forget why. Over the past seven years he had kept a wary eye over his shoulder. Was fate playing tricks? Snapping at his heels? He had been interviewed by the police and eliminated from their list of potential suspects. In fact, they all had. Was his imagination going into overdrive? Or something else?

The envelope was plain, white, standard business type, no identifier. Frank smudged but just visible was NW3 and dated yesterday. PRIVATE AND CONFIDENTIAL typed in the top left-hand corner. The address:

Lewis Green Esq
Lewis Green Literary Agency
17 Marble House
Fellows Drive
London NW3

He asked Margaret if anything similar had arrived in the past, although she would have told him if there had. He gave her instructions: anything similarly addressed in the future was to be handed to him. The last thing that he wanted was for Joan to find it and start asking questions.

The meeting came and went. A positive result. They would meet again in two weeks.

Seven days later. The envelope identical to the last. Posted yesterday in NW3. PRIVATE AND CONFIDENTIAL in the top left-hand corner. A single tri-fold sheet of cream wove. A single line of italic text across the centre:

Two down three to go!

Like a full-blooded thump in the gut. Everything came flooding back. That bitter taste. No doubt that was what was intended. Just what could: *Two down three to go,* mean? Traced? Handed to the police? Murdered? But there had been nothing in the press with all that it implied.

The thoughts stampeded through his brain. *Wait a minute. Get a grip, it's probably nothing to do with what happened in Leeds.*

He had a quiet word with Margaret. Nothing to worry about. Some sick joker.

All thoughts of the two unwelcome notes were locked in the top left-hand drawer of the bureau in his apartment. Friday morning, he worked on the Slushpile in his apartment. There would be more work for Joan to deal with when she returned from her latest jaunt; visiting her mother in Huddersfield. Send out their apologetic *not for us* letters. But sometimes there was a glimpse of that bright shining something that made it all worthwhile. And it might just be the next manuscript. A quick glance at the title in the covering letter didn't look too promising: *Where My Bones Lie.* However, the typed letter was a welcome change. It looked professional. He leant back in his antiquated but very comfortable swivel chair, feet on the stool:

17 Seven Oaks Fold
Sharp Lane
Almondbury
Huddersfield
West Riding of Yorkshire

No telephone number. And the address - Sharp Lane? How far is that from Dark Lane? Joan's parents live there, it can't be that far.

Lewis Green Esq

Lewis Green Literary Agency

47 Marble House

Fellows Drive

London NW3

15th March 1966

Dear Mr Green

Please excuse my unsolicited approach. I am seeking representation for my debut novel, Where My Bones Lie. A 120,000 word police procedural. A crime thriller set in the West Riding of Yorkshire. I am writing to you because I have been a fan of Douglas Marchant's work for several years. Marchant's writing style in particular has been an inspiration to me. I see my writing in the same vein.

Marchant's good, excellent writing style, doing very well. Where My Bones Lie? A bit odd, he thought, talking about their own body. However. And 120,000 words a bit long for a debut – should be able to trim 20 or 30,000 off that.

The story opens with five noisy, happy, well-heeled rugby-playing undergraduates being refused entry to the Mecca Locarno Ballroom situated in the County Arcade in Leeds City Centre. They collect half a dozen girls and go back to the house they rent for a party. Eventually, five of the girls leave. The sixth, still naked, passes out on a bed. The boys take their pleasure. The girl comes to and is suffocated when she begins to protest. The body is disposed of and has never been recovered. Police enquiries come to naught.

He thought his heart had stopped. Christ! It's not possible. Another one! This can't be chance. The scream heading rapidly for his vocal cords choked. No! Grasping the bundle his hands hovered over the waste bin, but something compelled him to continue.

However, this is not the heart of the story, and you may think this is too close to home, but one of the murderers changes his name by deed poll. On leaving university with a degree in English Literature he secures a position with a major publishing house, later becoming a literary agent. About the same time the murdered girl's friend unearths some information and begins to track the murderers down and kill them in the most brutal manner.

For Christ's sake I changed my bloody name from Martin Beck to Lewis Green to avoid this. I live at the other end of the country. What the Hell is going on? His hands shook like Aspen leaves in a storm. Rivulets of sweat trickled down his forehead into his eyes

I'm a thirty something investigative journalist, who after many years of promising, has finally put pen to paper and begun to write fiction, based on true crime. When working I do write under a nom de plume. I hope that my material is of interest, and I look forward to hearing from you.

Yours Truly
Granville Rodahl

Five

He poured himself a generous measure of Glen Morangie. Downed it in one. Settle the nausea. Gritted his teeth, shuddered and put the letter and manuscript on the bureau. He dialled Directory Enquiries. 'It's a Huddersfield number,' he said. 'The name is Rodahl, R-O-D-A-H-L, Granville Rodahl. Sorry, I don't know the address.'

It was a long moment. The second-hand froze. 'Sorry, caller. There is no Granville Rodahl listed in the Huddersfield area.'

'Any Rodahl?'

'Sorry, no. Would there be anything else?'

He looked out of his apartment window as he replaced the handset.

Time stood still. Staring down at the world beneath wondering if it could be a coincidence. The answer, a firm No. He took his keys from his trouser pocket and unlocked the top left-hand drawer in the bureau. The only drawer to which Joan did not have access. The blue manilla folder was at the bottom. Inside, the two typed notes glider-clipped to their envelopes. Both envelopes bearing NW3 franks, addressed to him at the office. Both marked private and confidential. Neither dated. The top one franked ten days ago:

Be sure your sins have found you out

The second, three days ago:

Two down three to go!

Now the manuscript. What exactly did it all mean? Don't be stupid. You know exactly what it means. Someone has talked. He poured a second helping of Glen Morangie and sat.

Jeremy worked for Reuters. Had his finger on the national pulse. 'Jeremy!' He cried. 'What's happening in this world that you can't tell me about? Do tell.'

'Fishing again?' he laughed. 'Trying to find plots for your worked-out clients.'

'Not really.' He tried to keep the tremor out of his voice. 'Just a trifle bored.'

'Hmm, there's the usual havoc and mayhem in London and the Home Counties. Up in the West Riding the police are in a bit of a sweat over a murder. Very cagey.'

Green's stomach twisted itself into a knot, his heart pounding. 'Any details?'

'They're very tight lipped. All we know is from the press release. No conference. Which is not like them.'

'I'm intrigued.' A hasty mouthful of scotch spilled down his chin.

'Aren't we all.'

Green broke out in a cold sweat, his shaking hand sending concentric ripples across the glass.

Jeremy continued. 'Twenty-six year-old lecturer in modern languages at York. Married with a twelve-month old son. Father, professor of history, mother, three sisters – all younger. Played in the pack for the varsity: second row. Goes by the name of ... just a sec ..'

His mind in turmoil the thoughts flashed through his brain. *Goes by the name of Bill Boxley. Nicknamed, Molière, because of his love of French literature. Christ*!

'Name of William Boxley, aka 'Bill'.'

It had become all too real. 'Is that all?'

The reply was terse. 'Don't sound so bloody disappointed, Lewis,' he said. 'The poor sod is dead.'

He couldn't prevent the stammer. 'S-Sorry, 'I-I didn't mean to. But it doesn't appear to warrant any reason why the police would be silent on the matter.'

Jeremy didn't pick up on the stammer. 'No, I agree, it doesn't. There's a whisper that it was a ritual killing. The body was mutilated. But they won't release any details.'

He caught sight of himself in the mirror. As pale as the proverbial. 'Christ. That sounds gruesome.'

'Hmm. He was an alumnus from Leeds. You went there if I remember correctly.'

Emotions once more under control. 'True,' he said. 'And I played rugger. But the name Boxley doesn't mean anything, sorry.' His lie was glib.

'Pity,' Jeremy said. 'Still, you can't have everything. Now, that's the end of the briefing. I've got work to do, Lewis, even if you haven't. Let's meet for a drink. Can you manage next Wednesday, usual place, say, one o'clock?'

Regular order placed with his newsagent for the northern edition of the Yorkshire Post he called Max Crawshaw: a retired detective from the West Riding: his latest client. 'Max? Lewis Green. How goes it?'

A delighted Max Crawshaw beamed at the phone. 'Very well, thank you, and for the call. It means a lot. I'd had so many refusals before you I was beginning to think I was wasting my time.'

'Not at all. Refusals are par for the course. But you already know that. How long do you think it will be before you're in a position to re-submit?'

'About another week, Lewis. Your comments hurt a bit, but it doesn't change the essentials, and it reads better

'That's excellent. Oh, before I go you might be able to shed a little light on something that I've heard about a murder in Yorkshire.'

'I'll try. But remember, Lewis, I'm no longer in the club.'

'I will. Apparently, it was someone who used to go to Leeds University at the same time as I did. Called him Box, Boxer or something like that. And the police aren't giving anything away.'

The reply was immediate. 'It's Boxley.'

'That's the name!' His tongue clove to the roof of his mouth. His throat dry as dust. He took a drink. 'There was a suggestion it might be a ritual killing because the body was mutilated.'

The laughter percolated the two hundred miles from Yorkshire. 'Whenever the police are tight-lipped, or to use police parlance, as tight as a duck's arse, rumours proliferate. Stories get made up simply because people want to believe the worst that their imagination can produce. To be honest, Lewis, I can't help because I don't know. I don't believe that guessing does any good.'

'No, you're probably right, Max Thanks. I look forward to your re-submission.' Phone down. Glass emptied. He put the kettle on. It was too early in the day. He attempted to rationalise his thoughts. In the end they were too nebulous to be threaded together and fit his scenario. There must be, had to be, some sort of rational explanation, even if it wasn't obvious. Annoying and unwelcome it might be but not a threat. He returned the documents to the folder and locked the drawer. For now, they could wait. He had to get to Almondbury. Joan's railway timetable on the pinboard. He had thirty-five minutes to get to Kings Cross. It would be tight.

Blake

Six

DI Priestly, given the choice, would not have been at the mortuary. Never a lover of murder cases or the sight of murder victims. This was one case where he could not designate. It was in his career interests to get on with it.

Blake watched the DI out of-his eye corner. He didn't look well. Yesterday's incident appeared to have had a lasting deleterious effect on him.

On the slab the body had been washed. Approximately six feet three inches tall. Well-muscled. No abundance of body fat. The groin was a mess although the incision to remove his penis and testicles looked professional and not a series of cuts or slashes, as did the stitching. The penis with attendant testicles were removed from his mouth and placed in a dish. That was followed by the tape. Everything in separate evidence bags. I was right about his age, late twenties. He had been a handsome lad. There were a few scars, particularly around his eyes and ears, that reminded me of a rugby player. A punch biopsy taken from the right deltoid. The sample should identify any substance that might have been injected that was relevant.

The professor's assistant got busy with his circular saw. Once the photographer and I were out of the way he split the sternum. The thorax and abdomen were opened. It didn't smell too bad. The wound to the heart plain to see.

'I will have to see what the lab says about any substance used to subdue this man. However, I can tell you that the knife wound to the heart was the cause of death. Also, that the removal of his genitals and subsequent stitching was carried out by someone with the requisite training.'

Seven

There were a dozen officers present. Both crimes now being run as a single incident. Just like old times, except this time I really was a detective, not just a uniformed officer with acting status. I know it's irrational, but when I was appointed a DC, I visited my biological father's grave and told him. It was something I owed to his memory.

I'd already spoken with several officers that I knew and a few more who pumped me with questions concerning Wainwright. A large wall-mounted board covered by a cloth. Across the room WDC Liz 'Penny' Farthing. I caught her attention and waved. But the first person I collided with was DI Kenton from York, accompanied by DS Dixon. He asked to catch up later.

The door opened. ACC Mithering entered accompanied by Detective Superintendent Wallace and Hazel Granby. She had been the Office Manager on the Wainwright case. She must have impressed. The chatter died. 'Settle down,' Mr Mithering looked around. 'Has DI Cartwright arrived yet?'

'Just parking the car, sir,' came an anonymous reply.

He nodded. 'You all know why you're here. So, we'll cover a bit of Admin first. The lady on my left is Hazel Granby. She will be the office manager and handle all the admin. Any claims for expenses, overtime etc. will go through your sergeants and inspectors as normal then to Mrs Granby. Should DI Cartwright not be present she will be the conduit. A warning,' he paused and smiled. 'She takes fewer prisoners than I do.' No-one tried to take advantage of Hazel twice.

'WDC Liz Farthing, she won't mind if you call her, Penny,' she waved as the laughter rang round the room, 'is the Exhibits Officer. No matter what you think about female officers she is not here to make tea or listen to your sob-stories, so forget it. And make sure that any exhibits you submit are correctly labelled, it makes the job simpler. Right, we have two crime scenes some distance apart, however, both appear to have been committed in DS Creighton's area, so he is in overall charge of the enquiry. DIs Priestly and Firth will head up the individual teams. Anyone not know which team they're in?'

Silence. 'Good.' The door opened as DI Cartwright entered. 'Good, you're here. For those that don't know him this is DI Cartwright. He will be in day-to-day charge of the incident room until the job is done. DI Kenton and DS Dixon are from York. The first victim hails from York. The second victim we now know is from Keighley, hence Detective Superintendent Wallace's presence.

Now, there's been a lot of comment about the lack of information emanating from us with regard to the first case. When you see the photographs you will understand why. If I hear of any talk outside of this room in the presence of any other officer, or member of the public or Press, those responsible will no longer be a member of CID and, I will deal with them in the same manner as the murderer dealt with his victims. I hope you all understand ... Farthing?'

Penny stepped forward and removed the cover from the board.

There was total silence as the detail of the photographs was absorbed, followed by numerous imprecations, expletives not deleted. 'Thank you, gentlemen,' Mr Mithering interrupted. 'We all share your disgust. Channel your feelings into your professionalism. Mr Kenton?'

He stepped to the front. 'DI Kenton, York. Good morning,' he said. 'It's nice to see some familiar faces. Would it have been under more pleasant circumstances.' He pointed to the first photograph. 'William Boxley, twenty-six years of age, lecturer in modern languages at York university. Married with a twelve-month old son. Hails from Oxford where his father is a Professor of Medieval History. Mother is still alive and there are three younger sisters. He played rugby for the Leeds varsity. Six feet tall and weighed fourteen stones. Reported missing thirteen days ago when he did not return home from work. Found nine days ago in Batley as you see him. Estimate of death was four days earlier. So where was he kept for those missing days? According to forensic there is no evidence that he was refrigerated.'

DI Firth took up the presentation. 'Working with DI Kenton and his team we have been splitting the enquiries. Although there are several lines of enquiry still running, so far, we have made little progress. What I can tell you is that according to the pathologist the wound to the chest was, in this case, the fatal blow. Delivered several minutes after the genitals were removed. We are still awaiting the result from the forensic lab as to what substance, if any, was administered to incapacitate the victim. Has anyone any questions?'

There were none. DI Priestly swapped places with DI Firth. 'The second victim,' he pointed at the photograph. 'Patrick Newsome, also twenty-six years of age, six feet three inches tall, sixteen stones in weight. A single man. Reported missing two days ago and discovered at approximately seven a.m. yesterday. As you can see from the photographs apparently identical to the first. Hails from Keighley and is a physiologist at Queen Mary's Hospital, Bradford. Estimated time of death was six hours prior to his arrival, so, approximately two thirty that morning.' He turned to me. 'Did you contact the Met office, Blake?'

'Yes sir. They estimate that in that area the rain started between four and four fifteen a.m.'

DI Priestly nodded. 'There were no traces of muddy footprints anywhere near to the body so that gives us a probable window of two a.m. to four fifteen a.m. Are there any questions?'

I had one. 'Sir, both victims are of the same age. If Newsome is a physiologist he will have a degree. Do we know if the victims attended the same university?'

'No, we don't, Blake. Well volunteered,' he almost smiled. There was a fair amount of laughter.

I returned the smile. 'Yes sir.'

'Right, gentlemen,' DS Creighton put his piece in. 'Before you're allocated your assignments this is how it will work. No wandering. Do the enquiries but, if they lead you somewhere else ensure that you inform DI Cartwright. Get permission before you go swanning off. This is a complicated enquiry and hopefully our list of victims remains at two. We need to know where you are. Keep us informed. Woe betide anyone who ignores the advice. Mr Cartwright?'

Whilst DI Cartwright was dishing out the assignments: House-to-house. Outlets that might have sold the whisky drunk by Tom Carver. Companies that ran night shifts. Taxi companies etc. I took the opportunity to have a quick word with DI Kenton and DS Dixon.

Apart from passing on Superintendent Patrickson's best wishes and reiterating his offer of a transfer to York CID, what I really required was a contact at York university from whom I could make the necessary enquiries. Safely in my pocketbook I promised to have a longer chat as soon as practicable. Then I sought out Detective Superintendent Wallace as to who to contact at Keighley as to where Patrick Newsome gained his degree.

A memory from the Wainwright case popped into my mind. 'Excuse me, sir,' I said to DS Wallace. 'Could I have a quick word?'

'Of course,' he smiled. 'How are you liking CID?'

'Brilliant .. It's about the Wainwright case. Something I've just remembered from when we searched the storeroom at Keighley.'

'And?'

'It was a photo of a murder victim. A man naked from the waist down propped up against a door frame of a semi-derelict house. Someone had cut his penis off and stuck it in his mouth.'

'Just a photo?'

'Sorry, yes. There was some writing on the back but I can't remember what it was.'

'No trace of the associated file?'

'No sir. It might be nothing but, in the circumstances.'

He nodded. 'What did you do with the photo?'

'I think it was on a shelf to the right. Penny,' I pointed across the room. 'WDC Farthing was there, she might be able to remember something.'

'Unusual, though, all major files end up in HQ. But thanks. You get off.'

An hour later sandwiches and coffee consumed, a chat with Penny, and the answer to my question: Leeds. Both Boxley and Newsome were alumni from Leeds. I passed the details on to both DI Cartwright and DI Priestly and left for Leeds University along with Max Cavendish, another refugee from the Wainwright case. We worked, or should that be hunted, in pairs.

In the hour or so it took us to reach Leeds University we'd caught up on the last six months. Me with my appendicitis and him with an addition to his family. He now had two boys aged six and eight and, an infant daughter.

Parking at Leeds was at a premium. An unexpected encounter in the car park with my brother-in-law, Gerald Vernon BSc PhD, now senior lecturer in mechanical engineering solved the issue. He knew enough not to ask questions. Told us where to park and directed us to the right person.

Miss Priscilla Walshaw, who looked more like my Mum than she did but dressed ten years older, had worked at the university for thirty years. What she didn't know wasn't worth knowing, and she liked to conspire. It had been a long time since she had had two young men in suits all to herself. She was only too willing, when prompted by the right questions, to spill the beans. In return for which she received nothing new. A couple of phone calls saw us escorted to the cellar with instructions of where to look for the records for 1954 to 1957, where she assured us, we would find details of Bill Boxley.

There was a problem. An electrical fault in the cellar two days earlier. The resulting fire had burned overnight. Several years records had been damaged or destroyed. Bert, one of the college security officers took us down. The cellar was a mess. The wooden shelving was badly damaged. However, tightly packed cards are, for the most part, impervious to flame, it only burns the edges. To a certain extent also impervious to water, unfortunately a high-pressure hose had removed any semblance of filing order. The sodden cards were spread across the floor. How long it would take to sort them out was anyone's guess.

'Sorry gentlemen,' said Bert. 'This is it.'

A cursory glance was all that was necessary. 'Ok, Brian,' Max grinned. 'You know your way round universities, what's next?'

I returned the grin. 'All is not lost, Max They're the same age. Both here at the same time and both played rugby. We'll check the sports records and the Accommodation Office.'

Safely deposited at Reception by Bert, we began again. This time with the Year Book for 1953 and sport.

‘Boxley and Newsome, you say?’ The librarian frowned then smiled. ‘That rings a bell,’ she said. ‘Just a tick.’ Two minutes later she returned carrying a couple of red bound books. ‘Here we are,’ she flipped the top book open at a paper marker and spun the book round pointed to a half-page photograph of five young men in evening dress. The photograph entitled ‘*The Famous Five*’. From left to right: *Neville Waters, William Boxley, Martin Beck, Charles Nash, Patrick Newsome.*

‘A good-looking bunch, but Famous Five?’ I said.

She laughed. ‘I do remember them. Played for the varsity. I think four in the scrum and a three-quarter. Thick as thieves. You’ll have to check with Accommodation, but I think they shared a house in the city centre. At the back of my mind there was a spot of bother regarding a girl – that was Beck. And a change of name. But I might be wrong. You’ll have to check.’

‘The usual?’

‘No, they used to hold *parties*,’ she smiled as she emphasised the word. ‘Pick girls up and take them back to their pad. Free food, wine and, whatever. One girl disappeared, never seen again. I don’t know the details, but the police were involved.’

Ten minutes later Max called DI Cartwright stressing our need to get to Millgarth Street. The Station that covered Leeds City Centre. No problem provided we informed them of the urgency on arrival.

The file on the Millgarth DI’s desk related to an Emily Reid. Murder. Defendant - Kevin Sharpe. During interview he had admitted raping Reid but there was no complaint – criminals would often admit what they saw as lesser offences in the hope it would stave off a murder charge. Sometimes it worked. He had always denied involvement in Emily Reid’s disappearance. Although no body had been recovered, he was now serving life in Sheffield. Traces of Emily Reid’s blood had been found on the flick knife he carried.

Green

Eight

The train was moving when Lewis Green clambered on board and sank into his seat in First Class. Although he should have remembered, the exact date was a blur. Over the past seven years he'd put all his efforts into his career. His memories, formerly buried, now emblazoned across his pineal eye. Vivid. Crisp. Disconcerting. Some clocks should not be turned back.

Saturday. Early September, warm, dry and sunny. The Turncoat Bar, Leeds, was busy. People going out for a good time. They certainly were. Dressed to kill. Black tie from shoes to dicky-bow. The ritual continued. Facing each other '*Molière*' snapped his fingers once:

'We're-on-the-hunt, we're-on-the-hunt, we're-on-the-hunt, we're-on-the-hunt,' They chanted. 'We're-hunting-for-some ... girls.' Glasses raised. Drinks drained, they turned and bowed to the regulars, and to calls of *good hunting,* left. They would meet up in fifteen minutes at the Locarno in the County Arcade.

'Bard, have palms yet been crossed with silver?' was asked as they left the Turncoat.

'No Newton,' he replied. 'But we are expected. All is in hand.'

'Good grief,' Newton replied. 'It'll be a bad night if it is.' A raucous laugh. They went their separate ways.

The County Arcade beckoned. Even for a stranger it was difficult to miss. The weather had brought out the droves. Jump into the flow and be swept by the current.

Thirty yards in front a situation developing. One female reveller, not dressed as most of the others who wore their ever shorter mini-skirts: five six, honey-blonde, pageboy hair do, an elegant figure-hugging blue patterned dress, hem-line just above the knee. She was facing the Locarno door looking around as if seeking friends. What she couldn't see were half-a-dozen teddy-boys to her left. Whilst most of the youth were now wearing Beatle jackets and mop-tops, the teddy-boys stuck religiously to their drape jackets, brocade waistcoats, white shirts, drainpipes, brothel creepers and elephant's trunk. At their head, 'Sharpie', Kevin Sharpe, a five feet four inch weed, had spotted the female in question. He said something to his acolytes. They all laughed. Not noted for his subtlety Sharpie headed in the wrong direction.

The man Bard had come to see, the man with the union jack haircut, spotted him and nodded. He'd also spotted Sharpie but made no move to interfere; It wasn't his patch. That was the Locarno.

Slowed by the crush, Bard was still ten yards away when Sharpie parked himself in front of his intended conquest. 'That's a great dress, darlin',' he said looking her up and down. 'It'd look great on my bedroom floor.'

She glared at him in astonishment. 'Go away,' she said and continued looking for her friends. 'You're annoying.'

Never one to refuse a challenge Sharpie grinned and grabbed her left wrist. 'Why you snotty cow,' a few revellers stopped to watch. 'Come on, you're dancin' wiv me.'

The slap attracted several revellers. 'Get your hand off!' she demanded, trying to break the grip. Sharpie wouldn't like losing face; his left cheek was glowing.

Before he could react, Bard grabbed his wrist with his left hand. 'You've had your answer, Sharpie,' he said. 'Now, let go of the lady's wrist.'

His acolytes arrived. 'Bugger off,' he said. 'Get your own bint.'

'I said, let go.'

Things started to get silly. 'Shall we do 'im?' came a voice from the rear of the group. It wasn't unknown for these wallies to carry razors or styling combs with sharpened handles.

Sanity reigned with two voices from behind. 'What ho, Sharpie,' Molière's voice from my right. 'Annoying the ladies, again?

'Look ladies,' the voice came from on high; Leonardo was six three against his five ten. 'Sharpie's brought his garden gnomes out to play.' No doubt he'd got two girls, he usually had. The giggles confirmed it.

'Well?' Bard looked Sharpie in the eye. 'What's it to be?

Sharpie let go with a bad grace. 'Sod you,' he said. 'One of these days you won't 'ave these two behind you.'

'Nice to see you as well,' Bard replied turning to his right and looked straight into the most beautiful blue eyes that he had ever seen. She took his breath away. A vision in blue with a flawless complexion. Realising he was staring he swallowed, feeling himself blush. 'Are you all right?'

'Yes, thank you. I'm glad you were here,' she smiled. Her accent was indefinable. Cultured and definitely not Yorkshire.

Two equally smartly dressed ladies of a similar age hurried towards them: one brunette dressed in red and the other, black haired in lilac. 'We could see what was happening from over there,' one of them said, indicating with her head. 'Who on earth was that horrid little man?

The knot of bystanders dispersed. King Tut and Newton, the last pair, arrived on their lonesome. The manager with the union jack haircut, all smiles and *bon homi*, name *Jimmy* on the badge, came walking towards them. 'Now then guys and gals,' he said. 'What was all that about? People are out for a good time. Can't have trouble.'

'You're going to tell us we can't go in, aren't you?' said a downcast Bard.

'Sorry fellas, you know how it is. If I were to let you in and there was trouble between you it's my job on the line. I hope you understand.'

Bard nodded and held his hand out. As they shook hands he palmed him the pre-arranged fee - a couple of quid. Jimmy was about to lose the company several entrance fees. A couple of quid for his trouble was more than worth it. The rest was up to them.

The stream was just as busy as the ladies broke up their conversation. 'He won't let you in?' said our puzzled friend in blue. 'That seems unfair. It wasn't your fault.'

'It certainly wasn't yours,' Bard replied. 'I hope your evening's not been spoilt.'

'Well ... What will you do now?'

'We do have an alternative,' said Molière.

'And you're more than welcome to join us if you wish,' Bard continued. 'We five share a house just a five-minute walk from here. We have a dance floor and the latest records. Fine wine and something to eat. There won't be the crowds you'll find in the Locarno but there won't be any trouble.'

The vision in blue glanced at her friends. 'Can we discuss it amongst ourselves for a minute?'

'Of course, take your time.'

Three of them got into a huddle as Leonardo was whispering to his escorts eliciting fits of giggles. 'Excuse me,' said a tremulous voice. 'Can I come. Kevin Sharpe's in there. I don't want to see him.'

She was very pretty. Slightly built, blue eyed with mousy hair and wearing a short black dress. 'Of course you can, I'll be your escort,' said Molière. 'What's your name?'

'Emily, Emily Reid. What's yours?'

'Molière.'

'That's an odd name.'

'He was a French writer,' he answered with a smile. 'I just borrow the name from time to time.'

'Oh.' She didn't pursue the matter, just looked a little puzzled.

The three ladies concluded their confab. 'All right,' said Blue, smiling. 'No strings?'

'None whatsoever,' Bard replied.

'And your names?'

Bard took on the MC's role. 'This is Leo, Leonardo,' he indicated his six feet three inch friend. As usual feeding his prodigious appetite. Jenny was becoming a regular. She and her friend dressed to the nines. 'With Jenny and?'

'Ruth,' replied the other.

He turned to his right. 'This is Molière and Emily and, on my left are King Tut and Newton.'

'And you are?' she said.

'Bard.'

'Nicknames of famous people?'

'Famous, character driven and relevant.'

'Linked to your degrees?'

He nodded.

'And you're Bard, as in the Bard of Avon?'

'Not quite,' he said and smiled. 'Bard as in the grim archer.'

She thought for a moment. 'Tolkien?' she said. 'You're a toxophilite?'

'I couldn't hit a barn door at three feet,' he grinned in return. 'I just like Tolkien's writing. And what do we call you?'

Blue indicated herself: Clare, Grace in red and Christine in lilac.

He wasn't a betting man, but Bard knew his mother and sister both liked French couture. Clare, Grace and Christine graced their wardrobes. None of their new friends were wearing wedding rings although the signs were there. So!

The gentle rain was annoying. 'Coats gentlemen,' was the call from Newton as he draped his jacket around Grace's shoulders.

Staying close to the building line either side of The Headrow they avoided the worst taking temporary shelter beneath the Grand Theatre canopy. Crossing New Briggate turning left into Merrion Street, seconds later right, along the ginnel that led to Merrion Lodge. Built around 1870 in a sort of subdued Palladian style. It was impressive. The house hadn't been officially occupied since 1947 when it had been used by some element of the security services. Since then, it had had a few temporary residents but now scheduled to be demolished; its new owner a property developer friend of Leo's father. Patched up they had been caretakers for two years; rent free. The grandeur long gone. No artwork on the walls. However, the plasterwork on the ceiling was as sumptuous as ever, if a little grubby. It was clean and tidy. The roof was sound. The gas, electricity and plumbing were safe.

The visit producing several 'Wows'.

'Sorry about the garden, ladies,' said Newton. 'The gardener has taken the weekend off.' It was a cross between a hay meadow and a jungle.

'What's it like inside?' said Ruth.

'Come in and have a look.'

With skill borne of practice they had the fire blazing, furniture moved and the music playing in less than three minutes, followed by the wine trolley – five bottles of a 14.5% Californian red from an estate in the Nappa Valley, a dozen wine glasses and a similar number of half-pint beer glasses for the recently released Watney's Party Seven. Everyone had their drink of choice and advised of the potency of the wine. Clare picked up the nearest bottle and they scrutinized the labels. Grace mouthed, 'fourteen and a half percent!' to Clare and looked at Bard who grinned and nodded.

After a couple of dances Bard picked up his and Clare's glasses. 'Follow me,' he said and headed for the corner of the room.

'Where are we going?' said Clare. No-one bothered. They were either dancing or smooching.

Bard introduced her to the kitchen. 'I'm the duty cook, tonight.'

'Ah,' she said. 'I did wonder. And bacon sandwiches. I haven't had one of those in years.'

She really was beautiful, standing just inside the kitchen door, arms folded and wine glass in her right hand.

'Worried?'

'Just wondering,' she replied and smiled. There was no apprehension. 'And, if I said, no, bearing in mind that the door is locked.'

'The key is in the lock,' Bard replied. 'All we ask is that should anyone leave, lock the door and post the key through the letterbox.'

She nodded.

'Although I suggest that you wait for Grace and Christine and we'll walk you to your hotel or wherever you want to go. It would be safer.'

'If I did decide to leave?'

'I would simply cry into my pillow, dream of you all night and tomorrow. I would become a Trappist monk.'

She put her glass down on the table threw her head back and laughed. Then with one hand either side of his face kissed him softly on the lips. He responded more firmly, holding her tight, left hand across her behind. His erection almost instantaneous. She noticed. How could she not? She broke the kiss, looked up at him and grinned. 'You are keen, and you're blushing.'

'Have you done this before?' he said, unable to prevent the broad grin.

'Sorely tempted,' she said. Her expression inscrutable.

'You're a long way from home and no-one knows your husband.'

'Enough questions. You haven't brought me here to talk, have you?' she said taking a bite from the proffered sandwich. Do we stay and eat with the others?'

'Not if you don't want.'

'There's a servant's staircase?'

'Behind me in the corner.'

'I'm not playing musical beds, if that's what you think.'

He frowned. 'I should think not, you're much too beautiful to share.'

Their empty plates on the table. Newton and Grace entered.

'Good, the food's ready. Are you off?'

Bard flicked his head towards the back staircase as they heard Jenny shriek. This was her third visit.

There were three golden rules on party nights: Clean bed linen. Spotless bathroom and toilet. If a bedroom door is closed, ignore it.

She passed him her wine. 'I need the bathroom.'

They stood face-to-face. Bard's hands clasped behind her hips. Claire with hers behind her neck.

'I'm surprised at you.'

'Why?' she had a wonderful smile. 'I'm here for the same reason that you are. I'm human.' She pulled his head towards her. As their lips met, he began to unzip her dress. She moaned softly as he ran his hands up her back feeling for something that wasn't there. Her lips twitched. 'It's fitted,' she whispered.

'Ah.'

She stopped him as he was sliding the dress from her shoulders. 'I'm obviously not your first, but when you're about to have sex do you ask the woman what she prefers, or assume you know?'

She found his hesitancy amusing. 'I thought so. But would you be willing to delay your own pleasure for my benefit. I guarantee that the rewards would more than make up for it. Let me use my own experience to help you become a better lover.'

There was only one answer. She dropped her arms. He slid her dress from her shoulders easing is over her hips. She gasped and pulled his head closer as he teased her nipples. Gasping and pressing his face into her bush as he slid her panties down to her ankles. Whatever she used was exotic and heady. He helped her out of her shoes and, as he stood, trailed his right fore and ring fingers up the inside of her thighs his middle finger through her bush beginning a gentle massage. She squealed and kissed him hard on the lips then dropped her hands and began to tear at his belt. She clasped his hands, 'No, stop. Too close. I don't think you need much help, And I don't want my first orgasm like this.'

Between the sheets her heart beat against his chest as they kissed.

She introduced him to fellatio. It was mind blowing. She lifted her head and smiled. He reciprocated. Slid down the bed hooking his arms under her thighs and buried his face. This time she wouldn't stop him. This is what she had been deprived of. The movements of her pelvis, her breathing and the noises she was making told him that she was close, grabbing his hair with both hands seconds later slammed her knees together trapping his head rendering him temporarily deaf and depriving him of oxygen. He took several seconds to extricate himself. Propped up on one elbow he watched her face. She opened her eyes and smiled. 'Excuse the pun,' he said returning the smile, 'but are you pleased you came?'

She reached up and pull his head towards her. Two seconds later a sharp knock at the door followed by an urgent voice. 'Carol! You screamed. Are you all right?'

He looked down and smiled, 'Carol?'

She hit him playfully on the chest and returned the smile, 'Shut up ... Yes Grace, I'm fine,' she replied. 'I'm more than fine .. Thank you,' she said her left hand behind his head. She slid her right behind his hip pulling him forward.

The feeling was sublime. She locked her ankles behind his hips. Her face told the story. She gasped and began to match him. 'Fuck me, hard,' Who was he to argue? It was a short but incredibly sweet paroxysm of pleasure. Her back arched. She had an almost wild look in her eyes. There was no scream. They lay locked together shudders running through Clare's, or was it Carol's, body. She opened her eyes. 'How soon before we can do that again?'

He smiled down at her. 'Soon .. But what you said. Your first?'

She nodded. 'My husband ejaculates immediately. He doesn't see it as anything to do with him.'

'Surely he's not inexperienced.'

'Far from it. And loses his temper just as quickly. Plus, he's infertile.'

'Isn't this a risk, being with me? I'm not using anything.'

'We're ships that pass in the night.' She rolled him onto his back, straddled him sighing as she felt him enter. Holding his hands on her breasts she began to roll her abdominal muscles.

He didn't check the time or keep score, but the tanks were empty. He was knackered. The hydraulics refused to cooperate. She lay at his side his arm around her, head and right arm on his chest. 'Comfortable?'

She nodded.

'Stay.'

She pushed herself into a sitting position twizzled towards him hugging her knees. 'I can't. Had things been different ...'

'But they're not, are they? And I don't suppose you'll let me know if I father any children.'

Her tone was smiling. 'Please, Martin. Forget me. You don't understand. We have no future and you will never see me again .. I'm not doing this to hurt you. Please do not cloud the issue.'

Under normal circumstances it would have been straight forward, no strings attached, consensual sex. This was turning into something altogether. He was beginning to want something that wasn't on offer. 'No, Carol,' He admitted and smiled. 'You're quite right but I've never known anyone like you.'

'Perhaps,' she said and smiled.

'Grace and Christine?'

'Their husbands have other interests. What's sauce for the goose ... When I told my husband I was taking a break with them he gave them enough to cover their expenses. They will confirm that our trip was celibate. Today was a bonus.'

'This is going to become a habit?'

She could scowl as well. 'Take that look off your face.'

It struck eleven. There was a knock at the door. It was Newton. 'Are you coming, or have you got Clare tied to the bed?'

'No, he hasn't,' she laughed. 'We'll be out in a couple of minutes.'

There was just her dress to fasten. 'I'll never forget you,' he slid his arms round her waist and nuzzled her neck. 'Are you sure you can't stay?'

She spun round. He was on the end of another exasperated scowl. She put her arms round his neck. They kissed. 'I'll never forget you either. It's been wonderful .. I have a favour to ask, well two actually.'

'Of course you can stay,' He grinned and received another scowl. 'They're yours.'

'Stop it!' she couldn't stop the grin. 'Could I have a bottle of that wine as a keepsake?

'You can have a dozen if you like.'

She looked puzzled. 'Family. My father is a partner in that vinyard.'

Her eyes widened. 'Really?'

He nodded. 'We're vintners. In Bristol.'

'Oh, excellent,' she smiled then looked doubtful. 'Too many.'

'One it is then. And what was the second?'

She paused and smiled. 'Well, you know my first name is Carol. My middle names Frances Elizabeth. What are yours?'

'Martin Graeme. Without the aitch. G-r-a-e-m-e.'

The rain had cleared. All except the brightest stars swamped by the glare of the streetlights as they walked Clare, Grace and Christine along Boar Lane towards City Square and The Queens Hotel. Jenny and Ruth had left about nine. Emily, still blotto, asleep on Molière's bed. He'd stayed behind to make sure she was all right. With the four of them, there was no risk that they would be subject to any unwanted attention.

At the door Clare slipped Bard's father's flying jacket from her shoulders. They shared a last kiss. That was that. A wonderful evening with a beautiful married woman. It had to have been a *what if* instead of a *no chance*. That was irrelevant. She was gone.

Nine

Reception in The Queens was busy. Clare, Grace and Christine occupying three easy chairs and an occasional table in a corner. Clare's bottle of wine, carefully wrapped, in her lap.

'Can we stop using these names yet?'

'Once we're in the taxi, Christine, although someone might have given the game away, mightn't they?' said Clare with a pointed look at Grace.

'Sorry, but when you screamed.'

'You did?'

Clare smiled. 'Mmm, rather intense.'

The others smiled. 'Worth it?'

'Oh yes, Grace. Definitely.'

'But you used ...'

Clare smiled.

'But what if?'

'It won't matter. Gordon can't. Never has been able to. But won't accept the test results. They were an affront to his manhood.'

'And we're going to guarantee your celibacy.'

Clare smiled and nodded.

'And you're going to make sure he thinks any offspring is his.'

'I am. It will confirm in his mind his assertion that the tests were wrong.'

'But doesn't this boy's age and background bother you?'

She smiled to herself. 'Not in the least. He's intelligent and fun.'

There was a long pause whilst they exchanged long glances. 'You haven't perchance fallen in love with him?'

Clare paused and smiled. 'Honestly, Christine? I don't know.'

'But he doesn't know who or what you are?'

'Somehow he found out my name is Carol,' she said grinning at Grace. 'Other than that, no.'

'Sorry.'

'No matter. He knows we won't see each other again .. They should be clear now. Will you get us a taxi?'

Ten

Bard's very pleasant dreams of Carol ruled out any thoughts of him becoming a Trapist Monk.

The Town Hall clock struck three. Bladder empty he was returning to his room still decorated by lingering traces of Carol's perfume. Passing Molière on the opposite journey, Emily still visible. 'What's she like?' he said.

'God knows how much she put away,' said Molière. 'She's still half asleep and every time I move she's making a grab at me. I'm fucked.'

'Sounds like fun,' Bard laughed.

'See if you've got any life left in you. You give her one for a change. I need a leak then I'll put the kettle on. Tea?'

'Ok.'

Bard hadn't seen anything of Emily since leaving to make the sandwiches. In the landing light she was naked, flat on her back her arms and legs spread and smiling. He began a gentle massage. 'That's nice,' she whispered and lifted her arms. 'Come on.' He entered slowly. She matched his rhythm and pulled his head down. They kissed. 'That feels so good.' She stopped. He glanced down. Her eyes wide open. A look of horror on her face. Her scream would have wakened the dead. 'Kevin, you bastard. No! Get the fuck off me.'

She brought her right knee up hard catching him in the rocks. She screamed again, breathing rapidly and sweating. So was he.

He took a deep breath. 'Emily, I'm not Kevin, I'm Bard, remember?'

'Get off me, you bastard.'

'Emily calm down.' He put his left hand over her mouth. She bit down hard and began to lash out with her fists. He changed hands. His right hand over her mouth and laid on her left arm pinning it to the bed. His left hand under her chin trying to keep her mouth closed and right fist and nails away from his face. It might have been just after three, but some clubs were turning out. Sound carries. The last thing they needed were calls to the police about a woman screaming.

The cavalry arrived *en masse.* Molière was first. Emily was still creating. 'What the Hell's going on. Emily, what's the matter? Bard?' He asked as Emily began to claw at Bard's hands.

'Haven't a clue. She just kicked off. Thought I was Kevin. She screamed and bit me.'

Emily went limp. 'Thank God for that,' he said and relaxed.

Leo was reading physiology. He stepped forward and looked down. 'Don't be too sure,' he said placing his fingers on Emily's throat. 'No carotid pulse,' he leaned forward his ear close to her mouth. 'Shit.' He closed her eye and opened it again, 'No response to light.' He studied her eye whilst the others wondered.

Bard, his brain all over the place broke the silence. 'Shouldn't I go and call an ambulance?'

'Not yet.' Leo stood took a deep breath and exhaled. 'Emily's dead,' he said.

'What the fuck! We need an ambulance,' Bard iterated.

'But how?' From Newton.

Leo pulled her eyelid back once more. 'See those red dots?'

They crowded round. 'And?' Bard said.

'They're called petechial haemorrhages. Caused by pressure on the throat. Basically strangulation, throttling.'

'It was an accident,' Bard protested.

'We know that,' said Leo. 'But the police don't ...'

King Tut, our archaeologist butted in – his father was a solicitor. '... and when the circumstances come out it could be a murder charge. Or possibly manslaughter,' he put his hand up as we all began to talk at once.

Leo, captain of the rugger team, took over. 'Look, we all saw and heard what was happening. It could have happened to any one of us. As I see it our options are to throw ourselves, or rather Bard, on the mercy of the police and the courts or, something else.'

'You mean bury her,' Bard offered. 'Then forget about it?'

'We can't do anything for her, that's true. But people, including Jenny and Ruth, know that she was here. Not forgetting Clare, Grace and Christine. We need a plan. Between us we can think of something.

Bard's brain was well and truly frazzled. He'd just killed a girl. It had been a delightful evening with Carol. Now this. Looking round, the others they weren't too far behind. Newton took a spare bedsheet from the cupboard. Between them they laid Emily on the sheet. Her clothes, shoes, ear-rings, handbag and watch followed, covered her up and sat in the kitchen to talk it through. Leo took the chair.

'We can't turn the clock back and what we decide has to be unanimous. If we do anything other than go to the police, if Emily's body is ever traced and identified it will turn round to bite us *all* in the balls. We play as a team and now is not the time to do anything else. I think we heard enough from King Tut earlier to understand the ramifications in regard to the law, the university and, the impact on our careers.' Everyone agreed. Bard knew how he and his family would have felt and reacted had it been his sister, Elizabeth, who suddenly failed to arrive home, never mind her husband. Selfish bastards to the nth degree they might have been, but it's called being human – just what Carol had said to him. We all have our reasons.

The plan was simple. Separate Emily from her clothes etc, burn the clothes and scatter the remainder including shoes and handbag throughout the rubbish bins the university and City Centre.

Emily, they decided to bury in an excavated gas trench that Newton knew of between Leeds and Harrogate. Then swimming in Eccup reservoir. Something they had done several times. Followed by a trip to Charlie Fortes, a twenty-four hour Transport Cafe on the A1 at Ferrybridge for a fry-up. As university students they did what normal people consider barmy.

Sooner or later Emily would be reported missing and the police involved. They would be interviewed. Answer the questions truthfully but stick to what we had individually witnessed until they went to bed. At three thirty am when they got up to go swimming, Emily, who had been asleep in Molière's bed, was no longer there. She and her clothes had gone. We searched the house but not the grounds. The front door key was on the mat below the letter box. He, and we, made the obvious assumption.

If the police start asking open-ended questions inviting an opinion, do not get drawn in.

Leo went to fetch his car. Emily's body was put in the boot. Her clothes on the fire. How long he stared through the fireguard into the flames he didn't know. Newton put his hand on *Bard's* shoulder. 'Come on, you can't bring her back.'

Like a black slash across the field the gaping maw of the trench appeared out of the starless night. The trench, one hundred yards from the road, northeast of Leeds, somewhere between Thorner and Collingham. About thirty yards of welded pipe exposed. Bard and Molière took possession of Emily in her shroud and slid her almost beneath the pipe with as much dignity as possible. King Tut and

Leo started a nearby bulldozer, pushed about ten yards of soil back into the trench and replaced it as near as possible to where it had been. Within fifteen minutes they were away. There was no point in hanging around.

It was a silent twenty-five minute ride to Eccup and down the track that skirted the Golf Club. It wasn't much better in the water. Normally once the water was at groin level there was an increase in levity. Today a blanket of despond had settled over them. After splashing around for perhaps ten minutes they got out to be met by their friend with the shotgun. Five nine. Stocky build. Dark hair protruding from beneath a deerstalker and a caped top-coat. A luxuriant growth of facial hair. His moustache so thick and untrimmed it looked like baleen. They never knew who he was, gamekeeper, poacher or Lord of the Manor, but he always seemed to be there or thereabouts with his shotgun. Broken. Perhaps he just liked looking at naked young men. They didn't know. 'You lads back again?' he'd say and smile. 'That water's bloody cold .. You'll catch your death ... Going to Charlie Fortes?'

A quick rub-down, dressed, they said farewell and left. Charlie Fortes was calling.

Through Collingham and onto the A1 south. They hadn't travelled more than a mile when a police car drew alongside and signalled them to pull over causing a few flutters. 'Come on,' Leo said as the police car stopped in front of them. Two police officers emerged. 'They're not looking for us. No blue lights. Let's see what they want.'

Early hours of the morning. Five young men in an almost new car. They were simply curious. With both front windows wound down they had a police officer either side, illuminating the interior with their torches and taking deep breaths. 'Have you been drinking?' said Constable nearside.

'Between eight pm last night, officer,' Bard volunteered, 'and now, between us, we've consumed approximately two bottles of wine.'

'That's two bottles each?' said Constable nearside.

'No officer, between us.'

'Really?' He straightened up and nodded to Constable offside.

Leo was invited to step out of the vehicle and sit in the police car. Constable nearside looked at them all in turn. 'You look wet. Where've you been?'

King Tut smiled and told him. 'Swimming, officer. In Eccup reservoir. Now we're en route to Charlie Fortes for a fry up.'

He pulled an unbelieving faux-pained expression. 'You're university students aren't you?' We agreed. He smiled and shook his head. 'And my daughter's wanting to go to university. Honestly.'

That caused a laugh. 'We're not that bad,' Bard said, grateful about the change in subject. Hoping his heart rate would slow. 'What does your daughter want to do?'

'Modern languages. She got seven O levels, JMB (Joint Matriculation Board), including French, German and Latin. She sits her A levels next term.'

'That's excellent,' said Bard. 'We hope she does well.'

He nodded, walked round the car and sat in the driver's seat. 'Right gentlemen,' he said, 'we'll have some names. Starting with your friend who's currently being tested to see if we consider him fit to drive.'

'How?'

'Can he walk in a straight line, heel to toe. Stand on one leg with his eyes closed. If he fails, you're all going to Wetherby police station whilst we call the police surgeon out. Keep your fingers crossed. When this new breathalyser comes in it will be much easier. Now, his name.'

'It's Leo,' said Newton. 'Sorry, that's a nickname. Short for Leonardo de ...'

'Leonardo de Vinci,' interrupted the officer. 'Italian polymath born April 15th, 1452. Probably most famous for his drawing called the Vitruvian Man based on the work of the Roman architect, Vitruvius,' he paused and made eye contact with them all. 'Just because I'm a constable does not make me or my colleagues stupid. Now, I want straight answers, or what I said earlier applies and for the next four or five hours instead of partaking of Charlie Fortes' finest, you will be in Wetherby police station, hungry and unloved, whilst we carry out background checks with your parents and the Dean of the university. Bearing in mind the time, I don't think they would be too pleased. Do you understand?'

Five minutes later he skimmed through several pages of his pocketbook. All their names, dates of birth, addresses in Leeds, Home addresses and telephone numbers, subjects we were reading and nicknames and, why we had them. They wondered whether he might regale his daughter with a tale of the barmy students that he'd met. She would probably think that it was *cool*. 'Does anyone wish to make any changes?'

There was £1.3.6d in Emily's purse. That went into the charity box at Fortes. Breakfast, as good as ever. The atmosphere subdued. Thankfully, thought Bard, it's not just me, although he felt it more than the others.

The rest of the day he kept to himself. He threw all his efforts at his latest essay, now three days late. On the Wednesday it came back: *See ME!!* Emblazoned across the top IN GREEN.

It was contagious. Everyone felt the same. Returning to the house in the evening reinforced the feeling. The next morning, Thursday, Bard announced that he was leaving and would see the Accommodations Office and look for somewhere else. That was also contagious. A decision made easier when, on the Friday morning a letter arrived to say that the owner was planning to commence demolition on the twenty second of the following month. He was most apologetic, but could they please make alternative arrangements. There were no complaints.

Eleven

The following Tuesday, ten days after Emily's death, Bard arrived back at the house to find Tweedle Dum and Tweedle Dee waiting for him. Both five eleven, black shoes, dark suits and matching beige raincoats, one carrying a briefcase. By this time, he was beginning to feel better. Even if he had no right to.

'Detective Sergeant Giles and Detective Constable Smith. You'll be Martin Beck, known as Bard,' said the elder of the two. His heart began to thump. Just how serious was this about to become?

He agreed, hoping there were no signs of nervousness, 'How can I help?'

They sat around the kitchen table. The kettle on, mugs, milk and sugar at the ready. 'Right, Martin. You don't mind of I call you Martin?' asked the detective sergeant.

'Not at all.'

'We're making enquiries about a missing girl,' he said. 'Perhaps you've seen the bit in the Evening Post, goes by the name of Emily Reid. I understand you know her?'

'Sorry, don't read the Evening Post,' he said, truthfully. 'Not sure about the Reid bit but the name Emily does ring a bell. A week last Saturday, pretty girl wearing a black dress.'

Detective Sergeant Giles nodded and took a buff manilla file from his briefcase. From the file he passed a photograph. 'Is this the girl?'

He looked at the photograph and passed it back. 'That's her. Outside the Locarno. She's a bit older than in the photograph, but it's her.'

'And you picked her up?'

'No, Sergeant, definitely not. She invited herself, or rather asked if she could come with us.'

'Why?'

'She didn't want to meet Kevin Sharpe.'

'What did she say, exactly?'

'Exactly?' He studied for a moment. 'As I recall it was: "Can I come. Kevin Sharpe's in there, I don't want to see him."'

'Did she allude as to why?'

'No, just that she didn't want to see Kevin Sharpe. She looked and sounded nervous.'

'But able to ask complete strangers if she could go with them?'

'Yes, but there were several other women present.'

'That's as maybe. Did you have sex with her?'

That was a yes/no question. They knew! 'No. I had sex with Clare. Nobody else. Emily was with Bill, Bill Boxley.'

'Ok,' he acknowledged. 'He's the last one we need to speak to. When's he due back?' He checked his watch. 'Generally speaking, in around an hour but I couldn't guarantee it.'

He narrowed his eyes. 'You call them Party Nights I understand. Tell me how they work.'

If Bill was to be the last it meant that the sergeant had already spoken to the other three and they already knew the answer. All he could do was to keep it straight. It took a few seconds to mash the tea. Apart from detailing their arrangement with the manager and what happened when they paired off and in the early hours, he told exactly what had occurred.

'Let me get this straight,' Sergeant Giles said. 'You're in your monkey suits .. The manager comes up and bars *you* because he doesn't want any trouble inside, even though it was Sharpe that caused it in the first place. How's that so far?'

'Ok,' he replied.

'One of your mates suggests that you all repair here where you have good music, a dance floor, wine and food .. and you charge for the booze and the food?'

'No, we don't.'

'It's all free?' he sounded as if he didn't believe me. 'What do you feed 'em?'

'Yes, it is,' he grinned. 'Bacon sandwiches. Quick and easy.'

The sergeant smiled. 'Interesting combination, red wine and bacon sandwiches.'

'We had a Watney's Seven as well this time. Should anyone not want wine.'

The detective sergeant grimaced. 'Watneys? That's witch piss.'

'I agree. We had to finish it later.'

'Serves you right ... Before we move on what names did these women give?'

'Jenny, she's been three times. Ruth, I don't recall seeing her before. There was Emily, she'd not been before. She had nearly a bottle of wine to herself. And the other three gave their names as Clare, Grace and Christine.'

'Married?'

'No rings, but you could see the marks on their ring fingers.'

The sergeant smiled and nodded. 'Any further details?'

'Not about those three, Sergeant. No questions. No lies. Except they were staying at the Queens. We walked them back around eleven.'

'Very gallant. What about the others?'

'Jenny and Ruth left together around nine, or so I was told. Emily was fast asleep, so Bill stayed with her. She was still asleep in Bill's bed when we returned. It was three thirty when we got up that anyone realised that she'd gone.'

'She just upped and went?'

This was the time to be careful. 'It appears so. We have our own keys, but we leave a spare in the lock and ask that if someone wants to leave and none of us are around, lock the door from the outside and post the key.'

'And?'

'The key was on the mat behind the door.'

'So, you assumed that she'd left. It didn't appear strange?'

'Not really. Although we always said that we would see them safe if they wanted to leave, not just leave them on their own in the city centre.'

'Fair enough. Did you search the house and grounds?'

'We had a quick look round the house to see if she'd wandered off and fallen. Not the grounds, it's like a jungle.'

'No trace? No property of hers anywhere?'

'Not a sausage.'

'Any further contact details?'

'I can't speak for anyone else, but I didn't. Ships that pass in the night.'

The sergeant smiled and nodded. 'I'd like a look round, but before that are there any independent witnesses to this confrontation outside the Mecca?'

'Yes, your colleague was there,' Bard nodded at the other policeman. The penny had just dropped. He had been in the crowd watching at the time.

'DC Smith?' he repeated looking at his colleague. 'Are you sure?'

'Certainly. He was standing about three yards away from me.'

Sergeant Giles turned to his colleague. He did not look happy. 'I rang Gail that Saturday evening. She said that you'd gone to your brother's in Tadcaster.'

'I did,' he protested.

'You'd better hope this fella's made a mistake,' then he turned to Bard. 'Was there anyone else with this man?'

Bard thought for a second. 'Yes, a young woman, five two, peroxide blonde, pretty, white top, and I think a black skirt ... Oh, she had pierced ears. The ear-rings were like small daggers. They stood out. When it broke up, they wandered off together towards the Locarno.'

If looks could have killed. 'That's the little tart from the typing pool,' Sergeant Giles snapped. 'She wears ear rings like that. I'll get to the bottom of this. You'd better pray that you've got a doppelganger. Now get your arse outside and search the garden. Then wait outside. Move.' He waited until the door closed and turned to me. 'Sorry about that,' he said. 'My son-in-law. I've had my suspicions about the little bastard for a while. Lesson number one. Don't shit on my doorstep.' he took a deep breath. 'Now,' he said and smiled. 'Before we do a search, why did you get up at three thirty?'

'We sometimes go swimming at Eccup reservoir.'

'Seriously? At that time in the morning. You must be daft. No witnesses at that time of course.'

'On the contrary. An old guy. Deerstalker, caped topcoat, dark hair and luxuriant facial hair and carrying a shotgun.'

'I thought he'd died years ago. It's the old man from the manor house. Harmless old bodger. He didn't take a pot-shot at you?'

'No, nothing like that. He's a man of few words though. He should remember us he's seen us a few times.'

He laughed. 'True, he wasn't known as a conversationalist. And we will see him. Was there anyone else?'

'We were stopped on the A1 south by two bobbies in an Austin Westminster. Patrick had to heel and toe a straight line, and stand on one leg with his eyes closed. Then we went for a fry-up at Fortes. They'll remember us.'

'Okay. Now then, these girls. Have you ever seen them outside of your Party Nights?'

'I can't speak for the others, but I haven't.'

'Do you know their full names or where they live.'

'Sorry, only the names they gave us. And that was just their Christian names.'

'If you saw them again, would you recognise them?'

'Perhaps.'

'Would you be prepared to work with us and try?'

'If you think it would help.'

'We will let you know ... This wine, could I see it, please?'

Bard poured him a glass. 'Try it, it's not a bribe.'

'True,' He smiled and took a drink. 'But it's good. It would be ok for our bar. Where can we get it.'

'From my father, here,' he took a business card from his pocket. 'Write to him. A senior officer's signature would help'

The house was searched from the cellar upwards. They'd had the foresight to sift the ashes disposing of anything untoward in various bins either in town or at the university. Lastly upstairs, with particular attention to Bill's room. Hoping that showing due concern for the fact that Emily was now on record as missing was all that was picked up. Perhaps the altercation with DC Smith over his possible adultery had swayed his judgement.

'Before I forget,' said Bard fetching the letter from a kitchen drawer and handing it to the sergeant. 'From the developer that owns the building. You can contact us through the Accommodations Office.'

DS Giles nodded and added the details to his pocketbook. He was on the point of leaving when Bill arrived. DC Smith was mooching about and ordered to re-do the search.

He invited Bill into the kitchen for a chat. Bard took himself off to his room.

Bill hadn't mentioned it earlier, but Emily had been far more forthcoming about *Sharpie* when she was under the influence. He'd raped her. Although she had no problem with Bill – perhaps that was the wine. Only later when she thought Bard was Kevin Sharpe.

Eight o'clock. Seated round the kitchen table. Doors locked. 'Right,' said Leo. 'We've all been spoken to by the police. Any doubts or problems? Did the police apply any serious pressure?'

They hadn't. It appeared they were following a pattern and asking us all the same questions. Give them something to compare notes against. As long as we didn't all quote verbatim from the same hymn sheet. That would be suspicious.

The police turned up the next morning and carried out a full fingerprint sweep. The aluminium powder they used to highlight any fingerprints stuck to everything. Especially clothes. In addition, a half dozen officers armed with a scythe and a couple of logging saws flattened everything. Nothing.

They started to buy the Evening Post. A few days later a article that an unidentified male had been arrested for questioning regarding the disappearance of Emily Reid. Enquiries were continuing. Rumoured to be Kevin Sharpe it made them wonder what other evidence they might have. All they had provided was suspicion.

That was the last party at Merrion Lodge. Via the Accommodation Office new lodgings were found in various houses around Woodhouse Moor, much closer to the university. The police were notified.

They worked with the police on three occasions, but the only girl they found was Ruth. She had no complaints and as far as possible backed up their version of events. She was disappointed when she found out there would be no further party nights.

Twelve

The train arrived at Bristol Temple Meads on time. There would be no reports about Emily in the local press. A hug from his mother and luggage in the boot it was a fifty-minute drive. However, there was something a little odd. His mother was usually cheerful and smiling. Today the smile never left her face.

'Something I should know?'

'No,' she made eye-contact via the rear-view mirror. 'Well, there's something that your father and I would like to know.'

'Fire away.'

The smile broadened. 'Let's wait until we get home.'

At home it was worse. His father was smiling almost as broadly as his mother. No explanation forthcoming. A table had been booked at the golf club. They could discuss it there.

Surprise, sister Elizabeth and husband Steve had also been invited – an hour earlier. What was so important for a gathering of the clan at such short notice? Booked in they occupied the last table in the corner of the bar for a preprandial drink. Bard looked at his parents' smiling faces. 'Right. What's all this about?'

His father nodded.

'Who do you know who is entitled to use the title, Her Ladyship?' his mother said. Elizabeth and Steve gave him a strange look.

'That's easy,' He replied and took a drink. 'Nobody. Does that answer your question?'

'Nobody?'

'In that case, Martin,' said his father. 'I don't suppose you know anyone who is entitled to use the title who also owns a new Rolls Royce Silver Shadow and employs a liveried chauffeur.'

That raised eyebrows a notch or two. 'No, I don't. Why?'

'Because, at half past ten this morning such a gentleman called at the office and asked for me by name. Confirmed that I had a son called Martin who was a student at Leeds university and handed me these.' He reached into his inside jacket pocket removed an envelope and handed it over.

Bard glanced at the envelope. 'Don't know the writing.'

His mother passed him a neatly wrapped package tied with blue ribbon.

'He had been instructed by Her Ladyship to hand them to me, in person.'

'For me?' Said Bard. The envelope was certainly not from Woolworths. He took a sniff. No scent.

'Yes, yes,' mother was getting agitated. 'Aren't you going to open them?'

He put them on the table and took another drink. 'Actually, Mum, I thought I'd leave them until I got home.' His father smiled. In spite of what she had said, could this possibly be Carol?

Elizabeth and Steve acted as though they were on the centre line of the Centre Court at Wimbledon, mid-rally.

His mother looked as if she were going to have a fit. He put his glass down. 'Just joking,' he picked the envelope up and ran his thumb along the fold. There was a single tri-fold sheet of unaddressed, undated, high-quality cream-wove paper bearing a short hand-written message. One look and his heart gave a bounce.

Dear Martin,

Many thanks for everything. This is a small gift to show my appreciation.

Best wishes for the future.
C.

No mistake. This was from the lady with those beautiful blue eyes. At least she hadn't underlined the word *everything.* Although with half a clue his mother would be down at the public library leafing through De Brett's and Burkes Peerage. Better stick to Clare. He passed the letter round. Her indefinable accent gave nothing away. And the promise she extracted?

'Does this initial C mean anything,' His mother asked. If she thought she was getting warm it would be all round her circle of friends and the Ladies Golf Section by this time tomorrow.

'Well, all I can think of was something that happened in Leeds a few weeks ago. There was a bit of a kerfuffle outside of the Locarno when one of the local oiks made some ungentlemanly comments to a young woman and grabbed hold of her wrist. I was close by and stepped in. Her name was Clare. But that was all.' Had his mother known she would have had a fit. His father would have been jealous.

'And that's all?'

'Mum, we went to a bar and just sat and talked and a few drinks. Then I walked her back to her hotel. She didn't know Leeds at all. No great romance, sorry.' *Pity,* He added mentally and collected the package. 'I'd better open this, hadn't I?'

Removing the wrapping he caught his breath. A royal blue box with the word ROLEX in gold impressed across the lid. This was the trigger they were looking for.

'That's some small gift,' said Steve.

His internal smile asked the question. *Forget me, she said. Looks like she hasn't. It's five weeks since. Two periods missed? Is she trying to tell me she's pregnant? Otherwise, why?*

'To someone with a Silver Shadow it might be,' Bard replied knowing that no-one would believe him. You buy someone a wristwatch because it fulfils a purpose. Every time the wearer looks at it, it reminds them of the giver. This was a Rolex Tudor Royal gold wristwatch costing several hundred pounds.

He had to stop the interrogation before his mother got into full flow. The decibels increasing. 'Martin, you have to send it back. You can't accept a present like this from a girl you hardly know.'

He raised his hand. 'Mum, whoa. You drilled it into us when we were younger that it was vulgar to talk about money or wealth in public. People are starting to listen.' He removed his wristwatch replacing it with Carol's. The engraved message pressed against his skin:

I will always
remember
C

His mother was shocked into silence.

'It's an incredibly nice present which I assume is from Clare. I only have a Christian name,' he looked at his father. 'I don't suppose you remembered the registration number,' he shook his head. 'Why she sent it I couldn't say, but I intend to keep it. She sent it to me through Dad, why you've taken such an interest I have no idea.' He paused and looked at his father.

'Your mother was in the office when the chauffeur arrived,' he replied with a *sorry* expression.

'Mum, you only turned against the idea of Clare when you realised there was nobody *you* could vet. I have no wish to fall out but if you persist in this interrogation I shall leave. I'm not a child anymore.'

He felt his father's hand on his shoulder. 'It's all right. Martin,' he said and turned to his wife. 'He's right, Pat. You have to let go.'

'... But I'm proud of you,' she said at last.

'Then be proud,' he said. 'Just don't try to get involved in my personal life.'

Rumours reached him that she had been talking to her friends about this mysterious '*Ladyship*' he had befriended. Three days later he put a small ad in the Times. *Clare, thank you for the watch,. Martin.* There was an answer five days later. *Martin, remember to wind it up. Remember me to Molière.* The emotional boost was enormous. Remembering what Carol had said about her husband's hair-trigger temper, it was under control.

The trouble began four weeks after they vacated Merrion Lodge. Being doorstepped by the Press. Ambushed on campus. Detective Sergeant Giles confirmed they were not suspects and would do what he could with the Press.

A Solicitor's letter sent with little effect. There was a piece in the Evening Post not identifying him directly but ... The continuing harassment led him to believe that Detective Constable Smith was responsible. He changed his lodgings three times. Early in the New Year he applied for interviews with several publishers, all of whom would offer him a position provided he obtained a two-one or higher. That was well within his compass. Top of the list was Finsbury Templeton Books.

It was never-ending. Bard discussed it with Branden Inglis of Moriarty and Sutcliffe. Brandon Inglis's suggestion was to change his name by deed poll. There was no problem with the university provided everything was completed within the next four weeks. Bard had already spoken with his father who wasn't thrilled by the idea but accepted the necessity. He would speak with his mother. To Finsbury Templeton Books it made no difference.

We had our final get together. Apart from the hassle we all had been through there had been no further interviews with the police, perhaps because we had all cooperated with their enquiries. It was not a cause for celebration. We took our final drink and went our separate ways. We would not contact each other again.

Three days later it was *Lewis Alexander Green* and not *Martin Graeme Beck* who was awarded his first-class honours degree and quietly moved to London.

Twelve months later he got a shock. Early for a dental appointment he was leafing through the magazines. The latest one being *Country Life*. A couple of photographs caught his eye. One showed a couple standing in front of the open door of the Libero Wing, St Stephen's Hospital in London. A woman with a beaming smile holding two babies in her arms. Slightly behind her left shoulder an older man, also smiling. The second photograph. A close-up of the woman. It was Carol, or, to give her proper name: Lady Carol Frances Elizabeth Sylverton. The man, her husband, Gordon Ignatius Gladius Sylverton, 9th Earl of Oldeney, Oldeney Carr House, North Riding of Yorkshire. That made Carol a Countess. Had he sired twins with a Countess? Justified or not, he felt an enormous surge of pride and there was nothing he could do about it. Laughing to himself at the thought of his mother's reaction had she known. The babies, twin boys, were named Martin Gordon and Graeme Alexander. When asked if he was bothered by the choice of names in breaking with family tradition, Lord Oldeney was dismissive, and said that his wife's choice was her affair and caused him no concern whatsoever.

Lord Oldeney, the man whose conviction for murder had been quashed on a technicality two weeks earlier by the House of Lords. That in turn lead to questions in the tabloid press about one law for the rich.

A copy of that issue of *Country Life* resided in his bureau drawer.

The six-year old picture faded. He was back in the present. Five minutes later the train pulled into Leeds station. The connection to Huddersfield three platforms away, his stomach churning.

Blake

Thirteen

Detective Inspector Michael "Mick" Giles closed the Emily Reid file and looked across his desk at Cavendish and Blake. 'I dealt with the Emily Reid job when I was a DS,' he said. 'There were five at Merrion Lodge at that time. You say that Boxley was the first victim and Newsome the second?'

'Yes sir,' Blake replied.

'The other three were,' Giles glanced out of the window and collected his thoughts. 'Nash. ... Walters? ... No, Waters and Beck. No, Beck changed his name to Green. He was hounded by the Press over Reid's disappearance although there was no evidence to connect him to anything untoward. And you want to ensure they're not next in line. I don't think there's anything to be gained from lending you the file but take whatever notes you want. You can always come back later if need be.'

As the junior of the team Blake took out his pen, when, 'You're the same Blake as in the Wainwright case?'

He agreed. Max smiled and began to make the notes. 'Good job. Well done. But that final pursuit and confrontation in the church must have been harrowing, especially for your wife.'

'It was, sir. ...' There was a sharp rap at the open door. The plain clothes officer strode rapidly and spoke softly. The DI frowned and nodded. 'Secure the building and surrounds. Make a note of everyone present or has been. Nobody leaves. No exceptions.'

Without a word he left. 'It looks as though we might have number three.' That was a show-stopper. 'I don't suppose either of you viewed either of the others.'

'I did, sir,' Blake replied. 'Newsome.'

'Right, I'd like to borrow you. I suppose you have to notify someone, use my phone. Just dial 9 for a line. Cavendish, when you've got what you want, follow us down. It's Old Mill Lane off Hunslet Low Road. You can't miss it.'

Another partially demolished mill. Up one flight of stairs. It *was* number three. The DI wanted to know if it was identical to Newsome. I walked him round. The victim was a well-built lad, six feet tall, all right for the pack, late twenties and wearing a wedding ring. There was one slight difference. It was identical in all regards right down to the five cuts on the right forearm and the stab wound between the ribs. The blood on both chair and floor was fully congealed. The extra something was a wound at the back of his head. One for the pathologist.

On the ground floor the demolition crew who found the body were standing to one side in a silent sick-looking huddle whilst a DC took their details. They were *politely* asked not to broadcast what they had seen. Whether that would have the desired effect remained to be seen.

Four men in suits rolled up. DI Giles just addressed them as, sir. Fair enough. Blake took a discreet step back waiting for their questions and Max

'DC Blake.' DI Giles beckoned him over. 'This,' the DI indicated a florid, thick-set man around five eleven, 'is Detective Superintendent Western.' Blake had heard of him. On a good day the detective superintendent was reputed to have a temper like a bear with a sore arse. This was not a good day. His aura of whisky fumes could have felled an ox.

'Blake, what's all this bollocks you've been spouting about these cuts to the forearm being some kind of,' he pulled a face. 'What did you call them?'

'Cardiac countdown, sir,' I replied.

'Bollocks,' he declared with disdain. 'Who's told you that?'

'No-one, sir,' I replied. 'It seemed reasonable bearing ...'

'Enough! I don't care what seems reasonable to you. I'm telling you it's tosh. Some kind of torture that's been inflicted on this poor bastard. Anything beyond that is irrelevant. I understand you've only been in the job for two minutes. Open your ears and close your mouth. A few lucky guesses might have worked in Wainwright, but they won't work in this enquiry.'

Weston glared at Blake over his glasses daring him to challenge. *County coppers? He'd shit 'em. Useless tosspots to a man.*

Blake realised very quickly that he was banging his head against a brick wall. 'Yes, sir,' he said.

Weston's self-satisfied smirk claimed a victory.

A tall lugubrious man in a dark grey suit stopped examining the corpse, straightened and turned to his right. 'Mr Western.'

Western ignored him.

Max arrived followed a few seconds later by DS Creighton and an officer aged about thirty-five that he didn't know. They exchanged nods.

'Mr Western,' the man repeated.

'Detective Superintendent Creighton,' said Western, as if it was a nasty taste and ignored the other. 'Detective? Pah. Couldn't detect your own arse with a map.'

'Good morning, Donald,' DS Creighton replied. 'Under the weather?'

'George,' said the tall man to the barrel-chested suit next to him. 'Get him out of here. Make sure he gets home in one piece and that he stays there.'

'Sir,' he acknowledged. 'Mr Western,' the barrel-chested man said, taking the detective superintendent by the arm. 'Come with me, we have some enquiries to make.'

'But,' Western protested as he was guided forcibly towards the door.

'No buts. Come on,' seconds later and still protesting he was gone.

The tall man managed a thin smile. 'Mr Western has been under a lot of stress of late,' he said. 'Good morning, Mr Creighton, you and DC Blake I've met. Who are the others?

'DS Ryder, sir,' he replied, indicating the man on his left. 'Just returned from leave, and DC Cavendish. Gentlemen, this is Mr Carlisle, Chief Constable of the Leeds City Police.'

He nodded. 'Blake,' said Mr Carlisle. 'You were saying you thought these cuts were a cardiac countdown. That was because the amount of blood was less the higher up the arm?' 'Yes sir.'

'Did you mention that to anyone?'

'Professor Snodgrass, sir, when he attended at the last body.'

'Did he have an opinion?'

I smiled. 'He thought it was novel, sir.'

'Yes, I'll bet he did. And he asked you to guess because he couldn't?'

'Yes sir.'

'Par for the course,' he smiled and continued, 'Giles, you will be OIC in this case and you will liaise fully with Mr Creighton and his team. If there is no objection? he added with a wry smile.

DS Creighton returned the smile. 'Certainly not, sir.'

'Good. Giles, how long do you think it will take to identify this victim?'

'With luck sir, thanks to DC's Blake and Cavendish, very quickly.'

Carlisle studied him over his glasses. 'Really?'

'Yes sir. Apparently the first two victims, Boxley and Newsome attended Leeds university at the same time and were living at Merrion Lodge together. It was from there that Emily Reid disappeared seven years ago.'

'Weren't there five students involved. Some kind of sex party if I remember. And you believe there is a connection between these murders and Reid's disappearance?'

'I don't know about Reid, sir, but from what we do know and the similarity between the three deaths, there is a connection of some description.'

'Mr Creighton?'

'We only found out about Emily Reid after Blake and Cavendish spoke with DI Giles. However, I agree with Mr Giles, there is a connection. The first enquiries should be with the information we have to trace and speak to the families of the three students on the list not currently accounted for.'

'Agreed. You have the contact details?'

'Yes sir,' replied Max

'Right,' said DS Creighton. 'You two get back to the office. That takes priority. Let Mr Cartwright know and keep it under your hats ... And Blake, before you go. I've had a call from Superintendent Wallace. You can fill me in with the details later but that photograph you mentioned is from a murder case over 30 years ago and not connected. But worth a mention.'

'Sir.'

As the door closed behind them Mr Carlile caught his eye. 'Photo?'

'Yes, sir. Relates back to the Wainwright case and a search at Keighley. Murder victim, semi-naked with his penis removed and stuck in his mouth. It was thirty years ago. Coincidental.'

'He's a bright lad.'

The DS smiled. 'He is. Now, Emily Reid doesn't ring any bells. How long ago?'

'Seven years, sir,' answered DI Giles. 'There were five students sharing an old house off Merrion Street. Merrion Lodge. They used to have what they termed Party Nights. Emily Reid hasn't been seen since. Parents filed a Misper which I dealt with. Not a sausage.

Dribs and drabs about a Kevin Sharpe and other girls drifted in. Pretty handy with his knife apparently. Something we were unaware of. Eventually we had him in. Traces of Reid's blood was found in the locking mechanism of the knife. Eventually he coughed Reid's rape and others. Once he was remanded complainants came out of the woodwork. The DPP said to charge murder. We had enough to send him down for a long time on the rapes alone. I have to say the QC was a genius and Sharpe was convicted. He's in Sheffield at the moment.'

'And, outside of that evening, there was nothing at all to link these five undergraduates to Reid, Mr Giles?' queried Carlisle.

'Nothing that I could find, sir,' he replied. 'It was ten days after Reid's disappearance before it landed on my desk. I interviewed all five plus Mr Baron at the Manor House at Eccup, two road traffic officers from Tadcaster and the night staff at Fortes. all of whom verified their stories. The search of Merrion Lodge and grounds revealed nothing.'

'So, apart from questioning the morals of these young people there was nothing?'

'No sir. Not a thing.'

Green

Fourteen

Emerging from the cloud of steam and smoke Joan greeted him with an embrace.

'Darling, what an unexpected pleasure. You made it sound quite mysterious. How long can you stay?'

'Not long,' he said. 'There is something I need to find out as a matter of urgency.'

'A problem? You haven't mentioned anything.'

His stomach was telling him to avoid any possible confrontation. 'Can we go, darling. I have to get back tonight.' He needed to get to the bottom of this as soon as possible.

'Tonight? But you've brought your overnight.'

'Please, Joan.'

'You're being very mysterious,' she said with a half-smile. 'Are you all right, you look a bit peaky?'

'Fine, really.'

Sir John Betjeman had described the portico of Huddersfield railway station as *the finest in England.* It might have been a scheduled Grade 1 monument and he usually took a few seconds to admire it. Today? He didn't give a damn.

'Where are we going?' she said and thrust her Austin Healey 3000 convertible into the St George's Square traffic. The heavens opened. His umbrella still on the train! Thank goodness the hood was up.

'Seven Oaks Fold, Sharpe Lane, Almondbury. Number 17,' he said.

'That will be difficult,' Joan laughed. 'None of the houses have numbers, only names.'

'No numbers?' Are you sure?' This was getting sillier. First no Rodahl now no house numbers.

'Absolutely. It used to be a part of Oaks Farm. There are seventeen new-builds and it's covenanted. The original purchasers were given a list of oak related names from which they could choose. It can't be changed. A friend of mine, Theresa, lives at Red Oaks. That's the fifth house. There's even one house called Gog and Magog, named after two ancient oak trees somewhere down south.'

'Gog and Magog are at Glastonbury Tor,' he said. 'I've seen them.'

'You have?'

'Yup,' He needed to divert the conversation. 'The names Gog and Magog seem to be biblical in origin. I've read somewhere that Gog was believed to be a figure empowered by evil: bent on the destruction of God's people and seen by some biblical scholars as a template for the Antichrist. Magog possibly the country from which he came. Nobody knows. Typical pre-historical myth.'

Joan laughed. 'I wonder if the householders know?'

'I wouldn't have thought they were bothered.'

It took ten minutes to reach Northgate, Almondbury's main street, lined with a blend of small terrace houses, shops and a terminus for trolley buses. The war memorial at the junction with Kaye Lane when turning right from Northgate. One minute later left into Sharpe Lane. Seven Oaks Fold on the right. His heart thumping. His gut churning. *Come on pull yourself together.*

His flat in north London would have fetched a good price but any one of this crescent in front of him would have been a stretch. Architecturally designed. Straight from the Ideal Home Exhibition and, as Joan had said, no house numbers. She stopped adjacent to the first house: White Oaks in Gothic script carved in a four-inch-thick diagonal slice of oak picked out in black.

'What do you want to do?'

'Not sure,' he said. 'The address I've got is 17. In the circumstances that gives me three possible numbers, always assuming that Seven Oaks Fold is correct. Of course it may be a hoax. I'll try the first, seventh and last houses. Are you coming with me?'

She studied his face. 'No, you're like a cat on a hot tin roof,' she paused. 'I'll give you some space and pay a call on Theresa. Just knock on the door of Red Oaks when you're finished.'

From his previous visit to Joan's parent's house in Dark Lane he knew that Almondbury was a very old village. The buildings told the story. Less than a half mile from where he was standing was King James Grammar School. Its Charter granted by James I in 1608. But these houses must have stretched the planning regulations to the limit. Looking at White Oaks, he heard Joan lock the car and the sound of her heels clicking on the pavement. The knock on the door followed seconds later by. 'Joan, how lovely to see you, come in.'

Why he was being so wound up he don't know. Was this escapade to do with Emily Reid? They had all been interviewed by the police and cleared. So, why worry? The second note *two down and three to go* could mean anything. The manuscript? The clock on the parish church struck three. He pressed the bell and stepped back, waiting should the hounds of hell burst forth.

He only had to wait a few seconds. Five-four. Brunette. Attractive. Mid-thirties. Green dress. She smiled. 'Can I help you?'

'I'm sorry to trouble you, but I'm trying to locate the whereabouts of Granville Rodahl. I understand he lives in this crescent.'

Her face lit up. 'You must be Mr Green, Lewis Green. We've been expecting you. Just a moment.' Before he could speak, she about-turned returning in less than a minute with an envelope about eight by six inches and handed it over. 'He said you'd be here today.'

What sort of mind-twisting wretch was this? 'He delivered the letter here so you could give it to me?'

She was all smiles. 'Yes. He said he had written to you, and you would be unable to resist the challenge.'.

'I must admit that I'm as a loss to understand what's going on.'

She smiled again. 'I understand you're a literary agent and live in London?'

'Yes, I am,' he replied, his churning gut now in overdrive. This was ridiculous.

'And your fiancée, what did he say her name was? Oh, Joan, she lives just over the fields in Dark Lane. They were such a nice couple. He was tall with a clipped moustache and very well spoken. She was older but very smartly dressed. He said you liked puzzles and would enjoy working this one out and would see you in a few days.'

Now he was rattled. Potential threats are one thing but details about Joan? She obviously noticed my expression. 'Is there a problem, Mr Green. He thought you would enjoy the irony. He told me that he's sent you a manuscript for a novel that he's writing and this trip of yours was part of the plot.'

'That could be true,' he replied. The bitter taste of digestive acid raked his throat. 'Although I've never met him and there is no-one in the Huddersfield area by the name of Rodahl.'

'How strange. But I know that he left messages for you at two other houses: Gog and Magog, and Victory Oaks.'

'That would be the seventh and last houses.'

'He said you were clever. Yes, exactly.'

All he could do was nod and smile. 'Well thank you, Mrs?'

'Watson, Angela Watson.'

'Thank you, Mrs Watson. I'm sorry you've been troubled.' She smiled and closed the door. Bard ran his thumb under the flap and removed the contents. A photograph of a Windsor armchair. All the way from London to look at a photo of a wooden armchair. What the bloody hell was his game? What was at the other two houses?

Gog and Magog? Someone's idea of a joke? Ah, well they're stuck with it. Before Bard could ring the bell the occupant, a big man in all regards, met him at the door, envelope in hand. 'Jack Jackson,' he introduced himself. 'So, you're Lewis Green the literary agent. You'll be wanting this,' he said, handing him an envelope identical to the one Angela Watson had given him.

'Thank you,' he replied hoping it wasn't another Windsor chair. You could have too much of a good thing. 'Mr Rodahl, whoever he is, likes playing games.'

'So Angela told me,' Jackson said. He had noticed Green's puzzled look. 'She called before you arrived.'

He nodded.

Jackson smiled. 'Tell me,' he said. 'What does a literary agent do?'

It took a minute to explain. 'No good to me,' Jackson said. 'Can't read or write. I'm dyslexic, letters are just a jumble. Business is not a problem. I'm a builders' merchant. I can look at someone's plans and work out the numbers in my head in a trice. Letters? No chance. Just have to have someone to write it down and read it back. People I can handle. Know your products. Know your people. Provide what they want.' He glanced over his shoulder.

'You're obviously successful.'

Jackson grinned. 'Yup. I supplied my own materials and my mate built it. Keeps the cost down. I use it as a Show House and it becomes tax deductible,' he said and winked.

'Show house?' Jackson had the broadest grin. 'You built this crescent?'

His grin became even broader as he raised his eyebrows. 'I paid over the odds for the land. Supplied the architect. Dealt with the planners, supplied the builder and basically retired. They got the full package far cheaper than they would have done if they'd done it themselves.' There wasn't much to say. 'Look, if you've a minute how about a cuppa? What you said about books. My daughter might be interested. She's at Leeds University and interested in writing for a living.'

It was a welcome break and an interesting chat. Her tutor was Dr Hollis, the same as he had had. How's that for coincidence. He gave him a business card and suggested that she call the office. Inform them Lewis Green was involved and ask for an information pack. Conversation ended he was just getting ready to leave.

'I know it's nothing to do with me,' said Jackson. 'I'm just a nosey bugger, but could I ask what's in the envelope?'

Green smiled. What was there to lose? 'Why not?' He opened the envelope. Another photo. He almost vomited. Just managing to push the photo of Molière's mutilated body, taped into what appeared to be a Windsor armchair, back into the envelope. He broke out in a cold sweat. His knees buckled. A huge hand grasped his shoulder hauling him to his feet before sitting him in an easy chair. He slid the envelope into his coat pocket. Now he knew! What had Angela Watson told him. Rodahl would see him in a few days. Not if he could help it.

'Are you all right?' Jackson sounded concerned. 'I could see it was a photo. What the Hell was it?'

Green shook his head. 'Sorry, it's private.'

Jackson didn't argue. 'Wait there,' he said and walked to a large cabinet. Returning with a bottle of Teachers and a glass. He poured a healthy measure and handed him the glass. 'Get this down you. You look as though you need it.'

It went down in one.

'More?'

He declined. Another call to make and Joan to consider.

'Well, if you're sure.'

'It's very kind of you, Jack. I've another call to make before meeting Joan, my fiancée, at Red Oaks?'

'That's right. Two down.' Not the most apposite comment to make. 'Your third call is Victory Oaks, I think. The last house. You sure you're all right?'

He needed to get this over with.

They shook hands extracting a promise that Jackson would not divulge the effect the envelope's contents had had on him. With trepidation he crossed the crescent to Victory Oaks. Jack had telephoned ahead. Envelope in pocket courtesy of Mrs. Christine Jessop he retreated to Red Oaks.

Curiosity got the better of him. It couldn't be worse. Another Windsor armchair but with a card bearing his true name, Martin Beck. The message loud and clear. Time to get to home ground and call the police in the West Riding. It would have been so much easier to call from Joan's parents but the thought of involving Joan or her parents, anathema.

Joan must not, under any circumstances, see the second photograph. A task that became difficult when she insisted on returning to London with him and staying at his flat instead of her own. Swings and roundabouts. Understandably she was curious. Understandably she became frosty when he declined to discuss it.

There was a knock on the door. Joan answered. Zelda Jenkins, the nosey neighbour opposite clasping something in both hands. She looked and sounded worried.

'Joan, it's nice to see you again.'

There was a difficult pause.

'Is something wrong, Zelda?'

'Mmm, it's a bit difficult. Can I come in?'

Joan closed the door behind her.

Bard took the funereal wreath in at a glance. A cold sweat broke out on his brow. 'Is that what I think it is, Zelda?'

'Sorry, Lewis,' she sounded apologetic. 'I found it propped against your door about an hour ago and thought I'd better take it in.'

He managed a smile, walked across taking it from her. 'Thank you very much, Zelda. It was good of you ... It's an annoying practical joke. I've been plagued with them over the past week or so. Nothing to worry about. Thank you again.' He guided her out of the door before she could speak.

He didn't realise just how tight a grip he had on the wreath until Joan prised his fingers open and lifted it in both hands. '*What the cobbler threw at his wife*,' she read. '*In Memoriam. Lewis Green. Gone & Forgotten* ...' At least it didn't say Martin Beck. Any doubt in Joan's mind had gone. She was frightened. He wasn't far behind. At least she hadn't seen what was in his pocket. Sending correspondence to the office was one thing. Leaving a funereal wreath propped up against the door to his flat was a different order of magnitude. Joan looked at him and read the card again. '*What the cobbler threw at his wife?* ... You're *the last*? The last what? Lewis, what the Hell is going on? You've been as fidgety as I don't know what since this morning. I saw your face when you came out of Jackson's, you looked terrible. Now this. You owe me an explanation.'

'Joan, please. It's a sick prank. Let me deal with it.'

'That's rubbish,' she said, her voice quivering with emotion. 'Lewis. Just look at your hands, they're shaking. We're engaged to be married. For God's sake tell me what's happening.'

A knock at the door saved him from having to answer. Joan gave him a hard stare and walked to the door.

Listening to the voice didn't make the situation any better.

'Can I help you?'

'Mrs Green,' the voice cultured, sonorous and familiar. 'May I extend my deepest condolences on the death of your husband. This is my card, Geoffrey Niven, funeral directors. We spoke earlier.'

Joan's voice was completely flat. 'You'd better come in, Mr Niven.'

Lewis and Niven's son, Bernard, were members of Hampstead Riders Rugby Club. Geoffrey was middle aged, five seven, dark greying hair slicked back, bespoke suit, immaculate shoes. Dying was obviously a lucrative business. He stopped when he saw Lewis standing by the window. A look a total shock on his face. 'L-Lewis, but ...'

'Somewhat premature, Geoffrey,' he managed a weak smile. 'Would you care to explain?

'I don't understand,' he said and looked at Joan. 'I spoke with your wife only this morning.'

'This morning, Geoffrey, I was en route to Huddersfield by train where I met Joan, my fiancée. There is no wife. Never has been. We arrived back here less than thirty minutes ago.'

There wasn't a great deal Geoffrey Niven could tell them. True, Geoffrey didn't know whether he was married or not but assumed from this morning's phone call, purporting to be from Joan, that he was. Female voice, name, address, telephone number all off pat. Geoffrey provided his contact details and with profuse apologies he left.

Lewis's head was spinning. Should he tell Joan the whole story. Should he tell her that for her own good he couldn't explain. Her own protection. That wouldn't work. Joan would demand to know. Protection from what? Would she let it slide? That was easy. No, she would not. Show her the photograph? No, she would be straight onto her mother. As for calling the police with her in the room? What a mess.

'Lewis,' she said, her voice emotional. 'I want the truth. What is going on? If you don't trust me, I can't live with that, and we're finished. I am not joking.'

Decision time. 'Sorry, Joan. I promise, once it's straightened out, I will tell you. But not just now.'

She looked devastated. Tears in her eyes. She removed her engagement ring and handed it back. 'I'm sorry I mean so little to you,' she said. 'I'm going to pack. Will you call me a taxi?'

It was pointless to discuss it any longer. He carried her case to the kerb. Without a word or a look passing between them Joan climbed into the taxi. A green van advertising Carson & Son, Cabinet Makers, pulled up nose to nose with the cab. Two men looking like father and son exited studying the flats, a piece of paper in the elder's hands. He had no idea why they were here, but it gave him a bad feeling.

'I wish you'd learn to bloody write properly,' the elder said and thrust the paper in front of the other. 'What's this flat number?'

'Dunno.'

'Excuse me. I live here,' he said. 'Can I help?'

'Thanks, mate. Can you read this address?' He passed him the paper.

A quick glance was sufficient. 'It's flat nineteen,' he said, handing the paper back.

The man gave him a disbelieving look. 'Is it? I'm buggered if I can make it out. But you're sure.'

In spite of everything he smiled. 'Believe me it's nineteen. But could I ask what you want?'

'Yup, poor sod's carked. His widow's ordered this,' he slid open the side door to reveal what appeared to be a mahogany coffin.

Lewis felt sick. 'I'm afraid you've been had,' he said.

The elder Carson whipped his head round and looked Lewis straight in the eye. 'What do you mean?'

'Flat nineteen is mine,' he said. 'And, as you can see, I'm very much alive. Furthermore, there is no Mrs Green. I'm not married and never have been.'

'You're sure?'

'I'm sure I'm still alive, yes. And there is no Mrs Green.'

The elder Carson's face clouded over. 'Who the chuff's going to pay for this?' He indicated the coffin and looked at Lewis Green.

For the first time in several hours, he smiled. 'Well, I can't, I'm supposed to be dead.'

Carson frowned and managed a grin. 'No, I don't suppose you can. A bit of a bastard this is. It's bloody expensive.'

'Look, you're not the first. Three quarters of an hour ago, I had an undertaker, Geoffrey Niven, knocking at the door. Somebody is having a go at me, and I don't know who,' the elder Carson looked shocked. 'Why don't you call at Nivens and tell him your story, see if you can come to an arrangement. You never know.'

The elder Carson nodded. 'Aye, It's worth a try. Sorry about your problem, Mr Green. I hope you catch the bastard. Come on Carl. Let's go.'

'A quick question before you go, Mr Carson. When were you asked to supply this coffin?'

He glanced at the paper in his hand. 'Five days ago and told to deliver it now. If you weren't in to return later.' Lewis Green nodded.

He stood and watched as Mr Carson U-turned followed a few seconds later by Joan in her taxi, winding the window up as she passed. She had heard every word. There was no attempt to make eye-contact.

He gazed through the window at the London skyline; the dome of St Pauls catching the late sunshine. Phone in hand he sat back in his chair listening to the ringtone, wondering. A female voice broke his reverie. 'West Riding Police.'

He hesitated. His gut churned. 'Can I speak to someone who is dealing with these murders, please.'

'Are you a member of the Press?'

He took a deep breath. 'No, I believe that I'm the next victim.'

Blake
Fifteen

We caught DI Cartwright in the kitchen making himself a coffee and brought him up to speed. 'You think this is definitely number three?'

'Yes sir,' I said. 'Apart from the scalp wound it appears identical to Newsome.'

He nodded and turned to Max 'What else have you got?'

Max detailed what we had found at the university and also from DI Giles at Millgarth.

'Right, we have five undergrads at Leeds Uni who share a house where this girl disappeared. At least two of them played rugby for the varsity. This latest victim is built like a forward?' I agreed. 'Three victims and three names which we can't account for. There's a strong possibility that the latest victim is one of the three. That's a careful phone call.'

'I was going to suggest a call to force control,' I offered. 'That's where incoming teleprinter and telex messages will appear first. Follow that with a call to M.O. (Criminal Record Office) in case one of the names has already arrived but not been circulated.'

'Good point. You do that, and Max, start with the first name on the list. Nash, wasn't it?'

'Yes sir.'

'Grab yourselves a drink whilst I copy the details and then get cracking.'

Calls to both the Force Control Room and M.O. took a few minutes. In the meantime, Max had obtained contact details of

Charles Nash and commenced trying to contact Neville Waters. That left me with Lewis Green.

It was a bit of a shock when a male voice answered. 'Clive Beck.'

'I'm sorry to trouble you Mr Beck but I was under the impression that Lewis Green lived there.'

He sounded suspicious. 'Who am I speaking with, please?'

'Detective Constable Blake from the West Riding. Does he live there?'

'No officer, he both lives and works in London.'

'We have that telephone number down as being at his home address. And can you please confirm that you are his father.'

'Yes, I am. But he hasn't lived here since he left university. Could I ask what this is about?'

'I'm sorry Mr Beck, I'm not at liberty to say. It is a matter of some urgency that we contact him.'

'The West Riding you say? Is this anything to do with that girl that went missing about seven years ago?'

'I'm sorry, Mr Beck, but I'm not at liberty to say. Will you confirm that he changed his name?'

There was a silence. 'Yes, he did,' he said. 'His name is Martin Graeme Beck. That's G-r-a-e-m-e. After that girl's disappearance he was being hounded by the Press and others. It's the route he took to avoid the hassle. Nobody liked the idea, but it seemed best at the time.'

'I see.' Change of name? This was new and Max hadn't mentioned anything. 'Could I have his contact details, please?' He gave me the numbers for both The Lewis Green Literary Agency and his flat. Our conversation ended with an exhortation that his son get in touch with us should the opportunity arise.

It was the middle of the working day. A Margaret Kelly answered my call. I sensed a very protective lady. No, Lewis Green was not on the premises. He had been working from home and called to say he was taking the train to Huddersfield. Something to do with a manuscript. She had no idea what the issue was. Plus, his fiancée was visiting her mother who lived there. Kill two birds with one stone.

'Was the manuscript linked to anything else? Any other correspondence perhaps?'

'Possibly. A couple of letters arrived a week or so ago that seemed to upset him. I didn't see the contents. All he said was that should anything similar arrive that I should hand them directly to him and not to Joan, his secretary.'

'So, they could have been anything?'

'Yes, except they arrived a few days prior to the manuscript.'

'And the manuscript? To do with his work as an Agent.'

'I would assume so, they usually are.'

There were no internal problems in the Agency, at least none that she would divulge. So, that was it for now. She confirmed the flat address and telephone number and gave me his secretary's parent's telephone number in Huddersfield.

There was no reply from the flat and no answering machine. Likewise, from Huddersfield.

Max and I had a confab with DI Cartwright. Max was aware of the change of name and apologised for not telling us. He had no success in trying to call Charles Nash. The board was brought up to date.

A phone call from M.O. A Neville Waters had been reported as missing.

An hour later in company with DS Creighton, DS Ryder and Max, I was en route to what could be number four. It was becoming a tsunami. Another derelict mill. This time Bradford Road, Batley.

First floors of former weaving mills were in high demand. The victim identical to Newsome in the manner he had been trussed and mutilated, but no wound to the back of the head. Another male big enough to play in the pack and assuming that he was one of the five it must be Nash. Green, or Beck had been alive earlier in the day and it was the smell that drew whoever it was that found the body to the scene. I hoped beyond hope that we would locate the last of the five before the killer.

Green / Blake

Sixteen

Everyone laughed when DS Creighton announced. 'Well gentlemen, it's been one Hell of a day. The corpse found in Leeds this morning we now know to be Neville Waters, a teacher from Manchester. Investigating Officer DI Giles. This afternoon's addition to the tally is Charles Nash, and, from the state of the body, preceded Waters. Nash hails from Eastbourne and works for the Atomic Energy Authority. That team lead by DI Weaver from Batley.

'We now know there are definite links. They all attended Leeds University. Shared the same address. All played rugby for the varsity. There was one more in the group, and as yet, we have been unable to make contact. His name is Lewis Green, changed from Martin Beck approx. seven years ago. We know Green was alive this morning when he travelled from Kings Cross to Huddersfield. Messages have been left with his parents in Bristol and at his business in London should he get in contact. The Met have been round to his flat but there is no reply.

'There is one further link. Apparently, they used to hold sex parties at their house,' DS Creighton held his hands up to subdue the laughter. 'Yes, I know, we were all young once. A girl, Emily Reid, disappeared after one of their parties. There has been no trace of her since. It was investigated by Detective Sergeant Giles, now DI. He interviewed all five and eliminated them from the enquiry. A local Ted was arrested and during interview admitted raping Reid. He later admitted other similar offences but denied murder. He carried a flick knife. Reid's blood was found in the locking mechanism. He is now serving life in Sheffield for the girl's rape and murder. For the time being, that is not a part of this enquiry.'

'Blake?' DI Priestly pointed as the phone began to ring.

'Incident room, DC Blake.' I could hear breathing. 'Hello, who is it?'

'M-my name is L-Lewis Green I ...' His voice tremulous.

I interjected. 'Hold the line Mr Green. We know who you are. Just a second.'

I raised my hand and snapped my fingers. Beckoned to DI Cartwright. 'Where exactly are you?'

'In my flat.

'Are you on your own?

'Yes.'

DI Cartwright arrived.

'Please make sure the door is secure.' The phone clattered against a wooden surface.

I turned to DI Cartwright. 'Lewis Green, sir,' I said. He scurried off.

> I could hear him breathing again. 'Mr Green, are you all right?'

There was a silence. 'They gave me a photo of Bill in the chair,' he said his voice emotional. 'And another with a chair and my name on it.'

If he had seen a photo of Bill Boxley, he must be crapping himself.

'I understand. I have spoken with your father and a lady in your office. Would you like me to call them and let them know you're all right? I won't pass on any details.'

'No, thank you,' he said, his voice more settled. 'It would be better coming from me.' DS Creighton appeared at my shoulder.

'Give me your telephone number again, please,' I wrote it down. 'Very well. Mr Green, I will call you back in ten minutes.'

I put the phone down and told DS Creighton what I knew.

'Ok. Mr Cartwright, call Hampstead. See if they have any secure accommodation where we can put Green until we can get to him. Failing that, do they have sufficient manpower to put someone outside his flat overnight. Tell them any officer who attends Green's flat is to say that DC Blake sent him. What's your collar number?

'547, sir.'

'Mr Priestley, whilst DI Cartwright is sorting that out, get the message out to the other DI's that Green is alive and well. They don't need to know anything else. And Blake, Green knows your voice so you will be his handler. When you reconnect just let him talk. See what he can tell you about this Reid girl. The more information the better,' he paused and looked over his shoulder. 'Sergeant Ryder, you and Blake will be going to London first thing in the morning. Leave at six, you should get to Green's address by ten. Contact HQ Garage see if they have a spare car. If not, claim mileage.'

Green answered at the first ring. I explained that we hoped to put him somewhere safe and the alternative, plus the questions he had to ask. Then the questions he would ask me when I arrived:

- What was my mother's maiden name – Westmoreland.
- Second, what was special about the day before my daughter was born – it was Christmas Day and five days prior to my wife Lucy's twenty second birthday.

Satisfied, I asked him to start with the day they met Emily Reid and progress to the arrival of the two mysterious letters. He worked his way through the past weeks and the revelations of his journey to Huddersfield. The photographs, manuscript and other documents were in a blue manilla folder in the top left-hand drawer of his desk. I was making my own notes. Details of the wreath, undertaker and cabinet maker, that completed that part of the exercise. What he recounted to me matched what I remembered of the Emily Reid file. There was nothing new, but why would there be unless he had lied earlier and was now telling the truth. Under no circumstances, short of fleeing fire, should he open the door.

The Boss pointed at the phone.

'Mr Green, Detective Superintendent Creighton. Unfortunately, there is no secure accommodation available. However, an officer should be with you shortly. You know what question to ask?'

'Yes, who sent you? and the answer should be DC 547 Blake.'

'Good. They have been told they cannot have access to your flat, even if they are desperate. DC Blake and DS Ryder will hopefully arrive around ten a.m. I have consulted with the officer-in-charge of the Metropolitan Police Information Room, if there is anything that makes you feel at risk then please ring 999. Your call will be given priority.'

Seventeen

The gentle hum of the lift silenced. The doors opened. A woman wearing a beige top-coat over a nurse's uniform stepped out. Followed by two men in their thirties one of them wearing a genuine police uniform. The other angry looking wearing a dark suit.

He almost spat the words. 'What the hell do we do now there's a policeman on the door. From what the others said, Green or whatever his name is, is the guilty one.'

'Take it easy.'

She turned to the man in police uniform. 'If it hadn't been for you, we might never have known about Emily. And if there's one thing I learned from the indigenous tribes of Africa over the past years, it's a life for a life. They're all guilty and they'll all die. For now? We have to wait.

It had been a nightmare. Road works and diversions. 10.55 a.m. Almost an hour late. A confirmatory check of the A-Z. 'Next right, Sarge. Flats on the left. I hope.'

'Let's bloody hope so.'

That was too simple. 'For crying out loud. Nobody warned us about this.' Cones. Pneumatic drills. Men and noise everywhere. As far as you could see. The Gas Board were doing what they did best – digging a trench down the nearside of the road.

'Drop me off here, Sarge. He's expecting me. It's flat nineteen. Oh, hang on.' I grabbed hold of a passing hard hat. Showed my warrant card. He waved his arms a bit. I just managed to make out six hundred yards. I thanked him.

He wandered off. I poked my head inside the car. 'As far as I could make out you take the left turn in about six hundred yards. I'll see you up there.'

After crossing the trench, it was simple. Flat nineteen. Third floor. Policeman outside the door. 'DC Blake, Brian Blake, from the West Riding,' I said showing my warrant card. 'Sorry we're late. Roadworks and diversions.'

'Tell me about it,' he laughed. We shook hands. 'Bill Cameron,' he replied. 'What's all this about? All we've been told is to stick fast and not move until you got here.'

'He's a witness in those murders we're dealing with,' I said. 'He's had a few threats.'

'You're taking him back to Yorkshire?'

'We are. Look, why don't you get off, my sergeant is just parking the car. He'll be up in a minute.'

'Once Green has let you in.'

'Fair enough,' said Blake. They were taking the job seriously.

'Who is it?' Was the response to my knocking on the door.

'DC 547 Blake, Mr Green. We spoke on the telephone yesterday. Sorry we're late.'

The response was immediate. 'What is your mother's maiden name?

'Westmoreland, Dorothy Westmoreland.'

'What was special about the day before your daughter was born?'

Pc Cameron gave me a strange look. I smiled in return. 'It was Christmas Day and five days prior to my wife's twenty second birthday.'

'Just a minute.'

From the sounds not only was the door locked there was something very heavy preventing it from being opened. Eventually a stress-lined face appeared. 'Can I see your warrant card, please?' After brief scrutiny it was handed back and the door opened. He stepped out. 'I thought you said there would be a Detective Sergeant Ryder with you.'

'There is, Mr Green,' I said. 'But with the mess outside he's trying to find somewhere to park. He'll be up in a minute.' He seemed satisfied and retreated to the confines of his flat.

'Right,' said Bill Cameron. 'I'm off. My bike's in the garage. I might see your sergeant, Ryder? was it?' I nodded. We went our separate ways.

There was a deep sigh and a wan smile. 'How are you feeling Mr Green?' I said as he closed the door.

'Better now you've arrived. Since Huddersfield it's not been good.'

I wasn't surprised. It was bad enough for me and I'd seen plenty. But to be caught cold and confronted by a photograph of someone you knew in those circumstances? It didn't bear thinking about. As for a chair with your name on it.

'Can I see these photographs and the other documents you mentioned, please?'

'Adrienne, we can't just hang around down here,' the man in the suit said. 'We stand out like sore thumbs.'

'I know,' she replied as PC Cameron, who had heard the latter part of the exchange, walked round the corner. A glance was all he required. A police uniform that wasn't the Met. The other two? It smelled wrong. 'You're not Sergeant Ryder.'

'Ah, you've been relieved,' the man in the police uniform said. The woman took a discrete step to her left. Opened her handbag. Took the syringe from the silver snap-shut case. Depressed the plunger causing a spurt of liquid before stabbing Bill Cameron in the neck emptying the syringe. He fell like a stone.

The man in the police uniform dropped to one knee placing two fingers along the side of Cameron's windpipe. 'There's no pulse, Adrienne,' he said. 'He's dead. This wasn't in the plan.'

Adrienne crouched and felt for the carotid pulse. The chance of anyone surviving an injection directly into the neck was remote. The possibility of anyone being able to establish just what the compound was, even less so. 'No, he's fine. It's the same as the others. He'll just be out longer and wake up with the mother and father of headaches. Now shift him into the corner behind the Rover. We've got a chance.'

I put the photograph of Boxley on the desk. 'I'm not surprised you nearly vomited, Mr Green. Anyone would feel the same.'

'Did you see him?'

'Boxley? No. The others? Yes. But not him.'

'Were they all the same?'

I nodded. 'They were.' I wanted to get his mind off that image if possible. 'Can I see the two letters you received and the manuscript.' I had a quick look and handed them back. He returned them to the folder. 'Have you got your bag packed?'

'It's on the sofa.'

'Fine, just as soon as Sergeant Ryder arrives, we can leave. Before then can I use your bathroom?'

'Of course,' he said pointing to a door behind the sofa. 'Facing you at the end.'

First door either side were bedrooms. I pulled the lounge door to behind me.

Lewis Green was gazing out of the window. There was a sharp knock at the door. 'Mr Green, Sergeant Ryder.'

There were two men standing there. One in a dark suit. The other a policeman in uniform, although it looked different from the first. The dark suit stepped forward and shook hands. "Where's the other officer," he said. There was a distinct whiff of aniseed. He brushed passed Green as he pointed to the door. Green turned and felt a searing crack on the back of his head. Then nothing.

Adrienne stepped over Lewis Green's legs. Together they dragged him into the room. 'Help him with that door,' she said. 'We haven't a moment to lose. That sergeant, Ryder, might be here at any moment.' Whilst she was refilling the syringe from the phial in her pocket the other two were manhandling an upright piano and sofa across the door.

'Quickly!' Adrienne said. 'Get hold of him and leave everything else.'

I came out of the toilet to hear furniture being moved behind the lounge door. Something was wrong. The door was shut fast. I slammed my fist against it. 'Mr Green!' I shouted. 'Lewis!' There was no answer to either call. 'Who's there? I'm a police officer. Open this door.' I might as well have kept my mouth shut. There were voices. Two males and one female. Shouting was no good. I turned the handle, got my shoulder to the door and pushed. There was some movement but it would take a long time. I hoped DS Ryder would arrive soon. I looked through a bedroom window. Third floor. No-one in sight.

DS Ryder parked at the side of a beige Rover 3.5 and alighted. Lift with doors open. He was about to step in when he glanced to his left. The sight of an occupied boot caught his attention. There was no carotid pulse. PC Bill Cameron was dead. Brian and Lewis Green? 'God almighty,' he cursed under his breath. The lift doors closed silently. He took one look at the indicator and headed for the doorway marked - STAIRS.

It was slow progress but now I could get my arm through, which did give some extra purchase. I heard DS Ryder as he came through the door. 'Sarge!' I shouted and waved my arm. 'Over here.' I could almost hear the refrain: *Oh dear, what can the matter be? Poor old Brian's locked in the lavatory.*

I was back in the carpark. A buffet from Green's kitchen preventing the lift doors from closing. The beige Rover had gone. I had blocked the garage entrance with the sergeant's car.

Sergeant Ryder? He was calling the Met Information Room.

Eighteen

Three cars arrived in convoy disgorging eight plain clothes officers. 'DI Tomlinson,' the lead driver said. 'Who are you?'

'DC Blake, sir, West Riding,' I turned and pointed. 'PC Cameron is in the corner to the left of the lift.'

The officer standing at the DI's shoulder turned. 'Walker, Smith, you two, come with me.'

'Hold it, sergeant,' said the DI. 'Blake, who's been to the body?'

'Those who put him in the corner and DS Ryder, sir, when he spotted the officer's boot.'

'Not you?'

'No, sir.'

He nodded as someone entered the garage from the stairs. 'Who in heaven's name has blocked the lift?' the man said.

'Don't touch that.' I shouted running towards him as he pulled the buffet clear of the door. I just managed to get my hand in the doors before they closed.

Mr Forsythe, an elderly well-dressed man needed the lift so that he could take his invalid wife for her hospital appointment. Four DC's were despatched to carry Mrs Forsythe downstairs. I moved Sergeant Ryder's car. After DI Tomlinson had taken a quick look at PC Cameron's body, I accompanied him to the flat. DS Ball organised door to door enquiries and security of the block.

The DI's first call was to the Information Room – circulate details of the beige Rover 3.5, containing two males and a female, wanted re the investigation into the abduction of Lewis Green and death of an on-duty police officer within the last hour. The second call to his divisional commander.

Within minutes a preliminary Express Message and All Ports Warning had been circulated nationwide re the beige Rover 3.5 and occupants. At the same time the nurse, having departed the Rover 3.5 at Camden tube station left the toilets at Kings Cross, now wearing a cream Givenchy suit with matching shoes. Nurse's uniform and shoes in her holdall. There was just time for her to catch the Edinburgh train. Her seat - First Class. The police uniform in the boot of the Rover along with Lewis Green, her associates worked their way through the London traffic heading for the A1.

A grim-faced DI Tomlinson handed back the Boxley photograph from Lewis Green's folder. 'And they're all the same?'

'Yes sir. This is the first victim, Boxley. I hadn't seen him, but the others are identical, except the third had a head wound, otherwise ...'

'That answers a lot of questions, thanks.'

DS Ryder held the phone out. 'Sir, DI Cartwright would like a word.'

'Mr Cartwright, DI Dave Tomlinson ...'

I took one look at DS Ryder's expression. 'They're not happy?'

'Not delirious, but pleased that neither of us is in PC Cameron's situation. They've got the Express, so everyone will now be aware. Obs have been ramped up and CID given a kick up the arse. All BTP offices notified. We're to make our statements and head north.'

The flats and the area in general had been crawling with detectives when we left. An hour later we were on our way north to face whatever music they were playing.

Nineteen

The main thing we achieved on the journey was the time scale of the events that morning. Frighteningly small.

We had an audience: DS Creighton, DIs Cartwright, Priestly and Weaver.

'I entered the flats via the front door and used the stairs. Made contact with Cameron and when I cleared the security with Lewis Green, Cameron left. That was near enough 11:00. Those responsible must have been in the garage when Cameron arrived to collect his bike. Did he use Sergeant Ryder's name when he saw them? Did Green challenge them at the door because I'd told him the sergeant was behind me? Did they use Sergeant Ryder's name to gain access? There was no sign of any disturbance in the flat so, was Lewis Green happy to let them in?

When Sergeant Ryder parked the car, the lift doors in the garage were open. They closed as he was examining Cameron's body. Whilst Sergeant Ryder legged it upstairs and I was trying to open the door into the lounge they must have been in the lift going the other way. By the time I was free they'd have gone. Had I stayed in the car with Sergeant Ryder and we had gone to meet Lewis Green together, in all probability he would not have been kidnapped and we stood a good chance of apprehending some or all of those responsible. Plus, PC Cameron may have still been alive.'

DS Creighton broke the silence. 'Everybody has perfect hindsight,' he said. 'Had I sent you both to London by train last night and arranged for the Met to collect him and meet you at King's Cross it would all have been different. You had no way of knowing what lay ahead, so it was the correct thing to do. Get to the flat as soon as possible and make contact. Release PC Cameron who then went to collect his bike. Had he been waiting for transport from a police vehicle there would have been other officers present or he could have left the building via the front door. The fact that matters developed as they did was completely out of your control. As for using the bathroom, don't we all. But, had there been no roadworks or diversions you could have been there for ten and on your way in less than five minutes. No comebacks. You've been on duty for almost thirteen hours straight. Get yourself off home the pair of you. Get some rest and be here for eight a.m.'

I hesitated. 'Sir, if this was a simple matter of killing Green why didn't they just do it in London? They had the means and the opportunity. And they took the risk of moving Green and shipping him in the Rover. All the victims were brought back here. I can't see them hanging about. This is going to be over tonight. I can't speak for Sergeant Ryder ...'

'I agree with Blake, sir,' he interjected. 'It will be over tonight. Two extra pairs of eyes?'

'Logically, sir,' I said. 'They'll finish where it began, Merrion Lodge.'

There was a look of annoyance gracing DI Priestley's face, a smile on DI Cartwright's and a narrowing of DI Weaver's eyes.

DI Cartwright left the group to answer his phone.

DS Creighton smiled. 'I agree with you, Blake. But you should know. According to DI Giles, Merrion Lodge was demolished two weeks ago.'

That was a kick in the guts.

DI Cartwright re-joined us.

'Good news?'

He smiled and nodded. 'At approximately 11:20 this morning a local beat officer in Camden saw a C registered, beige Rover 3.5

stop in a prohibited area adjacent to Camden Town tube station. A woman in a nurse's uniform alighted. He spoke to her. She apologised and said the two remaining male occupants had given her a lift because her car had broken down and she was due to start work at Guy's Hospital. When the officer looked round the car had gone. When he turned back so had the nurse. She apparently caught the next in-bound tube. A nurse was seen leaving the underground at King's Cross, which is north of the river. Guys Hospital is south of the river. There were no other nurses on that train. No reported sightings after that. Enquiries at Guy's Hospital reveal that there were no nurses commencing work today. However, the Edinburgh train left King's Cross fifteen minutes after her tube arrived. That train stops in Leeds. I've had a quick word with the Transport Police at Leeds City Station and they are making enquiries.'

'That's good to know. Initially, obs were broadcast for a car containing two men and a woman. Changing the number of occupants was well planned. But we can surmise that is our car. There aren't large numbers of the Rover 3.5 on the road. However, you're correct and we can look for the Rover. You two get the area from Regent Street up the hill towards Briggate, Merrion Street and the Grand. See if Millgarth Street have any spare radios. Mr Cartwright ...'

Twenty

'Christ, Adrienne, how much did you give him?' The three of them stared at the last of the five. Unconscious. Naked, except for his wristwatch, and pinioned in the Windsor armchair exactly as the others had been. Eyes and mouth taped.

'Perhaps a little bit more than the others, nothing untoward. And don't worry you'll get your beauty sleep.'

'It's not that, I was just thinking about that copper in London.'

'Don't worry,' she said and laughed. 'He'll be fine.'

'He didn't look it. Went down like a sack of spuds.'

'Don't worry. That's a normal response when you inject it in the neck. It works very fast.'

Lewis Green became aware of the light and strained to move towards it, but couldn't. Somewhere in the distance what could have been human voices, but more real was the headache and the deep throbbing ache in his right shoulder. For some reason he was cold. *My hands, I can't move my hands or legs. My legs are bare. Why are my hands on my legs? My clothes?* The photo of Molliere flashed into his pineal eye. *Where are the police? For god's sake. I can't open my mouth or my eyes.* Try as he might he was pinioned. '*The voices. Got to get help.*' His heart was pounding as he began to thrash. The noise that emanated from his vocal chords unintelligible.

A gloved hand on his shoulder. Tape was ripped from his mouth leaving a terrified Martin sweating and gasping.

'Get me out.' A sharp stab in his left thigh. 'Arrgh! What was that for?'

A female voice snapped. 'Be quiet. That was the point of an amputation knife. I take it you remember the photograph of your friend? I suggest you listen ... Nothing to say?'

'I've got plen.' Another stab in the thigh. 'Arrgh!'

'We'll dispense with this charade of calling you Lewis Green, Mr Beck. Martin wasn't it? If you shout or scream I will replace the tape and this time it will cover your nose as well. Do you agree?'

'Yes. 'W-why are you doing this.'.

'Uncomfortable? Now you know how Emily felt as you choked the life out of her.'

'Who are you? Why are you doing this?'

'Arrgh!'

'You're not here to ask questions. It's time to tell the truth.'

'You haven't asked me any questions yet.' He yelped again. 'Emily? The girl who disappeared seven years ago?'

'The girl you murdered seven years ago,' she added under her breath and seized him by his penis and testicles, pulled and held the amputation knife behind his scrotum. 'Now, Mr Beck if you don't want to look pretty with these sown into your mouth, I suggest you pay attention. I am going to ask you some questions. You are going to tell me what I want to hear. Do you understand?'

'W-why? Y-yes.'

She looked at her colleagues. 'Ready?'

Twenty One

Evening traffic, both vehicular and pedestrian was building steadily as DS Ryder and DC Blake crossed New Briggate from the Grand Theatre.

'We've checked everything this side of Regent Street, Brian, only the Merrion Street area left.'

'I know sarge. But if this is about Emily Reid it would make sense to finish it where it was supposed to have started.'

'I agree. But if Merrion House had been demolished, where?'

He shrugged helplessly. 'No idea.'

'And Green will be dead. The sooner we get this done the better.'

Merrion Street checked they stood by the side of the road. 'Well, sarge,' I said. 'Any ideas?'

'If only ...'

'Sergeant Ryder,' interrupted a voice. 'You know they shoot county coppers in Leeds. What are you doing here?'

We spun round to see a young PC walking up the hill towards us. 'Hello Neville,' he said. 'We're looking for this Rover.' He turned to me. 'Neville Brown, his parents are my next-door neighbours.'

'There's no Rovers of any shape down here,' said Neville. 'I've checked.'

'There bloody is,' said an angry voice behind them. 'It's blocking my loading doors. I rang Millgarth Street near thirty minutes ago.'

'Rover? What model is it?' said Sergeant Ryder.

He frowned as if to say what's the bloody difference. 'Rover 3.5. Bloody nuisance.'

'Show us.'

Within seconds it was in view. A beige Rover 3.5. It had to be the one. Whilst Sergeant Ryder was checking the car, I told Neville to let Millgarth know and to arrange recovery as a matter of urgency.

'Have you touched it at all?' said Sergeant Ryder.

'I had a look in the boot and sat in the driver's seat.'

'Anything else inside?'

'Might have touched the steering wheel.' Which means he had, what man wouldn't?

'They're arranging recovery now, Sarge. And telling the incident room.'

'Right, get this gentleman's details,' he turned to the shop keeper. 'Thanks very much. We shall need your fingerprints for elimination purposes either tonight or tomorrow.'

'It's important then?'

'A man's life is at stake,' I said. 'Now where? It's a pity that Merrion Lodge has been demolished. That would be our next stop.'

'Demolished?' the shop keeper laughed. 'It hasn't been demolished. It's being dismantled. Some Yank with more brass than brains is having it shipped across to the States.'

'Christ!'

DS Ryder took PC Brown's radio. 'Millgarth. DS Ryder, Incident Room. Urgent assistance required Merrion Lodge, Merrion Street. Inform DI Giles that the Lodge has not, repeat not, been demolished.' He handed the radio back. 'Wait here Neville, nobody but nobody touches the car except the recovery team.'

Without waiting for a reply and with directions that access to Merrion Lodge was across the road diagonally to the right, we left. I was faster. And there it was, enmeshed in an envelope of steel tubes. A couple of stacks of roof tiles on the garden. The door furniture had been removed. I gave the door a push. It didn't move. Through the hole where the escutcheon had been a length of one-inch square timber wedging it shut. I listened. 'There's someone inside. It's wedged. Look Sarge, I think I can shift it. As soon as I kick the door you go through. Stand back.'

Twenty-Two

Adrienne stood back with a look of utter contempt. 'Well, at last we have the truth. Blubber away Mr Beck. You're the lucky one. I'm going to call the police and let them know where you are. They can deal with you.'

The news received differently by her two accomplices. For one he was still angry, but it was all over and time to move on. The other? Aching to finish it the way he had the others – this one deserved it more than the rest.

Lewis Green / Martin Beck blocked everything out. Waiting for the cut.

The hammer blow against the door. The snap of the prop. The sound of the heavy oaken door slamming into the wall resounding through the cavernous interior like a thunderclap.

Sergeant Ryder dashed passed Blake as he struggled to his feet. 'POLICE OFFICERS,' he shouted at the top of his voice. 'The building is surrounded. Stay exactly where you are.' He stopped at what was the kitchen door. Silence.

I was fine. Much ado about nothing. Green was taped into a Windsor armchair just as the others had been. The one major difference being that he was hyperventilating and in full possession of his anatomy.

I put my hand on Green's shoulder. 'Mr Green, you're safe now,' I said. 'I'll have you out of there in a trice.' The tears rolled down Green's face as I draped my jacket across his lap, removed the tape from his eyes and severed his bonds. Within thirty seconds he was free

'Police officers. Stand exactly where you are.'

'DC BLAKE,' I shouted. 'Turn right through the door.'

There were half a dozen including Max Cavendish. 'All right, Brian?' Three more arrived.

'I'm fine. Will someone organise a search, they've blown. Sergeant Ryder's gone after them.'

'I'll do that,' said an unknown voice. 'I know this place. Smith and Jones, the cellar. Beardsley and Shearman, upstairs and there's a second staircase from the kitchen. The others outside, check the grounds.'

'Max, is there an ambulance anywhere near?'

'They're outside. I'll fetch 'em.'

Ambulancemen briefed and whilst they were getting Green settled on the stretcher. He of the unknown voice, Sergeant Burton, was smiling. 'Blake, your colleague tells me that you probably kicked the door open.'

'True Sarge, I did. There was just a baton wedging it shut. ...'

'Fair enough. You'll be travelling with him?'

'Yup.' The ambulance crew were ready.

The sergeant unclipped his radio. 'DS Burton. Lewis Green is enroute to LGI accompanied by DC Blake. Will you let the incident room know.'

By the time we reached the hospital Green had calmed.

Blake had a word with the Doctor and the Casualty Sister. A nurse despatched to get a pair of pyjamas.

Fifteen minutes later. 'Well done, Blake.' DS Creighton said, 'The birds had flown?'

'Yes, sir. We heard them running but they were clear.'

'No trace as yet. We'll get them. As soon as someone is available you will be relieved.'

'Was the Rover recovered, sir?'

'It was. It's a West Riding number. We have someone at St. John's North going through the records.'

A sixteen-hour shift. Green had been given a shot of something legal and was asleep.

I picked up the phone and dialled. 'Hello, love. I'll be home in about thirty minutes.'

Beck

Twenty-Three

The last words Lewis Green remembered were, 'This will help you to relax. Just a scratch.' How long ago that was he had no idea. Crisp bedsheets. The smell of antiseptic. Something sweet and floral. Hospital. The thoughts flooded his brain. He was the last of the five. Had the others confessed at the point of a knife? Or with the business edge of an amputation knife pressing into the tissue behind the scrotum as he had. The forlorn hope they might just be released so as not to have their genitals removed, followed by a knife being inserted between their ribs?

The sound of children's voices caught his attention.

'Could someone turn the light off, please?' he said. 'It's too bright.'

There was a scampering of small feet followed by a vaguely familiar, cultured, female voice. 'Can you reach, Graeme.' The soft click and sudden semi-darkness told him all he needed to know.

'Thank you,' he said. 'Sorry, I can't see you at the moment.'

'It's all right.' The voice was gentle, comforting. 'Take your time. Come here Graeme, stand by me.'

He'd heard the voice before. That he knew. But when? A long time ago. Some distant memory pressured its way forwards. It must have been what, six years or more. 'Carol?'

He could hear the smile. 'Yes, it's me. How are you feeling?'

'Better now I've heard your voice and that I'm still in one piece.' He didn't know what, if anything, she knew about the circumstances that lead to his incarceration in hospital. Time would dictate how much she became aware. But for now, nothing.

She chuckled. 'That's good.'

'Mummy,' said a small voice. 'What do we call him?'

Again, the humour. 'That's a good question, Martin,' she said. 'I'm not sure at the moment. It seems to change. However, I do know that he likes to be called, Bard.'

He opened his eyes carefully. There was no glare. A hospital room. On a bedside table a vase of flowers, jug of water and a glass. The blinds were drawn. Sitting on a chair near the foot of the bed was *the* woman with the most beautiful blue eyes. He had been in love with her almost since they first met. She had said they had no future. Now she was five feet away, as beautiful as ever. The twin babies from the photograph in *Country Life* now six years old and like peas from the same pod. Children that he believed he'd fathered. They exchanged smiles but before either could speak one of the boys suddenly spun to his right and pointed at the extinguished fluorescent light tube. 'Smaug,' he shouted. Together the boys bent their bows, nocked the arrows and took aim. 'Pyong!' They both said and lowered their bows as the arrows took flight. Carol sat there with a broad grin watching everything. 'Got him,' said one.

'That's not fair,' said the other with a look of real petulance. 'You shot him last time. It was my turn.'

'Then you should be faster,' a hint of triumph in the reply. 'You're too slow to shoot dragons.'

He couldn't help but smile. 'They were both excellent shots and both arrows struck Smaug,' he said beckoning the loser and whispering in his ear. 'All you have to do is to shout before your brother. Is that all right?'

He smiled and nodded. Then looked puzzled. 'Are you really, Bard?'

He reciprocated. 'No. As your mother said, I sometimes use different names.'

The loser put the back of his left hand against his right cheek. 'I'll bet you're a spy,' he whispered. 'Spies never use their own name.'

He knew about spies? What stories had he been exposed to? 'No, I'm not a spy,' He replied in kind. 'But don't tell anyone, will you?'

The loser shook his head and walked away grinning.

'What has he been telling you?' demanded the other. 'He's been telling you how to beat me, hasn't he?'

'No, your brother just wanted to know if I really was Bard. I'm not, but I like the story. But wait until you read *The Lord of The Rings*. It's much more exciting.'

'Even more exciting than the *Battle of the Five Armies*?' said the wide-eyed loser.

He smiled, leaning towards him and nodded. 'Far more exciting.'

Carol sat with an arm round each of them, her wedding and engagement rings clearly visible. 'These are *my* boys,' she said, 'This is Martin,' she squeezed the shoulders of the one nearest the bed. 'And this,' she squeezed the shoulders of the other, 'is Graeme.'

Before anyone could speak the door opened, a middle-aged man in chauffeur's livery entered. It was a good guess that this was the deliverer of the watch. He took a chance. 'I know it's a long time ago,' he said. 'But thank you for delivering the watch.'

He smiled thinly. 'My pleasure, sir,' he said turning to Carol, 'I have to move the car in thirty minutes, milady.'

Carol took one of the new fifty pence pieces from her purse and handed it to him. 'Will you get the boys a single 99 ice-cream please, John. My friend and I have a lot to talk about. And boys, stay with John. No running around the car park.'

The party left. 'Come on, I'll race you to the top of the stairs.' John didn't stand a chance.

Twenty-Four

His hopes that Carol would sit much nearer to him were dashed. She remained out of reach. She noticed the disappointment and smiled.

'So, you're a Countess,' he said, reciprocating.

A brief puzzled look crossed her face. 'You knew?'

'Dentists waiting room. An article in Country *Life* magazine six years ago.'

'I see,' she said and smiled.

'I haven't told anyone,' he said. 'Although after my mother saw John in Bristol and the watch later that day, she would have torn down the walls of Troy with her bare hands to try to find out who you were.'

'I'm pleased she didn't,' she smiled.

'Thank you, it was a beautiful present.' He held his wrist up. Why it hadn't been removed he had no idea. All his clothes had. Perhaps the police had arrived too quickly.

She smiled again. 'I felt it was the only thing I could do in the circumstances. John was one of the few people I could really trust. Had my husband discovered the truth there is every chance he would have had you or both of us killed; he had the contacts or, would have done it himself.'

'That sounds grim.'

'It wasn't the happiest time of my life.'

'It was a nice touch mentioning *Molière* in the small ad.' The thought of *Molière* in that chair brought the memory flooding back. For now, Carol didn't need to know anything.

'I wanted to make sure you understood it was from me.'

'It made me smile,' He looked into her eyes. 'I've really missed you.'

'And Joan?' she said averting her gaze.

Someone had been doing their homework. 'Ancient history I'm afraid,' he said and smiled. 'She left when things got bad. A wreath, an undertaker and a coffin arrived at my flat ... I know it sounds cheesy, but you were so far out of reach and there was this Carol-shaped hole in my future with no idea how I would fill it. Joan applied for the vacancy as my secretary. The rest was history.'

'And did she? Fill the hole?'

'Not really. Don't misunderstand me. She was intelligent, attractive, a good conversationalist and efficient, but she wasn't you.'

'If I remember rightly,' she had a winsome smile, 'we didn't spend much time talking.'

He semi-scowled. 'You were a hard taskmaster.'

Another smile. 'I don't remember many complaints.'

He replied in kind. 'I didn't hear any from you.'

'I wonder why,' she smiled, 'And you're wondering why I'm here'

'I am.' *And brought our sons.*

There was a lengthy pause. 'I was widowed over six months ago,' she announced to his astonishment.

It was important to get this next bit right and asked the question. 'Should I be sorry?' Was she saying she was available?

'No, you should not,' she pulled the chair closer taking hold of his hands. His reaction telling him the emotional trauma wasn't permanent. 'Most people that I know build a relationship before they have sex. We were the opposite, and it's not just about you and me. I have my boys to consider. I'm sure you realise there is far more than just sex involved.'

'And you want it, whatever *it* is, to work?'

'Of course I do, but I need to be sure.'

His mind was spinning like a top. He needed confirmation. 'Martin and Graeme?' he said. 'They are *our* sons?'

She smiled and nodded. 'Yes, they are. But please try and understand why I must always refer to them as *my sons* and not ours. I wish it could be different, but you can never lay claim to being their father.'

'Nevertheless, if we were compatible, you would want me to be their step-father?'

'If? Yes. Then you would be in a position to influence them for the good.'

He climbed back onto the spinning top. 'This is to do with inheriting their father's title?' He said at length.

'And more,' she said. 'Martin was the first born, if only by five minutes. However, it makes a world of difference. They are both sons of an Earl. Martin became Viscount Salton, Gordon's subsidiary title, and is now the Earl. I retain the courtesy title of Countess until such time as he marries and then I become the Dowager Countess. Martin inherits the estate.'

'That seems unfair, what about Graeme?'

'That will be decided in the fulness of time,' she said. 'At the moment he is entitled to be referred to as, Sir. However, they are six-year-old little boys who are good friends. It is my responsibility to run the estate on Martin's behalf. Really on everyone's behalf initially by putting right what Gordon did or neglected to do. The world is changing, thank goodness. One of my tasks will be to ensure that the boys understand that they cannot just swan around and do nothing, as Gordon did, and bugger his catamite.'

Catamite? What the? She was nothing if not blunt and smiled at my reaction. 'And you want some help?' He said tongue in cheek.

'A bit more than that,' she said and paused. 'You'll understand, at least I hope that you will when you hear my story, just how difficult it became for me. The memories of our short time together never far away. Call them a life raft if you like. I need to know whether we have a future or not. You have to understand the changes it would mean for you but more importantly, are we compatible enough?'

He gave her a quizzical look. 'You've taken the trouble to trace me and produce our sons .. are you proposing to me?' he teased.

She smiled in return. 'You've been on my mind for a long time, Martin,' she said. 'Call it musing aloud. But have you ever thought of reverting to Beck from Green?'

That brought a smile to his lips. 'You want me to change my name back to Beck?'

There was an answering smile. 'Yes,' she said. 'All the memories that I have of you are of that time. In my mind you are still Martin Beck.' She glanced at her watch. 'We don't have much time and I want to tell you what happened after we parted.'

'And you prefer Beck as your married surname instead of Green?' she could still scowl. 'I need a down payment. A kiss?'

> She gripped his hands and leaned forwards kissing him gently on the lips. 'Spoilsport,' he said as she sat back and laughed.

'You know you're supposed to rest, Martin. Too much excitement might be bad for you.'

He raised his eyebrows and flicked the covers back.

She managed to stop the laugh. 'Behave yourself.'

Twenty-Five

'If only things had been different. Melanie and Joan. That's Grace and Christine, thought I was falling in love with you. In spite of everything I couldn't get you out of my mind and after Gordon demanded sex that first evening back ... I knew I was. After that he didn't come near, which didn't bother me. When I told him I had missed two periods he was deliriously happy. The test results were obviously in error.

'He was staying at his club in London when I telephoned the estate in the Nappa Valley to confirm who their agent in the UK was and told Golding, the Butler to put them on the list of suppliers.

'It was during a visit to some friends in Surrey that I visited Bond Street and bought the watch.'

'My mother arranged a family get together just to find out what was in the letter and the parcel after John's appearance.'

She laughed. 'I'll bet you enjoyed it.'

'You have no idea. And when I saw the photographs, it was only the promise that stopped me from finding out where Oldeney Carr House was. And you being a Countess ... I thought, what would be the point,' he paused and smiled. 'And here you are. It's not just my magnetic personality.'

She reciprocated and squeezed his hands. 'To continue. When our sons were born, he threw a large party but his attitude didn't last.

'He'd never interacted with them in any meaningful way and when the boys were two they began to pick out words when I read to them, they learned quickly, especially Graeme. Mary, the ageing Nanny, previously Gordon's Nanny, must have told him and he demanded to know where this trait came from. I persuaded him it was part of my legacy. He only read the Times and accounts relating to the estate.

'It became worse. Our relationship soured. He installed his latest catamite into the House and then into his bedroom. The attitude of the staff split, there were those like John who I could always count on. Others clearly on Gordon's side but the most dangerous were those whose allegiances were unclear. Information was getting back to him. He took my car keys and banned me from leaving the estate. If I left the House I was accompanied. Even when I tried to smuggle notes out of the building they were returned, usually when I was attending to the boys during mealtimes, either by Gordon or perhaps *I had dropped them on the floor*. To all intents and purposes, I was under house arrest.

She paused and took a deep breath. He took the opportunity. 'Could I have my fingers back, please, milady.'

'What?' she looked at his hands, whilst telling him the story her grip was becoming uncomfortable. She grinned. 'Sorry,' she said, relaxed and kissed his fingers.

'That's quite some story. But what about his family?'

There was a deep sigh. 'His sister was the only one who tried to keep in touch with me; that became difficult after a while. As for the rest, including his mother, his father had died some years earlier, didn't bother at all. In fact, they basically ignored him and cut him off.'

'That can't have made it any easier,' said Bard after a few seconds. 'You ought to get it down in writing. I can think of several editors who would be delighted. Under a pseudonym of course and change any detail that could identify the source. But I think it would do well.'

'Perhaps ... I overheard a snippet of conversation between Gordon's manservant, Fletcher and Golding, our Butler, in which

Fletcher said His Lordship had intimated that the following day he was going to put the estate on the market and emigrate. I was furious. They were both on my mental list of Gordon's people. I knew that Gordon was in his garage - he had a collection of about twenty cars, some vintage, some rare and all very expensive. .

When I arrived, John was valeting the Rolls. Gordon, in his overalls was poking about in a toolbox. There was a car next to him jacked up at the front with the wheels off. "*Madam?*" he said, almost as a sneer as I slammed the door shut behind me. "*To what do I owe the pleasure?*"

'There was no point in beating about the bush. "I've just overheard your man, Fletcher, talking with Golding to the effect that tomorrow you're putting the estate on the market. Is that true?"

"*Really? Adding eavesdropping to your list of talents, I see.*"

"Never mind the sarcasm, is it true?"

'He looked up. "Get out!" he snapped at John. I was about to tell John to wait when 'Gordon continued. "No, on second thoughts wait. I don't mind you as a witness. Should my loving and devoted wife neglect to pass on the details, you will. Understood?"

'John acknowledged.

'I felt sorry for John having to hear this, however I ignored the barb and repeated the question. "Is it true?"

'He smirked and nodded. "Yes, it is. But you Madam will remain on the estate at all times. John, have the car ready for eight a.m. to take me to my solicitors. Once the documents are signed there is nothing, Madam, that you or your sainted father can do. A *fait accompli*."

'I asked him about the staff. What would happen to them. He said he hoped whoever bought the estate would keep them on, except Fletcher, it was difficult to get hold of a good manservant. Tulliver would also go with him.

'I didn't pick up on that for a minute or so but when I did the implications made my blood run cold.'

'You're squeezing my fingers again. What is it, Carol?'

She relaxed her grip and looked at me with fear in her eyes. 'How's your knowledge of Roman and Greek myth?'

'Fair,' Bard replied. 'Any in particular?'

'Ganymede,' she said, stony-faced

There was a pause whilst the cogs were busy. Then the penny dropped. That was evil. *Ganymede, in Roman mythology. Catamitus, the origin of the term catamite in Greek, was a beautiful Trojan male. Zeus, disguised as an eagle swooped to earth and carried him off. He became cup-bearer. The story is of homosexual love.* 'You're not serious?'

'Oh yes, I am. I asked him where we would live. His reply was that I could live where I wanted. Use my own money instead of his for a change. He was casting me off. At least I could make the necessary arrangements for myself and the boys and told him so.

'I'll never forget a single word of what followed next. I never thought that I could hate anyone with such intensity. Had I had the means to hand I would have killed him where he stood.'

'He shook his head and leaned towards me his face within inches of mine. He was almost hissing when he spoke.

"Oh no, the boys go with me. I am their father, am I not? ... Or am I?" He knew what I had done. Not who you were, but he knew. "There is not one aspect of either of them when compared to any family portrait which says *this boy is a Sylverton*. I took the test again and you were correct, I cannot father children. The question is, who is their father if it wasn't me? You will sign a statement before I leave in the morning that you were whoring with Beauchamp and de Vere's wives wherever it was and, as a result gave birth to these bastards. They will be disinherited. Your family will suffer the consequences of attempting to pass these cuckoos off as mine.

They are six years old now, but in two years they will make excellent cup bearers. In fact,' he paused and smiled, "Don't you think that Solomon would make the perfect teacher. I think they would enjoy watching their loving father explain everything to them." He took two steps back, looked me up and down and smiled. I've never seen such evil.

She paused. Her eyes moist. 'Our boys, our beautiful boys,' she said, 'when they were eight, he was going to use them as catamites. But he was incapable of understanding how hard a mother will fight to save her children.

'He blew me a kiss and got down on the floor. He had one of those boards with wheels on and slid headfirst under the front axle of the car that was jacked up. "You're an inhuman bastard, Gordon."

'There was no laughter. "Just two years, Carol .. I can feel it now. Such pleasure. Think about it."

'This was never going to happen. I didn't realise what I was doing when I screamed, "I hope you burn in Hell", and stood on the jacking handle.'

There was a pause. Bard's brow furrowed. 'But, that would release the pressure.'

'Very effectively. When he saw the car dropping, he shouted, "What the hell are you doing?" The scream as the axel hit his chest was short but very loud. "Saving my children from a monster," I replied.'

'I take it he was dead?'

'Oh, yes. There was no doubt about it.'

'He didn't use axle stands?'

'No, he never did. The next second John was by my side shaking me. "Did anyone know you were coming here, milady?"

I told him, "No"

"Quickly, milady," he said. "See if the keys are in the ignition." Whilst I was doing that, he fetched a trolley jack?'

I nodded.

She nodded. 'I told him the key was in the ignition. He acknowledged and jacked the car up again and placed this trolley jack beneath the axle. Then lifted the car slightly higher before adjusting the car jack beneath the axle. He lowered the car so that the axle was resting on the edge of the car jack. Trolley jack out of the way he climbed into the car, started the engine, and asked me quite firmly to stand by the door and face the other way. I heard the crack as he drove the car off the jack. When I turned round, he was putting the keys in Gordon's trouser pocket. I couldn't see Gordon's body and had no wish to. The significance of what John had done only became evident at the inquest a few weeks later.'

There was no resistance as I sat up and pulled her towards me. I even got a kiss for my trouble followed by a most satisfactory, 'I've missed you.' We didn't talk much for the next five minutes.

Carol pulled her chair closer so that we could hold hands without reaching. 'Was that it?'

'Oh no,' she said with an impish grin. 'I had no feeling whatsoever about Gordon's death but total trust in John. That was just the beginning. For the previous three years I had been increasingly isolated, degraded and humiliated. It was time to re-assert my authority. My instructions to John were that he should use the telephone in the Hall, firstly to call Dr Jessop, the village doctor, followed by a call to the Ambulance and then the police. I had other things to do.

'John opened the door for me. I flounced passed him. 'You know what to do, John?'

'Milady,' he acknowledged and picked up the telephone. 'We still have those where the earpiece hangs from the side. Then I spotted Christopher, one of the footmen, heading in my direction. I was blazing and snapped at him. 'Where is Tulliver?'

'In the Drawing Room, Milady.'

John, one of the gardeners appeared from the kitchen. 'What he was doing in the hall I had no idea, but he was just what I needed. 'Both of you follow me.' He looked shocked. I detested Tulliver as much as I did Gordon.'

'He was lounging in an easy chair looking at the Times. As usual clothed from head to foot at Gordon's largesse. A cream-coloured silk suit, peacock-blue silk shirt with a cream cravat and hand-made slip-ons.

'When he saw me, he said, "Carol, be a dear and order me some coffee."

'I pointed at Tulliver and turned to Christopher. 'This disgusting animal is a trespasser and barred from the estate. Take him to the gates as fast as you can. Use as much force as you deem necessary.'

A startled Tulliver dropped the newspaper. "Whoa, just a minute Carol."

'Lady Sylverton to you. His Lordship is dead. Do not show your face here again. Christopher?'

Tulliver was as unpopular with the staff as he was with me. 'I stood to one side as John and Christopher grabbed a protesting Tulliver by the arms and dragged him from the room.'

'You were enjoying this, weren't you?' I smiled at her.

She reciprocated 'You have no idea. For the past seven years I had been subjected to witnessing Gordon's depravity and my, for want of a better word, incarceration. His threat to our son's was the last straw.' she paused and smiled at me. 'It was cathartic.'

'From what you've told me there must have been quite a few who were trembling once the news spread.'

'It was necessary to be brutal, but fair. Let the staff know that there was a fresh pair of hands on the reins and that I was the boss and their positions were at risk .. I followed Christopher and John into the Hall.

'One of the maids was watching, open-mouthed. 'Anne!' Christopher's voice snapping her out of her trance. "The front door, quickly. Run girl."

'The door closed. Mrs Nesbit, the Housekeeper and several members of the domestic staff were in the staff entrance, including John Fletcher, Gordon's manservant. "Your Ladyship, I've just seen ..."

'Yes, Mr Tulliver is persona non grata. Lord Gordon is dead. There is a new Earl, my elder son, Martin, has inherited the title. Your services are no longer required. I want you packed and ready to leave within two hours. John will take you to your sister's in Beverley. I will pay you a month's salary and give you a good reference. 'John?'

'Yes, madam.'

"Could I ask how he died?"

'He was tinkering with one of his cars and it fell off the jack.'

"Not using axle stands, Your Ladyship?"

'"No, I was there with John when it happened. Two hours, Mr Fletcher." I think he was glad to go.'

'I went to speak with Mrs Nesbit and put her in the picture. I also told her that the members of her staff who had been openly against me had the option to leave voluntarily or be dismissed. To pass the word and keep a record.'

'Then the prize, Golding, the Butler. Always polite but Gordon's man. Plus, he had the keys to, amongst other things, the wine cellar. He realised that something serious had happened when I walked into his Pantry. The Butler's Pantry is where the silver is kept under lock and key. It was another of his responsibilities. He stood and glanced from me to John, standing in the doorway. "Milady?" I held my hand out and asked for his keys. He looked confused. He knew that I wouldn't have dared to do so under normal circumstances. So, I demanded that he hand his keys over. Still no reaction.

"His Lordship is dead. So, I would like the keys."

"But I was talking with him less than an hour ago, milady."

"Well, now he is dead: John?"

He turned towards the doorway. "It's true Mr Golding,' John told him. 'I was there when it happened. He never used axle stands and his car fell off the jack. The axle crushed his chest. I've called the doctor, ambulance and police."

He was like an automaton. His time was up and he knew it. He handed the keys over. I did thank him, then gave him an ultimatum. "Golding, you have a choice. You can either write your resignation now and I will pay you one month's salary in lieu of notice and give you a reference. You will quit your house within twenty-four hours, or I will have the police carry out an inventory of the wine cellar. I know how much wine is drunk in this house and how much we have delivered. There is a discrepancy. Only you and His Lordship had keys to the cellar. The question is, where did it go?" I knew Gordon never came down here and wouldn't soil his hands in selling it. It had to be Golding.'

'He resigned?'

'Yes, but didn't divulge where the wine had gone. I suspected that the coroner was the beneficiary. He lived rent free in one of the estate houses on the edge of the village. Why, I didn't know. I checked with the Land Agent in due course. According to the Wine Ledger about thirty percent of the wine was missing. That was an ongoing situation.

'The doctor and ambulance arrived at the same time. The police in the shape of an Inspector and a sergeant two minutes later.

John and Carol had their stories straight. He took the doctor *et al* to the garage. The police Inspector wanted the body leaving in situ whilst he summoned a police vehicle examiner and a photographer

'This was the story they both told. After all she was the wife of the Earl. John had been the loyal chauffeur for thirty years. Both above reproach. It was also the story she told her father when she spoke with him an hour later. Carol's parents arrived two and a half hours after that call.'

She sat there with a self-satisfied smile.

'That sounded exhausting.'

'Exhilarating, I would say. I had told no-one what I had been put through over the years, or about Gordon's sexual proclivities, although the staff knew. It was simply something that I had to do. It got rid of those who had nailed their colours to the wrong mast. They knew who was in charge..' She smiled to herself. 'The new Butler, George Givens, was recommended by my father. His previous employer was a drunk and had assaulted him, so he quit.'

Her husband's body was removed by ambulance. the vehicle and jack by a local garage to police headquarters for investigation.

An inquest was opened, identity established, and the body released for disposal. In this case, cremation. That did not sit well with the wider Sylverton family. However, it did meet with Carol's final comment that she hoped he burn in Hell.

Other than claims that accompanied the title she was the sole beneficiary of the will. Had it been the following week she would have received nothing other than the portrait of him which used to hang in the Old Library, now consigned to the flames along with his clothes, bedclothes and bedroom furniture.

The atmosphere at the full inquest four weeks later was frosty. She and John gave their evidence without problem. However, the Coroner was persistent in his questioning of the police officers to see if the fatal event could have somehow been engineered. And where were the ignition keys? In the ignition switch or elsewhere? The Inspector stated that the keys were in the Earl's trouser pocket. The vehicle examiner said that in his expert opinion the jack was in perfect working order and the death had been caused by the Earl not using axle stands and failing to ensure that the car was sitting on the jack safely. The verdict - misadventure.

'Then, I employed a private detective to find you. It took him a while because of your name change.'

That had been quite some tale. The last few years must have been Hell. He wouldn't have blamed her if she had trodden on the jacking handle deliberately. Anyone who would do that to children, theirs or not, deserved to die. She had trusted him with her story, that made him feel even more protective.

Twenty-Six

'It all began after we returned to the house after leaving you at The Queens ... ... It would never bring Emily back and the last few weeks have brought back the terrible memories of what I'd done.'

The silence was broken by Carol. 'You say Philip, *Leonardo*, was a physiologist?' he nodded. 'And these tiny haemorrhages are a possible indication of strangulation?' he nodded again. 'Would it have made a difference if I had stayed with you?'

That made me smile. 'Like you wanted to?' It was her turn to nod. 'You mustn't think like that, Carol. You can't shoulder any of this yourself. But I don't know. It wouldn't have been me, but it could have been any one of the others. She could have seen anyone as Kevin Sharpe and reacted in the same manner. But there? How would you have reacted. You would have been involved. Then what?'

'That would not have been good.'

'But what happened in the last two weeks. I was terrified ... when I came to, taped into that chair, just like Molière. Naked with that female threatening to emasculate me. I really thought I was going to be murdered as he had .. The next thing I knew DC Blake was talking to me ... it brought it all back.' Vivid memories flashed across his pineal eye. He felt the tears well up and trickle down his cheeks and began to sob.

Carol sat on the bed her arms round him with his head against her shoulder. She kissed his head. 'It's all over, Martin. You're safe now.'

He sniffed, sat up and blew his nose. 'Sorry.'

'There's nothing to apologise for. You're safe that's all that matters.'

Now she knew everything; except where Emily was buried. All he was waiting for now was to be interviewed by the police, wondering what they knew and what they might ask. Would she regret finding him?

'This is a pretty pickle,' she smiled and squeezed his hand. 'Unintended or not,' she said, 'we're both responsible for the death of someone. Do we throw ourselves on the mercy of the judicial system or keep quiet and live our lives with whatever guilt we might have. Bearing in mind the evidence that both John and I gave to the inquest? My vote is for the latter. I do not wish to add perjury and worse to the list.'

He only had chance to squeeze her hand before the door burst open and the boys walked in followed closely by John.

'Did you enjoy your ice creams?' Bard said.

'Yes, thank you,' the leader said, and smiled. 'John took us to the railway station and bought some platform tickets so we could get closer to the engines.'

'They're huge, smelly, noisy and dirty,' said the other, 'And some people were rude to John.'

'How?' said Carol

'They were being sarcastic about the uniform, milady,' he said. 'I asked one gentleman if he enjoyed his work. He said that he hated it but had to earn money. I sympathised with him and told him that I was employed by some wonderful people and was paid to drive a Rolls Royce. He walked away.'

They were still laughing as the door closed.

Blake

Twenty-Seven

DS Creighton arrived to a full room. The chatter died. 'Good morning ladies and gentlemen,' there was a rumble of replies. 'Yesterday was a day of small but significant margins. As far as I am now concerned the leader of these three murderers is female.' He lifted both hands to stifle the chatter. 'And-that-point-stays-in-this-room. Here's a run-down from yesterday. As you are no doubt aware Lewis Green is now in LGI with a uniformed officer on the door of his side-ward. However, because of the London traffic, diversions and road works it took Sergeant Ryder and Blake an hour longer to reach Lewis Green's flat than anticipated ...

... DC's Smith and Battersby entered the Lodge grounds from Belgrave Street at the rear where they encountered a male wearing a police uniform going the other way. He told them he was with the others and they were in the building. He continued into the street. It was only seconds later when they met DS Ryder leaving via the back door they realised. Also, the helmet this man was wearing had a top plate and not a comb, probably a County officer, if he was genuine. By the time that was realised all three had disappeared. Forensic have the beige Rover 3.5 so they must have had another means of transport.

As far as the woman is concerned, she was dressed as a nurse, however she may be a nurse, doctor, vet or just someone who knows how to use a hypodermic,' he paused. 'That makes her incredibly dangerous. So be careful. We do not want any further casualties. PC Cameron's staff was in his staff pocket and his cuffs tucked away.

There were no signs of a struggle. So, she probably stabbed him in the neck from behind and was still able to function normally when she dealt with Lewis Green. According to DC Blake, other than encouraging the two accompanying males to hurry up she didn't sound stressed .. How many firearms trained officers are there?'

Two hands were raised. 'That all? And you are?'

'DC Goodall, sir.'

'DC Smith, sir.'

'Draw revolvers and six rounds from DHQ, they're authorised. People aren't used to firearms, especially being carried by police officers, so keep quiet and them out of sight unless absolutely necessary, even in police stations. Is that clear?' There were a couple of acknowledgements. 'DI Cartwright will allocate the jobs and six of you are going to Huddersfield with an identikit operative. The first, seventh and seventeenth houses in Seven Oaks Fold, Almondbury. You six can get a verbal description and pass it through. The identikit will follow in time. Most of the remainder will be working in Leeds trying to identify the nurse and her two assistants. Sergeant Ryder, you and Blake are aware of your task?'

'Yes sir.'

'Right, everyone stay safe. Keep DI Cartwright informed.'

The Magnolias, West Grove, Middleton was the home of Margaret and Frederick Reid, parents of Emily; a detached bungalow with neat gardens and, as the name suggests, a magnolia either side of the path.

They sat side-by-side on the settee holding hands. From Emily's age I would have thought they would be in the mid to late forties possibly early fifties. Both were prematurely grey and looked a good ten years older. As soon as we appeared they realised why, Mrs Reid insisted on putting the kettle on.

'Is it to do with these terrible murders we've heard about?'

'Honestly, Mr Reid. We don't know if there is a link or not,' I said. 'But it is possible, and we have to check anything and everything that may lead us to those responsible.'

'I understand.'

'Mr Reid, DC Blake and myself have both read the missing person report in relation to Emily. I know that it's difficult, but can you think of anything at all that might help?'

The Reids looked at each other. 'Nothing that we didn't tell the other officers. And when Kevin Sharpe did what he did ... that was a dreadful shock. He used to be such a nice lad.'

This was new. 'You knew him?' I said.

'Well, yes. Emily was pals with his sister, Phyllis. They were in the same class at school. Kevin was a year older. He was a funny lively lad. They got on well together until ... it really changed her. She was a chatterbox but became depressed and morose, which wasn't like her at all. Blaise was devastated when she broke their engagement.'

There was nothing in the missing person's file, but we hadn't fully checked the crime file. We were on the point of leaving when Mrs Reid insisted that she show us some photographs. Amongst them were several of a supremely happy couple. Emily, with a tall moustachioed man in RAF pilot officer's uniform. This was Blaise, Blaise Lincoln. They made a good couple.

'Is Blaise still in the RAF?'

'No. He packed it in about a year later. I think he joined the prison service. He certainly talked about it. We haven't seen him for months.'

'That's quite a step. Do you happen to know which prison.'

'Sorry, no.'

Emily's bedroom was just as it had been seven years ago – clean and tidy and waiting for her return. I couldn't imagine what it must be like.

'Sergeant,' said Frederick Reid, 'We did speak with our solicitor about the length of time since Emily disappeared but ...'

'It's too final, Fred,' interrupted Margaret. 'I can't do it. Imagine how I would feel if we did apply for this Declaration of Presumed Death and she walked in through the front door. She still has a key. Or if she had suddenly got amnesia or she's in some hospital somewhere in a coma after an accident. I've got to keep hope alive.'

I couldn't argue with that.

The new information was on the board. We had permission to visit Sheffield prison to speak with Kevin Sharpe tomorrow.

Green
Twenty-Eight

It made his day. The policeman on the door held it open and acknowledged Carol as the excited twins bounded in.

'We're going home by train, Bard,' said the leader.

'John's going to collect us from York railway station,' said the other.

He smiled. 'I thought they were huge, smelly, noisy and dirty.'

'They are, but they look exciting.'

'It will be especially if you go through any tunnels..' Bard leaned forward speaking in hushed tones. 'If you ever go through Standedge Tunnel, it's very long and very dark. You have to close any windows otherwise the smoke will get in. So will the giant spiders, so have your bows at the ready.'

Their eyes were like saucers. 'Giant spiders? Are there really?'

'No, Martin,' Carol laughed. 'He's teasing you.'

They scowled at me. 'Aww.'

'Aww. No spiders, but some tunnels are very long and dark and you must make sure the windows are closed. Keep the smoke out.'

Carol stepped forwards and kissed him on the cheek. 'Hello, darling,' she said.

He kissed her on the lips. She didn't object. 'That's promising.'

She winked at me.

'You look as radiant as ever.'

She smiled. 'Thank you. We have about forty minutes and then have to get something to eat,'

` 'What time does your train leave?'

'In two hours..'

He was adjusting his pillows when one of the twins whispered something to Carol. She took a new hard-backed book from her bag and handed it to him. 'Bard, will you read to us, please,' he said and held it up for me to see.

The laugh was involuntary. Yesterday's suggestion springing to mind: Tolkien's masterpiece *The Lord of the Rings*. What was being held up was *The Fellowship of the Ring.* Way beyond a normal six-year old's ability, and, in many places not exactly bed-time reading, especially for children. The book bearer scowled. 'Is it a funny book, Bard?' he said. 'You said it was exciting.'

'There are funny bits in it,' He replied. 'But it is an adventure story, very exciting and contains far more scary things than *Smaug*. He leaned forwards eyes wide. '*The fighting Uruk-hai* and *Shelob,*' he sat back and smiled. 'I would be delighted to read some of it to you.'

They exchanged smiles as the twin's coats appeared in the easy chair to his left. Shoes lined up beneath. They scrambled onto the bed, Martin to his left. Graeme, the book bearer, the right. Carol pulled her chair closer and settled back resting her right hand on his right thigh. Smiles were exchanged.

Bard opened the book at the title page: 'The Fellowship of The Ring. Being the first part of The Lord of the Rings by JRR Tolkien. His full name is John Roland Reuel Tolkien.' There wasn't a peep from either of them. He turned the page. 'That's what I wanted to see,' he said. 'There's a verse here. I'll read it out, it will help you to understand what the story is about. Are you ready?' There were *three* answering yesses and a smile from Carol. He imparted just enough emphasis to indicate menace:

Three Rings for the Elven-kings under the sky,
Seven for the Dwarf-lords in their halls of stone,
Nine for the Mortal Men doomed to die,
One for the Dark Lord on his dark throne

In the land of Mordor where the shadows lie.
One Ring to rule them all, One Ring to find them,
One Ring to bring them all and in the darkness bind them
In the Land of Mordor where the shadows lie.'

He squeezed their shoulders and shuddered bringing out the expected giggle. Then asked them. 'In The Hobbit where did Bilbo Baggins first meet Gollum?'

The answer came straight back from Graeme. 'Under the Misty Mountains,' he said, looking up at Bard and smiling.

'Very good,' he said glancing at a smiling Carol.

'I wanted to answer that one,' said Martin, scowling.

'It's not a competition,' Bard replied, although it probably was for them. 'Here's another one. What did Gollum lose that Bilbo found?' He had hardly got the words out before the answer came straight back.

'A magic ring,' said Graeme laughing. 'When he put it on his finger, he became invisible.'

'Not fair!'

'Martin,' Carol's admonishing tone. 'You're better than Graeme at some things and he is better than you at others. You can't win at everything.' She glanced at me and rolled her eyes.

He stifled the smile. 'Right, last question. That ring is mentioned in the verse that I read. See if you can find it.'

Again Graeme. 'Well done. The story is about the ring that Bilbo found. The One Ring. The Ring of Power. Whoever can wear the Ring *and* control its power can conquer Middle Earth. The only one who can do that is Sauron, The Dark Lord mentioned in the verse. So, it has to be destroyed. That can only happen where it was made, right under Sauron's nose. In the Land of Mordor.'

Shivers were running down his spine. During the last few minutes whilst the boys were checking the text both had wriggled slightly closer. However, when he reached out for the book their heads were in the way, so arms were looped round their shoulders. They wriggled even closer. Circumstances had dictated that he couldn't be present at the birth. Missed their birthdays. Their first steps. Them learning to talk. In fact, he had been isolated from them and their mother for seven years. The feelings were unreal.

Carol was smiling at him. 'Are you all right?' She mouthed.

He replied in kind. 'Wonderful,' he turned to the book and took a deep breath.

'*Chapter 1. A Long-Expected Party.*

When Mr Bilbo Baggins of Bag End announced that he would shortly be celebrating his eleventy-first birthday of special magnificence, there was much talk and excitement in Hobbiton ...

... ... Thirdly and finally, I wish to make an ANNOUNCEMENT. He spoke this last word so loudly and suddenly that everyone sat up who still could. I regret to announce that – though, as I said, eleventy-one is far too short a time to spend among you – this is the END. I am going. I am leaving you NOW. GOOD BYE!

He stepped down and vanished ...'

He jumped almost as much as the boys did when Carol stood. 'I'm sorry, children, Bard.' she said. 'I've enjoyed the last forty minutes as much as you have, but we have to get something to eat and the engine driver won't wait for us. Quickly now, shoes and coats on; say thank you to Bard.'

It had been an impossible dream. It could never happen. But it had. It had been the most profound and emotionally satisfying experience he could imagine. Releasing some of the unrealised repressed tension that had been held in for the last seven years. With the exception of giggles at appropriate places the boys had been rapt. The presence of Carol had done nothing to lessen *his* pleasure.

In two minutes shoes were tied and coats fastened. One either side of Carol, her hands on his son's shoulders. They looked for all the world like Tweedle Dum and Tweedle Dee. There was a chorus of thank yous and, 'What happens next?' 'Will you read us some more?' 'Mummy, can he come to the House?'

'I think that might be possible,' she said and winked again.

Cards exchanged and the additional pleasure of a peck on the lips. We promised to write.

The door opened. Two men entered. The latter, Detective Constable Blake.

'Who might you be?' the first demanded of Carol. She would really like that approach.

She was put out and sounded it. 'From the look of you, you are policemen,' she said. 'As for who I *might* be. *I am* Lady Carol Sylverton, Countess of Oldeney. These are my sons, Lord Martin Sylverton, Earl of Oldeney and his younger brother Sir Graeme Sylverton .. Now, if you have nothing further to say, my children and I have a train to catch.

'Detective Inspector Priestly, Madam,' the unknown officer announced. 'I apologise. No, there is nothing further that we need to know. I'm sorry you've been inconvenienced.'

There was a curt nod from Carol as Detective Constable Blake opened the door. 'Thank you,' she said and flounced out followed by the twins.

DI Priestly and DC Blake took positions one either side of his bed. 'Nice looking woman. Mixing with the nobility, sir,' queried the detective inspector. 'You never mentioned her previously.'

'You never asked, Inspector.'

'Not one of your conquests on party nights, then?' He smirked.

Annoying. 'If you hurry Inspector,' He retorted, 'you could catch her before she gets to the stairs. You could ask her yourself. I'm sure she would appreciate your interest in her sex life.'

'This is a flying visit, sir,' the detective inspector ignored the comment, 'I understand that you will be released from Hospital either tomorrow or the day after. And before you return to London, we do need to interview you.

'Should I take legal advice beforehand?'

'That's not for me to say, sir. But I wouldn't have thought so.'

He nodded and glanced at Detective Constable Blake who gave the slightest of nods. Taking advice would be the sound thing to do.

The police clear, he used the public telephone in the corridor to call his solicitor in London. Five minutes later he took the return call: A Mr Trevor Bantling of Webman & Co. was aware and waiting. The good news was he was being released from hospital tomorrow. He made appointments to speak with Mr Bantling and later with the police.

Blake

Twenty-Nine

Kevin Sharpe looked pleased to see us. Probably because we were fresh faces, not because we were police officers. I indicated the chair opposite. 'Well?' he said as he sat. He could be as uncivil as he wanted, he wasn't going to serve any longer.

'How are you?' said Sergeant Ryder.

Sharpe stood. 'How do you think? If that's all you've come for, forget it. I don't have to talk to you.'

'Kevin, sit down, please.' I put a pack of twenty cigarettes on the table. He might smoke or he might not, but in prison cigarettes are currency. DS Ryder left the remainder of the interview to me.

He looked at us, and the cigarettes, and sat. 'What do you want?'

'We've spoken with Emily Reid's parents. They tell us that Emily and your sister, Phyllis, were friends and you were always round at their home. Tell us about Emily.'

'I didn't kill her if that's what you mean. The rape? Yes. She said no. I'll always be sorry for that. I thought she was playing hard to get and got carried away; but I didn't kill her.'

'What about the blood they found on your knife, that was hers.'

'I explained that,' he sat forward and was getting agitated. I caught the smell of something I couldn't identify. 'That blood had been there years. We were kids, ask Phyl she'll tell you. They were eleven. I was twelve. We'd been to the pictures, the matinée. It was a western. Just a kids trick. We were good together. Someone suggested we become blood brother and sisters. Just a nick in the thumb, some of the blood must have run down the blade.'

'And you told the police?'

'Of course I bloody well did. So did Phyl. No-one took a blind bit of notice. Why don't you ask Phyl?'

'Ok, apart from that, what about Emily.'

'She was best mates with Phyl. In the same class at school. Always together.'

'Mrs Reid said you were a regular visitor at their bungalow.'

He laughed. 'True. She baked every day, always something nice to eat.'

'Not at home?'

'Nah. My mother couldn't be arsed. Mrs Reid always made you feel welcome.'

'And you fancied Emily?'

'Not like that. Not then. When she was about fourteen she was getting really pretty. But I was just Phyl's brother. We were still friendly, but she had other boys in tow. Always sniffing round they were. And then ...'

'What about the night she disappeared? You had this run-in outside the Locarno.'

He frowned and thought. 'Oh, that? Those posh boys from the university. Always there looking for talent. Sticking their noses in.'

'I understand there was a young woman in a blue dress?'

'Her?' he said. His face lit up. 'Cracking looker. I really fancied her.'

'It got personal.'

'Yeah, she was a bit snooty. Real posh,' he laughed and put his hand to his left cheek. 'She gave me a good slap. Didn't like that, loosing face. Then *they* turned up and she went with them.'

'That's when Emily appeared on the scene. Asked if she could go with them because she'd seen you.'

'So I 'eard. I didn't see her outside the Locarno and I never saw her again. As God's my witness.'

There was nothing more forthcoming. I pushed the cigarettes across the table. Sharpe was escorted from the interview room and we left.

'And the sister, Phyllis, she backs up what Sharpe said about the blood-brother-sister thing?' said DS Creighton.

'Yes sir,' I said. 'They'd been to a matinee to watch some western film. That's where she got the idea. Although it doesn't negate what forensic said about Sharpe's blood.'

'No, it doesn't, but it could cloud the issue. However, we're not here to reinvestigate Emily Reid's disappearance. But, we now know a little more regarding Reid and Sharpe.

Thirty

11:30. Tuesday. Millgarth Street. DI Priestley and I were sitting opposite Lewis Green and Trevor Bantling, Webman & Co, solicitors of Albion Square. Lewis Green now kitted out by the hospital. All he had when we rescued him was his Rolex. How would he react to the next few minutes? His eyes fixed on the objects I placed on the table: green manilla folder, padded envelope and mini taper-recorder.

Introductions complete, Green informed us that he was in the process of reverting from Green to Beck. But for now, he was still Lewis Green. Time to progress.

'Under normal circumstances Mr Green,' I said, 'this would be a simple matter of obtaining a witness statement. However, in view of what we have here,' I placed my hand on the padded envelope. 'I'm going to have to caution you. Mr Bantling will explain it to you later .. Lewis Green, you are not obliged to say anything unless you wish to do so but that anything you say may be put into writing and used in evidence. Do you understand?

Lewis Green looked concerned and turned to his solicitor. 'But ...'

'It's all right, Mr Green, the officer is just doing what the law requires of him. We will understand when we see what is in the envelope. As we discussed, just answer his questions.' Mr Bantling nodded to me.

'In your own words, Mr Green,' I said, 'will you take us through what happened?'

He sat back, thinking, 'To be brutally honest there's not much I can tell you about what happened at the flat,' he looked at me. 'You had just gone through the door to the toilet when there was a knock at the door. I assumed it was the Sergeant Ryder you told me about. There were two men standing there. One in police uniform the other I assumed was the sergeant, he didn't identify himself and I didn't have time to ask. He stepped into the flat and waved a card in front of me which I took for some form of identity card.'

'Could you make out any details?'

'It was too fast. He asked where you were. Well, not you specifically, just where the other officer was. I turned and pointed to the door and someone, I assume the officer in uniform, hit me hard across the back of my head. That was it. When I came to, I had a cracking headache. A pain in my right shoulder, and was naked and trussed up in the chair where you found me. My eyes and mouth were taped shut.'

'You didn't recognise either of these two people you assumed were police officers?'

'Assumed? You mean they weren't police officers?'

'Not that we know of Mr Green. Did you recognise either of them?'

'Sorry, no.'

'Did both of them speak?'

'No, just the one in plain clothes.'

'What about the voice. Had you heard it before? What sort of accent did he have? Regional?'

'No,' he mused. 'Never heard it before. Not an identifiable accent per se. More received pronunciation, but not BBC, if you see what I mean.'

'Public school. Like your friend yesterday?'

'Carol? perhaps, but not as cut-glass.'

I nodded. 'Could you describe him: height, weight etc?'

'I'm five ten,' said Green. 'He was taller, maybe a couple of inches. I'm thirteen stone he would be about the same. About thirty. Dark hair well-trimmed, greying at the temples. Dark hooded eyes and trimmed moustache. That's about it really. Oh, and his breath smelled of aniseed. He breathed in my face as he passed, definitely aniseed.'

It came to me in a flash. Aniseed. That was the unidentified aroma on Sharpe's breath.

'Thank you. What about clothing?'

'Black shoes, dark suit, white shirt, dark red tie and a good black-overcoat, no hat. Suit well-pressed, good creases in the trousers. other than that, I couldn't say.'

'When you say a good overcoat. What did you mean?'

'Similar to a Crombie,' Green replied. 'Although I don't think it was. I've got a Crombie. It was similar.'

'And the policeman in uniform?'

'Don't they all look alike?' He replied. I forced a smile.

'Not quite, sir. If you would, please.'

'Twenty-five to maybe thirty-five, clean shaven, from what I could see brown hair, although it was a bit long.'

'Would you recognise him again?

'I don't know. I might. But I only saw him for about a second before the other pushed past me.'

'Could you describe his uniform?'

'Are there many differences?'

I listed some of the possible differences. 'Medal ribbons? Number of pockets? Number of buttons? Was the tunic belted or not?

'The tunic was belted and there were four pockets.'

I pushed the padded envelope across the table. 'The date is illegible, but it was posted in Leeds. Do you recognise the handwriting?'

Green scrutinised the envelope and slid it back to me. 'Sorry, no.' He glanced to his left as he did so. He pointed to the miniature tape cassette on the table. 'If that cassette came in this envelope,' he said. 'It's just brought a host of memories and emotions flooding back,' he paused. His breathing pattern changed as he began to hyperventilate.

'Are you all right, Mr Green?'

He took several deep breaths. Nodded. 'Just the thoughts taking me back.' His breathing eased. 'Yes, thank you .. Might I surmise the cassette contains some damming comments by me about Emily Reid? It would also explain the clicking noises that I heard whilst the female was torturing me at knife point. Mr Bantling knows the story but hasn't seen any photographs. Perhaps you could let him see those I handed to you.'

The DI nodded. I removed a blue manilla folder from my file and slid it across the table.

Trevor Bantling looked at the photographs for several seconds without comment. Eventually he placed them side-by-side on the table. 'Mr Green, this one,' he pointed to the one in the centre, the one of Bill Boxley's mutilated body in the chair, 'is the photograph you were given at the seventh house, your second call?'

'Yes, the first house, the Windsor chair. The third call, the last house in the crescent, the Windsor chair with my name attached. The two glider-clipped notes, the letter and manuscript are those I mentioned.'

'I see,' he said. 'Do you mind if I peruse them?'

'No.'

Eventually Trevor Bantling put the paperwork down. 'Mr Priestly, I cannot foresee any circumstances in which the Crown Prosecution Service would commence proceedings against Mr Green. Nevertheless, could I possibly have copies of everything, please?'

'Certainly,' the DI replied. 'You'll have them within the next two days.' Bantling nodded. 'Now Mr Green, you were about to say something about the cassette recorder.'

'.. Detective Inspector I don't need to listen to the tape. I know it by heart, and I did admit that I had sex with Emily Reid. That I strangled her whilst in the act and that I buried her body at Eccup reservoir. None of them true. I was trying to save my life, and a drowning man will clutch at straws. I didn't give much for my chances. I'm not married although I hope to be and have my own children but that photograph of *Molière*, Bill Boxley, told a different story.'

'I think you ought to listen, Mr Green,' I said. 'There is something you should hear.'

Lewis Green looked doubtful. 'Well, if you think so.'

I put the cassette in the player and pressed *play*. He had answered every question. There were tears. A few yelps – no doubt when he had been jabbed with the knife.

Complete and full admission of having had sex with Emily Reid. Her strangulation and burial

at Eccup reservoir. But who wouldn't if they thought they were going to suffer as his friends

had? What was different were the final seconds:

"*Well, Mr policeman. I've done your job for you. A full and complete admission of the*

manner in which Martin Graeme Beck murdered Emily Reid and disposed of her body. Now you know where to look so that she can be returned to her family. He's still alive and intact so at the very least he can be tried for his crimes".

The final sound was of the door being kicked open and a male voice shouting, "Run!"

Trevor Bantling said. 'And my client was the last of five victims. The first four trussed the same way, mutilated and killed in the same manner?'

I nodded. 'He was,' I said. 'Mr Green, did you hear this woman saying the words you've just heard on the cassette?'

'No, I didn't. I was waiting for the cut. I blocked everything else out.'

'Mr Green,' said the detective inspector, 'will you confirm that whilst you were being interrogated, some as yet unknown person had hold of your penis and testicles in their hand and was threatening to cut them off with a knife.'

'My eyes were taped so I couldn't see, but it was a woman. And, whenever I gave an answer she didn't like, I was jabbed. On the last occasion I could feel the knife pressing upwards into my body behind the scrotum. I admitted everything she'd demanded. The next second I heard the sound of the door crashing open. Whoever it was let go and I heard them running. The next voice was detective constable Blake's .. by the way I haven't thanked you yet.' We reached across the table and shook hands. He thanked me and for letting his parents know, and not passing any details on.

'I am truly sorry. Mr Green,' I said. 'I'm a martial arts instructor. Had I not been in the bathroom I can guarantee that it would not have happened at all.'

Lewis Green snorted a laugh, 'Ah well. At least you got there in time. Where was I been held by the way?'

'Merrion Lodge, where you used to hold the parties.'

Green looked shocked. 'But ... that was scheduled for demolition years ago. That's why we were given notice to quit.'

'An initial preservation order was served on the building,' I said. 'We were told that it had been demolished and didn't check. In fact, it was in the process of being dismantled before being shipped to the United States.'

Two hours later I saw Lewis Green board the Leeds – Kings Cross express. A new wardrobe courtesy of an advance from Webman and Co, and a first-class ticket – he needed peace and quiet.

Thirty-One

DS Creighton looked at those around hm. 'How did he react to the tape?'

'He wasn't happy, sir,' said DI Priestly, 'he said before we began, he didn't need a refresher. He could remember every word. Except he didn't remember the last few seconds of what the woman said about leaving him alive and intact so that we could deal with him.'

'Hmm ... We can't dig everything up. Blake, don't you have a relative at Leeds university?'

'Yes, sir, my brother-in-law, Gerald Vernon. Senior lecturer in physics.'

'Give him a ring and without telling him exactly why, see if there are any gizmos that could possibly help us narrow the field. Inspector, ring forensic and ask the same question, but you can tell them.'

Gerald Vernon smiled. There were few reasons why the police might need to look deep into the ground and Brian was working on a murder case. 'You looking for bodies or buried treasure?' he said.

Gerald was not stupid, but. 'Sorry, can't say.'

'You just have done, Brian. We have a metal detector and we can get hold of ground penetrating radar. I'll make some enquiries if you like.'

Gerald called back. The radar could penetrate up to one hundred feet.

Green

Thirty-Two

Keys once more in his possession he searched his flat; just in case. The takeaway from a new Italian restaurant: lasagne, focaccia, and bottle of pinot in front of him, the locksmith arranged by Mr Bantling arrived.

An hour later he was in possession of a door viewer, new five-lever locks, chain and mortice bolts.

Replete and half-drunk he flooded the flat with sound. The occupants of the top flat must have been deaf. He wanted his flat back. Getting rid of the detritus left by the fingerprint officers was the hardest thing.

In spite of his medication his sleep was fitful. Rose at six, showered and headed for Hampstead Heath, calling in at a local shop to top up his larder. He phoned his mother and tried to put her mind at rest with a modicum of success. He settled down to write to Carol. A clean sheet of cream wove, both addresses, date and 'My Darling Carol'. He put the pen down. They hadn't seen each other for seven years, yet a lot had been said in hospital. In the end it was six sides. Her telephone number etched onto his brain. He called her.

There was a bit of a squabble between two excited children as to who would be the first. 'You can both talk with him. But don't give too many secrets away or he won't need to read my letter. Graeme first. Hold this piece to your ear, hold the other in your other hand and speak. You don't have to shout.'

There was a giggle then Graeme's voice. 'Hello Bard. When we come to London will you take us to London Zoo and Madame Tussauds, please?'

Carole's voice cut in before he could answer. 'He's just come out of hospital, don't forget to ask him if he's feeling better.' That had him grinning.

'Are you feeling better?'

'I am feeling very much better Graeme, thank you. And, yes, I will take you all to the zoo and Madame Tussauds. Don't forget to bring the book.'

'I won't. Here you are, Mummy.'

'Martin, your turn.'

'Hello Bard, are you feeling better?'

'Yes, thank you, Martin. And where would you like to go?'

'Tower of London, please and Windsor Castle. Oh, and Hyde Park and Mummy wants to talk to you.'

'Hello darling.'

'Hello yourself, when are you coming?'

'Is Friday too soon? After school and returning Sunday about four.'

That provoked another grin. 'It's a good job you're not in a hurry.'

The humour in the reply was obvious. 'I'll forget you said that.'

'Just checking ... Not at all. It will be a bit tight to do it justice, but I'll arrange something.'

'Leave the Tower of London to me. I'll speak to someone.'

'Pulling strings?'

'Of course, that's why they're there. Oh, have you ever stayed at the Nelsonian before?'

London's newest 5-star hotel had quite a reputation. 'No.'

'Be there for six. Accommodation will be booked in your name, Martin Beck. And, the only rules are black tie and no jeans.'

Blake

Thirty-Three

Two days later we had the radar. In the interim the woods surrounding Eccup Reservoir were checked on foot. The body of water over a mile in length and half a mile at its widest. A rough calculation of the perimeter – four miles. Two teams working in opposite directions. No evidence of digging.

The university archaeology department did the honours. It wouldn't be easy. The tree roots would see to that.

DS Creighton looked round the huge area to be searched. 'Can we narrow the location down, Blake?'

'This is where they went swimming, sir. Reputed to be a popular spot .. In that case would this be a good choice?'

'Don't forget Mr Baron. Green told us he was always in the vicinity. '

'Yes, I'd forgotten him, sir.'

'You, forget?' he smiled and turned to Professor Chalkley. 'How long would it take to check where we are.'

'Depends on what's down there, Superintendent. The more clay there is underfoot the more difficult it will be, but about thirty minutes.'

Two students pulled the flat-bed behind them whilst others checked the display. We had the answer. Nothing.

The survey had picked out where the roots were fewest and the radar could be placed in direct contact with the ground. After four days DS Creighton was happy there was no body at Eccup.

I managed a quiet word with DS Creighton. 'You think there is a link with aniseed?' At least he didn't laugh.

'Yes, sir. Lewis Green noticed it on the breath of the kidnapper who wore the suit. I noticed it on Sharpe's breath when sergeant Ryder and I visited him in prison.'

'Even so, a bit tenuous don't you think? What does DI Priestly have to say about it? You have mentioned it to him?'

'Yes, sir. He gave me a scathing look and told me to do as I had been ordered. But there is something else.'

'And?'

'Until Sharpe raped her, Emily Reid had a fiancé. A Pilot Officer in the RAF. Tall. Well spoken. Clipped moustache. I've seen the photographs at the Reid's bungalow; Emily Reid and her fiancée, Blaise Lincoln. He fits that description. After Emily broke it off, he was devastated. Resigned his commission and thought to have joined the prison service. In Lewis's statement he made reference to one of the callers who left the photograph at the first house in Seven Oaks Fold. Two people. The man tall, very smart and moustachioed. The woman very smart but older.'

'I see what you're getting at. 'He gazed over my shoulder for a few seconds. 'All right, liaise with DI Cartwright. I'll clear it with DI Priestly. What do you intend?'

'Confirm the details with the prison service. Ascertain if they have a Blaise Lincoln. If so, when did he join etc and where has he served. I'll invest in some aniseed and go and see Sharpe again, see if he reacts when I put the aniseed on the table and invite him to help himself. It's possible that Sharpe knows more than he thinks he does. In fact, he probably knows Blaise Lincoln. And with your permission, sir, interview Blaise Lincoln, irrespective of whether he has ever served in the prison service.'

'One thing at a time, Blake. Whether you find anything or not, you come to me. Do not act on your own.'

Green/Beck

Thirty-Four

17:55. Friday. The Nelsonian reception desk. 'Martin Beck, I understand I have a reservation.'

'Indeed you have, sir. Sign here, please.' He spun the register round, lifted his hand and snapped his fingers. 'Jonathon. Suite 27 for Mr Beck.'

'Sir,' he said and bent to pick up Bard's holdall.

A couple of pocket battleships charged through reception, several yards behind an out of breath lady bearing a Nelsonian staff badge - Miriam.

'I'm going to carry Bard's case.'

'No you're not, I am, aren't I Bard?'

He smiled down on the expectant faces. 'You can both carry it. It's too heavy for just one.'

'Aww, not fair. I was here first.'

'Well, I am the Earl.'

'And I'm bigger than both of you.' They stood there grinning. He motioned to Jonathon to put the holdall down. 'Right you two. One either side .. Facing the same way. ... Good. Now, crouch. Lift a handle, put your arm and your head through ... stand ... Excellent, walk together. This is not a race.' He handed his suit carrier to a grinning Jonathon.

'Can I ask, sir,' said Miriam, 'How on earth did you get them to do that?'

He smiled in return. 'They are a bit of a handful, aren't they?'

Carol met him with a kiss outside of Suite 27. Her first task was to send his monkey suit to be pressed. To be worn tonight – dinner was at eight.

Everything away, he was grabbed, a pocket battleship on each hand, and propelled next door.

He didn't recall having seen an Earl in real life never mind a crestfallen one. Carol wasn't taking any prisoners. 'What did I say?' The boys stood there, heads hanging. 'This is the Nelsonian. They are entitled to expect you to be on your best behaviour. Not to run around like hooligans. If you disobey me again, you will find that Bard will no longer be here. Do you understand?' She looked at him and winked. A gesture not missed by Miriam.

'Yes Mummy,' the downcast pair looked at Miriam. 'Sorry, Miriam.'

Suit returned. Carol looked amazing in a full-length silver evening dress, a diamond necklace and earrings.

Carol looked down on her errant sons and frowned. 'Remember what I said?'

Pleading in their eyes they looked at Bard. 'You will stay, won't you Bard?'

'Well, you heard what your Mummy said.'

The door closed behind. Facing each other they smiled. 'Let me have a look at you.' A quick adjustment. 'Your tie wasn't straight. Other than that, very smart.'

There was a weak ending to the sentence. 'I sense a but.'

'Now, don't let's have any silly arguments over money.' It was the first time he'd heard Carol on the defensive. 'The people you will mix with judge all books, especially those they haven't read, by their covers. I'm not going to turn into your mother; however, it's going to cost a lot of money that you wouldn't otherwise have had to spend. Look upon it as my investment.'

'Long term?'

She smiled. 'I've had to wait seven years for tonight.'

After the agreed five minutes he opened the connecting door. She was waiting for him. This time there were no time constraints. A quick look at the boys, fast asleep. On impulse he gave them both a quick kiss on the forehead before Carol took his hand and led him into her bedroom.

'Can you remember the last time?

'Yes miss,' he said as he unzipped her dress.

It was a reprise of seven years ago except he was out of condition. She woke him at five. Clothes and watch gathered he returned to his cold and solitary bed. Hopefully to sleep.

Thirty-Five

'Mummy you promised,' said Martin as he shook Carol.'

Carol yawned and sat up looking at her two distraught sons.

'We've been good and you've sent Bard away,' sobbed Graeme. 'We went to the lavatory at two o'clock and Bard was there,' he pointed at the hollow in the pillow.

She put her arms round them both. 'Is that what you'd like to see?' she said and smiled.

They nodded.

'I haven't sent him anywhere. Don't forget he has his own suite next door. He's taking us to London Zoo after breakfast and we have a tour of the Tower of London at two pm.'

'Can we see him?'

The first Bard knew was a couple a dive bombers landing on his bed shaking him into consciousness. 'Bard, wake up it's almost six o'clock. You're taking us to London Zoo. We'll be late.'

He had never seen Carol first thing in the morning, never mind in her nightdress and negligee, but there she was, laughing and standing in the doorway. As beautiful as ever.

He sat up and grabbed them both. 'Good morning, boys. So, you think it's funny to jump on me and wake me up.' Was this what he'd missed for all those years.

They both nodded and giggled. 'Yes. Get-up.'

'London Zoo doesn't open until ten o'clock. There's plenty of time.'

'Aww.'

'Off you go. Clean your teeth and have a wash whilst I talk to Mummy.'

They scurried off. Carol sat on the bed and held his hand. 'Before you ask,' she said and smiled. 'We haven't time .. would you mind if they saw us in bed together?'

'Of course not,' he said and squeezed her hands. 'Carol, there's nothing I would like better, and I know what you told me about Gordon, but shouldn't you be like Caesar's wife?'

A pained expression clouded her face. 'I suppose so.'

'Will you marry me?'

'Yes. But that is just between you and me. It's too soon after Gordon for some.'

'And your family hasn't had the opportunity to run their eyes over me?'

'Especially my parents.'

'You said that Gordon had died over six months ago. How long would you have to wait?'

'At least six. Some think up to two years. That is not on my agenda. Those that don't like it?'

'Two years?' He leant forwards and kissed her lips. 'We could have more children by then.'

'I'm counting on it. If you have no objection I will come and stay at your flat next weekend, just you and me. Will you come to Oldeney the week after?'

It was a quarter past ten. Bard crouched in front of the boys. 'Today we only have a couple of hours here but we can always come back. We have to get something to eat before the Tower of London at 2pm. Please, do not run off. If you took the wrong turning you might just find yourselves face-to-face with a hungry lion.' He snarled and tapped his teeth together.

'We can run,' said a giggling Graeme.

'I'm sure you can,' he said stifling a laugh. 'But not as fast as a hungry lion.' He handed them a map of the zoo. 'Have a look. What do you want to see first? The lions are up here,' and pointed to the top.

Carol took his hand as he stood. 'Anyone would think you were their father,' she said.

He smiled. 'When I arrived at the Nelsonian yesterday, Miriam asked me how I got them to behave themselves.'

'Because you care. They were distraught this morning when they saw you weren't in my bed. They had seen you there when they went to the lavatory and thought I'd sent you away. Just look at them. No arguing. You've explained what we have to do and left them to choose what they want. They've never had a father figure. You are Bard. You're different.

'Bard?' said Graeme. 'What is a Komodo Dragon?'

He looked down and smiled at the expectant face. 'It doesn't breathe fire if that's what you're thinking.'

'Aww.'

'But full-grown ones are huge.'

Lions were first on the agenda followed by the Komodo Dragons. 11:45 they joined the queue to get something to eat. The boys had asked so many questions, most of which he couldn't answer, they must have been ready to burst.

'Carol. How's their writing?'

'Very good.'

'Good. When you get home, boys, why don't you write all your questions down in a letter. I'll find you the address and who to send it to and let your mummy know. I'm sure they would be happy that you're interested.'

It was the first time the boys had sampled hotdogs. They went down a treat. The journey from Camden Town to Tower Hill was twelve minutes and not a trace of giant spiders. A pleasant walk to the Tower and their tour. The Beefeater's presentation was age related with plenty of gory bits.

It was three miles to the Nelsonian so instead of the pleasant walk, the Tube called.

Less than fifty yards from the door Carol paled. 'I don't need this.' A man in smart evening dress and worse for wear was heading towards us. 'Come here boys,' she said. 'Stay with me. Bard, it's Christof Templeford. The son of the Duke of Crannock. He was a close friend of Gordon's. Be careful.'

Six feet tall, well-built, about thirty. He stopped in front of them rocking gently, uncertain what to do next. 'You WHORE!' he bellowed. 'Gordon promised you to me. And you're with this, this, this thing.' He waved his arms in Bard's direction.

'Carol,' he didn't take his eyes off Templeford. 'Take the boys. Leave this to me.'

Carol made her exit. Bard circled keeping himself between them and this drunk.

'Out of my way, you peasant,' Templeford took a swing at Bard who leaned backwards, Templeford overbalanced landing on his knees.

Bard helped him up. 'Don't you think you should go home and sleep it off?'

He looked Bard up and down trying to fell him with whisky fumes. 'Take your filthy hands off me,' he looked thoughtful. 'I know you. You're one of Gordon's Nancy boys. Did you take it up the arse or just suck his cock.'

`Disgusting,' said a voice by his side. 'Are you all right?'

'Of course I am. Just this peasant.' Templeford waved his right hand in Bard's direction.

'I wasn't speaking to you.'

The man to my right was five feet six, rotund and bald. I assumed it was his wife standing silently by his side. 'Yes,' said Bard. 'I'm fine, thank you.'

'Do you know this man? I say man. He's wearing a Guards Officer's tie and is certainly not a Guards Officer.'

'Oh yes I am,' smirked Templeford as he drew himself up to his full height. 'Lieutenant, Lord Christof Templeford, son of the Duke of Crannock.'

'No, I've never met him, but his father must be proud.'

'Of course he's proud,' said Templeford

'And this Gordon?'

'Carol's, that's Lady Carol Sylverton's deceased husband, the Earl of Oldeney. He died several months ago.'

'She murdered him you mean. Everyone knows that.'

'You're on thin ice young man. Those are serious allegations. I hope you have evidence.'

Whilst Templeford was making up his mind what to do next, the rotund witness put a business card in Bard's breast pocket. 'Should there be any ramifications from this exchange don't hesitate to call me.'

'Thank you. I'll remember.'

A small crowd had gathered, including, according to the badge, the Nelsonian Head of Security, when a police car drew up. A sergeant and PC exited.

'My Lord,' said the sergeant.

'What?' said Templeford. 'I didn't ask for the police. Go away.'

'No sir. I was speaking to the Lord Justice Nevison.'

Templeford looked confused. So did Bard.

'This young man will fill you in. He was escorting Lady Carol Sylverton and her two sons back to the Nelsonian when there was a foul-mouthed and potentially violent interlude. The least that Lord Templeford needs is to sleep it off. The rest is up to you, Sergeant.'

Lord Justice Nevison and his wife continued on their way. Bard provided his details for the sergeant. 'What will happen to him?'

'Up to the Inspector, sir. He is well known to us and most likely be handed to the military. They will be hard on him.'

After a five-minute confab with Carol, she said. 'Have you any objection to me calling my cousin?'

'No, but ...'

'He's in the military. He will know what to do.'

'... That's wonderful Bertie. I'll change the booking.'

Phone down Carol smiled at Bard. 'Bertie is my cousin. He and Alicia are joining us. They will be using one of the spare bedrooms, sorry. Don't say anything to the boys.'

'Ah well. They won't be joining us next week, will they?'

The suite doors were wide open. The boys waiting impatiently. 'Who's coming, Mummy?'

'Wait and see. Very soon.'

A couple in their thirties wearing evening dress appeared round the corner of the staircase. He was six feet plus. She five feet six. As one the boys shouted. 'Cousin Bertie,' and galloped along the corridor

Cousin Bertie put the case down as they launched themselves at him. In one well practised move he caught them both and spun, maintaining his balance.

'My you're getting heavy.'

'We're six now,' said Graeme.

'So you are. Say hello to Alicia.'

'Hello cousin Alicia.'

'Hello boys,' said a beaming Alicia. 'My how you've grown.'

They grinned and nodded.

'Right you little rapscallions, take me to your mummy.'

They put their hands over his eyes. 'Quick march,' said Graeme. 'Left-right-left-right.'

'Don't let me fall down the stairs or I'll squash you,' said Bertie arching towards Carol's suite.

'There aren't any stairs,' said Martin.

'Why, who's pinched them?'

'It's a hotel corridor.'

'Oh, that's all right then.'

Bard slipped past them and took the case from Alicia. 'Allow me.'

'Thank you. And you're the one who put the smile back in Carol's voice.'

'I think so. My name's Martin, or Bard. That's what the boys call me.'

'Bard?'

'Yes, it was my university nickname when I first met Carol seven or eight years ago. From Tolkien.'

'A long time since I read any of his.'

Boys on the floor and air kisses exchanged, Bertie stepped back. 'Now, where's the young man who put those roses back in your cheeks? And why are you blushing? Anyone would think you've been misbehaving.'

'I'm not blushing,' she said in vain.

'If you say so. Now, where is he? We need a chat.'

Connecting door closed. The boys safely on the other side they sat in the lounge of suite 27. Drinks in hand.

'Before we begin,' said Bard. 'You're Carol's cousin. How should I address you?'

He smiled. 'I'm Major Herbert fforde-Selk,' his voice pure liquid upper class. 'Major will do fine.'

'And your wife?'

'Ah. Stymied. Duchess.'

'I understand.'

'And you?'

'Martin or Bard, that's what the boys and Carol call me.'

'Shakespeare or Tolkien?'

'Tolkien.'

'Martin it is then. This altercation you had with Lieutenant Christoff Templeford, tell me about it.' He took a notebook from his pocket.

' ... and this was in the street outside? There were witnesses apart from Carol and the boys?'

'About a dozen including the Head of Security, and this man.' He walked to the wardrobe removing the business card from the breast pocket of his jacket.'

The Major's eyebrows raised a few notches when he read the name. 'May I borrow this for a few days. I will ensure that you get it back.'

'Of course.'

He nodded, walked across to the phone and dialled. 'Harvey. Major Selk. Ascertain which is the nearest Metropolitan Police Station to The Nelsonian, they will have Lieutenant Templeford languishing in their cells. Speak with the officer-in-charge and ask if they would release his body to us and save them the trouble. With luck we can keep it out of the Press … No, hang onto him. I understand that he will not be *compos mentis* until the morning when I will deal with him.'

'What happens now, Major?' Bard said and sat.

'Templeford has transgressed once too often. He has two options: either resign his commission and save some face. If he refuses, he will be cashiered. Although everyone will know.'

'Turfed out?'

'Simply put. But it is a ritual dismissal. His father is not a fool although the son is. The thought of his son being cashiered would be anathema. Tomorrow I will put the fear of God into Templeford. Out of courtesy to the Duke I will pay them a visit. Thankfully, Carol called me for advice without realising that I would be dealing with it.'

'I understand. Do either Lord Templeford or his father know where you stand in this?'

There was a grim smile. 'He certainly should, he holds a commission in the Guards. This is the end of Christoph Templeford's military career.'

The boys were tucking into their evening meal supervised by Miriam. Carol's warning working well.

'He's very good looking. When did you meet?'

'Do you want the truth, or what everyone has been told?'

A sly smile crossed Alicia's face. 'Sounds delicious. And I can keep a secret.'

'Wait and see. When did we meet? … Almost nine months to the day before the twins were born.'

'What!? But. Gordon? We thought that after you announced the pregnancy everything was well.'

'Let me tell you a few home truths about Gordon Ignatius Gladius Sylverton, 9th Earl of Oldeney ... '

'But that's appalling. Does Martin know?'

'About Gordon and the boys? Yes. He does accept that he can't make any claims. His only other regret is that he missed being with me and the first six years of their lives. The boys have no idea. Martin is becoming the father they never had. They think he's the bees' knees. He's wonderful with them and they reciprocate.'

'And you do love him?'

'Yes. I was apprehensive when I made contact with him in hospital, but when I saw his reaction and the way my boys reacted. Any doubt disappeared. He says he fell in love with me the first time he looked into my eyes.'

'He would. No other commitments?'

'He's certainly not married and I've told you about Joan.'

'The one who walked out when things got tough?'

Carol nodded.

'Do your parents know?'

There was a sharp intake of breath from Carol. 'No, I intend to tell them on Monday. The *whole* story.'

'However, when you get married, isn't it going to mean changes for the both of you?'

'Yes, but this time it will be Lady Carol Beck. And as soon as possible. I want to be rid of the Sylverton name and deliver him children that he can claim as his own. He deserves that. It's just time.'

'You must. You had a terrible time. It's over six months. Never mind what others think.'

'Martin is a literary agent, and he suggested that I write a book as a fiction.'

'Change the names to protect the guilty?

'Something like that. But I'm not so sure.'

'It might help to vent your spleen. Get it out into the open.'

'I'll give some thought to it.'

'Now,' Alicia paused and put her arm round Carol's shoulders. 'If we weren't here where would Martin be sleeping tonight?'

'What?'

'You're blushing. I take it with you.'

She grinned. 'I don't know about sleep.'

'Then don't let us stop you. He's got his own suite, hasn't he? Wake up with him,'

'But the boys.'

'Put a note on your pillow that you will see them before breakfast.'

Carol arm-in-arm with Bertie. Alicia and Bard followed. Being seen dining at the Nelsonian in intimate company with a Duke and Duchess, and a Countess was one way of becoming known.

'Carol and I had a heart to heart, Martin. No intimate details. However, she told me everything. Don't worry, secrets I can keep. And your sleeping arrangements for tonight have only switched next door. After what you both endured perhaps you could treat it as therapeutic.'

'She certainly is.'

'Good. That's settled.'

If anything, tonight's meal was even better than before. Or perhaps that was the wine. Much of the conversation revolving round the two families including Bard's interaction with the boys. The rest filled by asking him about being a literary agent and Bertie extolling his military adventures. It was an excellent night.

They looked so tiny and helpless lying there. I kissed my sons goodnight. Graeme woke. 'Shh,' I stroked his forehead. 'In the morning I will be next door as I was today. Don't worry.' He smiled and closed his eyes.

Carol collected what she required for the morning and followed me to suite 27.

We lay facing each other my right arm round her shoulders my left hand on her hip.

'So, you told Alicia everything.'

'I've kept that bottled up for seven years, Martin. Only you knew anything about what happened. I had to tell someone and I trust Alicia implicitly.'

'I do understand. Will they talk with each other?'

'Almost certainly. Alicia will speak with my parents on Monday morning. I will talk with them after lunch.'

'And that's what she told you. Martin is the boys' natural father?'

'It was heart rending.'

'I wish I'd known earlier what Oldeney was up to, I would have stepped in. Marrying Martin will not create many ripples. Apart from among those who thought they might be suitors.'

Thirty-Six

He opened his eyes to the very welcome feel of a left arm under his neck. The gentle pressure of a breast in his back and fingernails raking him. Wriggling over he kissed Carol's forehead. 'Good morning,' he said as she opened her eyes.

She rolled him over and straddled him. 'I've heard sex first thing in the morning is the best. Relax,' she caught her breath as she lowered herself. Two sets of running footsteps became louder. The combined thump on the connecting door was enough.

'Mummy, are you in there with Bard?'

She dropped her chin to her chest. 'Fuck,' she said under her breath.

He couldn't help but laugh. 'Not this morning, Darling. Next weekend will be different. Grab all your things and go to the bathroom. Leave yesterday's in the bin. I'll sort it when I've dealt with the invaders.'

Carol padded off, turned as she reached the door and blew a kiss.

Pyjama bottoms on and dressing gown tied the connecting door flung open. 'Good morning invaders, what do you seek?'

'Mummy,' they said together and giggled.

'We are not invaders,' said Martin. 'We're looking for Mummy.'

Rewarded with giggles when he crouched and tickled them. 'You were yesterday morning at six o'clock,' he said. 'Mummy's in the bathroom.' The book obvious in Graeme's hands. 'Is that a book I see before me?'

'Yes, will you read to us?'

'Carol, what time does your train leave King's Cross?'

'Five past four, why?'

'Madam Tussauds this morning, that was Graeme's second choice, so this afternoon is Martin's but his choice was Windsor Castle.'

'And there won't be enough time,' said Carol.

'A cruise on the Thames,' said Alicia. 'I've heard they're very good. Lasts about an hour.'

'Well, Martin. What do you think? We can go to Windsor Castle next time. A cruise on the River Thames?'

He was quivering with excitement. 'Are there any monsters?'

'Sure to be,' said Bard. 'But don't spend too much time looking for monsters that you miss everything else.'

'Let me know in advance when you're coming again and I will see what I can do,' said Cousin Bertie. 'Just as long as Her Majesty isn't there.'

Unexpected interruptions apart, it had been a great weekend. The gory bits of Madam Tussauds were the best.

By popular request it was hotdogs for lunch. It was a pity that high tide had restricted the journey upstream. Nevertheless, a good time was had by all. They made their farewells with Cousin Bertie and Alicia at the Nelsonian.

Bard dropped Carol and the boys off on the platform at King's Cross, parting with hugs from the boys and a kiss and embrace from Carol. He would collect her from here next Thursday around seven. The boys hanging out of the window until the train disappeared from sight.

Blake

Thirty-Seven

At last, I managed to get hold of the Prisons Department of the Home Office and passed on the enquiry. They promised to let me know as soon as possible. Don't hold your breath.

DI Cartwright brought up to date, DS Creighton gave his permission to visit the Reid's and borrow the photo of Blaise Lincoln and Emily Reid. We could pursue that line of enquiry.

Once again, we were sitting opposite Kevin Sharpe. I placed forty cigarettes on the table alongside a small bag of aniseed. I took a pinch, watching Sharpe's reaction when I didn't offer any to him. He became twitchy.

'Sorry, Kevin,' I said. 'I forgot you used aniseed. Help yourself.'

'Ta,' he said taking a pinch and sucking the small seeds into his mouth and licking his fingers.

'We're not wanting to rake up bad memories, Kevin, but did you ever meet Blaise Lincoln?'

He paled. 'Blaise? Yup. Not after I raped Emily. I think he would have killed me if he'd gotten hold of me before the police.' He laughed to himself. 'That's what happens when your prick overrules your brain.'

'Until then what was your relationship like?'

'Ok. He didn't think much of my gear or Teds in general. But he was friendly enough.'

'Is that where you got the habit of using aniseed, from Blaise.'

'Yeah. He even got Emily to use it for a bit. I'd always liked aniseed balls, so I scrounged some seed from Emily.'

We had the information we sought but kept the conversation going for a few minutes.

'One last question before we go, Kevin. Have you seen or heard from Blaise Lincoln at all since your arrest.'

He grimaced. 'Not a sausage.'

'Ok, we're off. You can have the aniseed and these.' I pushed a couple of packets of Kensitas across the table.

The ever-present prison officer came across. I picked the cigarettes up. 'Seal intact,' I said and smiled. He had a quick look and handed them to Sharpe.

'Thanks,' he said. 'You can come again.'

'Oh, one last thing. Do you know where Lincoln lived?'

He thought for a moment and shook his head. 'Nope.'

Sergeant Ryder laughed as we walked across the prison car park. 'That was a shot in the dark, Brian, to link Blaise Lincoln to aniseed.'

I grinned at him. 'A shot to nothing.'

'Can't fault you there. Photo ID next?'

'Yeah. If we get just one positive we can give Lincoln a tug.'

'If we can find him.'

10:00 a.m. the following day I collected a copy of Blaise Lincoln's headshot from Studio. It was fixed in the right-hand slot on the second row of four. Eleven police officers and Blaise Lincoln. All in the same age range and all moustachioed.

DS Ryder and I set off for Seven Oaks Fold, Almondbury.

White Oaks was the first house. 'Mrs Angela Watson?' I said to the lady who opened the door. I showed my warrant card. 'I'm DC Blake and this is DS Ryder. Could we have a few minutes of your time.'

Mrs Watson studied the twelve photos. 'Do I have to pick one?'

'If you are certain, it would be a great help.'

'But if it's the wrong man. Then what.'

'As I explained, Mrs Watson, one of these photos is of the man we believe came to your home with an older female and gave you an envelope concerning Lewis Green. Which do you think it is. If it is not our suspect, there is no harm done.'

'In that case. I think it was this one,' She pointed to number five.

Sergeant Ryder completed Mrs Watson's details and handed her the form. 'Will you enter the number of the photo in the space there,' he pointed with his pen. 'And then sign it in the space provided.'

'Was I right?' she said as she handed the statement back.

'Sorry, we can't tell you,' I said. 'Please don't contact anyone to discuss it for the next thirty minutes. We need people to make their own minds up.'

Jack Jackson at Gog and Magog was next. He took one look. 'Number six, gentlemen. No problem.'

His problem was his dyslexia. His wife was home and read the statement out to him and entered the number six in the appropriate space. He made his mark. She countersigned it as did DS Ryder and myself.

Jackson gave them a quizzical look. 'You're not going to confirm my choice, are you?'

'Sorry, We can't. But if you're certain.'

'I am.'

Mrs Christine Jessop at Victory Oaks was last. 'This is fun,' she said. 'I've often wondered what it would be like to be involved in a police enquiry. I think it was number six.'

'Number six,' I iterated.

'Yes.'

'Two out of three is good enough. All we have to do now is find the bastard.'

DS Creighton quietened the room. 'Good morning gentlemen. We have an answer from forensics regarding the substance used to subdue the five murder victims – The four students and Constable William Cameron, plus Lewis Green a.k.a. Martin Beck. They have identified curare. A plant derived neurotoxin, and used by certain South American tribes. It creates the same effect that police officers suffer when they turn over the promotion examination question paper.'

There was a burst of laughter. 'Would that be paralysis, sir?'

'It would DC Knight. It has several valuable medical uses and in our case the amount was minute. The remainder of the compound is still a mystery. That information stays in this room.

'Second. We now have reasonable grounds for believing that the male, accompanied by an older female, who delivered the envelopes to the houses in Seven Oaks Fold in Huddersfield was Blaise Lincoln, Emily Reid's former fiancée.

'We have an ongoing enquiry with the Home Office to ascertain whether the Reid's comment about his joining the Prison Service is true. Whether that will reach us this side of Christmas is anyone's guess.

'An Express Message and All Ports has been circulated. And until we have him, keep looking.

'We are still looking for the possible police officer and the female involved.' He paused and nodded, 'We are getting there. There will be a press release later this morning.'

Detective Inspector Tristram Priestley bristled as he closed the door to DS Creighton's office. 'Sir, this is outrageous.'

The Superintendent pointed to the chair. 'Aniseed?' he said as the Inspector sat.

'In words of one syllable, sir. Yes.'

'You dismissed Blake's comments out of hand. You didn't ask him to elucidate?'

'Sir, Blake's head is full of airy-fairy nonsense. He ought to be learning his trade not coming up with fanciful theories.'

'So, you chopped him off without hearing everything he wanted to say?'

DI Priestly frowned. 'I saw no merit in what he had to say.'

DS Creighton leant forwards resting his arms on his desk. 'This case revolves around the disappearance of Emily Reid some six years ago, for which Kevin Sharpe is currently serving life for her rape and murder; although no body has yet been recovered. Had you listened, Mr Priestly, not only did Blake mention about both the kidnapper and Sharpe smelling of aniseed, but according to Mr and Mrs Reid, Emily's fiancée, Blaise Lincoln, resigned his commission and was thought to have joined the prison service. The Reid's description of Lincoln was very similar to that given by Lewis Green of the kidnapper wearing the suit. In part verified by a photograph of Emily Reid and Blaise Lincoln at the Reid's home. Also, by the occupants of the three houses in Seven Oaks Fold.

'Bearing in mind that Sharpe's sister Phyllis was Emily Reid's best friend, I authorised Blake, accompanied by Sergeant Ryder, to visit Sharpe and find out what he knew about Lincoln. During the interview Blake slipped a question into the interview as to whether it was Lincoln who had introduced Sharpe to aniseed. It was. That gave us a viable link. On my instructions Blake and Ryder constructed a photo id folder of eleven moustachioed police officers and Lincoln. Two out of the three occupants in Seven Oaks Fold made positive Ids. More than enough to arrest on suspicion.

'Yes, he lacks experience. That will come with time. But he is intelligent and uses his brain. If he is correct and Lincoln is who we are looking for, that's great. If he's wrong, then we have excluded a possible suspect. We have lost nothing.'

Green

Thirty-Eight

Investing 2d in a platform ticket Bard met Carol as she stepped from the first-class compartment. A swift kiss and embrace. 'Are you hungry?'

'Yes, but the food can wait.'

Her ankles locked behind his hips and back arched she gave a deep sigh and sank to the mattress.

She opened her eyes reached up and stroked his face. 'I'm hungry now. You mentioned before there was a passable Italian nearby.'

'There is. About a twenty-minute walk. I booked the table for eight thirty,' he paused, 'When will you know?'

'If I'm possibly pregnant? Sunday.'

A last kiss. Bard threw the covers back. 'Ok, you get your shower. I'll put some music on.'

Carol reached out to him. 'No, come and join me.'

Water cascading over them she put her left arm round his neck and pressed her lips against his. Lowered her right hand and began a gentle massage.

'We'll be late,' He mumbled through the water as she began to rake him.

'We'll be later still if you don't stop talking.'

Bard's look was met with a beaming smile. 'That was nice.'

Try as he might, he couldn't stop the grin. 'Trying to hang onto a soapy wriggling countess whilst standing in the shower?'

'Any complaints?' from a wide-eyed-in-all-innocence Carol.

'Not a one. But that's why they call them knee-tremblers. I nearly went down.'

A quick flick of her eyebrows. 'Hmm.' The smile lit up her face.

He shook his head. 'You are incorrigible. Now I've got to learn to walk again.'

Carol's delicious giggle resulting in a tap on the rump as she stepped out of the shower.

He reached a decision. He needed to lose a stone.

The restaurant was full of couples waiting patiently. A smiling Aurelio, the restauranteur, approached. 'Signore e Signorina, everything was to your satisfaction?'

'It was excellent,' said Carol. 'The next time I come to London?'

'You will be most welcome, Signorina.'

The door closed behind them. 'Signorina?' Queried Bard. 'You're still wearing your wedding ring.'

'Mm, commonplace. Treat all women as young. Bolster the egos of the not so.'

Sitting up he hugged his knees. 'Ok, lunch time. What do you fancy? Apart from sex,' she smiled and pouted. 'Most of the restaurants around here open for the evening traffic. There are a couple of passable ones that open at lunchtime. Any favourite?'

She rolled onto her side and propped herself on her elbow. 'I've a nice bottle of red in my case that I was given almost seven years ago. I understand it goes well with bacon sandwiches. If you have any bacon, that is.'

'You still have it?'

She nodded. 'Mmm, never found the right opportunity. When Gordon began to get nasty, I used it as a memory enhancer. Now seems to be the perfect time.'

He leaned forward and gave her a kiss, 'I do love you.'

'I love you too but I'm still hungry. Now go,' she said pushing him away.

He grinned. Pulled on a pair of tracksuit bottoms and T-shirt leaving a sprawling Carol complained that she was pining away.

'Don't be silly,' He called from the kitchenette. 'You're beautiful.'

'I'll be a beautiful skeleton if you don't get a move on.'

Up to his elbows in bacon, tinned tomatoes and sliced bread the doorbell rang. 'Answer that, Carol.'

There was an answering grunt. 'I'm comfortable.'

'My dressing gown is behind the door.'

'You'll pay for this intrusion this afternoon,' she threw the covers back, got out of bed and hand on her belly smiled at her reflection, wondering.

'I look forward to it.'

She studied the mirror as she slowly wrapped the dressing gown round her; left over right as Martin would. After all what was the point in wearing a lover's dressing gown and fastening it as though he were a woman.

She was mid-twenties, slim, attractive, hazel eyes, slightly taller, elegantly turned out in a brown worsted two piece flecked with green, matching topcoat, black high-heeled shoes, and a concerned expression. 'You must be Joan,' said Carol.

It was impossible to miss the implications. She was beautiful, a honey-blonde, Lewis's dressing gown, bare legs and feet. 'Yes, I am,' she replied. 'I was looking for Lewis.'

This woman had travelled down from Huddersfield. This was not the time to be sympathetic. She was blunt. 'Lewis, Lewis Green? His name is Martin Beck. I'm afraid we're busy.'

'There must be some mistake,' Joan said and faltered as Carol lifted her left hand to her collar to make sure that Joan could see her wedding ring.

Carol noticed the switch of focus. 'There is no mistake, and yes, this is a wedding ring. No, we are not married. And, I have known him longer than you. His name *is* Martin Beck. Two things for you to consider before you go. If I loved someone enough to agree to marry them, I would never abandon them as you did when things became really tough. Secondly, I am carrying his child.'

Joan was silent. The thought lodged in her brain. If she knows she's pregnant they must have been sleeping together before I left. She put her hand in her pocket and handed Carol a key. 'I hope you'll be very happy,' she said in a defiant tone. 'You deserve each other.' She turned and walked away.

Carol smiled and put the key in the pocket for Martin to find later. 'She won't be back,' she said to herself then spotted the piano. 'How did I miss this earlier,' she smiled to herself, 'Oh yes,' and collected her case. Her explanation of the caller? A neighbour who enquired after him but gave no personal details, and she did not enquire.

Two perfectly poached eggs and two full rashers of crispy bacon each, tinned tomatoes plus an eight-year-old 14.5% Californian red and a half loaf of thick sliced bread to share. The toast: 'To us'.

They sat across the corner of the small kitchen table elbows touching. 'How long can you stay?'

Smiles were exchanged. 'Not as long as I would like,' said Carol, 'John is collecting me at three pm on Sunday. That gives us three nights together. He leant across the table and kissed her on the cheek. 'The boys wanted to come with me but it's too soon. There would be little or no privacy. But this is a two-bedroomed flat, isn't it.'

He nodded. 'Twin bedded; I can't wait to see them again.'

'How about next Friday? The boys have done nothing but talk about you and *The Lord of the Rings* since we left. Gordon wanted an heir, but he was not interested in them as his children, even when they began to develop their own personalities. Never kissed them goodnight, read to them. Never even spoke to them. You are exactly the opposite.

'You introduced them to The Hobbit and that I was called Bard.' he said.

'True,' she agreed, 'but from the start you talked with them about *Smaug* and *The Hobbit* and you smiled. I saw their reactions when you put your arms round them. That had never happened before. That's why I'm prepared to take the chance.

Carol yawned, stretched, stroked his cheek before rolling onto her stomach. 'Do you ever give any thought to what might have happened had we been together for the past seven and a bit years?'

'Initially. But after I discovered that you were a Countess?'

'Nevertheless, you still thought about me.'

'How could I not? Especially after your gift arrived. It reminds me every day. I know you said that money was not a problem but at the time it would have been,'

'Not really. Unless your pride was in the way. A bequest from my grandfather. And bequests from my parents, although should he pre-decease my mother she will have a life-interest: the estate and title will pass to Martin.'

'Your farther is?'

She smiled at him. 'Major-General Sir Lawrence Ingleby-Roberts, Duke of Tysor.'

'A Major-General *and* a Duke. Just what have I let myself in for?'

'Me!' she replied. 'Don't worry, he comes across as a bear but he's a pussy cat.'

'So is a tiger and they have sharp teeth and retractable claws.'

'Poor you. Getting cold feet?' she teased.

'No. Just wondering where I can buy some armour plate.'

'Don't be silly.'

'Changing the subject. I take it that beautiful gown hanging from the wardrobe is connected with the second of the two appointments you mentioned.'

'Yes, tomorrow. And it's black tie.'

'Ok.'

'Do you like ballet?'

'I've never seen a live performance.'

'Covent Garden. La Fille Mal Gardeé.'

'Erm, No, don't know that. What's it about?'

'It's a comedy. But you know what you told the boys? You'll just have to wait and see.'

Thirty Nine

'Hello, 2968.'

'Good morning. Roderick Bewley from the Royal Opera House. I have that a contact number for Lady Carol Sylverton. Would it be possible to speak with her, please?'

Bard turned 'It's for you Carol. Royal Opera House. A Mr Bewley.'

'Mr Bewley, good morning. Not bad news I hope.'

'... I see. Thank you for letting me know ... Yes, you can leave messages for me here or at Oldeney. Thank you again.'

She put the phone back on its cradle. 'Tonight's performance has been cancelled owing to a gas leak. I was looking forward to that. What else can we do?'

'Apart from the obvious?'

She had such a sweet smile. 'How's the stamina?'

'Point made. The Odeon at Camden has a classic Hitchcock, The 39 Steps. Robert Donat and Madeleine Carroll; there's a decent restaurant quite close. Or we could try the Italian again.'

'I haven't been to the cinema in ages. Let's go there.'

Rolls and Clarridges cancelled; umbrellas were the order of the day. Trafalgar Square and its' pigeons and The National Portrait Gallery. The portrait of her father, gazing down on unsuspecting observers:

Major-General Sir Lawrence Ingleby-Roberts.
DSO, MC & Bar. Duke of Tysor

Six feet three inches tall, Imposing in his Coldstream Guards uniform. Which probably accounted for the fact that Martin and

Graeme were tall for their age. Plus, there was something about the jaw

A stroll through Admiralty Arch and St. James Park to Buckingham Palace, and Langham's for lunch; courtesy of Carol. The afternoon was taken up by a visit to his office. Lady Carol Sylverton was introduced as his latest literary client. And a grilling re his absence.

The mixed grill at Neasby's was excellent and the red drinkable. We spent a couple of hours watching a nature film: Beaver Valley, a couple of Looney Tunes and Hitchcock at his finest. The taxi dropped up off as the heavens opened.

Pester power worked. John arrived precisely, accompanied by the twins. Carol had telephoned home each evening to speak with them, eventually acquiescing. It took them about thirty seconds to reconnoitre the flat. Graeme had even brought *The Fellowship of the Ring* in the forlorn hope that Bard might have time to read some to them. He would continue the story next weekend. A last passionate embrace. He walked her to the Rolls where the boys were waiting. He gave them a hug through the open window. 'Be good and I'll see you next week.' He stood at the kerb waving until the little Earl and his twin disappeared from view.

He felt on top of the world. His output that week was tremendous. Contracts exchanged. Marchant's book had been bought in the United States, France, Germany and the antipodes. Max Crawshaw's upgraded manuscript arrived Monday and went out to the commissioning editors. Two of the other agents had also had promising noises with regard to their manuscripts as well. Things had been good and were getting better. It might have been a cliché, but nothing really does succeed like success.'

Forty

10:00. Friday. Full tank of petrol and the 200-mile drive north to Oldeney.

2:30 and the finger post to Oldeney. His heart rate picked up when he came to the wall on the right, ten feet high with mature trees breaking the line of coping stones. A further ten minutes the entrance gates; just as Carol had described it: Fifteen feet tall, intricate wrought iron freshly painted in black and gold, were open. Without thinking he pulled between the gates across the cattle grid and stopped to check his map. Thirty seconds later there was a firm paarp to the rear. In the rear-view mirror was a Rolls Royce. A single lady in the rear seat. He acknowledged, pulled forwards and stopped. Carol leapt out, said something to the chauffeur and ran round to the passenger side as the chauffeur set off.

'You made it,' she said, put her arms round his neck and kissed him. 'Pull forwards to the point where the road disappears. Tell me what you think.'

The Rolls was about two hundred yards away. The view opened. A shallow valley. The mature woodland they had been driving through for the past five minutes disappeared to the right. On the left it followed the road as it curved to the right into the valley, for the most part occupied by a sizeable lake. A waterfall on the left. On the hilltop directly opposite, a huge mansion shaped like a letter 'H'. All the space between the house and the lake was open parkland with specimen trees.

'What I think is, WOW!. I'd expected something special, darling, but this is magnificent.'

'It is, isn't it,' she said and put her head on his shoulder. 'It can be a very lonely place at times. I want to fill the house with children, laughter and happiness. Is that so silly?'

He put his arm round her shoulders and kissed her head. 'Not a bit of it. We've made a start with the twins.'

She smiled. 'True, but they could be going away to school in a few years. I don't want to be here on my own. Yet, I have to look after the estate for Martin. That's only fair.'

'No-one else is listening. When can we get married?'

'I hope about six weeks. I spoke with my parents last Monday afternoon. Alicia had primed them. I told them everything about our evening. My father wants to meet you. Don't look so worried.' She ran the back of her right hand down his cheek. 'Come on. Front door.'

The house had three stories above ground and the closer you were the more magnificent it became.

A tall middle-aged man, smartly dressed in morning coat, waistcoat, dark grey pin-striped trousers, white shirt and tie, and black highly-polished shoes, opened the passenger door. 'The Blue Suite has been readied as instructed, Milady.'

'Givens, this is Mr Beck. He will be my house guest over the weekend and will become a regular house guest,' she turned to me. 'Are you able to stay until Monday, Martin?' The look in her eyes said please.

'That will be fine, Carol,' he said as she relaxed.

'Have Christopher park the car. And Mr Beck's bag taken to the suite. Leave the ignition keys on the bedside table. I will speak with Mrs Nesbitt.'

I handed him the keys, thanked him and left him to it.

'What are you laughing at?' Said Carol as they entered the House.

'This,' he replied taking in what was in front of them. 'Just comparing this to Merrion Lodge.'

'I see,; she returned his smile. 'But Merrion Lodge would have been nice in its day.' She took him by the hand. 'Come on.' She introduced him to the Housekeeper, Mrs Nesbitt. Our evening meal in the family dining room at five pm.

A whistle-stop tour of the house. Built in 1783 by Robert Adam. Every room was an eye-opener. the paintings, wall-hangings, furniture and porcelain were stunning. Decoration and plasterwork equally so. It would take some time to learn his way around. Libraries – books by the thousand. Dining rooms, including The State Dining Room – so named after a visit by King George and Queen Mary in 1936. Ballroom and music room, both with Grand Pianos . Another in the drawing room. Billiard room. Over twenty bedrooms – his separated from Carol's by a shared bathroom. Galleries. Salons. Ante-rooms and at least eight staircases, one of which took them to the roof. The view north, was spectacular: a deep terrace between the east and west wings with full width parterre. Beyond that, parkland with deer. Away to the left, the farm. To the right the stables and coach house, behind which was a walled garden; sides at least one hundred yards, beyond that an enormous glasshouse. To the right the garage block where, presumably, his car was parked. Carol must have felt as though she was rattling round like a pea in a drum.

'Have you ever thought of opening the House to the public?'

'Not seriously, but ... perhaps.'

The twins were expected home at four thirty. They passed a very pleasant hour in Carol's suite.

Bard, book in hand, was waiting on the Chesterfield when the Rolls drove past. Carol telling the boys they had a visitor in the Drawing Room. Graeme asked if it was Bard arriving early. They were permitted twenty minutes of hearing about Bilbo leaving his eleventy-first birthday party. Frodo leaving Hobbiton and heading for Rivendell, before Carol ushered them upstairs to get washed and changed for dinner. The food, roast chicken, fresh vegetables with a dangerous trifle to finish.

Piano practise next and then feed the ponies. Carol clapped her hands twice. 'Sorry boys. You have some homework to do and then it's bath-time. Bard will come and say goodnight and perhaps he will read to you tomorrow.'

They both looked at me. 'Promise?' said Graeme.

'I promise.' With that in mind they ran to the door and disappeared.

'Homework?'

'A little each day. Misspelt words to correct. Simple comprehension and a short paragraph of writing practise.'

'They're only six. It sounds a lot.'

'It takes about thirty minutes. They enjoy it. They like puzzles. That is how they see it.'

We were standing face-to-face. My hands clasped behind Carol's waist. She had her hands behind his neck. 'A penny?'

'Just a thought. What time do you have breakfast?'

'Whenever you want. Why?'

'Have you ever been to Blackpool?'

'We're only ten miles from Bridlington. Why Blackpool?

'The twins. They ride?'

'Like the wind, if I'd let them. Is that relevant?'

'I think so. I'm going to be their stepfather.' The thought made him smile. 'I'd like to give them the kind of upbringing that I had. I went through scouting, pioneering, backwoods cooking and camping. How to do things safely and have fun. It's about trust, in people and in themselves.'

'All right,' she said after a think. 'And Blackpool?'

'Some of the rides in the pleasure beach are scary. But if they're sat between us, they'll know they'll be safe. They'll still be frightened but it will be enjoyable.'

She looked at me suspiciously. 'I'm doing this as well?'

'But Carol, if you don't *who* is going to hold *my* hand?'

She was still laughing after the children were in bed. On impulse he stroked their hair, kissed them both on the forehead and tucked them in. That was when he first met Mary; the children's elderly nanny. Originally Lord Gordon's nanny she looked at Bard as if he were an interloper..

The next issue was to arrange somewhere to sleep tomorrow night. Being a Countess, Carol could open many doors.

Bard checked his address book. His father had a client in Blackpool. That took care of their evening meal.

Time for bed.

Forty-One

The forecast was good. Sunny periods, light winds with the chance of showers later in the day.

The pale green Austin A40 Farina that had followed them discretely from Oldeney parked three rows behind. The lone female occupant observing. 'Happy families? Make the most of it.' she said under her breath.

Walking north from Squire's Gate car park towards the Tower the boys reacted when they saw the Big dipper. 'Ooo, can we go on that, please?'

The front carriage. 'You first, Carol,' she climbed in followed by Martin, Graeme and Bard. A bit of wriggling from the centre. Safety bar engaged. He looked across at Carol. 'Hold tight everybody.'

The attendant made one lest check. 'Hold tight boys.'

There was a jerk as the brakes were released. Gravity took over.

> Feet braced he reached across in front of the boys taking hold of Carol's hand.

The train hit the drag chain and faltered. The clatter as the train engaged. With a jerk they were away. 'Look at the view,' he said. 'The higher we go the better it gets. You might even see *Smaug*.'

The train detached from the chain and rolled sedately round the curve picking up speed. In front Bard could just make out the edge of the drop.

'Don't be silly, Bard. Dragons don't exist,' said Martin.

'Really? he said. 'You're riding in one. Just imagine what *Smaug* saw when he attacked Dale. Just-like-this.' The acceleration was phenomenal. The roar and thunder of the cars combined with the screams and noise of the passengers was tremendous, not to mention the sensation of speed as they flashed through the structure. The boys hanging onto the rail for grim death and laughing. Carol screamed which made her look even more beautiful. What a rush.

Outside, the twins were jumping up and down. 'Everybody OK?' Said Bard.

'Can we go on again, please?' said Graeme.

Later, perhaps. But there's an entire fun fair to choose from and Blackpool Tower. Besides, Mummy looks as though she could do with a cup of coffee. How about a drink of pop and a cake?'

Carol found an empty table. Bard and the boys joined the queue. Two glasses of orange pop, two coffees and two Eccles cakes. They were huge so they had half each. The boys were happily munching their way through the Eccles cakes when Martin surprised them both. 'Mummy, are you and Bard going to get married?'

'We've seen you holding hands and kissing,' added Graeme with a sly grin.

'We haven't hidden it, have we?' Carol smiled and put her arm round Martin, giving him a squeeze. 'Would you like that, if we did get married?'

They both nodded. 'Bard reads to us and he's kind to you.' said Martin.

'And he taught us those funny songs,' added Graeme.

What Martin had said worried him in view of Carol's history.

'Martin, what did you mean when you said I was kind to your mummy.'

'You don't shout at her or hit her,' he said. It was so matter of fact. Just how commonplace had it been?

Carol looked tearful. Memories? Or just because the boys were aware? 'Was it often that your Daddy lost his temper?'

They both nodded. 'We used to run and hide.'

It was all coming out now. 'Did you tell anyone?' I said.

Graeme nodded. 'We told nanny. She hit us for telling tales. Said that if Daddy had had to do that, it was Mummy's fault.'

'Has she hit you often?' said Carol.

They both nodded.

'When was the last time?'

'When we didn't cry when Daddy died. She made *us* cry.'

'How?'

'She told us we should be sad and cry because Daddy died. I said he was nasty to you, and I wasn't sad. She tried to smack me, but I ducked. Then she hit Graeme and me with her walking stick. That hurt.'

'Where did she hit you? On what part of your bodies?'

'On our heads,' said Graeme.

Carol put her arms round them both. She had tears in her eyes. 'I am so sorry,' she said. 'She had no right to do that and I promise it will never happen again.'

'It didn't hurt for long,' said Graeme.

'She had no right to hit you at all.'

Several pairs of eyes followed as they left. That couldn't be helped. 'We didn't answer your question, did we?' Bard said when they were clear, 'About your mummy and me getting married. We're thinking about it. We first met a long time before you were born but your mummy was already married to your daddy, so we couldn't.'

'But you are going to get married now,' said Graeme.

'Nothing is finally decided. The fact that you two are in favour is good. But you must not tell anyone about what we have discussed today. Not your grandpa or your grandma, your friends or the teachers at school and certainly not the staff at the House. I want your promise, do you understand?'

After that they sampled almost every amusement in the Pleasure Beach, the faster and wilder the better. The most fun was Carol winning five consecutive games on the *Camel* Donkey Derby and winning a large teddy bear. Under protest they left the pleasure beach walking north towards The Tower.

Stomachs were rumbling. Bard checked his watch. 'I know it's early but if we don't want to queue for something to eat, we ought to find a restaurant now. All in favour?' It was unanimous. Fresh fish and chips followed by a trip up Blackpool Tower. No-one lost their dinner.

The tide was out. A football purchased from a promenade gift shop. A kick-about on the sand. They would sleep well.

A slow visit to the two remaining piers, arriving at The Blackpool Grill as the twins were protesting their hunger.

They left the car-park in failing light.

'Switch on in five minutes,' said Bard. The number of pedestrians would increase soon enough. He looked in the rear view mirror. 'Martin, pass your rug to Mummy so she can keep warm. I'm going to open the sunshine-roof, you and Graeme can stand on that bump in the centre of the car with your head and shoulders poking through. You will see more clearly. Fasten your coats.'

Martin claimed the front spot.

A chorus of 'Oohs' and 'Aahs welcomed the switch-on'. They were in the nearside lane and travelling slowly, Carol asked. 'How long does it take?'

'At this speed about an hour. But this is fast. Good, aren't they?'

'Brilliant. Far better than you see on the television.'

'From the Metropole Hotel north there are fewer of these overhead lights, but more tableaux. Then it will slow down.'

Had it not been for a minor collision just north of the Tower it might have been non-stop. The number of bumper-hoppers many with young children and pushchairs made things interesting. At the Metropole Carol had the boys switch round, under protest from Martin but it went without a hitch. Illuminations cleared in one and a half hours. The boys were back in the car and sunshine roof closed as it began to rain. 'Has everyone enjoyed today?

The general consensus was positive.

Fifteen minutes later it became very quiet. Carol half turned. 'Both fast asleep.'

'I'm not surprised. Now, where do you want to get married?'

'The vicar was in Gordon's clique so I'd be happy with a civic ceremony; preferably York. Are you happy with that?'

'Yes, I've never been what you might call religious. When?'

'Announce our engagement within six weeks. The ceremony a few weeks later. Those that do not like our itinerary? They can deal with it ... We haven't discussed the number of children. How many would you like?'

'Would *I* like? You're the one giving birth,'

'I am aware of how it works,' she said and laughed. 'I was wondering if you had a figure in mind.'

'I've always got your figure in mind.'

She scowled at him. 'Number?'

He grinned at her through the rearview mirror. 'Two or three?'

'The more children I deliver that carry your name the happier I shall be. Get rid of the Sylverton memories.'

The Bowland Court Hotel was a red brick Victorian pile with an enviable reputation. The A55 stood out between the Daimlers, Jaguars and the odd Bentley. Bard managed to pick the boys up as they both put their arms round his neck. A member of staff dashed out took the cases and followed them inside.

A burst pipe had rendered his suite out of order and so he would have to occupy the third bedroom of Carol's. That would be difficult. And, 'A Mrs Nesbitt called. Would you call her back.'

Francois Leroy, the manager chipped in. 'You can use my office, Countess, follow me please. James escort Mr Beck and his charges to the Fylde Suite.'

When Carol arrived, the twins were sound asleep. 'Mary has been admitted to the QEII Hospital York. Suspected heart attack. Better than she deserves. I'll retire her. She can go and live with her daughter in the village,'

After a nightcap they retired to Carol's bed.

The next morning she lay there, eyes closed, a contented smile. She stretched both arms to the ceiling, folded them behind his neck and pulled him down into the waiting kiss. 'Is there a better way to start the day,' she said at last. 'What time is it?'

'There's a clock on your left.'

'Too comfortable,' she replied. 'Besides, I thought you loved me.'

'You're incorrigible,' she smiled and nodded in agreement. 'Quarter to seven. Better get up.'

'You first.'

She had her legs locked behind his hips. 'Uncross your legs.'

She was in a playful mood, opened her eyes and grinned. 'Nope. You'll have to wriggle.'

'You want me to floss my teeth on the way through?'

She began to giggle. 'Sounds like fun.'

He grinned in return, pushed hard sliding downwards planting the biggest raspberry that he could.

'That tickles,' she said and made a grab at his head.

'Missed me.' he said, put his dressing gown on, deposited Carol's on her teddy bear and sat. 'Happy?'

'Mmm, thank you for yesterday,' she said and smiled. 'The way you and the boys interacted you'd think you were their father.'

'I wonder why,' he said leaned over and kissed her.

'Oh, whilst you were away buying ice creams yesterday, they asked if, after we were married, could they call you daddy.'

That brought a lump to his throat. 'What did you say?'

'That you would be pleased. You have the right, it's just that ...'

'I know. It's got to remain a secret.'

Any further conversation was brought to a halt with the twins hammering on the bedroom door.

He flicked the bed covers back, bent down and kissed her breast. 'You are so beautiful,' he said. 'Even without your clothes.' The pillow missed by inches.

'Out!'

It was an hour to QEII Hospital. Bard took the boys for a drink and a cake whilst Carol paid Mary a visit. It was confirmed, Mary had suffered a heart attack and would be kept in for observations.

Back at Oldeney, Carol telephoned Mary's daughter and explained that in the circumstances Mary would be retired on pension. That caused problems because Carol's late husband had allegedly promised Mary could have the post as long as she wanted. In other words, her daughter didn't want the hassle. Carol insisted, saying that it was either accepting retirement or being dismissed for hitting the boys with her walking stick. She would see Mary in hospital the following day and explain. The last thing that Carol needed was for a re-occurrence and the boys coming across a body when they woke up.

Forty-Two

Carol loved her horses and had bought him a pair of very expensive looking boots for his first lesson.

It was sixty degrees with the forecast promising a fine day.

Daisy, a ten-year-old black mare with a white blaze and front left sock, was already saddled. The next time that would be one of his tasks.

A swift leg up, he was lead to the rear of the garage block. 'Remember Martin this is a manège and not ménage. Do not get it wrong.'

With the boys on their Shetland ponies, Dapple and Apple, buzzing round like angry wasps whilst he managed not to fall off. After ten minutes he was declared safe.

It was beautiful undulating parkland with deer in the distance. Large wooded areas that gave him some ideas for the boys' adventure playground. Providing it was safe Carol agreed. Yesterday had been wonderful. Today, the four of them together on horseback. No one else in sight. It was at this point that Carol told him something he hadn't considered. She would lose the title Countess. However, as the daughter of a Duke she would retain her courtesy title of Lady. She would be known as Lady Carol Frances Elizabeth Beck.

Inaugural ride completed unscathed they dismounted. Carol grinned at Bard. 'You're going to ache in the morning. Don't worry, what brings it on will take it off.'

'Thanks.'

Over a light lunch He outlined his ideas and asked the boys what they liked best about the pleasure beach: 'Going fast,' the boys said together. 'Being so high up. It felt dangerous but you and Mummy were there.'

'We can build our own. Not like Blackpool but it will be fun. And, while you're visiting Mary this afternoon, Carol, why don't the boys and I see the lie of the land?'

Blake

Forty-Three

The Press Conference was to be held in the Sports Hall at Bishopgarth. The conversation settled as the Chief and his entourage entered and took their seats.

'Good morning ladies and gentlemen. I'm Ray Barton, the Chief Constable. On my left is Commander Jameson from the Metropolitan Police. The reason that he is here is because the murder of a Metropolitan police constable is linked to our enquiry. Not because the Metropolitan Police are being brought in to take charge. On my right is ACC Mithering. On his right Detective Superintendent Creighton who is in overall charge of our enquiry.

As you are aware our enquiry concerns the murder of four young men from different parts of the country and whose bodies were discovered in the West Riding. Also the subsequent associated murder of a Metropolitan police officer. The reason this press conference was called is because we have someone we need to interview and eliminate from out enquiries. You will be provided with what we believe to be an accurate photograph when you leave the Hall. In the meantime, this is the man.' The ACC held up a 24" x 12" black and white photograph. 'His name is Blaise Lincoln, a former RAF Pilot Officer. We are awaiting confirmation from the Home Office as to whether he joined the prison service or not and if he did, where. Described as six feet to six feet two inches tall. Proportionate build. Military bearing. May have a clipped moustache. As far as we can ascertain he poses no risk to the public at large. Are there any questions?'

The Chief Constable pointed at an upraised arm. 'Yes?'

'Alistair McDonald, Telegraph and Argus. I've heard rumours that this enquiry is linked to the report of a missing girl from seven years ago. Would you care to comment?'

'I don't comment on rumours, Mr McDonald. In my experience all that does is to introduce confusion.' He looked round and pointed to another arm. 'Yes?'

'Norman Smith, Daily Mirror. The last time I was here during the Wainwright case we were introduced to a constable, Brian Blake. Could you tell us, is he involved in this enquiry?'

The Chief Constable broke into a broad smile. 'Yes, he is now a detective constable and one of many detectives involved in the case. To pre-empt a possible further question, he will not be attending today.'

He pointed at another raised arm. 'Yes?'

'Could I ask a question of Commander Jameson?'

The Chief Constable glanced to his left. 'Commander?'

The Commander smiled. 'What would you like to know?

'Neville Coustache, York Evening Herald. Why would an officer of your rank make a personal trip so far into the wilds of the north when an officer of lower rank could have accomplished the same. What's the real reason you're here?'

The burst of laughter subsided. 'Judging from your accent Mr Coustache you hail from Essex. I was born in Yorkshire and have many relatives in the county. And Yorkshire has lots of what London does not.'

'Yorkshiremen?'

'Yes, Mr Coustache,' he said through the laughter. 'Men and women. My wife, who also hails from Yorkshire, and I return to recharge our batteries. However, Mr Barton was correct. Today I am here primarily to liaise over the enquiry concerning the death of a metropolitan police constable.'

'That would be PC Cameron?'

'Yes, it is.'

No further information was forthcoming the conference ended.

Beck

Forty-Four

The Old Library was far from being the largest in the house, but it was magnificent. Even the air smelled of history.

Carol showed Bard where the original plans, documents and maps were kept before she left for the hospital, taking a bunch of flowers from the garden.

'We're not allowed to look at these without Mummy present,' said Graeme. 'Daddy wouldn't let us in here at all.'

'One morning we followed him,' said Martin. 'When he saw us, he shouted and chased us out then locked the door.'

What could he say. 'Well, I won't. But these maps and charts are very old and easy to damage. If Mummy says you have to be accompanied then find your mummy or me.' They both nodded.

The maps of the estate were in the top drawer. There was something reminiscent of a draughtman's table. It looked period. The twins fetched a buffet apiece. Martin standing on Bard's left and Graeme on his right. This was becoming a very comfortable pattern. 'Maps are wonderful,' he said. 'Just like works of art. This,' he pointed at the ornate drawing in the top right-hand corner. 'is called a Compass Rose and the arrow points to the north.'

'But there's no lake,' said a confused Graeme.

'Or House,' said Martin.

Bard spotted the clue. 'If you know where to look this map tells you why the house is called what it is. What's the name of the house?'

'Oldeney Carr House,' said Martin.

'What does that say?' He pointed to the map.

'The Carr with two r's.' said Graeme

'This is the land before the house was built. What's this wiggly line next to Carr?'

Graeme twisted his head round. 'It says Oldeney Brook,'

'So, why do you think it's written next to Oldeney Brook? What do you think Carr means?'

'It's boggy?'

'It does.'

'The house is named after a bog? Yuk.'

The looks on their faces had him laughing. 'But in those days that is just what they did. And there's more. The word Brook is an old English name for a stream. The word Carr isn't.' He leaned forward and whispered. 'It's Viking.'

That fired their imaginations. 'We've got Vikings?' said Martin.

Graeme followed. 'Can we go and look for them?'

'Whoa, slow down. The name is probably more than a thousand years old. We have to do some research and there's plenty of time.'

It only took a minute or so to point out that *The Carr* was where the lake is. The House to the north. The next map was more modern. Everything looked to be there. Entering through the gates, Dark Wood was on the left, South Wood on the right. The New Plantation behind the walled garden.

It was a ten-minute walk to the Dark Wood. The conifers were too dense; not enough variety, although the carpet of pine needles would make for a softer landing. It was dark and oppressive even in the daytime. The boys called it Mirkwood, even in the absence of giant spiders.

The boys were chasing Bard puffing and panting like old men by the time they reached the New Plantation. He 'tripped'. They took advantage and piled on top. He surrendered and picked the giggling pair up, one under each arm, and carried them into the wood. About twenty yards in there were signs that there had been a large fire.

According to the boys, "Mummy had a large bonfire after Daddy died". That he knew about. New Plantation it might have been on the map dated 1790, but not now. It was mature and perfect for what he had in mind. An extensive range of broadleaf, including several varieties of oak, sweet and horse chestnut, some conifers and masses of shrubs, copious quantities of dead wood lying around and not a few rabbits. Try as they might they didn't catch any. The air was full of birdsong. An hour of wandering brought them back to the fire-ground.

'I think this is perfect for our adventure playground,' said Bard

'Where?' came the puzzled reply.

'Here,' he said and walked the twenty yards to a large oak tree. Followed by the two inquisitives. 'Look,' he pointed to the lower branches. 'We can put ropes over this branch to make swings or ropes to climb. On that spruce tree over there,' He pointed to one thirty yards away, 'we can make a type of roundabout. We can make ladders. When you know a little more, we can build towers and bridges and a zip-line so you can slide down. I'll teach you to abseil, just like mountaineers do.'

That did the trick. All they wanted to know was, when? They would start the following Sunday. But first of all, he had to teach them how to tie a running bowline. All ideas of hunting down the Vikings were set aside.

Mrs Nesbitt was in her office. One ball of thick string and a pair of scissors were produced. Each an arm's length piece of string. 'Right, follow what I do. String under the back rail and down the front ... Good. Now hold the upper end in your right hand and the lower one in your left ... Now we're going to tie a knot in the right-hand piece around the left. You do what I do, ready?'

There was an instantaneous 'Yes, Bard.'

> 'Good. Now pass the right-hand piece under the left and tuck the end under your thumb, but don't pull ... that's good. Now we pretend that's a little rabbit and he's hungry, so we have to build him a burrow so he can go out and eat.'
>
> Step by step Bard showed them how to construct the knot. 'Nip it between your left thumb and forefinger. That's good. Now, where did we put the rabbit?'
>
> 'Here Bard,' said Martin and let go of his string.
>
> 'Oops. Not to worry. We'll wait for you to catch up.'
>
> Martin's funny bone had just taken a bruising. 'Not funny, Graeme. Stop laughing.'
>
> 'No, he's just pleased it wasn't him. From the beginning ... Good, all together again.

Now keep the loop nipped and hold the rabbit in your right hand ... now push him up through the hole and let him have a look round,'

Three pieces of string appeared. 'Without anybody dropping anything, take hold of your rabbit and pull him through. ... Good. There's a fox coming. What would the rabbit do?'

'Run back down his burrow.'

'Correct, but first he has to run behind the tree ... Carefully. Don't drop anything ... Excellent. Now slowly pull everything together ... Well done, both of you. You have just tied a very complicated knot called a running bowline. Very useful for the adventure playground. It will help to keep you safe. Now, I will leave mine where it is, and I want you to unfasten yours and tie it again. Can you do that?

They both nodded and started again.

Mrs Nesbitt appeared beside him. 'You get on well with His Lordship and his brother, sir,' she observed softly.

'They're delightful. That was a difficult knot to tie, especially for children so young with no previous experience. They did well.'

They could hear the boys muttering to themselves as they retied their knots.

'I understand that their father wasn't the easiest of men.'

'He was a man of strong opinions, sir,' she said.

'Childhood should be for having fun and learning. But it's difficult to take on board that the title lies on Martin's shoulders.'

Before Mrs Nesbitt could answer Martin said. 'Bard, I've finished and it looks like yours.' Followed immediately by Graeme's. 'So does mine.'

He smiled at the expectant faces. 'That was quick. Let's have a look, shall we?' Smiling he peered at the knots. 'They both look all right.' He tightened the knots. Both held. 'Well done. That was very good.' There were two happy little boys. He crouched down to talk at their eye level. 'It's easier to tie with rope because it's not as floppy as string. And, when you have bigger hands like mine. Try it again.'

Only practice could improve it.

Carol was not in a good frame of mind. 'Later,' was the answer to his quizzical glance.

Sitting on the Chesterfield in the Drawing Room she put her arms round the twins. 'Right, what have you two been up to in my absence?'

Graeme got in first. 'Did you know the House is named after a Viking bog, Mummy?

She frowned. 'Is it?'

'That's what Carr means. Bard showed us on the map.'

'He'll have to show me,' she said.

'Can we come?'

'We can do that later. Now, what else have you been doing?'

'Chasing rabbits in The New Plantation, Mummy,' said Graeme.

She smiled. 'Did you catch any?'

'No, they ran away.'

'That is a surprise. Anything else?'

'Bard taught us to tie a knot called a running bowline so we can have a swing.'

She looked at her elder son. 'A running bowline? Can it run as fast as a rabbit?' she teased.

Martin looked puzzled. 'But, it doesn't have any legs, Mummy,' he said. 'It's a knot.'

'Well,' she smiled. 'Will you tie one for me.'

'Hold your arms out, Mummy,' said Martin as they took their strings from their pockets. You could hear the mumbled recitations as Carol sat there, arms outstretched with the cords dangling from her forearms and the twins beaming at her. 'That was very proficient,' she said.

'Don't you think that Mummy looks like a Christmas tree. We could decorate her instead.'

The twins just giggled. I was on the end of a wrinkled nose. 'You would say that,' she smiled as she took the string from her arms. 'That looked complicated.'

I nodded. 'It is. If they can tie that the others will appear simple.'

A trip to the stables, give the horses a treat of apple. The coach house: five landaus and two coaches. The 10,000 square yard walled garden and the huge glasshouse, which had seen better days. Exactly what specimens were supposed to be in there Carol had no idea. Last, the New Plantation the scene of the proposed playground,

'That woman. Even the nursing staff described her as unpleasant. When I told her she was being retired because of her heart condition and she had struck the boys with her stick she became worse.

'The boys were Sylvertons and needed discipline. Spare the rod and spoil the child. And you can't force me to retire. My son promised me that I could work as long as I wished. When he arrives you will wish you had never been born. I pointed out that Gordon was dead, and Martin was the Earl. That any promise she claimed Gordon may have made died with him. Because of her assault on Martin and Graeme she was banned from the House permanently and fortunate to receive a pension instead of being dismissed. She would live with her daughter in the village. Then she claimed that Gordon was her son and knew how to deal with the likes of me.'

'You're serious?'

'I told her. Whether she liked it or not I wasn't going to change my mind. She was furious and said Martin would never achieve his majority.'

'That's a terrible threat.'

'I'll tell Givens to ensure that the rest of the staff are made aware. She is not to be allowed into the house. Outside is a different matter. Also, they have all been told to report any strangers paying particular attention to the house. Givens and Mrs Nesbitt have been told why. After your episode and those responsible not being in custody, I'm not having you at risk on the estate. I've also passed the message on to the Farm Manager and, the Game Keeper and his staff. They know all the locals so any strangers will stand out.'

Forty-Five

Strenholme opened as a school in 1870 by the Rev. Zachariah Wilmot and now had four hundred and thirty students. Eighty percent of whom were boarders. The school grounds, over four hundred acres of buildings, sports fields, woodland and a sixty acre farm largely run by the senior boys with a small permanent staff. The farm producing milk, cheese, butter, and vegetables, plus a small number of calves and pigs. The twins were in the pre-preparatory school for students aged from four to eight years. the Principal, Dr Ivan Hollis was standing in the doorway welcoming students returning from the weekend at home. Bard had driven south with Carol and the twins on his way to London. John following behind to take Carol home.

'Countess!' he beamed a smile. 'How nice to see you. It seems a long time since you were here.'

'Too long, Dr Hollis. I thought that it was time.' Carol's enforced separation from anything outside of Oldeney now being unravelled. 'My boys insisted that we both accompany them here this morning. May I introduce my house-guest, Mr. Beck.'

Pleasantries exchanged and hands shaken, the twins were ushered into school leaving Carol and Bard at the front door. They were just about to return to the car, 'Before you go, Countess, might I have a confidential word?'

'There is a problem, Headmaster?'

'Nothing that I would call a problem. However, it does affect your children.'

'Do you have a problem with Mr Beck sitting in?'

He looked surprised. 'Not if you don't. If you go and see my secretary she will show you into my office. I will be along shortly.'

'May I get you some more refreshment?' he said when he saw the empty cups. They declined. He sat behind his desk.

It was too much of a coincidence. 'Dr Hollis,' said Bard. 'Do you by any chance happen to have a male relative on the academic staff at Leeds University?'

His face lit up. 'Indeed I do, Mr Beck. My cousin Gregory. You know him?'

'My tutor.'

'Excellent. Truly excellent,' he raised a quizzical eyebrow. 'And?'

'A first,' I smiled.

'Wonderful,' he said as he broke into a broad grin. 'And does he still use green ink to express his displeasure?'

I remembered it well. 'He certainly does.'

He shook his head and laughed. 'Green is not important. If, however, green doesn't work and he uses red, then beware .. It has stood you in good stead?'

'Indeed. I secured a position with Finsbury Templeton Books. Now I work under contract to them and also independently as a literary agent. The Lewis Green Literary Agency.'

'Excellent! What I have to say to the Countess you will find interesting.'

He settled down. Carol advised him of our forthcoming engagement. And should he hear anything from the boys to please do his best to dampen any rumour. This time he came round the desk, offered his congratulations and shook our hands. He made no comment about the death of Carol's husband.

He leant forward resting his forearms on the edge of his desk. 'Can I take it Mr Beck that you are the Bard that Graeme has written about?'

He smiled at the memory. 'I am.'

'And you read Tolkien to them.'

'I'm reading The Fellowship of The Ring to them at the moment.'

He nodded. Paused for a few seconds. 'I thought you must be ... As far as Martin is concerned, in all lessons he is in advance of where we might expect for someone of his age to be. However, in mathematics he is almost ready for the move from pre-prep to prep. At the end of the year, with a little extra work he should be ready. What I have done is to prepare a learning plan for him to achieve that in all subjects. However because he is a day student it will necessitate some of the work being carried out at home. Nothing too arduous but it will help. Is that all right?'

'Certainly, as long as he has some time to be six years old.'

Dr Hollis smiled. 'Of course. Graeme is different. He is ready in all subjects to move now.' The shock on Bard's face equal to Carol's. 'He is almost six and a half and has a reading age of twelve.' He paused whilst he took a pocketed beige manilla folder from his desk drawer. 'On a Monday morning they have a period set aside for creative writing. Most students simply write what they did with their parents and siblings over the weekend. We don't make too much fuss about the spelling or grammar at this stage, although it is corrected. The main thing is to get them putting pen to paper,' he passed several sheets of paper to Carol. 'This is some of Graeme's work.'

Carol quickly scanned the pages before passing them to Bard. 'What do you think?'

It was obviously a child's hand although most of the letters were joined. The writing was neat and on the line. The thing that hit him was the content:

The Last Dragon Ryder.

I am Ulrick, last of the Dragon Ryders. From my seat on the shoulders of Ulysses I could see through the smoke to the flames in the township below ...

He took a deep breath and exhaled before handing the papers back to Dr Hollis. 'Had I been handed that as a typed manuscript and asked to estimate the age of the author I would have said mid-teens.'

'I would agree with you. But you see what I mean, his vocabulary and comprehension are outstanding for a child of his age. His other subjects are of a standard equal to the first year in prep, or better. And you may find these of interest.' He handed several other sheets to Carol.

'Would you like these also?' She said to Bard.

'Please.'

'Would it be possible to have copies, Dr Hollis?'

'Certainly, Countess,' he said and handed them to his secretary.

Bard had nothing to do with non-adult literature. He wanted to show them to someone who did.

Dr Hollis suggested a reading regime that would keep the boys interested. One where the boys read to them rather than the other way round. He suggested that Carol order The Children's Newspaper. He also gave us a list of suitable authors: He would post details to Carol of other subjects within the next week.

Forty-Six

Christine Honeydew, Finsbury Templeton Books Director of Children's Literature put Graeme's work on the coffee table and leant back in her easy chair. Looked at him quizzically. 'The hand-writing is that of a child. However, the storyline and the syntax are not. From the smile on your face, Martin, this work is not what it appears at first glance, is it?

He shook his head. 'Nope. The original work of a six-year-old boy.'

This was the first time he had ever seen Christine's face show emotion. 'You're serious?'

'Yup. And hopefully, with his elder twin will shortly become my stepsons.'

The mask slipped. 'Congratulations, you kept that quiet. Who's the lucky lady.'

'Lady Carol Sylverton, Countess of Oldeney.'

'Marrying into nobility, eh?' She smiled then narrowed her eyes. 'Husband was an Earl. Widowed or divorced?'

'Widowed.'

'Oldeney. Where do I know that name from? ... Never mind. She obviously knows that you have these manuscripts.'

'She does. Also, that I'm bringing them here.'

'Right. Is there any more artwork?'

'Not that I'm aware of.'

'Fair enough. There's enough to give us an idea. Can't guarantee it at the moment. I'll call you at your office tomorrow morning around ten. Give you a definitive answer. If it's a go-ahead I'll need to speak with them both next week, here, say Wednesday. Two pm. Is that all right?'

That was quick. Under normal circumstances this process could take anything from four to six weeks. 'I'll confirm it.'

The next couple of hours he spent on errands concerning the adventure playground. Beales ships chandlers in Seven Dials. A nearby supplier of climbing equipment and, a visit to both a toy and a book shop. A five-minute chat with Carol promising to let her know as soon as possible the result of Christine's meeting. The fact that a positive result for Graeme would exclude Martin and require a certain amount of diplomacy. In this, Martin would definitely come second.

Forty-Seven

Tuesday a.m., Christine called. The company was fully committed. However, they would accept Graeme's manuscript but not commit to further progress. In other words it was good but, they wanted to mothball it until they saw fit. No guarantee. As an independent agent who had approached them and not under contract, he took possession of Graeme's documents. Called Carol appraising her of the situation and suggested that he put Graeme's work out to all the companies specialising in children's literature. Provoke a response. She agreed.

Friday came round at a rush. Three pm he headed north, destination: Tewksbury Grange Country House Hotel, Stratford.

He arrived at five thirty. A huge Victorian red brick pile. His Austin A55 standing out against two Bentleys, three Daimlers, several Jaguars and a Jenson.

Immaculate inside as well as out. A swift embrace and an unexpected hug from the twins. Booked in he was taken to his suite; with a connecting door to Carol's. Dinner had been booked for six thirty. He handed the twins the two packages. They opened the heaviest one first: a Chambers etymological dictionary. The second was Scrabble. They hadn't played before. They had a twenty-minute session explaining the rules; then they played. This was going to be competitive.

The askance looks as we entered the restaurant rapidly faded. The twins behaved impeccably, as they could when necessary. The food was excellent: Tomato soup with fresh basil. Grilled sole with Mediterranean vegetables, a lemon garlic and butter sauce followed by tiramisu – ice cream for the boys. Accompanied by a Californian Chardonnay. Orange juice for the boys. However, all they wanted to do was to finish their meal and play Scrabble. They even walked, until they left the restaurant leaving us to drink our wine in peace.

There was a quizzical smile as she put her glass down. 'There's a lot of rope in the garage.'

He nodded. 'Good. Three balls of sisal string. Seven hundred yards of 8mm sisal. The same of 10mm and 10mm nylon rope. a hundred yards of climbing rope. Two reels of coloured whipping twine and several other bits and pieces. There should have been a box as well.'

'There was. Very heavy. Christopher put it in your office.'

'Good,' he said and smiled. 'There's something in there for you.'

He saw the quizzical look appearing. 'Well, you don't want to miss out on all the fun, do you?'

She picked her glass up and took a sip. 'Hmm, we will see. Now, tell me again about your meeting with this Christine.'

'They want to mothball it so I did what we agreed,' he said. 'I've sent copies of Graeme's work to all the editors who publish non-adult fiction. All we have to do is to sit back and see who bites.'

'You make it sound like an auction.'

'That's just what it is. See who wants it most. In the interim, as Graeme's mother I need a contract agreeing that Graeme can become my client. And if he doesn't have his own bank account, he will need one'

'And what commission will you take. You're not doing this for nothing just because of your relationship.'

'Yes, I am. You would do the same in my place, wouldn't you?'

She smiled and nodded. 'Yes, I would ... An income from writing would be a great advantage. Until recently the younger son of an Earl was expected to join the church. And there may yet be pressure for that to happen. I will ensure it doesn't.'

Blake

Forty-Eight

DI Cartwright put the phone back on the cradle. 'At bloody last,' he said to himself. He opened the office door, 'Sergeant Ryder!'

'Just coming.' He galloped downstairs. 'Sir?'

'Who's free?'

'Blake's just left, other than him everyone else is out.'

'OK. Grab him and bring him back. Two minutes.'

The two officers looked at the smiling face. 'Sir?'

'Blaise Lincoln saw his face plastered across the TV last night and handed himself in at Reading; accompanied by a solicitor.'

'Reading, sir?' I said.

The DI laughed. 'Reading.'

'Has he been arrested?'

'No. You can do that. We know that he had been Emily Reid's fiancée and appeared to be the male involved at Seven Oaks Fold. So, rattle his cage. Point out the allegations but we need to make sure it is not misidentification. I'll notify Reading. They can expect you about 2pm. ID parade Monday.'

Forty-Nine

We arrived just after eleven. My parent's home, a 1940s six bedroomed detached house in an acre of garden was in the throes of autumn colour. The virginia-creeper across the front of the house was beginning its inexorable progression from its normal dull green to the flaming crimson-vermillion in competition with the roof tiles. He parked between Stephen's Volvo and his father's new burgundy Jaguar 4.2 XJ6. Business was already doing well with the busiest time of the year looming.

In answer to the twins closing of the car doors the family came to greet us.

'Carol, this is my family, Mum – Patricia, Dad – Clive, Sister – Elizabeth, Brother-in-law - Steven and last but by no means least my Nephew - Peter. Everybody this is Carol and her boys, Martin and Graeme. You two can call them Aunt Elizabeth and Uncle Steve'

His father and sister picked up on the names straight away. There would be interesting conversations ahead. There were hugs and handshakes all round with Mum and Dad insisting on first names. So far so good. Mum almost pounced on the twins.

'Aren't you two adorable,' she gushed. 'How do people tell you apart?'

'There is no easy way, Mum. Just practise and honesty. This is Martin,' he put his hand on Martin's shoulder. 'And this one, is Graeme.'

Dad was chuckling to himself. 'How old are you boys?'

'Six, Mr Beck,' they said together.

'I see,' he said and raised his eyebrows. I'll have to keep an eye on you.'

It was going well. Carol was playing the game accepting condolences on the death of her husband. That must have hurt. Glenda, the maid, had brought the coffee and soft drinks. Mother had been getting a little forgetful over the past twelve months, except where gossip was concerned. Dad had thought a little domestic help might be useful. The twins were examining the books in the large bookcase that Bard had cut his teeth on. It wasn't a surprise when schoolteacher-sister Elizabeth went for a chat with Peter in tow. 'Peter likes books, do you?'

'Yes, Aunt Elizabeth,' they both replied.

'I've read that one,' said Graeme pointing. 'Masterman Ready.'

Liz looked down at the pair of six-year-olds in semi-disbelief. '*You've* read it?'

Graeme nodded. 'Yes.'

'We both have,' said Martin, making sure that he wasn't missed out.

'When did you read it?'

'Easter, in the school holidays.

'Did you like it?'

Graeme nodded again. 'Yes,' he replied. 'Mummy helped me with a few words, and I liked the story more than The Swiss Family Robinson.'

'Why do you say that?'

'Swiss Family Robinson was too easy,' he replied. 'Not like a proper shipwreck. Bard's reading The Fellowship of The Ring to us. That's exciting.'

'Bard?' she said looking at me. 'That was your nickname.'

'Guilty,' he said and grinned. 'Just got something to find. Back in two minutes.'

'Can we come?'

'Not this time, Martin. Won't be long.'

'When you come to our house, Peter, you can play on our swings.'

Bard carried the three boxes from the loft.

'What have you got in there?' said Martin.

'Models for what we're going to build.'

Boxes in the boot, Bard was confronted by both father and sister, questions coming out of their ears.

'All right,' he said smiling at them both. 'Who's first?'

Seniority made its claim. 'It's a hell of a thing you're doing, Martin, taking on another man's children. Yes, Carol is young, certainly beautiful and the boys are a couple of crackers. Should you two get together we would love more grandchildren. But it was only a few months ago you were engaged to that other girl. What do they call her? Joan, wasn't it? You can't have known Carol for more than five minutes. Are you certain?'

He didn't get a chance to answer. 'You've missed the point, Dad. They've known each other for over seven years,' she returned the smile. 'How is your watch?' She always was smart.

He smiled and pulled the sleeve back. 'It keeps perfect time.'

The fog cleared. 'Are you telling me, you young sod,' Dad laughed. 'That the mysterious '**C**' is Carol? The 'milady' and owner of the Silver Shadow? The time we spent discussing that and you never let on.'

We hadn't been sure how the news would be received but his sister's leap into the dark had just ripped it open wide. How would dad react. Thankfully, laughter is contagious.

'Dad, I couldn't. Initially I didn't know, or at least I wasn't sure until I got an answer to a small ad I put in The Times. Even then I had no idea about wealth or titles.'

His expression became serious. 'Then the watch was because she was pregnant?'

'So it would appear,' He said trying to deflect what might be coming next.

'But why you?'

'Simply because I was in the right place at the right time. Serendipitous. And, had things been different we would have married years ago with more children. The result would have been the same.'

He didn't give up. Perhaps he thought there were problems on the horizon. 'Her

husband?'

'A private episode in her life that she had drawn a line through. And why she employed a private investigator to find me. And that, Dad, is as much as you're getting.'

His father visibly relaxed, 'But still... the boys *are* our grandsons?'

'What do they say in parliament? I refer the honourable gentleman to the answer I gave some time ago.'

At least they laughed. Then Liz added her bit. 'Dad, you're beginning to sound like Mum. We'll have to wait until next weekend. Hopefully, things will be clearer then.'

'Thanks, Liz. This is just for you two. Not even Mum.' She wasn't a malicious gossip. It's just that when the ladies golf team were taking their ease, discretion went out of the window. She could blather for Bristol. 'We are getting married in a few months. However, it must stay under wraps for now. Let us stick to *our* time scale. Afterwards, I will be the boys' stepfather and it is imperative that they must not know what we've just discussed. We will have to be happy with half a loaf. Once Carol and I marry you will become grandparents, and aunt and uncle. But come next weekend Mum will have enough to chat about, believe me. Promise me that you won't breathe a word of what you're thinking.'

'Ok son, sorry,' he said and put his hand on Bard's shoulder. 'It's your decision. And we'll take up Carol's offer of a weekend at Oldeney; although we'll need an overnight stop. Let's go eat.'

There had been a shower over lunch but now the sun was making a brave effort to break through. The golf club car park was full. Carol, Liz and Mum, plus the boys were in a huddle close to the doors. Clive, Steve and Bard were pouring over Bard's AA roadmap on the bonnet of his car.

'If we set off Friday straight after lunch and stop between Birmingham and Derby, it should be ok. That all right with you, Steve?'

'Fine. A flying start on Saturday we should make it by eleven. What's it like, Martin.'

'Beautiful. You'll like it.' Bard closed the roadmap. 'We'll see you a week today.'

Handshakes, hugs and kisses all round they were ready to leave. Carol suddenly paused and turned to the others. 'Don't forget your riding gear.'

They stood and waved until the A55 turned right out of the car park. 'What a lovely girl, and what adorable boys. They haven't said anything, but it would be nice if they did get married, even if those boys aren't his.'

'We'll just have to wait and see, Pat. And I agree those boys are livewires.'

'In your family chat, Clive, did either you or Liz manage to glean anything new?'

'In words of one syllable, Steve. No. We'll just have to wait.'

Beck/Blake

Fifty

Carl Oscarson was not happy. An arrest for conspiracy to kidnap was a very serious offence and not one his client had led him to believe was likely. Now the police were wanting to cart him off to Yorkshire. 'Sergeant, is this really necessary?'

'It is, sir. And the sooner we leave the better for all concerned. You are more than welcome to travel to Yorkshire, although I'm sure you are aware that your client does not have an automatic right to have a solicitor present. Now, if you will excuse us. Brian.'

I took hold of Lincoln's arm. 'This way Mr Lincoln,' and led him to the door. He could think about what he had done, overnight.

Blake

Fifty-One

10:00. Monday. 'Gentlemen,' Inspector Fisher waited until the chatter stopped. 'Form a line, please' The eight police officers in plain clothes plus three civilians of the same height and build shuffled into some semblance of order.' Solicitor Jeffrey George, clipboard in hand waited patiently for his client to appear. Inspector Fisher turned to his left. 'Sergeant Ruddock, Mr Lincoln.'

'Sir,' he said and left returning two minutes later.

'Mr Lincoln, with you there will be twelve people in the line. You may choose to stand wherever you want. There will be two witnesses. After the first witness you may change your position if you wish. Because of your height we have had to include several police officers. They will do nothing to identify themselves as such, they are merely members of the line. The witnesses have been kept separate from each other and will not have the opportunity to converse after their attendance; neither have the members of the line seen either of the witnesses. If the witnesses think they recognise the person, they will touch that person on the shoulder. Should they select you they will not speak to you. Neither should you speak to them. Have you any questions?

Lincoln shook his head. 'No, Inspector.'

'Where do you want to stand?'

'Next to the last?' he said. Lincoln took his place.

The Inspector nodded. 'Sergeant, Mrs Watson.'

Angela Watson looked apprehensive as she entered. 'Oh, there are a lot, Inspector,' she said.

`Inspector Fisher smiled. 'Laid down by the Home Office, Mrs Watson. To be seen to be fair to any possible suspect. What we would like you to do is to see if you can identify the man you saw, accompanied by the female who handed you an envelope addressed to a Lewis Green. I have to tell you that the person you saw may or not be present. Taking as much time as you require, walk along the line. Should you identify the man touch him on the shoulder. Do not speak to them. They will not speak to you.'

'What if I touch the wrong person?'

'That person may be here or not, Mrs Watson. There is no wrong person just someone you may think is the person you saw. If you think he is that person touch him on the shoulder.'

Angela Watson nodded and began the lonely walk, conscious of the eyes boring into her. 'I'm not quite sure, Inspector,' she said when she reached the last one. 'Could I hear them speak?'

'Certainly. Is there anything in particular that you would like them to say?'

She thought for a moment and smiled. 'Yes. One of the things he said was, "He enjoys puzzles and will enjoy working this one out".

Inspector Fisher and Jeffrey George wrote it down.

"He enjoys puzzles and will enjoy working this one out?" the Inspector iterated.

'Yes, I remember that, it seemed strange at the time.'

'Very well. Gentlemen, Mrs Watson will walk along the line again. She will stop in front of each of you. When she does, in your normal speaking voice, say the words, "He enjoys puzzles and will enjoy working this one out. In your own time, Mrs Watson.'

Slowly, Inspector Fisher with Jeffrey George close behind, Angela Watson stood in front of each as they repeated the words. The closer she was to the end the more nervous Blaise Lincoln looked.

'I'm happy now Inspector. It was this one,' she stepped forwards and touched Blaise Lincoln on the shoulder.'

'You are certain, Mrs Watson?'

'As I can be, Inspector.'

'Thank you. The sergeant will take you back to the interview room. We will require you to make a statement. Sergeant, when Mrs Watson is settled bring in Mr Beck.'

At the sound of Beck's name Lincoln quailed.

'Mr Lincoln, would you like to change your place in the line?'

'Yes,' he said fighting to conquer his emotion.

'Take the place you want.'

Blaise Lincoln walked to his right taking the third place from the beginning. The line settled. Martin Beck entered.

I'd hung back until Martin Beck entered the ID parade and waited outside the door, listening. I recognised the voice of Inspector Fisher.

'Mr Beck, the man that you saw at the door of your London flat the day you were kidnapped may be in this parade. Or not as the case may be.'

Unbeknown to me Martin Beck smiled to himself when he spotted Lincoln.

'The procedure is that you walk slowly along the line perusing each person in turn. Should that man be present you do not speak to him, just walk towards him and touch him on the shoulder. In your own time, Mr Beck.

'Inspector, I only saw that face for five seconds. It's engraved on my brain. Do I have to walk the full length because he is third in the line.'

That caught me by surprise.

'You are certain, Mr Beck?' the surprise evident in Inspector Fisher's voice.

'There is no doubt, Inspector.'

'In that case just confirm your choice by touching him on the shoulder.'

I opened the door and stepped inside as Martin Beck took the five steps, touched Blaise Lincoln on the shoulder and returned to the inspector. 'Mr Beck, the sergeant will return you to the interview room and take a short statement.' Then he turned to me. 'DC Blake. There have been two positive identifications.'

I walked across to Lincoln and took him by the arm. 'Blaise Lincoln, you are not obliged to say anything unless you wish to do so but whatever you say may be taken down and used in evidence. I am arresting you for the kidnap and false imprisonment of Martin Beck.' Lincoln made no reply. I took him by the arm and walked him back to the cells. 'Positive ID Sergeant,' I said. 'Mr Lincoln is now under arrest for kidnap and false imprisonment.'

'Number four, Blake. We've kept your cell warm for you Mr Lincoln.' He nodded to the gaoler.

There was the positive sound as the cell door closed and the double-click of the lock.

Inspector Fisher turned to the parade. 'Thank you, gentlemen. You are free to go. The three non-police officers, wait in the corridor please and I will take you to collect your expenses.'

They ambled out chatting amongst themselves.

Inspector Fisher, noted for being fastidious, turned to Jeffrey George. 'Any observations, Mr George?'

'No Inspector. I'm happy with the manner in which the parade was conducted.'

The atmosphere in the interview room was tense. Blaise Lincoln looked worried and picked at the cuticle of his right middle finger with his thumb nail. Sitting on his right side, Jeffrey George.

I sat opposite Jeffrey George. Sergeant Ryder opposite Lincoln.

'I'm Sergeant Ryder and my colleague is DC Blake. But of course you know our names don't you Mr Lincoln, we almost met in London and again in Leeds.'

There was a flash of recognition at the sound of DS Ryder's name.

The sergeant gave me the nod. 'May I remind you, Mr Lincoln,' I said, 'that you are still under caution?'

'I understand,' he said, his voice flat. 'Or rather, I don't understand why?'

'Why what?'

'Why is Lewis Green, or whatever his name is, walking free and I am under arrest for his so-called false imprisonment? He is the one who admitted killing Emily and burying her body outside Leeds. Yet he's the one who identified me. We gave you the evidence, why isn't he in custody? '

I was about to answer when Sergeant Ryder lifted his hand. 'It's all right, Brian,' he said. 'I'll deal with this.' He turned to the solicitor. 'Mr George, I don't know how much your client has told you about the circumstances leading to his arrest, but he is going to prison for a very long time. He may never be released.'

Blaise Lincoln's face paled as his solicitor spoke. 'But I thought it was a straightforward matter of kidnapping and false imprisonment. An indictable common law misdemeanour.'

DS Ryder shook his head. 'No, sir. Six or seven years ago your client was engaged to be married to a very pretty girl call Emily Reid. One day, the brother of a childhood friend of Emily's, Kevin Sharpe, raped her. She couldn't face Mr Lincoln and broke off the engagement ..

... There has been no trace of Emily then or since. Detective Sergeant, now Detective Inspector Giles carried out the investigation into the report.

'No sightings at all?'

'No sir.'

'That's a lie, sergeant. It's a police cover-up. Pandering to the rich parents of these undergraduates.'

'There is no evidence to substantiate that, Mr Lincoln. But let's move on, shall we? Brian.'

'You have been positively identified four times, Mr Lincoln.'

'But there were only two.'

'Today, yes. But you were identified on two previous occasions by photographs,' I took the folder from my briefcase showing it to Jeffrey George.

'This is my client, Mr Lincoln?' he said pointing to the sixth photograph.

'That is correct.'

'But what reason did you have to include my client?'

'All in good time, Mr George,' I said and slid the first of Lewis Green's anonymous notes across the table. '*Be sure your sins have found you out,*' I read. 'This was addressed to Lewis Green, or to give him his birth name, to which he has reverted, Martin Beck. What does this mean, Mr Lincoln?

'What it says, I suppose.'

'And what sins are those?'

'Why don't you ask him?'

I slid the second note across the table. 'This was also addressed to Lewis Green. *Two down three to go.* To what does it refer?'

'He knows, ask him.'

'Did you type these notes?'

'No.'

'Who did?'

'Not me.'

'But you do know?'

All he did was smile.

'Those two notes arrived one week apart. This,' I slid the letter across the table, 'arrived one week later. We have statements taken from the three addresses you visited in Seven Oaks Fold where you gave the name Granville Rodahl. This letter is signed with that name. Did you sign it?'

Lincoln and his solicitor perused the letter. 'I've never seen this before,' said Lincoln.

'In that case, who said for you to use the name Granville Rodahl? Was it the female who accompanied you to the house in Seven Oaks Fold?'

'I can't say.'

'Can't or won't, Mr Lincoln? Right, these envelopes that you and this mysterious female delivered. Shall we see what they contained?' Lincoln's face dropped. 'Ah, so you remember. It will be a surprise for Mr George. I hope he likes surprises.' I took the first. 'Of course, although the address shown on the letter is 17 Seven Oaks Fold, as you know the houses in Seven Oaks Fold are named, not numbered. This is the envelope you handed to Mrs Watson in the first house, White Oaks, and its contents.' I slid the photo across the table.

'A Windsor chair?' Jeffrey George looked confused.

'A Windsor chair. Now, this is the envelope you handed to Mr Jackson at the seventh house, strangely named Gog and Magog. What do you make of this?'

As though hypnotised Lincoln stared at the photograph of William Boxley.

Jeffrey George looked at the photograph as though unable to believe his eyes. Then at his client. Then at me. 'Is this why the police would not release details of the victims in this murder investigation?'

'It is Mr George. This is William Boxley, the first victim. Lecturer in English at York University, married with an infant son. He was the only victim that I haven't seen .. Admiring your handiwork, Mr Lincoln? The secure bindings. The finesse of the needlework fixing

Mr Boxley's genitals into his mouth. You can just make out the puncture wound in his right deltoid muscle where he was injected with some substance to immobilise him. We know that it contained curare; the remainder as yet unknown. Rest assured we will identify it .. Note the puncture wound that finally put this young man out of his misery. Something resembling a dagger inserted between his ribs into his heart ... was that you, or the man wearing the police uniform .. or, perhaps the woman wearing the nurse's uniform ... Well?'

There was no response from Lincoln.

I took the third envelope and tipped the photograph onto the table. 'Following what you see in the second photograph this is a statement of what would happen to Martin Beck when you got hold of him, isn't it. A Windsor chair with his name on it. A psychological horror show – *This is what you can expect* ... nothing to say Mr Lincoln? ... Then we should consider when he returned to his London flat. A visit from an undertaker, arranged by a female voice claiming to be his widow; he's never been married. A cabinetmaker trying to deliver a coffin to his home. But the first thing was a funereal wreath with a card bearing the inscription: *What the cobbler threw at his wife. In memoriam Lewis Green gone & forgotten.*

What did the cobbler throw at his wife, Mr Lincoln? ... The last? The last what? The last of the five undergraduates you and others are blaming for the disappearance and murder of Emily Reid. Or so you choose to believe. Five human beings going about their lawful business until you decided. What?'

'But Green, or Beck, is still alive.'

'You are quite correct, Mr Lincoln, but PC Cameron isn't. According to the Home Office pathologist he was dead from whatever was injected into his neck before he hit the floor. Four undergraduates and one Metropolitan police officer. He had been standing guard outside Mr Beck's flat and had been relieved by me. He was going home to his wife and family.'

'But we didn't do that.'

'Analysis of the compound that killed PC Cameron contained curare in the same proportions as the samples taken from the other victims. So, what happened? Did he surprise you when he entered the cellar?'

Lincoln nodded. 'Is that a 'yes', Mr Lincoln?' Sergeant Ryder said.

Lincoln nodded again. 'Yes,' he said.

'Who did the injecting?'

'Adrienne.' This was new. The Sergeant and I looked at each other. 'Her surname?'

'I don't know, honestly. But Green admitted to strangling Emily and then burying her body at Eccup. Why aren't you looking for her body.'

'Oh, we did. We had twenty officers check the circumference of the lake. Then the department of Physics from the university brought in ground penetrating radar. There is nothing there. Not even a dead dog.'

'So, he lied.'

'Wouldn't you?' I said indicating the evidence on the table, 'If you were trying to keep your anatomy intact and prevent someone inserting a sharp object between your ribs? What you put those other young men through defies imagination. For what? ... Exactly nothing! But assuming for one moment that you were correct and Mr Beck was guilty, what gave you the right to sidestep the law and assume the positions of Judge, Jury and Executioner?'

Sergeant Ryder lifted his hand. 'All right, Brian. Mr Lincoln. We're having a short break during which I hope Mr George will persuade you to co-operate. On our return we would like you to make a full statement. Any loyalty that you feel towards the man dressed in the police uniform and your female companion is misplaced. They are still dangerous and any help that you can give us to bring this enquiry to an end will sit well with the court. Should you be in any doubt I'm sure that Mr George will explain what acting in concert means, whether you believe you are culpable or not.

DS Creighton put Lincoln's statement on his desk as DS Ryder and I entered his office. 'Some statement. All they knew of this woman is the name, Adrienne, which may be false.'

'Yes, sir.' I said. 'She made the initial approach and pulled all the strings. She had obviously done a lot of digging and sold Lincoln and Smith the entire story.'

'And based on what she said they were prepared to torture those former undergraduates and eventually commit murder?'

'So it seems, sir,' said DS Ryder.

The superintendent shook his head. 'Unbelievable. You've spoken with Emily Reid's parents?'

'Yes sir,' I said. 'And DI Giles. The name Adrienne doesn't mean anything to him either.'

'Very well.' He put his hand on the statement. 'Smith's on a touring holiday. When's he due back?'

'Next week, sir.'

He nodded. 'We've nothing from forensic re the compound. They've sent samples to other labs. You keep your finger on the pulse with the universities.

'Sir.'

'Good. Sergeant, hold back on any charges relating to PC Cameron. The Met will probably want a say in that. Keep me posted.'

Beck
Fifty-Two

He stared at the door at the base of the north-west corner turret of the stable block. 'I thought it was just unused.' he said.

'It's our own private fire station.' Carol laughed at his expression.

'Fire station?. Why am I carrying this oilcan?'

'It hasn't been opened for years.' She brushed the cobwebs away sending a few spiders running for cover. The key hanging in the recess was large and ornate as befitting its age and turned as smoothly as if it were brand new. 'The oil is for the hinges.'

Of course it was. The lock was brass.

' WOW!' A four-wheeled early 19th century fire-fighting engine. Hand-drawn. He guessed a hundred-gallon tank on the back; filled by bucket chain. Somewhere there would be a hose. Operated by two men either side by means of large handles along the back of the engine. First one side pulled down then the other. Dragging on the shafts we re-introduced this mechanical wonder to daylight. There was just a rumble as the iron wheels bit into the gravel. It was beautiful. The coachwork, complete with the Sylverton coat of arms, was in pristine condition.

Spiders or no spiders, within seconds it was occupied by two six year old firemen.

'Uncle Steve's an engineer,' said Bard. 'He would love this.'

Carol laughed. 'Boys and their toys?'

'Of course,' He grinned.

'Let's put the fire engine back for now. Then you can help Bard with your swing before it rains.'

Over the next 90 minutes three swings appeared from the bottom branch of the large oak tree. One with a stick as a seat, another with an eye splice and the last for climbing. Even Carol joined in the construction and swinging. The twins spent most their time giggling, but they would have something to write about the next morning.

He knew he was biased, but his sons were a delight. So was Carol. The twins would never know how or why this strange man, who came into their life just a few short weeks ago, was having such a marked effect on them, or vice versa. He owed it to them. They repaid in trust. Soaked up information like sponges and wanted to learn whatever it was that he wanted to teach.

Today, Home Farm. A rare mixture of sights, sounds and exotic aromas. Introduced to the farm manager, Jonathan Beale. Bard told him what he would like in terms of both hardwood and softwood.

Could I ask what you need it for?'

'I will be doing some pioneering with the boys, including an aerial platform.'

'Sweet chestnut splits well. That would be the best for your platform, sir. Where would you like me to drop it?'

'By the bonfire site.'

'It'll be there, sir.'

The week had been manic but now everything was clear: Slushpile. Desk. Commissions. Rejections posted. Finally, confirmed details with his father regarding tomorrow. Oldeney was fast becoming an oasis of calm. It was dark when he arrived. Carol had been in a bit of a flap. Mary had been found wandering in the kitchens. Warnings were repeated to all staff and Mary returned to her daughter's.

The first pie of the winter. What could be better to keep out the autumnal chill than meat and potato pie? Followed by an eve pudding, with apples from the estate, and proper custard.

In company with Mrs Nesbitt, they intruded on Mrs Evans's kitchen.

'We don't often see you down here, milady.'

'True, Mrs Evans, but this,' she indicated me. 'is my houseguest, Mr Beck. He asked to meet you.'

'There's nothing wrong, I hope, sir?'

'On the contrary, it was excellent. You set a high standard Mrs, Evans. They say that the way to a man's heart is through his stomach. I can see Her Ladyship having to look to her laurels.'

She blushed to the roots of her hair.

Carol's knowing smile said, really?

'Does your repertoire extend to Italian and Indian food.'

'It does, but Lord Gordon could not abide the smell or taste of garlic, curry or any other strong flavours. But if you wish I'll speak with Mrs Nesbitt.'

'Thank you, that would be appreciated.'

The burst of chatter as they left the kitchen was silenced by Mrs Evans. 'If you haven't enough to keep you occupied, I'll find you something.'

There was one dissenter. 'Mrs. Evans, do you think they'll get married. He's been here several times and he is good looking.'

'Patricia, if that is what is planned my girl, you will find out in good time. Now get on with your work.'

The boys in bed, they sat in Carol's private quarters. Ten responses from the publishing houses on the table in front of them. 'So many? Who do you go with? There is a lot of money on offer, Martin.'

'OK. We can ignore Finsbury Templeton. They want the manuscript and they're prepared to pay. That confirms how good it is. And, as his mother, you will decide to go for them.

'Just because of the money?'

'Yup. We can ignore these. He selected another four. These are all big players. They want the book as a back-up, but will not publish until the run up to next Easter. Of these last five, the one we should go with is this one.' He pointed to the last one.'

'Why? They're the lowest.'

'They are the smallest. But they are taking market share and growing fast. In any company there is only so much money available per project, especially for a new author; it's just spread out in different ways. They don't have the resources that the others do, so the amount they've offered is the lowest at £500, which is good. However, the royalties will kick in sooner. They're hungry and will throw everything at the project to get it on the shelves in time for Christmas. And, they have the best illustrator in the industry. If you agree, I'll set up a preliminary meeting.

Half an hour later Carol began to yawn. Hint, hint. We had some catching up to do, You never know, a full-time children's nurse might be required before too long.

Not just yet was the pronouncement the following morning. C'est la vie.

Breakfast time. A knock on the door. Givens entered. 'Pardon my intrusion Your Ladyship. There is a telephone call for Mr Beck in his office. A Mr Bright of Raymond Bright Publishing.'

Bard winked at Graeme and stood. 'Thank you, Givens. I'd better go and see what he wants, hadn't I.'

'Good morning, Raymond.'

'Good morning to you. Who was it that answered the phone?

'Givens, the butler.'

'Butler? You implied it was a big house. Just how big?'

He laughed. 'Very big.'

There was an answering laugh. 'Can you make eleven on Tuesday.'

'No problem. Same address?'

'It is. Will the little boy and his mother be coming with you?'

'In all probability.'

'We will see you then.'

Fifty-Three

10:45. Both landaus, spruced up, were drawn up in echelon at the top of the hill. Grooms Geraldine and Angela by the horses. John and William both in livery to transport the cars in advance of the landaus. Carol, myself and the twins waiting. Some less patiently than others. Thankfully the clouds were breaking and the sun shining. It was a pleasant autumnal day.

The Jaguar coasted to a standstill at the gates. The Volvo behind. 'Are you sure this is right, Clive, it looks very grand.'

'This fits the description that Martin gave me, so? He said and set off followed by the Volvo.

Bard's mother stared all around. 'There are a lot of trees, Clive.'

'So there are, Pat. They will meet us where the road bends to the right and the trees on the right end. The road bends just ahead. 'And there they are. A welcoming committee: horses, carriages and uniforms. And two little boys.'

Martin and Graeme came haring towards the group. 'They're coming, Mummy.'

The cars drew to a halt twenty yards short of where they needed to be to see the House and parkland. A thoroughly confused group of adults exited. Handshakes and hugs were the order of the day. First things first. 'Dad, will you give your keys to John. Steve yours to William. We've got something different for you.'

John had just opened the Jaguar door when Mum said. 'Excuse me, I've seen you before. But I can't remember where.'

'Indeed you have, madam,' said a smiling John. 'It was several years ago at your husband's workplace. Now, if you will excuse me.'

From the look on her face, she didn't remember. 'Sorry,' she said and stepped back.

The cars disappeared over the crest. Now it was Carol's turn. 'You can only do or see something for the first time, once. We thought you might like to travel in authentic style, hence the landaus. When you see the view, you will understand. Walk with me, please.' Peter walked with Martin and Graeme. Bard knew that his sister and father were furiously trying to work it out. Carol stopped. 'There you are,' she said and stood on my left.

The look on Liz's face was *what the hell is going on*. Dad was just puzzled as were Mum and Steve.

There were comments of: magnificent, beautiful and 'Wow' before Mum spoke. 'Carol, Martin said that you live on a house on the estate. Where is it?'

'There, Pat,' she replied and smiled, inclining her head towards the House. 'Courtesy of the Earl.'

'Earl!? Does he live there as well?'

'Yes, he does.'

Martin was grinning like the proverbial. I put my fingers to my lips. A move not missed by Liz. She caught my eye and raised an eyebrow looked at Martin and glanced to the house. I nodded. The spark of realisation was like a roman candle being ignited on bonfire night.

Mum was completely in the dark. 'But what do we say if we meet him?'

'You already have, Mum,' I said.

That made it worse. 'I don't understand.'

Carol nodded. 'Will the Earl of Oldeney please step forward.' A grinning Martin obliged.

I heard a joint, 'My God,' from Dad and Liz. 'The penny's just dropped,' Dad said, He looked at Carol. 'So, Carol, you're a Countess?'

'Yes, Clive, I am. Sorry for the deception. Martin thought it would be for the best.'

'But what do we call you?'

'In private or like this, first names. If you're referring to me to my staff or to anyone else, Countess or Her Ladyship .. Shall we mount up? Pat, you and Clive in front with me and His Lordship and brother. Liz you, Steve, Peter and Bard in the second. And Steve you're an engineer I understand?'

'Yes, I am.'

'We have a surprise for you. You can't quite see it from here but there's plenty of time.'

'What do you think of it so far, Liz?' I said.

'If you had described the house and parkland and said we would be travelling there in a landau, I wouldn't have believed you. But it's brilliant?'

'Early 18th century. George the Second. Not sure of the year.'

'What about this landau?' Steve asked.

'Carol thought around 1850 but couldn't find any relevant paperwork.'

'But whatever, it's in excellent condition and more comfortable than it looks.'

'What about you, Peter?'

He had his priorities right. 'Graeme said I could play on the swings, Uncle Martin.'

'And so you can.'

The scale of the house unfolded as you drew closer. Both east and west wings wrapping round the three shallow-flights of steps and statuary leading the visitor to the huge doors. Everything said this was power.

It took seven minutes to reach the House. Givens had the staff out in force. We stopped behind Geraldine. Steve reached out to open the door. 'Hold it, Steve. We're doing things properly.'

Givens opened the door. Carol stepped out and introduced Mum and Dad. Geraldine moved off as we took her place.

We followed likewise. 'And this is Mr and Mrs Wilson, and their son, Peter. Mrs Wilson is Mr Beck's sister.'

'Sir, madam, and master Peter,' Givens said and smiled. 'Welcome to Oldeney Carr House,' he turned to Carol. 'Everything will be ready in five minutes, Madam.'

They stood and stared up at the edifice. 'We'll go through the house.' As she turned to climb the steps past the staff Liz whispered to her. She smiled. 'Of course. Follow me.' Peter needed to pee.

Back in the group Carol took us to the northern terrace overlooking the parterre. The general consensus being it was *so beautiful*. 'Normally we would have refreshments here,' she said. 'But today is different, we're going to have them on the manège.' Which meant nothing to most, but they followed unquestioning. Past the stables. The landaus, in the inner courtyard, clearly visible. The horses stabled.

Waiting was Christopher, a table set for five adults awaiting the coffee and whatever Mrs Evans would dispense. Alongside, a small table for three children. Facing the gate were the twins mounted on Dapple and Apple with a saddled Flash between them, waiting. Peter laughed and pointed at the blaze, 'Flash!' he said and ran over.

We all followed whilst Peter stroked Flash's muzzle.

'Right young man,' said Steve and sat Peter on the saddle. 'Let's hand you over to Aunty Carol.'

'Right, Peter,' said Carol. 'Are you comfortable?'

The coffee and orange juice arrived.

'Yes, thank you, Aunty Carol.'

'Good. Let's get you started.' The next minute or so were taken up with posture, holding the reins and where to put his feet. She led Flash into the centre of the manège, clipped a long rein to the harness and backed away. He couldn't hear what she was saying but the twins suddenly peeled away and fell in behind. 'And behave yourselves. This is Peter's first time in the saddle. Ready, Peter?' He nodded. She said, 'Walk-on.' The three ponies began to move as one, the cheeky grins on the twins' faces self-evident.

'What was this surprise that she has for Steve?' said Dad.

In spite of everything Bard laughed. 'He's an engineer. It's an early nineteenth century fire-fighting engine. The top side of the stable block.'

'Original?'

'Yes, and apart from a hose it appears complete. 'I'll show you when we leave here. It's brilliant.'

We looked up as Carol unclipped Flash. 'Right, Peter. Take him round the manège. Back straight, hands loose and eyes front. You know what to do.'

A tap of his heels and Flash began to walk. Carol watched him like a hawk. All they could hear was the occasional word as Peter rode Flash round the manège ... sit straight ... into the trot ... good .. keep your heels down ... eyes front ... use your heels ... back into a walk ... now stop, gently. Excellent. Time for a drink of orange juice.

Fresh coffee arrived. Carol joined them at the table. 'For a little boy and the first time that was very good. There's a lot to remember. It takes time,' she turned to the boys at their table. 'Did you enjoy that, Peter?'

'Yes, thank you. But I kept forgetting what to do.'

Carol smiled at him. 'If you knew what to do you wouldn't need to practice. All beginners forget. You will be better the next time.' On the table was a plate with an apple cut into three pieces. 'Take a piece of apple each. You as well Peter, watch what they do. Make sure you keep your fingers straight otherwise they might get nibbled. The apple is the treat for your pony not your fingers.'

'It tickles,' giggled Peter as Flash took the apple.

Refreshments finished they walked the ponies back to the stables. Carol finding herself side-by-side with Liz. 'Should you get married to my brother do you think you'll have any more children?'

'Good question,' Carol looked over her shoulder. 'My aim is to fill the house with children, laughter and music. So I'd better, or he gets the sack.'

'I am trying my best milady,' he replied.

There was a shocked, 'Martin!' from Mum. A squeezed shoulder from Dad. And laughter from him, Steve and Liz. That was that. Leaving the ponies to the grooms Carol took us on a mini-tour of the coach house where Steve began to drool. Through the rear doors to the walled garden, glasshouse; and last the fire engine.

Steve scanned it for all of five seconds before declaring. 'My God! This is a Tilley. It should be in a museum.' He started to circumnavigate the appliance.

'Do you work with fire engines, Steve?' said Carol.

'No,' he got to his knees and peered under the engine. 'Old vehicles, especially fire engines are a childhood passion. I never grew up.'

'That's true,' confirmed Liz to associated laughter.

'Thank you!' he said and joined in. 'They're as rare as hen's teeth.' He stood and dusted his trousers. We removed the three firemen from the engine. That was it for now. We had somewhere else to visit.

The three boys, pursued by Bard and Steve, more slowly by the others, headed for the swings.

Martin was using the centre rope with the large eye-splice. Graeme and Peter the left-hand swing. Feet on the seat. Both holding the rope trying to get it going and giggling fit to bust.

'You're telling me that two six-year-olds tied all the knots and the back splicing?'

'Under supervision, but yes,' Steve didn't believe him. 'Martin,' Bard called as he swung towards them. 'Tell uncle Steve what the first knot I taught you was?'

'Running bowline, Bard,' he said between grunts as he finally got the swing to cooperate.

'But that's in the First-Class badge,' Steve protested.

'True. Martin, what did I teach you last night?'

The swing was going well. 'An eye splice for a tether, Uncle Steve.'

From his expression Steve didn't believe that either. 'Can I see it?'

'Yes, it's at the house.'

Carol and Liz arrived and soon had Graeme and Peter working together. Dad wandered across. 'Carol tells me the boys did all this,' he said indicating the ropes.

'True, Dad,' he said and smiled. 'Do you want a go?'

'You're three stone too late, Martin,' he grimaced, 'But you've got plenty of raw material; what else do you intend to do?'

He outlined what he had in mind.

'That's quite adventurous,' said Steve. 'Have you considered a crawl line?'

'I hadn't, but it's a great idea for later.'

Steve and I spent a half hour introducing the boys to descenders; how to thread the rope with warnings to keep their fingers and hair clear. Steve examined the boy's belts. The last thing was to replace the three sisal ropes with the climbing rope. That entailed getting a line over the branch, tying a bowline in the end, and Bard demonstrating how to get to an eleven feet high branch without a ladder.

Fifty-Four

It could have been much worse.

'We ought to tell him whilst your parents, Liz and Steve are here. More of a distraction.'

'I suppose so,' said Bard. 'He's still not going to like it. We can't just say, that's tough get used to it.'

'No, we can't. Let me tell him.'

'... So next Tuesday. After we take you to school, we are taking Graeme to see the publishers in Chesterfield.'

There was a chorus of *wonderful* and *congratulations* from around the table followed by an immediate retort. The tone shocking the others round the table. 'That's not fair. I can write as well. He's always been Bard's favourite.'

'That is not true Martin and you know it. Bard loves you both the same. It was Dr. Hollis who told both of us about Graeme's writing. Yours is good. Far better than most children of your age. It's just that Graeme's is better. And it wasn't Bard's decision. He had to contact lots of publishers. They make the decision.'

'Who usually wins at Scrabble?' Said Bard.

Martin jabbed a petulant finger at his brother. 'He does.'

'He sees anagrams, Martin,' said Bard. 'He can make words out of the jumble of letters. It's something he was born with.'

'You're the Earl, Martin,' Dad joined the conversation.

'I know,' came the scowling reply.

'Martin! Where are your manners. Apologise to Mr Beck ... Now.'

Martin's head dropped. 'Sorry, Mr Beck.'

'That's all right, come and stand by me,' a dejected Martin trudged round the table. Dad put his arm round his shoulders. 'All this,' he gestured with his hands. 'is yours. Looked after by your mummy until you are old enough. Because you were born first you are the Earl. You own everything. That will make you very rich.'

'But we're brothers,' was the plaintive reply. 'I'll give Graeme pocket money.'

There were smiles all-round the table. 'I'm sure you would. But supposing you fell out. You could stop. Then where would Graeme be?' There was no reply. 'Now, this argument is about being different. That is good. It would be very boring if we were all the same, wouldn't it?'

'Suppose.'

There were a few suppressed grimaces. 'When mummies decide to have a baby it all starts with an egg.'

'Like a chicken?' said Martin.

'But tiny by comparison. So small you could only just see it. And it begins to divide. After the nine months that your mother has carried you it's time for you to be born. However, in your case, that's both you and Graeme, that egg was very special. After a day or so the egg split into two. So, instead of having one baby your mummy had?'

'Two.'

'That's right. But it wasn't an exact split. Yes, you look very similar but there are differences. Your hair parts on the opposite side to Graeme. And I'll bet that one of you is left-handed.'

'I am,' said Graeme.

'You both inherit some of the characteristics of your parents; even your grandparents. No-one knows who will inherit which. It's completely random.'

The thought - *all the Becks were left-handed therefore there was a good chance. Whether Lord Gordon had been he had no idea.*

'It makes you different. It's not something to fight over, it just happens that Graeme is very good at Scrabble and he has written a nice story; but your mummy loves you both; more than anyone else in the world.'

'Even more than Bard?'

'Yes, Graeme,' laughed Carol. 'Even more than Bard.'

'But in London we saw you in bed together. But next morning he wasn't there. We thought that you *had* sent him away.'

The broad grins and his mother's confused look were distracting. Bard feigned a look of innocence and shrugged.

Carol was laughing. 'No, I'm not going to send him away. I promise.'

Martin looked at Graeme and nodded. 'Bard, are you and Mummy going to get married?' said Graeme.

'Yes, we are.'

There was a round of applause around the table accompanied by 'Congratulations'.

Carol turned to Holly waiting patiently by the door. 'Have Givens assemble the staff in the Drawing Room in ten minutes, please. And not a word about what you may have just overheard.'

'Milady,' she said, smiled and left.

'Right, young man. Try to remember that Graeme hasn't caused a fuss over you getting all the estate. You're different from him as he is from you. The last thing your mother wants is for you and Graeme to fall out. Remember, your mother gave you both life. Why don't you go and give her a big hug.'

Carol and Bard standing side-by-side, the boys in front; everyone else seated behind. Givens, Mrs Nesbitt and Mrs Evans standing opposite, the remainder of the staff behind them.

'You will have noticed that the gentleman on my right has become a regular houseguest. And, has an office on the first floor. We have decided to make the situation permanent.' There was a flurry at the back as the stage whisper of, *I told you, they're getting married* carried across the Drawing Room.

'Yes, we are. Thank you for stealing my news, Patricia.' Was the curt reply. Carol made eye contact with Mrs Nesbitt who nodded. 'We are getting married and that will mean changes. Because my late husband was an Earl, I carry the courtesy title of Countess; unless I remarry. Once married I will no longer carry the title. However, because my father is a Duke, I automatically carry the courtesy title of Lady, for life. So, I will be known as Lady Carol Frances Elizabeth Beck, and addressed as Your Ladyship or Madam. My husband has no title so he will be addressed as, Sir. You will also be aware that my sons refer to him as Bard. You will not. There will be no change as far as my sons are concerned.

Mrs Evans, I will speak with you, Mrs Nesbitt and Givens on Monday to discuss details, but in two weeks there will be a dinner party for twenty guests when our engagement becomes official. Until then, anything that I have told you today will remain confidential,' Carol's eyes bored into the chamber maids. 'Do you understand, Patricia?'

The dejected maid dropped her head. 'Yes, Your Ladyship.'

'Good. Thank you all. Givens, Mrs Nesbitt, a moment.'

'Excuse me your Ladyship,' said Givens. 'May I on behalf of myself, Mrs Nesbitt and all the staff offer heartfelt congratulations on the news of your engagement to Mr Beck.'

'You can and they are much appreciated. Thank you.'

Bard nodded. 'Thank you.'

Carol took a deep breath and exhaled. 'What is the matter with that girl, Mrs Nesbitt. Final warning.'

Mrs Nesbitt smiled. 'This is the third final warning, Madam.'

She returned the smile. 'Yes, I know. Before you speak with her fetch me the Staff Register and I will endorse it myself. Perhaps that will get through to her. I'm not having a loose cannon on the staff. If she is incapable of discretion she will have to go.'

'Yes, Madam.'

'And, before you both go, and this is only for you two at the moment, I will inform Mrs Evans on Monday. Our wedding will take place in six weeks at the York Registry Office.

'Oh, before I forget. I have had a request from a Dr. Katherine Butters, a Lexicographer from St James' College, Oxford. She would like to do some research in the West Wing Library, starting next Monday. She apparently spoke with Lord Gordon last year and he agreed, although I can't find any record. However, that is not a problem. She does not wish to intrude on us too much and has accommodation booked at the Arms. I said we will provide her with a light lunch whenever she is here.'

'Do we know for how long, Madam?'

'No we don't. Will that cause any problems?'

'None that I can think of.'

Annette Nesbitt sat forward in her chair, pushed the Staff Register across her desk towards the Maid. 'To repeat what Her Ladyship said to me. "What on earth is the matter with that girl? She wanted to announce to the staff that she and Mr Beck are getting married. What do you do? You spoil it for her.' She pointed at the Register. 'Read that. In all my time here I have never seen the Master or Mistress of this house resort to that. You have a loose tongue, Patricia, and if you do not curb it you will be dismissed.'

'But I was only ..'

Annette Nesbitt interjected. 'You were talking out of turn. You were there to listen. If you had bridled your tongue and listened, you could have made your comments to whoever it was afterwards. Be warned. If there are any more indiscretions you know the consequences. Had it been Lord Gordon he would have sacked you long ago. Do not take advantage.'

Clive Beck turned his back to the lake. 'Just look at that, Martin. If I were the jealous type I would say that you've fallen on your feet.'

Bard looked up at the House. 'You mean you're not? His father laughed and shrugged his shoulders. 'I had Carol with me the first time. She had me stop on the crest where we were waiting for you. I couldn't believe my eyes.'

'And you have an office?'

'I have. Carol's late husband's bedroom. Where he used to bugger his catamite.'

'What!? She was married to one of those?'

'Yup. Name of Solomon Tulliver. She found out after they married. Moved him into his bedroom. Carol was a vehicle to produce a son. Other than that there was nothing from him. And what I'm going to tell you goes no further ...'

' ... Good God. that's evil. The thought of it makes me sick.'

'It did me as well.'

'And when he told her, the car just happened to fall off the jack?'

Bard caught his breath. 'Don't go there, Dad. It's a closed book.'

'No, I won't. And, if the car had a helping hand, I for one wouldn't blame her.'

'I couldn't agree more.'

'And the boys? We can see you get on well. Apart from today?'

'They're six. Martin is the elder and as such sees himself as the leader. Doesn't like being bested. It's not the sort of thing they can understand at that age, but they're brilliant kids. Martin is the fix bayonets and charge man. He should be moving to the next tier in the autumn term, that's a year early. Graeme is more of a thinker and ready now but the Head wanted to keep them together.'

'They're very close.'

'Yeah, apart from school they have no-one to play with, at least not of their own age. They will find it difficult to be separated from the other even for a few hours. This business of Graeme's book? It's like a wedge being forced between them. With luck it shouldn't need to happen again.'

'Cross your fingers. Look, there's a bridge at the far end of the lake. Let's take a walk round before dinner.'

The rain set in around six. We had a cluster round the piano evening. The twins got to air their lungs with The Runaway Train and The National Anthem of the Ancient Britons; Steve and Bard joining in. The latter receiving applause from an unexpected quarter. Two of the maids, Holly and Valerie who came to ensure that the twins got to bed.

Clive Beck raising a few laughs with his comment: 'If you young ladies are going to stand there and applaud you can come over here and sing.'

Their embarrassment quashed by Carol. 'Not tonight, Clive. Come on boys, time for bed.'

Met by a combined, 'Aww.' All thoughts of conflict appearing to be reconciled. At least for now.

10:15. One look out of the window said there would be no seeking the herd of Fallow deer this morning.

Whilst the boys played in their room. Carol, at Liz and Pat's request took them to the Tapestry Gallery.

After lunch with a clear sky and brilliant sunshine the guests left with a promise from Carol that the search for the deer would continue when they next visited Oldeney.

Blake

Fifty-Five

We had our mysterious policeman in custody. Patrick Smith, former detective constable and now haulage contractor, was not a happy man.

'Why am I here?'

'I've told you,' said Sergeant Ryder. 'For conspiracy to murder.'

'That's crap. Who am I supposed to have conspired to murder?'

'You're still under caution.'

'I know the score. I've interviewed enough villains. Who?'

'William Boxley, Patrick Newsam, Neville Waters, Charles Nash and Martin Beck.'

'What!? Those bloody undergrads. That's' rubbish.'

'You remembered them quick enough.'

'I should think I did. That twat Beck, what did he change his name to? Oh aye, Lewis Green, dropped me right in the shit with Gail. Giles almost hounded me out of the job; said I was shagging that little tart from the typing pool. In the end I jacked it in.'

'And?'

He smiled to himself. 'Drive a lorry now. Bought my own last month. No Giles. No drunken bosses. More money. Keep my nose clean. Sound.'

'And were you? Shagging the little tart?'

'Once or twice, that's all. She shagged for nuts. Passing information on to her boyfriend, Jason Jepson, a real tearaway. Drank at the Fisherman's Hut. As a typist she had access to everything. She started making sheep's eyes at me so I took her out a few times to see just what she was up to. I was right, she was after the criminal intelligence we had on Jepson and his mates.'

'So, you're not involved in the murders of those undergraduates.'

'My God, Sergeant, you are quick. No, I was not,'

'You deny the allegation?'

'Of course I bloody do. Vicky spent more time horizontal than vertical. If I hadn't given her one, she would have become suspicious. Gave her some duff gen as a thank you.'

'Did you report back about her trying to prize information from you?'

'For what it's worth, yes. But Giles got his oar in first. No-one took a blind bit of notice. It's their problem.'

'Do you still see her?'

'Vicky? No chance. Is there anything else, sergeant? I have a contract to fulfil.'

'No sir, there was no statement on file from the typist. She left police employment shortly afterwards. Smith was bailed to the station in four weeks.'

'He would fit the bill, but we need something concrete. Keep digging. Sergeant, Check with DI Giles. Lincoln's on remand. Pay him a visit see what he has to say.

Beck

Fifty-Six

10:55. Tuesday. It was overcast with a promise of rain. Bard, Carol and Graeme alighted from Bard's car. The Rolls pulled up behind. John remaining at the wheel.

Raymond Bright and Victoria Mellors, the graphic illustrator, stepped forward to meet them.

'Nice car, Raymond,' whispered Victoria

'You can say that again. Just who the hell are they?'

'Hello Raymond,' said Bard as they shook hands. 'Vicky.'

'Allow me to introduce my fiancée, Lady Carol Sylverton, Countess of Oldeney and her younger son, Sir Graeme Sylverton, the young man you want to meet,' he turned to Carol. 'This is Raymond of Raymond Bright Publishing and Victoria, 'Vicky', who, I believe, is the best illustrator in the country.'

'You kept that quiet, Martin,' he said turning to Carol. 'It's not often I'm lost for words, Countess,' he said. 'But congratulations to you both and welcome.' They shook hands. 'And you are Sir Graeme?' he said shaking hands.

'You may call him, Graeme,' said Carol.

'Graeme it is. That's a very special little book you've written, Graeme,' Raymond said. 'Please come in. We have some refreshments waiting.'

' ... Martin said it was Givens, the Butler. I hadn't expected that and asked how big the house was. He said it was very big.'

'It is,' said Graeme. 'We have thirty bedrooms.'

'Thirty?

Graeme laughed and nodded. He enjoyed teasing people. 'And a deer park.'

Carol took over. 'It is a big house and early 18th century. Subject to a satisfactory meeting this morning I will invite you.'

That was some carrot. Who doesn't want to know how the other half live?

'Thank you. That's very kind. Now, before I hand you over to Vicky for a tour of the Print Shop can we talk about the contract; unless of course Graeme would find it boring.'

There was a wide-eyed response. 'How much will I earn?'

'I see,' was the smiling reply. 'Right. It won't seem much but when the contract is signed, I will send Martin, as your agent, a cheque to the amount of £500. That is yours to keep no matter how well the book sells. Once the sales have covered that amount you will earn royalties. For a brand new author, it would normally be 5% of the retail price. However, I'm certain the book will sell well and we will pay 10%. In the shops the book will cost five shillings which means you will earn six pence for each book sold. As I said, it doesn't sound a lot. However, the initial print run is 25,000. So, taking the advance payment into account there could be additional royalties of £125.00.

'£625! That is a lot of money,' said Carol.

'I know, and many authors don't earn large amounts. But this is a well-written children's book, written by a child. Christmas is not far away. It's perfect timing.'

'Can I ask a question?'

Raymand smiled at the six-year-old sitting in front of him swinging his legs. 'Yes, of course?'

'Where does the rest of the money go?'

That was a surprise. 'Well, there are the costs of making your book. We will show you some of those later. I have to pay my staff. There are transport costs, advertising and booksellers have to make a profit. We have editors and proofreaders to pay and maybe have the book translated if it is sold overseas. I get to keep what is left.'

'Is it going to be sold in other countries?'

He smiled at Graeme. 'That's a very astute question, young man. The answer is yes,' he looked at Bard. 'You're ok with your nickname?'

'No problem.'

'Once I had the phone call from Bard, apart from beginning work here, I made enquiries. There is dragon folklore in the Scandinavian and Germanic speaking countries; they call them worms; also in the far east. There is interest but no orders, yet. If I do?'

'What territories are you interested in?' said Bard.

He didn't need to think. 'British Isles, Europe and the Commonwealth including Hong Kong.'

'Not the United States?' said Carol.

'Too big for us, Countess. In a few years, perhaps. However, I'm happy with those I've mentioned. I'm waiting for a call from a friend of yours Bard, Levi Steiner of Consolidated Books. I sent them a copy and they're champing at the bit.'

Bard laughed. 'I'll bet they are. And they will sign. They can have everything you don't want?'

'In words of one syllable, yes.'

'Consolidated Books?'

'They control the children's book market in the US, Carol. Once they sign, they will go hell for leather. The Christmas market, especially the children's sector, is when these companies make most of their money. If it takes off in the States, you will need a York P.O. Box No. to protect your privacy. Worth thinking about.'

'If Levi does come over ... could we put him up for a night or so?'

'Not a problem.'

'Thanks. If he does, give him our address but no details about Graeme, Something to tempt him.'

'Excuse me,' said Carol. 'Is this what you meant when you talked about companies mothballing the book. The advance that they pay is, in reality, them buying the book. It becomes their property?'

'As far as publication is concerned it is. Except Raymond will not be mothballing anything. And he will deal with other companies without our input. He will let us know what is happening. And Graeme will get paid.'

'Should I send the contract to my solicitor?'

'If you wish, Countess. That is not a problem.'

Raymond's secretary returned with the prepared contracts five minutes later. Everyone signed, including Graeme.

'There's just one more thing before Vicky whisks you off. This is an excellent book.' Bard knew what was coming. 'But a series would be better. A bit like the Enid Blyton books, People like to follow stories,' he turned to Graeme. 'Have you any more stories?'

'Lots. None about dragons though.'

'Where are you going with this, Mr Bright,' interjected Carol, her eyes narrowed.

I could almost see the cogs spinning inside Raymond's head at Carol's tone of voice. 'I was thinking of perhaps four Dragon Ryder stories a year. A Christmas Annual of Graeme's other stories. He writes them once and ...'

'I'm not so sure about that, Mr Bright,' said Carol. 'I will discuss it with Martin and let you know in due course.'

Raymond was bright enough not to pursue the matter.

'Of course, Countess .. Graeme, do you like puzzles?'

His eyes lit up. 'I like Scrabble.'

'He's very good at anagrams,' said Bard.

He handed Graeme a sheet of paper. 'This is a new type of puzzle. It's called a Word Search. Words are hidden in a grid: Up, down, side to side, forwards and backwards, diagonally. You find them from the list on the other side then put a line through them. My children like it. See what you think.'

Leaving Raymond to think of new ways of extracting work from Graeme, Vicky whisked us off to her studio. 'How do you like this, Graeme?' Vicky smiled and removed a cover from her drawing table. Side-by-side were Graeme's drawing and hers.

'Wow! That's brilliant. Mine is rubbish.'

'Thank you. But yours is not rubbish. You are six years old and I am a trained illustrator. Yours is very good. All I've done is to polish it. Is there anything you want me to change? For example, is the colour right? Ulrick's armour?'

'No. I like it.'

'You weren't shown how to draw?'

'No, there was a picture of a dragon in the cupboard at school, I copied it.'

'Well, it's very good hand-eye coordination. Now, look at these.' She open her portfolio and removed six drawings. 'These relate to various stages of your story. Do you like them?'

'Mmm, they're great. I wish I could do that.'

'There's plenty of time for you to learn.'

A shiver ran down my spine as Carol planted the gentlest of kisses on my nape.

'What a shame you're spending the night at your flat,' she whispered.

The Print Room was noisy. Nevertheless, we managed to follow the process from blank paper to finished book. At the end of the tour Vicky presented Graeme with a cardboard box. 'This is for you to give to your friends, grandparents, aunts and uncles etc. There's a table over here,' she pointed. 'Take a look.'

He opened the box, removed the top copy and laughed. 'Look Mummy, that's me. Graeme Sylverton.' And passed it over.

'That's wonderful,' and looked through the book. 'We can give one to Dr. Hollis when we collect Martin.'

'That will always be you,' said Vicky. 'What does it feel like to see your name in print.'

He frowned. 'I don't know.'

'You will,' said Vicky laughing. 'I think, Countess, that what Raymond was trying to say, albeit in a clumsy fashion, this book is the first. The name Graeme Sylverton will become known and that is what people will look for. People buy people.'

Blake
Fifty-Seven

'Anything further Blake?' DS Creighton looked up from his desk as I entered his office.

I had to laugh. 'Not really, sir. Smith insists he had sex with her once or twice because it was expected, bearing in mind the company she kept. Vallery Rangely, says he had his hand up her skirt as often as he could. Not that she objected. From what Smith said to her she thought he wasn't getting any at home. Apparently he struck up a conversation with her when she was first appointed. It developed from there.'

'Any confirmation?'

'From the other typists? To a degree. Rangely was young and very pretty. She attracted a lot of attention, but she zeroed in on Smith. What we have at the moment is a he-said-she-said scenario. Nothing more. As to whether he was involved in the murders? I wouldn't like to hazard a guess. Mr Giles might be able to help.'

'And your university checks?'

'I've got someone to speak to at Leeds tomorrow.'

Gerald Vernon waved across the refectory. 'Brian, this is Andrew Tyson, the scientist I told you about.' he indicated the short rotund and balding man to his left. 'Andrew, my brother-in-law, Brian Blake. Watch your pockets he's a policeman,' he said and smiled.

'So, you're the one who married the delightful Lucy,' he smiled as we shook hands.

'She threw herself at my feet. What was I to do?'

He smiled again. 'Now, how can I help?'

'We're trying to trace someone with a particular interest in curare.'

'Curare? Could I ask what it's about?'

'Sorry, I'm not at liberty to divulge any details.'

'Makes it difficult.'

I thought for a moment. 'Mixed with other compounds. Something that may enhance curare's properties. Maybe subdue people?'

'Hmm. Makes a difference ... Last year I attended a symposium in Edinburgh. Can't remember her name but she had worked in both South America and Southern Africa. A cultural anthropologist studying the hunting practises of the various tribes. Of course, curare comes from South America. What the Africans use I can't honestly remember. Curare is of great benefit to modern medicine. What the other compounds might be I'm afraid I can't help.'

'Thanks, that's useful.'

Andrew Tyson removed a business card holder from his briefcase. 'Here,' he said handing him a card. 'Call this number, they should be able to help.'

I could feel their eyes burning into my back as I left.

'Gerald, do you know what it's about?'

'Sorry Andrew, I'd only be guessing.'

'Strange questions though. A detective asking about tribal practices.'

'Perhaps he's investigating Parliamentarians.'

'About time someone did,' Tyson laughed as they headed for the queue.

''Dr. Adrienne Robertshaw? Didn't Lincoln mention an Adrienne?'

'He did, sir. But wouldn't or couldn't elucidate. However, it's an unusual name.'

'Do we know if she is a Dr. of medicine or simply a PhD?'

'No sir. But this one is a cultural anthropologist and has studied tribal practices in both South America and Southern Africa, so probably a PhD.'

DS Creighton steepled his hands on the desk and rested his chin. 'And your next step?'

'According to the organiser, St James College, Oxford is her *pied a terre.*'

'If there is anything of interest let me know straight away.'

The third ring. 'Anthropology.'

'Good afternoon. Detective Constable Blake. I'm making enquiries in regard to a Dr Adrienne Robertshaw.'

'Could I ask what it's about?'

Nosey sod. 'I need to speak with her as a matter of urgency. Is she working.'

'Not here. She's engaged in research into early Victorian plant hunters.'

'I see. Might I ask where?'

'Some stately house that I've never heard of before. I can't remember exactly but it sounded like Olden ...'

The line went dead.

I rattled the cradle but to no avail. A voice from down the corridor. 'What's the matter with these bloody phones?' That answered my thought.

Olden? .. Olden?. Where had I heard that name before? The voice of a six-year-old boy sprung to mind. "Are you in trouble because you're a spy?" Countess of Oldeney. Beck. Curare. Torture. Adrienne. That was too much of a coincidence.

The Super had a Gazetteer on his desk: Oldeney, North Yorkshire. Hamlet, population 119. Established C745.

AA roadmap. Somewhere off the A165 north of Beverley.

I scribbled three notes about where I was heading and asking for someone to ring Lucy. I left one on the open Gazetteer weighed down with a ruler. One on DI Cartwright's desk and the third on Sergeant Ryder's desk. Tried the phone again – still dead. Headed for my bike. Possibly a two-hour trip. What would I find when I got there?

Beck

Fifty-Eight

Laughing, the guests scattered as the two pocket battleships charged towards the stairs. 'Bard, Grandad wants to see you,' they grabbed him by the hands pulling him towards the Drawing Room.

Six feet three, moustache, ramrod straight. His wife, wearing a tiara and elegantly sheathed in a full-length dark green gown, at his side. Smiles playing round their mouths. 'This is Bard, Grandad.'

'We thought it might be,' he smiled.

Bard looked at a face that was used to command. Not to be trifled with. 'Your Grace, Duchess. This is a pleasure I've been anticipating ever since Carol explained that you were simply a pussycat. I didn't believe her.'

'Did she now?' he said as his wife broke into a broad smile. 'I shall have to have words with my daughter.'

Graeme was tugging my sleeve. 'Excuse me Your Grace,' said Bard and crouched in front of the twins. 'I would never have found your grandparents without your assistance.'

'We know,' Martin interjected.

'We wanted to make sure you got here.' Said Graeme.

'Well, thank you. Your mission is complete. You can go now. Shoo.'

'Aww, came the joint reply

'I want to talk with your grandparents. Go on, hop it.'.

They ran off giggling. 'They're delightful,' he said.

'It's a long time since I heard anyone tell an Earl to hop it.'

'They're six years old. I think the time for gravitas and responsibility is waiting for them. For now, they should be able to enjoy being six.'

'I agree,' said the Duchess. 'Carol told me all about you.'

'I sincerely hope not,' said Bard holding back a laugh.

The Duchess reciprocated. 'Well, enough. When did you realise who she was?'

'Whilst reading Country Life magazine in a dentist's waiting room. It came as a shock. And when I recovered consciousness in hospital and found Carol sitting there with the boys? At the time it was a feeling I didn't understand. And when she told me her story.'

'Harrowing.'

'Indeed it was, Duchess. I asked her to stay that first day and, had it not been for the fear of Lord Gordon having both of us killed she probably would have.'

'She said what?' The Duke looked as though he were about to explode.

'That her husband had the contacts to make it happen, or would carry out the threat himself. And because of that extracted a promise that I would make no attempt to trace her.'

The Duchess took her husband's arm. 'Lawrence, calm down. He's no longer here. Ancient history. You had a question to ask.'

The Duke patted his wife's hand. 'Quite. You're a literary agent, I understand. What does that entail?'

'I assess work sent to Finsbury Templeton Books to see if they have merit .. I get paid a rolling commission on sales, with one exception. I won't take a penny from any royalties paid to Graeme. He's a very talented little boy.'

'I've read that book he wrote,' said the Duchess. 'It's very good. Could he make a living from writing?'

'Most certainly. And the publisher would like more, plus a Christmas Annual of his stories, puzzles and games for next year.

According to Dr Hollis, the head teacher, Graeme wrote the story in little over an hour. What Carol and I have to do is to make sure that he doesn't try to do too much to the exclusion of everything else.'

'Absolutely,' said the Duchess.

The Duke nodded. 'Yes, I understand. And they've extracted a promise from me to use their playground and crawl across the rope tomorrow, weather permitting.'

The Duchess laughed. 'He's praying for rain.'

'Almost,' he said and laughed. 'It's a long time ago that I had to undergo such exercise.'

'The crawl line isn't up yet, Your Grace, so you're safe for the time being.'

The look of relief noticeable. Now. Do you write?'

'I have a couple of drafts for novels. Did you have something in mind?'

'Yes, I'm considering a history of the Ingleby-Roberts family. Would that be something that you might consider?'

'Very specialist genre, Sir. What did you have in mind? Something that is called a vanity project? .. i.e. You just want a copy for your own library. Or a wider audience.'

'Oh, the wider audience.'

'I see. What I would recommend is a ghostwriter. He, they are all men, will assess your work and will charge you a fee and then write it with your name on the cover. Or with both names on the cover. That may be cheaper, but he will expect to participate in the royalties.'

'And you, do you get paid?'

'For this I would. If that is the route you wish to take, I will write to you with the names of those who would be able to do what you wish. You can interview them and find someone with whom you can work. In the meantime, I will speak with the publishers and see what your potential market might be.'

Before the Duke could answer the pocket-battleships returned. 'Grandad, we want to sing a song for you. Bard will you play?'

'Of course, which one?' as if he didn't know.

'The National Anthem.' said Graeme without letting his face slip.

'The National Anthem?'

'Yes, Your Grace, but not as you know it.'

'I'm intrigued.'

The Duke clapped his hands twice. 'Ladies and gentlemen. Our grandsons would like to sing for us. They would like to sing The National Anthem. But, not as we know it?'

Cousins Bertie and Alicia with their four daughters were standing close by. The girls were not impressed. Everyone else standing quietly.

Bard sat at the piano and lifted the lid. 'The tune is Men of Harlech, if you know the words, join in.'

'Excellent,' said Bertie. 'Written by a housemaster at Eton, if I'm not mistaken.'

'Deep breath boys. On three .. Three.'

They sang with gusto:

What's the good of wearing braces
Vests and pants and boots with laces,
Spats or hats you buy in places
Down in Brompton Road?
What's the use of shirts of cot-ton,
Studs that always get for-gotten?
These affairs are simply rotten:
Better far is Woad.
Woad's the stuff to show, men.
Woad to scare your foemen:

Boil it to a brilliant hue
And rub it on your back and your ab-domen.
Ancient Britons ne'er did hit on
Anything as good as woad to fit on
Neck, or knees, or where you sit o-on.
Tailors, you be blowed.

Romans came across the Chann-el
All wrapped up in tin and flann-el:
Half a pint of woad per man'll
Dress us more than these.
Saxons, you can waste your stitches
Building beds for bugs in britches:
We have woad to clothe us, which is
Not a nest for fleas.
Romans keep your armours;
Saxons your pyjamas:
Hairy coats were meant for goats,
Gorillas, yaks, retriever dogs and llamas.
Tramp up Snowdon with our woad on:
Never mind if we get rained or blowed on.
Never want a button sewed o-on.
Go it, Ancient Bs

There was so much laughter and not a few tears, not to mention applause. Carol came across and gave them both a hug. Cousin Bertie's daughters wanted to learn the words. Liz and Steve were here but Peter had tonsilitis and was tucked up in bed.

It was the perfect opportunity for a group sing-song, beginning with There's a Hole in My Bucket. A couple of maids co-opted to swell the female ranks.

Blake

Fifty-Nine

The light was beginning to fade as I approached the junction with the A165 north from Beverley. Everything stopped as a convoy of fire engines, blue lights working overtime preceded me. I stopped at the side of the young policewoman controlling the traffic.

'DC Blake, West Riding,' I said and flashed my warrant card. 'Where are they going?'

'Big house in the middle of no-where, Oldeney.'

I started. 'Oldeney? That's where I'm heading.'

'Why?'

'Trying to prevent a murder.'

'You serious?'

'Yup. All the phones were out when I set off. Do you know where it is?'

'Yeah, nice place. Pity the House isn't open to the public. It's beautiful. Are you offering me a lift?'

'It'll be cold on the back.'

'I soon warm up. I'm off duty anyway. I'll just let them know,' she unclipped her radio. 'All the twos, over.'

'Go ahead, Jean.'

'It's six. Sign me off, will you. I'm with a West Riding DC wanting directions to Oldeney.'

The radio operators voice came across, 'Will do.'

Followed immediately by another voice, 'Probably some scrote trying to get in her knickers.'

'I heard that, Jack.'

'Sorry.'

'You will be tomorrow.'

She re-clipped her radio. 'Bastard,' the word spat out. 'Let's go.' She climbed on board.

'Ready?'

'Too true.'

Beck/Blake

Sixty

The conversation stopped as Givens, metal-tipped silver-capped staff in hand struck the floor three times. 'My Lords, Ladies and Gentlemen. Dinner is served.'

Carol and Alicia rounded up the children. 'Time to leave us I'm afraid,' said Carol.

'But I'm fourteen,' protested Christine. The eldest of Bertie's daughters.

Carol smiled. 'I know, fourteen is a terrible age. It could have been worse.'

'I know,' Christine replied with a resigned expression. 'I could have been fifteen.'

'True. But I promise when we get married you can stay up all night, if you want.'

Christine brightened up. 'Really?'

'I promise.'

Children and posse of four maids left the Drawing Room.

Carol and Bard leading. Carol's father with Bard's mother following, they processed to the State Dining Room. The table laid for twenty-four. The settings as they had been for the Royal Visit of 1936. Footmen, many of them actors and coached by Givens and Christopher behind every chair.

Blake stopped at the roadside. 'How far now, Jean?'

Not far. Fifteen minutes Max. Next turn right. Just a finger post, easy to miss.'

'Right,' I said and unzipped my jacket. 'You're wearing this or you'll get pneumonia.'

'You're sure?'

'Positive. How's that,' I said as she zipped the jacket.

The warmth soaked into her body. 'Wonderful. Are you married?'

I laughed. 'And with a little girl. Plus, Lucy's mother is a friend of the Chief.'

'Oh well. It was worth asking.'

'Next right.'

For seven years she had waited. Seven years ago the police had failed to find Emily and had simply given up. Over time the bitterness had turned to hatred. Hatred of the incompetence of the Plod and of those who she held responsible.

It had been a chance encounter with an ex-detective; one of the incompetents that brought her to where she was. Good looking and amusing. But like most men thought with his genitals. She hadn't had a man since her husband died and it's surprising what men would betray for sex.

To be fair Patrick and Blaise had been useful. Now it was just her. She had allowed Beck to live. Even provided the police with evidence of Emily's murder and where the body was buried. Again, nothing. What more did they want?

Tonight it would end. Having watched this example of British nobility strut about as if they meant something, tonight would be poetic justice.

The door to the storeroom opened catching her by surprise. The old woman walked in and stared. 'What are you doing here. You have no right. I'm going to tell my son.'

'I'm afraid you aren't, come here,' she took Mary by the arm and pulled her further into the store.

'How dare you. Let go this instant.'

'Sorry, can't do that,' she replied and picked the chef's knife from the stone. Devoid of emotion, drove the blade into Mary's chest and watched as she slumped to the floor, the blood spreading across her apron and the cellar floor. 'Shouldn't be so bloody nosey.'

The voice echoed down the corridor. 'Who's there?'

My God another one, she thought. 'Just me, I found this old lady wandering in the cellar,' she said as she stepped outside.

'Dr? It sounded like Mary's voice.'

'Is that her name?'

'Yes, she's not supposed to be in here. I'll take her back.' said Patricia pushing past. 'But she's been stabbed. What on earth?'

'You shouldn't be here. I'm sorry.' For the second time that evening Adrienne Robertshaw withdrew the knife. A last look at the two bodies she locked the door leaving the key in situ.

Sixty-One

Carol's father rose to his feet and tapped his glass three times. 'My Lords ...' the clatter of a bell stopped him. He looked at his daughter. 'Isn't that the fire bell?'

Carol stood. 'Yes, it is,' she said.

'Fire?' said Bard. 'The children!' He raced from the chair pushing the footman out of the way.

The door opened. Gregory, the Under Footman stepped inside. 'Countess, the stairs are on fire. No-on can get through.'

Flames two to three feet high. Billowing smoke. Just visible on the top step a gallon canister with paraffin running down the stairs. Mrs Nesbitt struggling with two buckets of water reached the stairs and put them down.

'Mrs Nesbitt, hold it there,' shouted Bard as he ripped his coat off. Dunked the jacket into the water. 'Pour the water over my head, please.'

'Same goes for me, Nessie,' said Bertie following suit.

She smiled at the name as she poured the water over Bard's head.

'Catch me up, Major' said Bard, took a deep breath, arms across his face he plunged into the flames. The heat was intense.

'Ready, sir?'

'When you are ready, Nessie,' he said and followed Bard into the inferno.

Carol and Alicia, hearts in mouths, tears in their eyes watched helplessly as the flames set fire to the huge velvet drapes. Who had set the fire and why.

Their six children and maid on the wrong side of the flames

There were twelve steps before the turn to the left. A further twelve to the top. Bard was six steps from the top when he heard the scream. A blazing drape had fallen enveloping Major fforde-Selk in flames. Bard kept going but half-turned to see Carol's father and one of the temporary footmen dash into the flames and drag the unfortunate Major to safety.

Two steps from the top he saw the second canister. On its side, paraffin running down the stairs. Using the jacket sleeves, he picked both cannisters up. At the top of the stairs Bard leaned over the balustrade. 'Dad,' he shouted. His father looked up. 'Take care of these, will you. Be careful they're hot.'

Clive Beck removed his jacket catching one can then the other. When he looked back his son had disappeared. 'God speed,' he thought. 'Look after your sons.'

Orders were flying in all directions.

'I want six volunteers,' said Steve to the stand-in footmen. 'Now.'

'What do you want us to do?'

'Come with me,' he said and turned to the front door.

'Aren't we more use here,' said one.

'No, follow me.' With shrugged shoulders they followed at the run.

'What the Hell has he got in mind?'

'God knows.'

The door was half-open. It was a horror show. Pauline, who looked after the twins, was lying on her back, unmoving. Clothing heavily blood-stained, the wound in her left abdomen obvious. Graeme, kneeling on the floor and sitting back on his heels with Martin's head, face like tallow, resting on his knees. A wound in the right side of his abdomen. The rise and fall of his chest was shallow.

The drawn bow with nocked arrow in Graeme's hands pointed to Bard's left, the hinge side of the door, caught and held his attention. The arrows should have a suction cup but there was none and the arrow was sharpened. Graeme gave Bard a watery smile but didn't lower the bow.

What the hell was going on? Without speaking Bard took a step inside and felt a searing pain in the back of his left thigh. Graeme loosed the arrow. There was a scream from behind the door.

With his left hand he found a knife, still embedded.

The sound of running feet. Bertie's four daughters, in pyjamas and dressing gowns burst in. 'There's a fire.' They caught sight of Pauline and the scream's began.'

'Will you be quiet,' he shouted. 'For goodness sake.'

'You can't speak to us, like that,' said Christine, the eldest.

'Oh yes I can,' he said. 'And I will.'

She gave him a furious look. 'Then get rid of that,' she said pointing at Pauline.

'That, has a name, it's Pauline. She was stabbed by whoever is sitting behind the door while trying to protect his Lordship and his brother. Treat her with some respect.'

The voice that answered turned his knees to water. 'So, we meet again Mr Beck.' His torturer was sitting there, Graeme's arrow protruding from her left upper chest below the clavicle.

'Why?'

'I think it's fair. First born for first born.'

'What?'

'Don't play the innocent. You know what I mean.'

'I haven't a clue.'

'Have it your way. It makes no difference you're all going to die.'

The screams began again.

'Will you be quiet,' Bard shouted. 'No one is going to die. Listen.' Just audible and getting louder the sound of the first emergency vehicles approaching. 'Christine,' she looked at him. 'I want you to be brave. Take hold of this knife handle and pull it out in a straight line, please.'

She looked at him again.

'Slowly and steadily. You're the eldest. You're in charge. No fuss. Then I want you and your sisters to go and get dressed in your riding habit and jumpers. Be back here fully dressed and with all the bed sheets you can find from all the bedrooms. Five minutes.'

'Just hold the handle and pull?'

'Please. Straight line. Let me hold the door.'

They all moved to one side. 'If you don't want to watch, stand in the corridor.' Susan and Jessica, the two youngest left. Annabelle stared as Christine grasped the knife and drew it out.

His leg hurt like hell and wouldn't bear his weight but the knife was out. The tip was missing. What were the chances it was still in his thigh? Worry about that later. 'Thank you. That was very brave.' Bard took the knife. 'Now hurry. Five minutes. Fully dressed and all the bed sheets you can find.

The footsteps disappeared. Bard knelt by Graeme's side and put his hand on his shoulder. 'That was a very brave thing to do.'

'Is Martin going to die?' he said holding back the tears.

'I hope not and the faster we are the better it will be. You can tell me about it later. All right?'

He nodded.

'Good boy. Now, have you got any rope up here?'

'No, but we've got our harnesses and belts.'

'Great. Get them for me. Get dressed as quick as you can. I need your bedding and mattresses.'

Bard held Martin's head whilst Graeme slid a cushion beneath it, then stood. 'Bard, she's gone.'

'This note Blake left, has he timed it?'

'5.05pm, sir. He's left your gazetteer open with a ruler under the name Oldeney. I called North Yorks control. All services are attending a reported major fire at Oldeney Carr House. Off the A165 south of Bridlington.'

'Did he put what his enquiry was?'

'No, sir. There's a jotting here about St James' College and a Dr Adrienne Robertshaw. He couldn't let anyone know because the phones were out.'

'Very well. Call his wife and let her know and that he is likely to be some time. I'll pick you up in fifteen minutes.'

Steve extracted the Fire Station key from its cubby hole.

'What the hell is that?' said one of the men when he opened the doors.

The last member arrived. 'Bloody Hell. That's a Tilley.'

It took a concerted effort to get the Tilley up the steps to the door.

'Remember, pull down. Do not push up. You'll break it! Steve looked round. 'Where's our fireman? Here, take the hose.'

'Pick up the speed he shouted. 'Pull down then let go!'

A jet of water shot up to the top of the stairs. 'That's it! Keep going!

The bucket-chain was working well. The water level constant.

The sight was unbelievable. Smoke issuing from numerous windows. Sheets of flame from the rear of the building. Was this the mysterious Dr Robertshaw's doing?

'Good grief.'

'Enough to make you cry,' said Jean.

'Climb aboard.'

'Stop at the bridge, Brian. From the look of the way cars have been dumped they need sorting. Then you can have your jacket back.'

A minute later. 'You'll be all right?'

'I can vent my spleen over that pillock Jack Holroyd if anyone gets awkward.'

I didn't comment

Jean dismounted, handed me my jacket and homed in on one car disgorging what appeared to be a family. 'Move your car, sir. You're blocking the way for the Fire brigade and the ambulances.'

'Everybody else is.'

'Well, you're not. Move your car onto the grass out of the way.'

'I don't like your attitude. I shall complain.'

'Good, then my Chief Constable will know that I'm working. Now, are you going to move your car or not? And you and your family stay this side of the bridge. That's a tragedy over there not a peep-show.'

I left my bike at the foot of the stairs and ran into the chaos. A Victorian fire pump. It was remarkable, a small jet but with a good range as long as those operating the two handles didn't falter.

One man stood out. Tall, distinguished, moustachioed and dishevelled. Warrant card in hand. Excuse me, sir. I'm Detective

Constable Blake from the West Riding,' I held out my warrant card. 'This may seem a bizarre thing to ask but is there an academic from St James College, Oxford doing plant research.

'I couldn't say, officer,' he said. 'But there's a man who will.' And nodded in the direction of the smartest man in the room. 'Givens, can you help this officer?'

'I will do my best, Your Grace. How can I help.'

I outlined my question again.

'Yes sir, a Dr Katherine Butters. She has been researching the work of the Third Earl, in the West Wing Library.'

'Not Adrienne Robertshaw?'

'Definitely not, sir.'

'However, it was St James' College?'

'Most certainly, sir.'

'Thank you, that's most useful.'

'Is there anything else.'

'Yes, a Mr Beck, Martin Beck.'

'I can answer that, Givens. I'm sure you have plenty to keep you occupied.'

'Thank you, Your Grace,' he said and left.

'That man is unflappable,' he said. 'Now, Mr Beck. I know his story and you think that this academic is involved?'

'I have no direct evidence, sir, but I believe so. Mr Beck is here?'

'Yes, today's shindig is to celebrate his engagement to my daughter.'

I had to smile. 'The Countess?'

'You know her?'

'In passing. When Mr Beck was in hospital. Where is he?'

'Martin is up there. There are six children including my grandsons and a maid up there on their own. He ran through the flames. Another guest followed and got caught when a blazing drape dropped. We don't know what is happening.'

'Which room are they in?'

He pointed at the balcony. 'Down that corridor. Third on the left.'

'That balcony, sir? It's not too high. If it's sound enough dropping the children might be an option. Could you?'

'Of course. But how will you ascertain that?'

'Trial and error, Your Grace.' I pulled my visor down and put my gauntlets on and ran for the stairs. I'd read that the wood nearest the wall was often the strongest but I wanted something to grab hold of if required. I ran close to the handrail.

'Where the hell is he going?' Someone shouted.

'Never mind,' said the Duke. 'Turn the hose on him.'

I felt the water hit me in the back as I took the steps two at a time. Three steps from the top, the staircase gave way accompanied by screams. With my left arm over the balustrade, I managed to stop myself falling through. The water jet now playing around my lower back. It was getting hotter by the second. I managed to haul myself out and climbed the remaining steps. My legs were sore.

There were a couple of cheers and shouts of, 'Are you all right?' There was no sign of the Duke. I waved and turned into the corridor.

The sound of voices passing below distracted him. Bard opened the window and shouted, 'Who's there?'

The party came back. 'John, sir, the Gardener.'

'Mr Beck, Bard. I want you to find the Duke, the Countess's father. All the children are here. His Lordship is seriously injured and requires an ambulance, urgently. There's a maid here unfortunately she is dead. I'm going to lower them out of this window. Some long ladders would be useful.'

'Yes sir,' he said and turned. 'Charlie, you and Eric get round to the garden bring back the long ladders ... don't just stand there like bloody lemons, run.'

'They won't be long, sir.'

I removed my helmet and gauntlets and knocked on the door and entered. 'Hello Martin, it's DC Blake.' I took the scene in one glance. Five terrified children, one adult bleeding from a leg wound and one of the twins with an abdominal wound.

'Hello, ladies, my name is Brian. I'm a policeman. We're going to get you down from the balcony. Martin you'll be all right 'til I get back.'

He looked Blake up and down taking in the scorched leathers. 'Yes. Not suitable for this one. But go ahead.'

I smiled at the other twin. 'You're the one who thought that Bard was a spy, aren't you?'

His thin smile did nothing to lift the mood. He nodded.

'Are you coming with us?'

'I want to stay with my brother.'

It was what I expected.

I smiled at him and nodded. 'I'll be back and we'll get you down.'

I crouched in front of the smallest tear-stained face and smiled. 'Now what's your name?'

'Jessica. I'm four.'

'Jessica, that's a pretty name. I've got a daughter much smaller than you; her name is Claire. *I* think you're the bravest of all. Shall we go and find your mummy and daddy?'

The smoke was noticeably thicker when I opened the door; a point not missed by the girls. Holding Jessica by the hand I stopped just short of the balcony. 'Jessica, stay back here with your sisters.' And nodded to Annabelle who took her by the hand and crouched.

'Don't worry, Jess, we'll soon be down,'

The bucket chain was working smoothly and the two men either side of the pump were doing a sterling job. The jet from the old fire engine was having some effect, nevertheless, the stairs were an inferno, flames several feet high and clouds of smoke. I'm glad I wasn't trying to climb them. How the girls would react I don't know.

There were shouts as I appeared on the balcony. I raised my hands and the noise stopped. The Duke and several others had tight hold of what appeared to be a curtain. 'I've got the four girls. They're frightened but uninjured. The Earl has an abdominal stab wound and needs a doctor as soon as possible. We're going to lower him and his brother from the window. First to come down will be Jessica.'

One tear-stained very smartly dressed woman called. 'My baby, is she all right?'

'She's fine, just frightened, and missing her mother.'

I crouched in front of Jessica. 'Your mummy's waiting for you. But the way you get down is going to seem like magic. Do you like magic?'

Her eyes opened wide. 'Fairy magic?'

I nodded. 'Just like fairy magic. I'm going to pick you up and I want you to close your eyes as tight as you can. Then put your hands over your eyes and keep them there. When I say, now, I want you to start counting from one to ten. Can you do that?'

'I'm not silly, of course I can count.'

At least her three sisters were smiling. 'Ready?' she nodded. 'Here we go.' I scooped her up. 'Close your eyes tight ... Good, now put your hands over your eyes.' There were gasps as I held Jessica over the balustrade. 'Ready, start counting, now.' I let go. Jessica dropped smoothly into the curtain. 'Four, five, six,'

Her mother grabbed her and carried her away from the balcony. 'You can open your eyes now Jessica.'

'No, I have to count to ten or the magic won't work. Seven, eight, nine, ten. Hello Mummy.'

Her mother clutched her to her chest and looked up. 'Thank you,' she mouthed.

I grinned and waved. There was a round of applause as I returned to the others

I smiled at the three remaining sisters. 'The stairs are on fire but don't worry too much. Right, you're next. What's your name?'

'Susan.'

'What I did to your sister isn't going to work with you, is it?'

'No. How do *I* get down?'

'Come on I'll show you.'

The sight of the flames unnerved her. I felt the balcony move beneath my feet.

'Quickly now. Don't look at the flames just concentrate on getting down.'

Even so ... 'Hello Mummy, Daddy, Carol, Uncle Lawrence.' There were answering waves.

'Quickly.' I leaned over the balustrade. 'Ready?'

'Let her jump,' was the reply.

'Climb over, I'll count from three to one, let go and fall backwards. Try to land on your back. It is safe, trust me.'

'You're sure?'

'Positive,' I said and nodded.

There was a creaking sound from the top of the stairs. The balcony lurched. 'From Three,' I said. 'Three two one GO!'

Susan shrieked as gravity took over. It must have seemed like an eternity until she landed safely. She was seized by Uncle Lawrence and carried away to her parents.

'Well done,' he shouted.

'The balcony is breaking away. We'll have to do the remainder through the window.' I said as a group of Firemen rushed in followed by two ambulancemen and someone in a white coat. 'What the! Bloody hell it's a Tilley. Well done gentlemen. We'll take over, now'

Whilst the firemen brought their higher-pressure hose to bear, the man in the white coat shouted up. 'I'm a doctor. Where's this child with the abdominal wound?'

'In the third room along this way,' I pointed towards the room. 'We'll have to lower him from the window. The balcony isn't safe.'

'What about servant's staircases?'

'Sorry, I don't know.'

'That's where the fire is,' someone said.

I left them to it. 'Come on ladies, we'll all have to take the scenic route.'

WPC 222 Jean Murray flinched at the sight of the three police vehicles: two cars and a personnel carrier. The first car stopped. A senior officer exited. She stood to attention. 'Sir.'

'ACC Patrickson. OK. Easy. Looks like you're fighting a losing battle.'

'Yes, sir. Trying to keep the road clear for the fire brigade and ambulances. But they're just abandoning their vehicles and, well, you can see.'

> 'Yes,' he said. 'Your collar number, 222, you're not one of ours. Where are you from. 'Beverley, sir ...'

'...Your topcoat is in Beverley? You look frozen.'

'A bit sir.'

'I'll bet. Now, does this mysterious C.I.D. officer have a name?'

'Brian Blake, sir.'

'That's a name to conjure with, Inspector,' the ACC said as several officers burst out laughing, unlike the Inspector. 'He's trespassing again. It's time he transferred. Where is he now, Murray?'

'In the house, sir.'

'Good, you come with me. Mac and Wilberforce also. Inspector Flake sort this mess out.'

'Sir?'

'Someone on the bridge to do what WPC Murray has been doing. A team over there,' he indicated with his hand. Get everyone back this side of the bridge and most important get these vehicles off the road onto the grass. Can you manage that?'

'Yes sir.'

'Oh, members of the Press can walk over the bridge once their cars are on the grass. And an officer on each corner of the house.'

'Give me strength,' the ACC said as they crossed the bridge. 'Mac, make a quick circuit of the house to see just how extensive the fire is. You'll find me inside.'

'Yes sir.' he ran towards the corner of the House.

'My name's Jean. What's yours?'

'Pete.'

'Wouldn't it be normal for the inspector to accompany the ACC?'

'Yes, but this is Simon Nigel Oliver Flake behind his back known as ...?'

She puckered her brow. 'Snoflake?'

'The same. About as much use as a chocolate fireguard. Need I say more?'

'I understand. Oops,' she said as she staggered into Pete Wilberforce. 'Sorry, just went a bit dizzy.'

'You OK?'

'Think so.'

He took hold of her hand. 'You're like ice.'

She nodded. 'Why did you laugh at Brian Blake's name?'

'Do you remember the Wainwright case?'

'That serial killer, foreign name.'

'He's the one. Iago Yarney. It was Brian's wife and daughter that were kidnapped in York. ... .. Inspector Flake challenged what Brian said about his arrest of Yarney. Made himself look a fool. Mr Patrickson's been trying to get Brian to transfer over here ever since. Here we are, soon get warm.'

'You've been busy, Martin,' I said. In my absence the sheets had been torn into strips and tied together to make a rope of sorts with some type of knot constructed at the end with two huge loops. Graeme was fully dressed and wearing a harness.

He looked at the girls. 'Only two?'

'The balcony is starting to break away.'

He nodded. 'Just got to remove the window. 'Graeme, Christine and Annabelle just step into the bedroom for a moment and close the door,' without a word they left. 'Good, I'm glad you're here. I can't put any weight on my leg,'

'What do you want me to do?'

'Open the window and tell everybody to move out of the way. Then smash it with that chair. I'll protect Martin with a blanket.'

I leaned out of the window. 'I'm going to smash the window. Everyone get back at least twenty yards.' Without waiting for any comments, I picked the chair up. It was noisy. It took a minute to remove the glass fragments from the frame. When I turned round the children were back in the room.

'OK. Now we lift Martin onto the mattress. Graeme, you support Martin's head. Brian, one arm under the small of his back and the other hand under his thighs. I'll do the other side. Annabelle, just hold Martin's feet together, gently. Christine, when we lift, manipulate the mattress beneath him ... On three. ... lift.'

There were moans from Martin, but the task was completed in a few seconds. 'Brian, take that loop nearest you and feed it beneath the mattress and work it towards his hips. I'll do the other end ...Damn! I forgot this.' He held up what looked like a ladder made of strips of sheet. 'Brian, we need to lift Martin and the mattress. Girls, I need you to slide this beneath the mattress when we lift. It's to stop the mattress bending and Martin falling through.'

'I'll switch sides' I said.

In position. 'On three. ... three, lift,' Excellent. He passed me two strips of sheet. 'Tie the end cross pieces to the loop, as tight as you can ... Right, now we're in business. Martin pulled himself to his feet. Tied a long piece of knotted sheet to the knot. 'Graeme, fix your carabiner to the loop near to Martin's head and lock the gate,' He smiled at him, 'Good boy. Are you ready?'

It was a thin smile. Graeme nodded.

'Remember what I taught you about abseiling?'

'Feet against the wall and walk down.'

'Excellent.' He leaned against the outer wall. 'I'm sending Martin and Graeme down now. When they're down please do not cut anything. We need them again,' he turned to Graeme. 'When we lift you move into the window but don't fall. As you begin to descend just talk to him.'

It went far smoother than I thought it would. There were gasps from the assembled when Graeme appeared hanging from the Heath Robinson stretcher. The ropes held. Within two minutes Martin was on the stretcher. He, Graeme, his mother and the injured would-be rescuer were en route to hospital with Dr Clarke. Reassurances from Bard that he was all right didn't make the Countess feel any better.

'Your Grace,' the Duke spun round.

'Mr Patrickson,' he said as they shook hands. 'Unhappy times.'

'Excuse me, Sir. I just need a quick word with Mrs Nesbitt. Both of you come with me ... Ah, Mrs Nesbitt.'

'Mr. Patrickson, how can I help?'

'This, is Jean. She travelled up from Beverley on the back of a motorbike and without a topcoat. She's a bit cold. Could you?'

'Of course. Come with me, dear.'

Ten steps later. 'Sorry, Mrs Nesbitt.' Jean Murray slumped against her and slid to the floor.

'Christopher!' She crouched at her side.

'Take this young lady to the Butler's Pantry and put her in his cot with a blanket, keep her warm. I'll speak to Mrs Evans.'

Elsie, at sixteen the youngest maid and in floods of tears almost collapsed at Mrs Nesbitt's feet. 'What on earth is the matter, girl. Talk to me.'

'It's terrible, Mrs Nesbitt,' she sobbed. 'They're both dead. Old Mary and Patricia. In the cellar. They're on the floor they've been stabbed.'

ACC Patrickson took one look at the distraught maid. 'Mrs Nesbitt?'

'It's Elsie, she says that Mary, the old Nanny, and Patricia one of the maids have been stabbed. They're in the cellar.

'Elsie,' said the ACC. 'Is this true.'

'Yes, sir. Honest.'

The ACC turned. 'Wilberforce. With me. Elsie, show us where.'

'Do I have to?'

'Yes, you do. Be brave. You don't have to go in the room.'

The frightened maid retraced her steps along the corridor towards the servant's staircase. She stopped and pointed. 'In there, sir.'

ACC Patrickson eased the door open. 'Mrs Nesbitt can you confirm their identity please?'

'Yes,' said Mrs Nesbitt. 'Patricia is lying across Mary's body. Although what Mary was doing here, I don't know. She is banned from entering the House.'

'We can worry about that later. Wilberforce, find Sergeant MacAllister. He's to contact the Control Room. On my authority I want the Duty Superintendent here yesterday. And every available detective plus fingerprints and photographer. The Duty Officer is to contact the Chief. When you've done that find me. And I do not want Inspector Flake in the building. Is that clear?'

'Yes sir,' he said and ran down the corridor.

'Bard checked his *ropes*. You weigh quite a bit more than your little sisters,' he said.

'Will you teach us to do what you taught Graeme, please,' said Christine. 'And I'm sorry for what I said about Pauline. Daddy's always telling us about *noblesse oblige*. It was wrong of me.'

He smiled at the girls. 'You were frightened, anyone would be. Let's say no more about it and yes, I'll teach you but not today. There,' he put the ropes down. 'Annabelle, pick up the loops and put your head and arms through ... Good. Now grasp it tightly in front of your chest. That will stop it slipping ... Great. Now sit on the blanket in the window frame and slide off, but don't let go of the rope. Turn to face the wall and put your feet on it, as Graeme did. Then it's your turn Christine.

'Slide when you're ready and turn towards the wall.'

Within seconds. 'Help, I'm falling.'

I dived to the window. She had a tight hold of the rope but she was lifting her elbows. 'Annabelle, tuck your elbows into your sides. Keep them tight.' With a struggle she managed. 'Well done.. Bring your feet up against the wall. That will stop you banging against it. Keep your elbows tight. Good. We're going to lower you now. That's good. Keep your elbows tight against your sides.'

Willing hands grabbed her when she was in range. She looked up. I could see the tears in her eyes. 'Thank you. That was scary.'

Christine pushed alongside me and poked her head out of the window. 'Are you all right, Anna?'

'Yes, thanks.' She slid her arms out of the loop. 'Your turn Chris. Keep your elbows tucked in.'

There was an answering grin. 'OK.'

'Ready, Christine,' said Bard.

'Ready.'

Whether it was her age or perhaps her athleticism, but she slid off the window ledge and turned in one move. She almost ran down the wall. She slipped the loop from her shoulders, waved and ran to join her mother and siblings.

No-one had mentioned it, but the smell of the fire was getting stronger.

'We'll send Pauline next.'

'Good idea.'

I stuck my head out of the window to be met by a voice I'd heard several times before. 'DC Blake, fancy seeing you on my patch.'

It took me a while to spot the shoulder tabs and locate the owner of the voice. 'Oh, hello, sir. Before we lower the next one will you ensure that all children and anybody who doesn't need to be here is removed.' I saw the puzzled look. 'One for the coroner's officer.'

He turned to the Officer on his left. 'I'll see to it, sir. Sergeant lets clear the roadway. Ladies and gentlemen will you clear the roadway, please, back to the corner of the house.'

'One of the maids looking after the Earl and his brother whilst they got ready for bed.'

The roadway clear, an ambulance reversed and parked five yards away.

Pauline in a double loop, the rope behind and arms bound to her sides, we manipulated Pauline to the window. Bard held the rope whilst I slid her off then joined Bard. Try as we might it was impossible to prevent any contact with the wall. Hopefully not too much.

Bard was next. 'Did you know who it was who did the stabbing?' I said.

'Never seen her before, but when I heard her voice after she stabbed me my knees buckled. It was the voice from the tape and when I was being threatened with castration.'

'You're certain.'

'Believe me, that is a voice I will never forget. And she said something strange. "I think it's fair. First born for first born." That doesn't make sense, at least to me. And before I forget, you'll want this,' he handed me a ten-inch chef's knife. 'This is what she stabbed me with. The point's broken. Whether it's in my leg or not I don't know.'

I lowered him. He fended himself off the wall with his good leg, departing by ambulance.

Next job, wrap the blade in a couple of towels, put the package in a pillowcase and tuck it under my belt inside my leathers.

Helmet on head and gauntlets in my teeth, I shinned down the rope which broke when I was six feet from the ground only to be helped to my feet by the ACC. 'Now, I've spoken with your navigator, WPC Murray from Beverley. What exactly are you doing here?'

It didn't take long for me to join the dots.

'Then this incident would appear to be linked to the murder of those four former undergraduates. Martin Beck would have been the fifth. And he recognised the voice from when he was held captive and from the tape?'

'That's what he told me.'

'And a link to St James's College?'

'Yes sir. However, the names Drs Katherine Butters and Adrienne Robertshaw, as far as I can recall are in no way connected to Emily Reid, the girl at the centre of everything.'

'Strange. Nothing else?

'Just something that the woman who stabbed the Earl ... Oh that reminds me, sir, you'll need this,' I reached inside my leathers, removed the package and handed it to the ACC. 'This is the knife used to stab the Earl, Martin Beck and the maid. The point is broken so it could still be in one of the victims.'

'Thanks. I wondered where that was.' He noticed my puzzled look. 'There are two more deaths in the cellar. One maid and the retired family nanny. Whoever she is, she's been busy. That would make seven deaths, eight if you include the Metropolitan police officer, plus attempted murder of the Earl and the wounding of Martin Beck ... Now what were you saying?'

'Er, oh yes. After she stabbed Martin Beck she said, and here I quote him. "I think it's fair. First born for a first born.'

'First born for a first born?' the ACC iterated. 'And as far as you know neither of those names have any link to Emily Reid?'

'I've read both misper and crime files and spoken with the Reids on more than one occasion, there's nothing.'

'Something for you to ponder on. Anything else?'

'Nothing that won't keep, sir. Jean Murray, is she all right. She was very cold.'

'She fainted. She's OK and has an admirer in Christopher, the First Footman. They seem quite taken with each other. She's asked if she can transfer from Beverley to North Yorkshire. Told me about the message that leaked out over the air when you two first met.'

'That was bad. A bit of banter is one thing but everybody within range of a radio would have heard that.'

He nodded. 'I'll deal with it later.'

'Excuse me, sir.' The officer gave me a hesitant look.

'DS Jones, this,' he indicated me, 'is DC Blake from the West Riding, you can speak freely.'

'Sir, we've searched the entire cellar and there is no trace of the murder weapon.'

The ACC lifted the pillowcase. 'I think you will find what we are looking for in here. It was in the Earl's bedroom. Left by the murderer and recovered by Martin Beck and DC Blake. Blake, what were the names she used?'

'Dr Adrienne Robertshaw is the name she is known by in the academic world. Dr Katherine Butters was the name by which she was known here. But I haven't seen her so I can't give you a description. Oh, the knife was handled by Christine fford-Selk, daughter of one of the guests; she extracted it from the back of Martin Beck's thigh. And the tip of the blade is missing.'

'Sergeant, you are aware of the third body and the attempt on the Earl's life, plus the stabbing of Martin Beck?'

'I am sir. I take it that the scene has not been examined.'

'Blake?'

'Only by me, sir. The corridor was beginning to fill with smoke.'

The reflected blue lights drew attention to the fire engine.

'I think we're in the way,' said the ACC walking to the side of the roadway.

A fireman leaned out of the window. 'Have any of you come from the room up there?' he said pointing at the broken window.

'I have,' I said.

'Any trace of the fire?'

'Smoke in the corridor was getting worse. There was no sign of any flames, but the door was closed.'

'That's fine, thanks.'

Within seconds there was a ladder at the window. Two firemen climbed through with the hose followed by two others. Two more ran towards us unrolling a length of hose and connected it to the fire engine. He waved to a fireman at the corner of the House. 'Water on.' Seconds later the hose expanded.

'Come on gentlemen, we're no use here.'

'Help yourself to tea, coffee and sandwiches,' was the call as we entered the kitchen.

'Come on Maisie,' said a stout, grey haired middle-aged woman. 'Get a move on with that bread.'

'Yes, Mrs Evans. I'm doing my best.'

'Not yet you're not, my girl.'

She would have made a good sergeant.

Jean Murray was working her way through her sandwich, coffee by her side. I grimaced and sat beside her, helping myself to freshly ground coffee and a beef sandwich.

'You OK?' I said. 'I heard you had a dizzy spell.'

She pulled an annoyed expression. 'You mean I fainted,' she said and smiled. 'It was embarrassing.'

'But you're all right now?'

'Yup,' she said and took another bite.

'I hear you've got a new friend?' I said, teasing.

She blushed. 'You mean Christopher? He's sweet. We're going to write.'

'Good. Will your transfer go through?'

'I think so. Mr Patrickson sounded positive.'

'I hope you'll both be very happy.'

She blushed to the roots of her hair. 'He is nice, and, well?'

'Who knows? Perhaps I'll see you later.'

'And if you hadn't stopped to ask directions we would never have met,' she leaned across and gave me a kiss on the cheek. 'Thank you.'

I bumped into Pete Wilberforce at the top of the steps. 'I heard you were here,' he said as we shook hands. 'Look at the state of your leathers.'

I grimaced. 'Yeah, heat treated.'

'Very funny.'

'The stairs collapsed. Managed to get my arm over the balustrade.'

'That was close. But ... you've been busy since Wainwright. Is this connected to the other job that your lot were being tight-lipped about.'

'It's looking that way,'

He raised his eyebrows and smiled. 'Like that is it?' I smiled and nodded. 'And Mr Patrickson wants a word.' He pointed to the ACC and the Duke.

'You wanted to see me, sir?'

'The Duke does,' he said.

'Sir?'

He seized my hand. 'I want to shake your hand young man. That was a damned brave thing you did. Thank you for saving my grandsons.'

I managed to rescue my hand. 'Thank you, sir. But it was Mr Beck's knowledge of

knots that made it possible.'

'Nevertheless, because of his injury without you ... So, thank you.'

'My pleasure, sir.'

He looked me up and down and frowned. 'Your leathers, they're a mite scorched.'

I followed suit and smiled. ‘Hmm. So are your trousers. I’ll have a chat with my insurance broker.’

‘You’ll do no such thing. I know you can’t accept gifts, but I think Mr Patrickson might be able to have a chat with your Chief, Mr Barton? Smooth things over.’ The Duke said looking at the ACC.

‘Indeed, I will Your Grace.’ he replied and nodded.

‘Now then, what did you say to Jessica. She was talking about you doing *fairy magic*.’

I couldn’t do anything but laugh. ‘Ah. It would have been a long way to drop a four year old ... she counted to ten.’

They both laughed. ‘That explains why she wouldn’t stop counting until she reached ten.’

‘Probably, your Grace .. Mr Patrickson, I don’t think I can help anymore, and I have something to work on. Is it all right for me to leave? And unless you have any objections, I would like to call at the hospital.’

‘You get off. I expect your wife would like to see you.’

‘Thank you, sir. I expect she would.’

They stood and watched as Blake put his helmet on. ‘Do you remember that case at the Old Bailey, the rogue MI5 Captain?’

‘Certainly do,’ the Duke growled. ‘Should have hanged.’

‘Blake was in his basic training at Pannal Ash, and was the arresting officer. Invested with the George Cross.’

I paused at the top of the drive and looked back. Massive sheets of flame dwarfing the west side of the House; the north-westerly wind not helping. At least a dozen fire appliances visible; blue lights everywhere. How much of the building could they save? Time to go.

Sixty-Two

The Accident Department at the QEII Hospital in York was busy. My first job to find a public telephone and call home. 'Do you know what time you'll be back?'

'Sorry, love, no. It's an hours plus ride from here so don't wait up.'

There was a snort down the line. 'Wait up? Do you know what time it is? I had to get out of bed to answer the phone.'

I looked at my watch. 23:30. 'Sorry. Forgot the time.'

'I saw the news about the fire, but they were light on possible casualties.'

The last thing Lucy needed was to hear about a six-year-old being stabbed and three other woman murdered. 'I'll fill you in tomorrow. You get back to sleep.'

'If I can. Just take care.'

I came across the four girls in the Waiting Room. 'Hello Ladies, recovering from your ordeal?'

'Mummy,' said Susan. 'That policeman's here.'

The tear-stained lady appeared from behind a screen, followed by Major Selk both hands bound.

'It was bad enough when Bertie was hit by the drapes and burned his hands. But the girls on the wrong side of the flames. It was as terrifying for us as it must have been for them. I don't know how we can thank you.'

'It's enough to know that everyone is safe. How are you, Sir.'

'Second and third degree burns to my hands. I forgot to duck,' he said and laughed. 'I won't do that again in a hurry. I can't even shake hands for the next three weeks.'

'I heard Susan address the Duke as uncle. How do I address you?'

'We are the Duke and Duchess of Keston, but after what you did today, in private, it's Bertie and Alicia, and you know the girl's names ... Now, I know as a police officer we can't give you a reward but if you like you can stay with us as our guests, I don't think that breaches police regulations.'

'That's very kind of you. I think you're correct and I'm sure Lucy would be delighted.'

She passed me a notepad. 'Just jot your contact details on there.'

Completed I handed the notepad back.

Jessica stood there her eyes like saucers. 'Can you show Mummy and Daddy how you made me float, please?'

This could be fun. He crouched. 'I'm sorry. I'm only ever allowed to do that once. That makes you *very* special.'

She puffed her chest out and grew. 'I'm special.'

'You are very special, darling,' said her mother giving her a hug.

'Now, please can you tell me where Mr Beck and Lady Carol are?'

The answer to the question was simple. Martin Beck was in theatre. Lady Carol Sylverton was in a sitting room with her younger son. The elder was in theatre. According to the doctor I spoke with, it was the toss of a coin. The next twenty-four hours would dictate whether he would live.

I tapped on the door and pushed it open. Lady Carol Sylverton was sitting on a settee with her arm round her son. She looked up. 'You're Detective Constable Blake, aren't you?'

I nodded and smiled. 'I am, your Ladyship. Do you mind if I sit?'

'Please,' she said indicating a nearby chair. 'Is this a social call?'

'In part.'

Before I had chance to say anything else her son said. 'Have you come to arrest me?'

His mother looked shocked.

Had it not been so serious and the look on the boy's face, I would have laughed. It was not appropriate. 'No, Graeme I haven't. But what on earth makes you think that I would?'

'I shot the doctor.'

'Dr Butters?'

He nodded.

'Graeme?'

'She hurt Pauline and Martin, Mummy, so I shot her.'

It was so matter of fact, just how traumatised was he? 'Do you want to tell me what happened?' I said. 'Believe me you are not in any trouble.'

'Go on, Graeme. Tell Mr Blake.'

'In your own time, Graeme,' I said

'Christine took the girls to their room and Pauline followed us into our room. She was telling us to get our pyjamas on, but we were shooting pillows instead.' He smiled at the thought.

'That sounds like fun.'

'It is,' he said.

'They have bows and arrows with suction cups, so they are safe.'

'No Mummy,' he said smiling. 'We took the cups off and sharpened them with Bard's pencil sharpener. The arrows stick in the pillows.'

His mother laughed. 'Oh, you did, did you?'

'Yes, it's more fun, 'he said and laughed.

'Then what happened?'

The door opened and Dr Butters walked in. She was carrying one of Mrs Evan's knives in her hand.'

'Then what?'

'Pauline walked towards her and said "You're supposed to be in the library. You're not allowed up here. These are family rooms." Then the doctor stabbed her and she fell down. Is Pauline dead?'

'I'm sorry,' I said. 'She is.'

'We liked Pauline. She was nice. Then Martin said, "I'm the Earl this is my room and my brother's, get out.'

'I know you are,' she said and stabbed Martin. So, I shot her.'

'You hit her?'

He nodded. 'Here, in the shoulder,' Graeme pointed to his right upper chest. 'The arrow stuck in.'

'Did she say anything?'

'She yelped and stepped backwards and sat in the chair behind the door.'

'She didn't say anything else?'

'No. Martin was crying and moaning so I put his head on my knee. She started to get up, so I nocked another arrow and she sat down.'

'Did you say anything?'

'No.'

'What happened then, darling?'

Graeme smiled at his mother. 'I drew the bow in case she tried to stab me. Then the door opened. Bard was standing there looking at us. He stepped inside and before I could fire, she leaned forwards and stabbed him in his leg. I fired again. This time the arrow stuck in her left shoulder. She called me a little bastard. What does that mean?'

'It's just a nasty word that adults sometimes use. Don't worry about it.'

'Then the girls arrived and started screaming ... Then you arrived.'

'You're a very brave little boy,' I said. But would anybody believe him?

Sixty-Three

I was on babysitting duty. The countess had gone to speak with the ffford-Selks.

'There's a bookcase over there,' I said, pointing. 'Do you like to read?'

Graeme nodded. 'Mmm. I like adventure stories.'

'Let me see.' I walked across the room, 'There's one here, Danger in Deep Space by Carey Rockwell. That sounds exciting. Would you like me to read some of it to you?'

'Please.'

I leant back in the easy chair with Graeme perched on my knee, my arm round him. 'Comfortable?'

He nodded.

'Sorry, can't hear a nod.'

He giggled. 'Yes.'

'Good. Pin back your ears,' I said to more giggles. "Chapter 1: "*Stand by to reduce thrust on main drive rockets!" The tall broad-shouldered officer in the uniform of the Solar Guard snapped out the order as he watched the telescanner screen and saw the Western Hemisphere of Earth looming larger and larger ...*

Graeme's head slumped. His rhythmic breathing telling me he wasn't listening anymore. *That didn't last very long. Still.* I closed the book and put it on a neighbouring table. *Sleep, you've earned it.*

'Countess.'

She turned round. 'Mr Patrickson, any news from the House.'

'The chief fire officer assured me the fire was under control and out within the hour.'

'Thank goodness for that.'

'Your father is holding the fort.'

'As always.'

'This is Detective Superintendent Creighton and Detective Inspector Cartwright. They're looking for their colleague, Detective Constable Blake.'

'He's down here, gentlemen. Looking after my son.'

I heard DI Cartwright's voice well before they reached the door.

'They're in here,' the Countess pushed the door open.

'I'll bet he's fast asleep,' said DI Cartwright. 'Ha! what did I tell you?'

I put my finger to my lips. 'Shh.'

'Has anyone got a camera?' said DS Creighton.

'I have,' I didn't know the voice. A man stepped forward, a PRESS badge round his neck. 'Would you mind?'

'As long as I get a copy.'

'I'll see you all do. Just close your eyes.'

Graeme stirred and settled down. 'All done. It will be in tomorrow's Post.'

I changed places with the Countess. 'Thank you so much,' she said.

'You're welcome. He's deserved his sleep after what he told us.'

'... That's what he told you?'

'Yes sir, and backed-up by what Martin Beck said. So?'

'Unbelievable. Then when we trace this mysterious academic, she should have two minor wounds, one to each shoulder?'

'Yes sir.'

When I said goodbye to Lord and Lady fforde-Selk neither Martin Sylverton nor Martin Beck had returned from theatre.

Lucy flinched as I put my arm under her neck. 'You smell of smoke and you're cold. Go away.'

'You're nice and warm. Come here.'

'Brian, you're freezing. That's cruelty and grounds for divorce.'

'I know. I think we should get warm.'

'I already am warm. Or at least I was.'

My right hand fully occupied I slid my left across her belly.

'What ... ?'

'You're forgiven. Even if it is nearly two.'

'Were you worried?'

'Peter called me. Said you were making urgent enquiries in North Yorkshire because the phones were out. He was a bit light on detail. I saw the northern news on the telly and assumed that's where you were when you hadn't come home. Now you smell of smoke. It looked horrendous.'

'It was and could have been a lot worse.'

'Want to talk about it? Or can't you?'

'I'll have my photo in the newspapers tomorrow.'

'You will? But why?' I felt her hand sliding south. 'That's a good reason to celebrate; seeing we're awake.'

Sixty-Four

Carol stroked the hair out of her son's eyes. 'Good morning, darling,' she said. 'Did you sleep?'

Graeme yawned. 'A little bit, Mummy. Is the house going to fall down?'

She laughed. 'No. The West Wing will have to be re-built. The library was destroyed. One or two pictures that belonged to Lord Gordon are burnt. Other than that. . .'

'Where did that nice policeman go.'

'Home. He lives about eighty miles from here. And he has a wife and little girl. Did you like him reading to you.'

Graeme nodded. 'Is Martin better?'

'Not yet. He's very poorly. I've spoken to the doctors; they told me that he is comfortable. When you've had your breakfast, we're going to see him.'

Sixty-Five

'Shouldn't we go and confront the Reids with what we know, sir?'

'No, Priestly. We don't know how this information fits into the investigation.'

'That's where Blake is? But Sergeant Ryder is still here. Surely, you're not letting him do this on his own?'

'That's just what I am doing. He is very thorough, and I trust him.'

I completed my call to St James's College. They promised to fax the information regarding Dr Robertshaw to Force Control for my information.

There was a problem. I was checking the details of Emily Reid's misper and the murder file I'd recorded previously. I hadn't noticed before but there was a variance in Emily Reid's date of birth. I called Millgarth and arranged to view both files.

Sure enough the misper report showed Emily Reid's date of birth as June 17th 1941 , the report taken by a PC Mulligan. The murder file, June 19th 1941, statement taken by the then Detective Sergeant Giles. Both documents signed by Margaret Reid, Emily's mother.

Was either of these a simple mistake when the officer wrote it down? Or had Margaret Reid made the mistake? But what mother doesn't know the date of birth of her child?

Yesterday's comment, reputedly made by Dr Butters, flashed into my brain: "I think it's fair. First born for first born" The questions queueing up were legion. There was only one way to find out.

'Sorry DC Blake, but there are no births registered by Frederick Reid.'

This was bizarre. 'None at all? ... In that case would you check for a marriage certificate in the same name, wife's name is Margaret. I don't know her maiden name'

She came back several minutes later. 'Yes, we have a record of a marriage between Frederick Reid and Margaret Butters on June 13th 1936.'

I had to smile. 'Butters?'

'Yes, there is a problem?'

'Not at all. Could I have a copy please?'

Time to play what if. Did Margaret have a sister? Younger or older? That would account for the comment about first borns. Single estranged mother with child brought up by sister and her husband, using the sister's surname and not the birth mother's name?

'This is a long shot. Would you check for children born to an Adrienne Robertshaw or Katherine Butters. I would think around ... 1941?'

She returned ten minutes later. There is nothing for Adrienne Robertshaw. However,' she smiled, 'Katherine Butters registered the birth of a girl child, born on June 18th, on June 24th. I've taken the liberty of printing them both off for you.'

She slid them across the counter.

'The birth certificate was on top. 'Good God,' I said when I read the details.

'So, they tell us,' came back the reply across the counter. 'A surprise?'

'Very much so,' I said. 'Will the library have copies of the National Censuses?'

'Yes, they do. They're on microfiche.'

'Thank you. That's very helpful.'

'Countess, I must counsel against your son seeing his brother under these circumstances. There is no telling what the sight of him under these circumstances might do for his mental state.'

'Mr Yarnal, I understand your concern. However, Graeme witnessed the murder of the maid seeing them to bed and the stabbing of his brother with the same knife.

Seeing Martin alive having survived the operation must be beneficial. They are identical twins and joined not only at the hip, but at the heart and head as well. He wants to read to him not play hunt the thimble. Sir Clive Weatherill is en route from Harley Street. If you refuse, I will ask him to arrange a transfer to a private facility.'

'Very well, Countess. But I don't think we have any books suitable for a six-year-old.'

'Oh, he's found one in that bookcase in the sitting room down the corridor.'

'They're not for six-year-olds.'

'They are for this one, Mr Yarnal.'

'Yes, officer. Censuses for 1921, 1939 and 1951 are on microfiche, are you familiar with them?'

'From university. But the 1931 Census?'

'Sorry, no. Destroyed by fire in 1942. But you can always try the Town Hall. They will have historic copies of the Electoral Registers.'

'Thank you, but they won't have records of children below voting age.'

'That is correct.'

They stood in silence taking in the sight of Martin, covers round his waist the leads to the ECG clearly visible.

Graeme pointed at the monitor. 'Does that tell you Martin is still alive?'

'It does,' said Sister Perkin. 'It's a long name, it's called an Electrocardiogram; we call them ECGs. Every one of those pulses on the screen is Martin's heart beating. Would you like a copy to show him when he comes home.'

He nodded. 'Yes, please.'

The Sister pressed the button for five seconds tore the trace off and handed it to Graeme. 'There, you've got your own record now.'

'Look, Mummy. Martin's heart beating.'

'So it is. We can put this in your bedroom later.'

'Can I read to Martin, now, please?'

'Of course you can. We have some books here,' said Sister Perkins indicating several books on a bedside table.

'Noddy and Big Ears? But they're for babies. I've got one here, it's an adventure story. Will he be able to hear me?'

'I don't know,' said the Sister smiling at him. 'We have given him something to help him sleep. If he can it might be a bit like a dream. All right?'

'Yes, thank you.'

'This is Sally,' she said as a young nurse entered. 'She will be with you whilst you're here.'

'Hello, can I call you, Graeme?'

He nodded, sat down and opened the book before taking hold of Martin's hand.

'Pin back your ears, Martin,' he said, glanced at his mother and giggled. 'It's what that policeman said to me.' he said and turned to his brother, *'Danger in Deep Space .. Chapter 1: Stand by to reduce thrust on main drive rockets! ...'*

Sister Perkins whispered to Carol. 'He's very good, especially for his age. He's even got Sally paying attention, which is not easy.'

'They both began reading when they were two years old. It's progressed from there.'

'Two? And you can see how close they are.'

'Identical twins and inseparable. He'll be lost without his brother. How long before he will be back to normal?'

'Well, there was internal damage. He had a catheter fitted because his bowel was cut. It has been repaired but it is very serious.'

Bard shot his arm round Carol's waist. 'Whoa, steady on. You ok.'

'Yes,' she said. 'It was hearing the words. Bowel problems are the sort of thing you read about involving the elderly, not six year olds.'

'Last night's operation was to clean his abdomen. When he wakes he's going to be sore.'

He picked the phone up at the third ring. 'DI Cartwright.'

'DC Blake, sir.'

'We thought you'd emigrated. What have you got?'

'How about, Emily Reid never existed.'

'Pardon?'

I had to smile. 'The Reid's are childless. There is no Emily Reid.'

'You'd better get back here, smart. I'll inform the Super.'

They stared at me in disbelief. 'And you'd better see this, sir.' I handed him the envelope containing the copy birth certificate.

DS Creighton blew out slowly. Without any comment he passed the birth certificate to DI Cartwright. 'But he carried out the enquiries into the misper report and took the statement for the murder file from Margaret Reid. He obviously didn't know.'

'And still doesn't,' added the Superintendent

'Either that or he's the best actor this country has ever produced,' I said. 'But I'm sure there's a photo of him in military uniform in his office.'

'Yet, he's shown as a police constable.

'An estrangement?' I said. 'Maybe she didn't tell him.'

'Single woman in wartime, Brian? Bearing in mind they both hail from Leeds and the birth registered in Leeds? It must have been something pretty drastic for that to happen.'

'We can play guessing games all day long. What do we do next?' the Superintendent was looking straight at me. 'This is bloody good work. What do *you* think we should do next?'

That caught me on the hop. 'Thank you, sir ... But there's this as well. It arrived at force control from St James College, yesterday evening.'

'What is it?'

'Dr Robertshaw's notes regarding the hunting practices of various southern African tribes. They use insect larvae. Without an antidote they can be fatal.'

He handed the notes back to Blake. 'That changes things. Continue with what you were saying.'

'We should visit the Reid's and invite DI Giles, but not inform him of what we know.'

'Spring it on him? That seems a bit cruel.'

'At the moment, sir, we don't know what he knows. We might get more truth with a sudden release of information.'

'Right, Peter, call Mr Giles and tell him that we are going to the Reids as a matter of some urgency. Would he meet us there. I will contact DI Priestly.'

They pulled up outside the Magnolias to be met by DI Giles. 'A little bit mysterious, sir.'

'It all stems from that fire at Oldeney, in the North Riding, yesterday.'

The DI furrowed his brow. 'They are all connected; the four murders and the fire?'

'Yes, but don't forget the Met officer, Cameron. There were three further murders and an attempted murder at Oldeney.'

Before DI Giles could respond the superintendent knocked at the door. Frederick Reid answered. Took one look and stepped back. 'We've been expecting you. Better come in. First door on the left.'

There was a good fire in the grate, but the atmosphere was chilly. Except for one thing, it hadn't changed since I was last here with Sergeant Ryder. Margaret Reid was sitting on the sofa and joined by Frederick; they held hands. The difference being the lady standing adjacent to the fireplace. Facially resembling Margeret Reid but with a tired and strained expression. A point of interest being the spreading dark stain on her green dress just below her left shoulder.

She watched us with interest and smiled. 'Hello, Michael. It's been a long time.'

The shock on Detective Inspector Giles's face was palpable. 'Katherine? But ...'

DS Creighton glanced over his shoulder. 'Blake?'

'Sir,' I turned to face the female we were looking for. 'You're Katherine Adrienne Robertshaw nee Butters?'

'Who are you?'

'Detective Constable Blake.'

'Well Detective Constable Blake, for your information, yes, I am. But five of you, what is this, a party?'

'I have to caution you,' I said. 'You are not obliged to say anything but anything you do say may be put into writing and given in evidence.'

DS Creighton handed DI Giles the birth certificate. 'I think you had better read this.'

A puzzled detective inspector began to absorb the details.

'Why the confusion, Michael? It's quite simple. I thought we had something special. We were engaged to be married. It was wartime.

We slept together and I became pregnant. I wrote to tell you, and you didn't answer. You dumped me.'

'We did have something special,' DI Giles protested. 'But on the date on this birth certificate I was in the Military Police. I wrote to you, gave you my service address. I knew you were involved in something secret so I sent the letters to Margaret so she could forward them.'

The realisation spread across her face. 'You mean you didn't receive anything from me?'

'Not a thing. As for dumping you. I love you as much now as I did then. I have two failed marriages because I couldn't get you out of my head.'

Katherine Butters glared at her sister. 'You didn't forward any of our letters. Why? What did you do with them?

Margaret Reid stared at the floor.

'She read them and burned them,' said Frederick. 'I did tell her.'

'Why didn't *you* write to us. We could have been married with a family instead of what we had. I sent you money to help with the expense. I even let you bring her up as your own, using your surname instead of mine ... Well, answer me, you sanctimonious bitch.' There was no reply.

She turned her glare to her brother-in-law. 'You knew what was happening, Fred. If Margaret refused to do anything, why didn't you? Why didn't you write to me or just contact Michael? Or was this a conspiracy to steal my, our, daughter? Why?'

'Margaret can't have children.' He said in a flat voice.

'That's an excuse? When did you find that out? Or was it a private message from God?'

'There's no need to blaspheme. She went to the doctors.'

'When?'

'Twelve months after we were wed.'

‘So, when I told you my news, you decided you would have mine and Michael’s child?’

‘No, it wasn’t like that.’

‘Well, what was it like? Michael and I had been writing to each other once a week for three months before the doctor confirmed I was pregnant. I told you straight away but after that not one single letter that either of us posted got through. Well, they couldn’t, could they? My beloved sister saw to that. Did she read them before she burned them?

Reid nodded. ‘Yes, she did.’

She turned on her sister and snapped. ‘You bitch. You planned this didn’t you? When you got my news, you hatched the plan. You couldn’t have a child so you decided you would do the sisterly thing when it was born and offer to raise it. Emily, as it happens.

A silence settled on the room.

I glanced over my shoulder. ‘Sir, this is looking like a section 56.’[*2]

‘I agree. Don’t do anything yet.’ I nodded.

DI Giles broke the silence. ‘You mean the Emily on the birth certificate is the Emily Reid who was reported missing?”

‘Yes, Michael, and we know who murdered her.’

‘If you’re meaning Martin Beck, no we don’t. I carried out the enquiries and there was nothing to suggest foul play.’

‘Doctor,’ DS Creighton interjected. ‘When the tape you made of Lewis Green or Martin Beck was received, I gave instructions to have the area around Eccup reservoir searched. Five full days. First on foot and then ground penetrating radar. There is not and never has been any bodies buried there. But what makes you so certain?’

‘They admitted it.’

‘Excuse me, sir,’ I said. ‘I’d like to ask, is it Dr Butters or Dr Robertshaw? A question.'

DS Creighton nodded.

DI Priestly tapped him on his elbow. 'Sir, Blake? Is this wise?'

'Let him run with it, for now.'

'It's Robertshaw.'

'Who are *they*, Dr Robertshaw?'

'All of them.'

'That's Neville Waters, William Boxley, Martin Beck, Charles Nash and Patrick Newsam.'

'Yes. Beck was the last.'

'And Boxley was first?'

'Yes, why.'

'Will you tell us how you met Boxley?'

She shrugged her shoulders. 'It won't make any difference now. At a conference in York. We were in adjacent seats. During a coffee break I overheard him talking to another delegate, Patrick Newsam. They were talking in a huddle. I couldn't hear everything but they were talking about my daughter on the night she disappeared.'

'So, you decided to intervene? Was that with your two colleagues, Blaise Lincoln and Patrick Smith?

'I don't know how you found out, but yes.'

'Who did you meet first?'

'Patrick. I was in Leeds and went to the Pimlico Club. I was on my own, my husband died several years ago and I was looking for some company. We got chatting. He was amusing. He told me he was an ex-police officer; some of the tales he told me were very funny. Then he told me about Beck and their sex parties; seven years of suppressed hatred released,' she said with a grim smile. 'About Blaise and Kevin Sharpe. I determined to use him, so we spent the night together, or most of it.' I could feel DI Giles's eyes boring into my back. 'He introduced me to Blaise.'

'You knew how to contact Boxley, but what about the others?'

'Patrick still had friends in the police.'

'And he got you the information?'

'He said it would be easy. It wasn't as easy as he suggested, but yes.'

'And you used the same compound which was based on curare and the preparations used by the San tribesmen of Namibia to knock them out.'

Dr Robertshaw bristled. 'How on earth did you know that?'

'Someone with similar interests was at a conference in Edinburgh where you were a speaker. The information he gave us led us to St James's College. Your dual identity and, Dr Stringer. He sent me your notes.'

You could cut the silence with a knife.

'When the victims came round and found themselves trussed as we saw them, how did they react?'

'Like frightened children. Crying and trying to fight their way out of the chair.'

'Is there any wonder?' I said. 'Boxley was the first victim. I know this is painful talking about your daughter in this manner, sir, but can you remember who he had sex with?'

'Boxley? That was Emily.'

'Did they stay with the same partner or play musical beds.'

'No, they were consistent in their statements. They kept one partner for the evening ... Just a minute. If that is so and Boxley was the first victim, why were the others killed and all the blame heaped on Beck?'

'Yes, sir. That is a good question .. Well Doctor? You had the man you blamed for the so-called murder of your daughter, why pursue the rest?'

There was no reply.

'Let's consider a different question. There is nothing we have been told to suggest that you are by nature a violent person. In fact, as a woman in a man's world and working in a foreign country with tribesmen used to killing wild animals, not only for food but defence, and your protection, you have to be thoughtful and caring to get them to accept you and to show you what you want to know. On the other hand, the violence exhibited in these murders is extreme. My question is: who drove the agenda? In fact, whose agenda was it? We know what the statements say. You've heard what DI Giles has said. So, which amongst you hated Martin Beck?'

'I don't understand what you mean.'

'Yes Doctor, you do. You know exactly what I mean. Whoever it was, you, Patrick Smith or Blaise Lincoln, you did not ask who killed Emily because the answer would have been, no-one. Yet, you state they all, except Beck, claimed that he did. From the injuries, it appears at the point of a knife. Or was it the threat to emasculate them? In fact, you extracted a confession from Beck to that effect at the point of a knife. We have Martin Beck's statement and the tape you sent. I'll ask again. Who wanted Beck to be named? Which of you hated Martin Beck?'

'Blaise hadn't the stomach for it. In fact, he was sickened by the whole thing.'

'So, Dr. was it you or Smith?'

'Patrick Smith,' she said, 'Although why I don't know.'

'Inspector Giles does. Sir?'

His voice was terse. 'Katherine, Smith is my son-in-law.'

'Seriously, Michael? I'm sorry I had no idea.'

'On the evening of this sex-party there was a bit of a confrontation outside the Locarno involving Beck and a Teddy Boy, Kevin Sharpe and his friends, when Sharpe grabbed hold of a well-spoken young woman. Beck and his friends stepped in. Patrick Smith was watching, holding hands with one of the typists; one of his bits on the side. He'd told my daughter he was visiting his brother in Tadcaster. Emily turned up and asked if she could join the party to avoid Sharpe, although, at the time, no one knew about Sharpe raping her.

'I interviewed Beck. Smith was present when Beck recalled seeing Smith with the typist, obviously together. Needless to say, I wasn't happy. The culmination being that Smith resigned from the police. He blamed Beck and initiated a campaign against him to such an extent that Beck changed his name to Green. That's the reason why.'

'I am so sorry.'

'How did you get Smith and Lincoln to go along with you?' I said.

'When Smith told me about Emily and Beck's sex party, I told him that I was Emily's aunt. He provided me with a lot more information. I asked him if he would help me to do what the police hadn't.'

'Did you say anything about murder?'

'Don't be stupid, Of course not.'

'But they went along with you?'

'Yes, Smith did a good job of winding Lincoln up. It was Lincoln who suggested writing to Beck, or Green as he was then. It was he who did the research at Huddersfield and sending the letter purported to be signed by Granville Rodahl. The occupants of Seven Oaks Fold were only too pleased to be involved. Put a bit of variety into their humdrum lives.'

'You did the typing?'

'Yes.'

'Who taped the victims into the chairs?'

'Smith. Very professional.'

'How did Lincoln react to the kidnap, trussing of the victims and what followed?'

'He wasn't impressed when Smith used his stiletto. But it was too late. He was compromised and went along. That's when he decided to emigrate.'

'Did either react when you carried out your threat to remove their penis and testicles and then sew them into their mouths?'

'Lincoln was shocked. Smith thought the episode funny.'

'But neither objected?'

'No. Lincoln was pleased when I decided not to do the same to Beck. Smith not so. I got the impression he wanted to finish the job. Then the police arrived.'

She put her hand in her pocket and removed a snap-shut case. Opened it and removed a hypodermic syringe and fixed the needle. 'I hope you know what this is.'

'It's lethal,' I said. 'Don't worry. I'm not going to try and take it from you.'

She smiled. 'Very wise.'

'Where did you obtain the sack-wheels and Windsor chairs?'

'That was Smith, he had contacts through his business.'

'Thank you. And you carried out the torture and Smith inserted the knife through the ribs?'

'Yes, Smith did the stabbing of the undergraduates; I did the rest.'

'He killed all four?'

'If the knife is what killed them, then yes.'

'You do realise, Doctor' said DS Creighton. 'That evidence obtained by torture is not admissible in court, however if you hadn't killed them, we would have been able to question them again. But now?'

There was no reply.

DS Creighton turned to his right. 'Mr Cartwright, find Smith. Take Sergeant Ryder and another half dozen. Goodall and Smith are firearms trained and armed.'

'Sir,' he said and left.

'I'll go with him, sir.'

'No Mr Giles, you are too closely engaged. You will stay here with me. Blake, caution the Reids, we will interview them tomorrow.'

'Sir,' I turned to the Reids. 'Frederick Reid, Margaret Reid, you are not obliged to say anything but whatever you say will be taken down in writing and may be given in evidence. You will be interviewed tomorrow regarding possible offences under Section 56 of the Offences Against the Persons Act 1861. Section 56 relates to child stealing. Have you anything to say?'

They remained silent.

'And the Doctor.'

'Sir. Katherine Robertshaw, you are not obliged to say anything unless you wish to do so but whatever you say will be taken down in writing and given in evidence. I am arresting you for the murder of William Boxley.'

'But?'

'It's called acting in concert. As far as the law is concerned you are just as guilty .. Now, why the three servants?'

She laughed down her nose. 'Wrong place, wrong time. The old woman in the cellar threatened to tell her son, whoever he was. She wouldn't stop. The other heard the conversation and came to investigate. As I said, wrong place, wrong time.

'The one in the bedroom? She wanted to be the hero. Stepped in front of His Lordship,' she said with a sneer. 'It had to be done. Then he opened his mouth and, well. It was fair, first born for a first born.'

'The last I heard the Earl was alive.'

'That's impossible.'

I opened my pocketbook and showed it to Frederick Reid. 'Ring that number will you, Mr Reid? Tell them you're calling on behalf of Detective Superintendent Creighton. Ask them how Martin Sylverton, the Earl of Oldeney is progressing, please.'

'I see. Thank you,' he said and replaced the phone. 'He regained consciousness ten minutes ago. His mother and family are with him.'

Katherine Robertshaw looked bleak. 'What about Lincoln?'

'We will deal with him in due course, Doctor,' said DS Creighton. 'Are you going to put that needle down?'

'No,' she said and turned to her sister. 'You really are a sanctimonious bitch, Margaret. The criticism I received from you because I was pregnant out of wedlock. But what you did? Michael and I would have married long before Emily was born. *None* of this would have happened at all if you hadn't interfered with the letters that Michael and I wrote to each other. Yes, I've done some terrible things, but it all stems from what *you* did. You two are as guilty as I am. I hope you rot in Hell!'

She stepped back and sighed. 'I'm tired. It's time to end it,' she said as she turned towards us, lifted the needle placing the point against her neck. 'It could have been so different, Michael, but I'm not going to prison.'

As Katherine Robertshaw pushed the needle into her neck and depressed the plunger Michael Giles screamed and threw himself across the room. I got my arm round him and with DS Creighton pulled him back. Within seconds Katherine Robertshaw was dead.

Frederick and Margaret Reid watched impassively.

Beck

Sixty-Six

The ECG displayed sinus rhythm. The heart rate elevated. The signs were promising.

Two nurses, Sally and Anne were sitting to one side as Graeme, holding Martin's hand, continued his reading. "*By the blessed rings of Saturn," exclaimed Connel, "it's almost too good to be true! ...* "*[1]

Graeme stopped reading. Martin's hand tightened its grip. His eyes flickered open. He smiled. 'Where's Mummy?'

'I'll find her,' said Graeme and dashed for the door. The policeman in the corridor outside stepped to one side and smiled. 'Steady on now, you'll trip.'

Sally smiled down at Martin. Who would have thought anyone so small could be an Earl. And why on earth would anyone want to hurt him. 'Hello, I'm Sally. Is it all right to call you, Martin?'

He looked up at her face and nodded. 'You're pretty.'

'Thank you,' she said and smiled. 'And you're a heart-breaker. Would you like to sit up?'

'Yes, please.'

'No,' she said as Martin tried to get his elbows underneath and winced. 'Don't try to do it by yourself. Leave it to us. You're going to be sore for a while. Anne?'

'My, you're a big boy for six,' said Anne as they supported him and extended the backrest.

'I'm nearly seven,' he protested.

'That's all right then,' said Anne as they grinned at each other and laid him back.

'Better?'

'Yes, thank you,' he said the sound of running feet caught his attention. 'That's Graeme's voice.'

'Thank you, officer,' Carol, pushing Bard in a wheelchair and accompanied by Graeme swept through the open door.

'Hello Darling,' she said as she sat. 'How do you feel?'

'Hungry and sore. What happened to me?'

'What do you remember?'

'Just Doctor Butters standing in the doorway ....'

Bard slid his arm round Graeme's waist. 'Are you all right?'

He nodded.

'No bad dreams?'

'I kept waking up, but I can't remember anything.'

'If you do get any bad dreams or you remember any of what you dreamt last night, tell me or Mummy.'

He nodded again and looked grim. 'Is Martin going to die?'

Bard laughed. 'When he's a very old man. If you look at the machine on the other side of his bed you can see his heart is beating normally.'

'I don't understand. If they switch the machine off will his heart stop?'

'No, it just measures the heartbeat. He's fine,' Bard crossed his metaphorical fingers. 'That book you were reading to Martin; can I see it?'

Graeme handed it over.

'Danger in Deep Space. Is this from the hospital?'

'The policeman who was with you in the bedroom found it and read it to me.'

'Mr Blake, he's a detective. He read it to you?'

'Yes, then I fell asleep. When I woke up, he wasn't there.

'No, he would be very busy. This is a Tom Corbett Space Cadet book. I've got a box of old books in the attic. I forgot about them. If you like, I'll call my father to dig them out.'

'Are they adventure stories?'

'All of ...'

'I DON'T WANT IT. TAKE IT AWAY,' Martin's raised voice drowning out the conversation.

'But Martin.'

'Mummy, please make them take it away. I don't like it.'

Sally leapt from her chair. 'Excuse me Countess,' she said easing Carol to one side, knelt, held Martin's hand and stroked his forehead. 'Martin, it's all right. Even adults are frightened when they have one of these. But it won't last forever.'

Martin sniffed. 'But why is it there?'

'When that lady attacked you,'

'It was Dr Butters. What did she do?'

'She stabbed you in the tummy.' Sally saw the look of fear in his eyes. 'No, she is not coming back. We have a policeman on the door and there are lots more looking for her. You are quite safe. Besides we have a big sign on the hospital doors saying, NO DOCTOR BUTTERS ALLOWED.'

Martin giggled and winced.

'Inside our tummies, and we all have them, is a long tube called intestines. A small intestine and a big one called a colon. When you eat and drink it goes into your stomach and then into the small intestine where all the goodness is taken out. What's left we pass out of our bottoms. When she stabbed you, it damaged your colon. The doctors had to operate to make it better. So, for the time being you have to have this contraption. But it will be reversed and no-one will ever know. So, will you be brave for me?'

He nodded. 'Yes.'

'Good boy,' she smiled. 'I want my heart-breaker back. I'll hand you back to your mummy.'

She stood, turned, raised her eyebrows and exhaled.

Carol put her hand on Sally's arm. 'Thank you,' she said and frowned. 'But, heart-breaker?'

'My pleasure, Countess,' she said and smiled, 'He's an Earl, six years old and told me I was pretty. It doesn't bode well for the fairer sex when he's a few years older.'

Blake

Sixty-Seven

'Morning Linda, what's happening?'

'Patrick, what the hell have you been up to?

'Nothing, why?'

'Why? Because the police have been here with a search warrant. A DI Cartwright and a DS Ryder with half a dozen other coppers. They turned the house, including the attic, shed and garage, upside-down. They took loads of stuff away. Why?'

Sweat began to run down his forehead. 'Buggered if I know, love. Did they say anything?'

'Just that if you rang, I should tell you to contact them.'

'DI Cartwright?'

'That's the name he gave me. Where are you going next?'

'Bernie's, for a think. I'll be in touch.'

The line went dead. She wrote the address down and handed the note to DI Cartwright. 'This is his brother Bernie's address. His bolthole. If he's where I think he is, he's got a bit on the side at Hipperholme, it will take him about twenty minutes.'

'Thank you, Mrs Smith. It can't have been easy.'

'It gets easier every time he goes to screw that bitch, Inspector. I've forgiven him so many times I've lost count.'

'Anything further on Mr Giles, sir?' said DS Creighton.

'I've spoken with Mr Carlisle and Giles is in a psychiatric ward under sedation. Whatever baggage he was carrying round was released when he heard the revelations and saw the lady who, by all accounts, would have been his wife, make the confession and commit suicide in front of him. The suggestion was that he remain on sick leave for the next three months when he will have enough time in to be retired on a full medical pension.'

'Under the circumstances that's only fair.'

'Agreed. Now Mr Creighton, Blake. Do you consider him ready for promotion?'

'If he's as good with men as he is with the job, sir, then he must be close. I've known sergeants and above with far more service who couldn't boil an egg without instructions. Blake doesn't suffer from that particular malady. But,' he paused and smiled, 'there's only one way to find out ... And from what I've heard he did very well in his promotion exam, and had he not had a ruptured appendix could well have made it onto the Special Course. In which case we would already know the answer to the question.'

'He was in the top five nationally,' said Mr Barton.

'With that service it's still sink or swim?' added ACC Mithering with a laugh. 'But he's a tendency to be too far the other way.'

'I agree,' said the chief constable. 'He can be impetuous but he's not afraid to make decisions.' The phone began to ring. 'Just a moment.' He picked the phone from the cradle. 'Barton ... Yes Professor, he's here ... Professor Snodgrass for you, Mr. Creighton.'

'Yes, Professor, what can I do for you?'

> 'More like what I can do for you, Superintendent. You are aware that Frederick and Margaret Reid committed suicide overnight?'
>
> 'Yes, they gassed themselves. Is there a problem?'

'More like a medical condition you may never have come across and may throw some light on your case. If you can get here within the next twenty minutes?'

ACC Mithering, DS Creighton and me were standing round the two dissection slabs. 'Margaret Reid had perfectly normal sex organs with one variation that you rarely see in a married woman. She was virgo intacta.'

'Professor,' I said. 'She told us that she couldn't have children.'

'Subject to some underlying medical condition she was capable of bearing children. However,' he removed the sheet from Frederick Reid's body. 'Her husband is a different matter. *Anorchia.* Under normal circumstances the embryo develops sex organs in the first few weeks of pregnancy. Mr Reid was born without testes. And in his case, it is known as *congenital anorchia* or, *vanishing testes syndrome.* The testes disappeared between 12- and 14-weeks gestation. As evidenced by the presence of penis and scrotum.

'Had his testes begun to develop perhaps 8 weeks into gestation, he would have been born a male child but with the sexual organs of a female.

'And, had the testes disappeared between 8 and 10 weeks he would have been born with *ambiguous genitalia*, meaning he would have had parts of both male and female sex organs.'

'An hermaphrodite?' I said.

'Exactly.'

'This will be in your report, Professor?'

'In full, Mr. Creighton.'

'It appears,' said DS Creighton, 'that Margaret Reid wanted children but never resorted to sexual activity outside of her marriage. She took the opportunity, whatever the circumstances to manipulate her sister's pregnancy and control the flow of information between Mr Giles and her sister, in order to acquire what she could not produce herself and with the full knowledge and complicity of her husband.'

Sixty-Eight

I was en route to hospital in York and maybe Oldeney, if the Countess and Martin Beck weren't there, to explain the present situation. DS Creighton didn't want the information passing over the phone.

In the meantime, DI Cartwright and Sergeant Ryder would be interviewing Patrick Smith.

I had a quick word with Martin Beck, giving him the basics before moving onto his namesake.

The Countess's father was present keeping his grandson occupied with tales of derring-do about his military exploits. After he had tried to dislocate my right shoulder for my actions at Oldeney Carr House and my visit to the Palace, I was making my excuses when his grandson said. 'Do you ride a motorbike?'

I smiled at him. 'Yes, I do.'

'Can I have a ride, please?'

'Once the doctors say that it's safe and your mother agrees. But it will be a while before you are well enough.'

'I know,' he said and hung his head.

'Better still,' I said. 'How would you like to drive a racing car. Perhaps race against your Grandfather?'

His eyes lit up. 'Oh yes. Can I?'

'I'll have to arrange it. But yes. It shouldn't be a problem.'

'Steady on, officer. That's going a bit far isn't it?'

'You've heard of go-carts, Sir.'

'Those little things that zip around as you trail your backside on the floor?'

'The same,' I said and laughed. 'My wife's mother owns the Spartans and they have a go-cart track at Tadcaster. Obviously it will be some time but a bit of adventure will be good for them all.'

'Are my grandsons old enough?'

'As long as they're six. Something for them to look forward to.'

'Well, if you think so.'

I turned back to Martin. 'Now, you've got to be a good boy, do exactly what the nurses say and eat all your food.'

'Oh, I will. Can Graeme race as well?'

I smiled at the expectation on the little boy's face. 'Of course he can. And the girls.'

His face clouded over. 'Girls?' he said. 'What do they know?'

'I think you would be surprised.' I said and smiled.

'Can we have a quiet word, officer.'

'You would like to know the present situation?'

'As much as you can tell me.'

'In truth it's a tragic and unnecessary story, Sir. All I can tell you at the moment is that Dr Butters committed suicide. So, there is no further risk to the family.'

'I can tell my grandsons?'

'You can, sir. Although, after what he's been through it might be better to tell him that she is simply in police custody. I will inform your daughter when I get to Oldeney.

I waved to the young Earl. Shook hands with his grandfather and left.

Showing my warrant card to the officer on the gates of Oldeney Carr House I paused for a few seconds to take in the view from the crest. The first time I'd seen the House in daylight. Even with the fire-damage it was magnificent. There was one fire appliance present. No trace of any smoke.

Inside was a hive of activity orchestrated by the Countess. 'Oh, I'm pleased you're here,' she said. 'I wanted to thank you properly for what you did. In the Drawing Room there is fresh tea and coffee. Help yourself and I will join you shortly.'

Fifteen minutes later. 'Sorry to have kept you, Mr Blake, what can I do for you? Oh, and it's Carol when we're in a family group. My father would not approve but I'm trying to drag the family into the 20th century.'

'Thank you. In that case my name is Brian, but please not when other officers are present .. There are a couple of things and one of them is for your younger son. And I would also like to tell him that Dr. Butters is in police custody and no longer a threat .. The truth, Carol, is that she committed suicide in front of me and other officers. But I don't think your son needs to be reminded about such things, bearing in mind what he witnessed.'

'I agree. He's lost without his brother and presently grooming his pony.'

'His eyes lit up like fireworks. 'Racing cars, yes please. Can we, Mummy?'

'I suppose so. But it will be some time before Martin can go.'

His head dropped. 'I know.'

'Carol, have they given you any idea how long it will be before Martin can come home?

'No date, but it will be weeks rather than days.'

Sixty-Nine

In spite of the recent lick of paint the atmosphere in the interview room was oppressive; still retaining faint aromas of sweat, unwashed bodies and fear. The same battered table and uncomfortable chairs.

DI Cartwright and DS Ryder sat opposite Patrick Smith who was giving the outward impression of calmness. Inside he was anything but. Blaise Lincoln could have said anything. Adrienne had too much to lose by shooting her mouth off.

'Patrick Smith,' began DS Ryder. 'You are not obliged to say anything but whatever you say will be taken down in writing and may be given in evidence.'

'Yes, I know the caution.'

'You know why you're here?'

'Some bollocks about suspicion of murder.'

'You think murder is bollocks, do you?'

'No I don't, so don't try to put words in my mouth, sergeant. But I don't have anything to do with murder.'

'Shall we get on, Mr Smith?' said the DI. You are Patrick Smith born 31st August 1928. A former police officer and now a self-employed haulage contractor.'

'Yes, I should have done it years ago.'

'Seven months ago you were in the Pimlico Bar in Park Row, Leeds where you made the acquaintance of one Katherine Adrianne Robertshaw.'

'Adrienne, yes, what of it.'

'She thought you were excellent company. Quite amusing. You told her numerous stories of events that occurred whilst you were a police officer, including the sex party organised by five undergraduates and the ladies they basically picked up in the city centre, including Emily Reid. In fact, she not only told you that she was Emily Reid's aunt but you spent the night with her and had an ongoing sexual affair.'

'True.'

'Even though you were married to the then Detective Sergeant Giles daughter.'

'I'm not the first copper to have sex outside marriage.'

'I know. You also introduced Adrienne to Blaise Lincoln, Emily Reid's former fiancée. And, when she hatched her plan to seek retribution against the undergraduates, you were the one who persuaded Lincoln to join you.'

'He didn't take much persuading.'

'But let's take a step back in time to the investigation following Emily's disappearance. Tell me about Martin Beck.'

'That bastard dropped me right in the shit.'

'Was he lying? You weren't watching the confrontation between Beck and his colleagues and Kevin Sharpe concerning the lady in the blue dress?'

There was no reply.

'Well, were you having sex with the typist that he reported you were with outside the Locarno?'

There was no reply.

'I take it from your silence that you were, and as a means of exacting revenge you instigated a campaign against him to such an extent he changed his name.'

'I don't remember that.'

'Really, your friend PC Jacobs remembers well what you told him about your hatred of Beck. Does that refresh your memory. I have his statement here. He remembers it very well.'

Anger flashed in Smith's eyes. 'The bastard should've kept his mouth shut.'

'According to his statement, he also accessed the misper file in relation to Emily Reid, and R v Sharpe file relating to the murder of Emily Reid, whilst he was working nights. Subsequently, passed details of the home addresses of the five undergraduates on to you. He also loaned you an old uniform, plus a uniform helmet formerly belonging to a West Riding officer he found following a fight during a rugby match at Keighley.'

'Twat!'

DI Cartwright smiled to himself. 'Things not looking too good, are they, Mr Smith?'

After a lengthy pause. 'Well, Mr Smith, have you anything to say?'

'No comment.'

'No comment? We have Blaise Lincoln's statement and Dr Robertshaw's dying declaration that you were the one who rendered the five victims insensible before Dr Robertshaw injected them. You supplied the sack wheels, Windsor chairs and bound the victims into the chairs. This is your opportunity to give your version of events.'

'Dying declaration?'

'Yes. She said she had had enough and injected herself in the neck, as she had done with PC Cameron in London. I was present along with DS Creighton and several other officers.'

Patrick Smith took a deep breath and sighed. 'She was a nice woman. But she had a violent streak. More than any woman I had ever come across. She got the answers she wanted.'

'None of which are admissible in evidence.'

'True. But she was single-minded in pursuit of her niece's killer.'

'Who she thought was her niece's killer, even though there is no body. But she was not Emily Reid's aunt. She was her mother.'

'But?'

'Nevertheless true.'

'I didn't kill anyone, that was Adrienne. She cut their bollocks and dicks off and stitched them into their mouths. That wasn't me.'

'Dr Robertshaw admitted that. Apart from impersonating a police officer, what did you do?'

Smith laughed down his nose. 'They were dead. I used a stiletto. Pushed it through the ribs into the heart.'

'And you were disappointed when Dr Robertshaw decided to let Beck live? That's what you wanted, isn't it. To kill the man who had, as you put it, dropped you in the shit? Your entire effort in this venture was to pin the blame for Emily's death on Beck. Emily's partner that night was Boxley; the first one who was killed, no-one else. But you wanted to pin it on Beck. And when Dr Robertshaw decided to let Beck live?'

'Aye, Beck deserved it.'

'You still decided to desecrate the bodies.'

'Other than outraging public decency, there's nothing in law that makes it an offence.'

'Almost right, Mr Smith ... The Pathologist disagrees with you. The fatal blow in each of the undergraduate killings came from your stiletto. That, Mr Smith, is murder.'

Seventy

Two weeks later.

The taxi coasted to a halt overlooking Oldeney Carr House; the mesh of scaffolding standing out against the fabric of the building. 'That's some beautiful house. And some fire. The family still live there?'

'Yes, they do, sir,' the driver said as he set off down the hill. 'At least I haven't heard otherwise.'

Two minutes later, 'You'll probably find the butler, Givens, answers the door. The Countess, Lady Carol Sylverton, owns the place.'

'I'm much obliged, here this should cover it.'

Frank Senior stared at the £5 note in his hand. 'This is far too much, sir.'

Levi Steiner smiled. 'Keep it. I might need a favour someday.' He turned and took in the grandeur of the house. 'To describe this as a house makes it sound mundane,' he said to himself. At the top of the stairs, suitcase in hand, he paused before taking the seven paces to the door

The door opened before he could knock. Givens, through years of practise glanced him up and down: tailored suit, highly polished shoes and smart haircut. 'Yes sir, how may I help?

He handed Givens his card. 'My name is Levi Steiner. I have an invitation from Martin Beck.'

'Indeed you have, sir. Please come this way. May I take your valise? Mr Beck is in the Drawing Room.'

Bard put down the latest synopsis. Another, I can make you rich attempt, when Givens entered. 'Excuse me, sir. Mr Steiner.'

Bard smiled to himself and levered himself from the chair.

'This way, sir.' Givens stepped back allowing Levi Steiner to enter.

'Levi, good to see you again.' He said and walked to greet his old friend. They shook hands and hugged.

Levi Steiner took a step back. 'And you, been in the wars?'

'Cut to the back of my thigh during the fire.'

'Excuse me, Mr Steiner, would you care for some refreshment?'

'Thank you,' said Levi. 'English tea with lemon.'

'Certainly, sir. And your usual, sir?' he said to Bard.

Bard grinned and nodded.

'You still drinking nothing but coffee? You want to be careful with that stuff, Martin. It will addle your brain.'

'Eventually. Now then Levi, you've been to Bright's.'

'I have, why did you turn Finsbury down for the book?'

'They wanted to mothball it. And, once they had a contract?'

Levi Steiner nodded. 'Understood. I don't understand why they would. They're buckling.'

Bard frowned. 'Really? That's odd. But it could explain why their bid was so much higher than the next highest.'

'But Brights have Vicky and promised to get the book out for the Christmas market?'

'Yes, they did.'

'Fair enough.'

'Million-dollar question.'

'Of course I signed. My grandfather would have skinned me otherwise.'

'And?'

'Two thousand advance and 12.5% royalty.'

'That's high for a first book and a picture book at that.'

'It's exceptional. It's rarely you find an adult who can write like that, making it look as though it was a child. Remarkable.'

'There's a good reason for that; Graeme is only six years old.'

'You're joshing me. No child of six can write like that. The spelling and syntax are way beyond a six-year old's ability.'

'Not this one.'

'You're serious?'

'Very. You've seen the book?'

'Richard sent me a copy.'

'That was damn quick.'

'I was in London.'

In London and knows that Finsbury is faltering? 'Don't tell me, you're in negotiation with Finsbury.'

'Can't deny it. But it will safeguard your existing clients.'

'I was wondering about that. Thanks.' But what pressure will he try to impose if he does? 'Can you tell me how you knew?'

'An eavesdropped conversation.'

There was a brief hiatus when the refreshments were delivered. 'Thank you, Mary. We'll see to that.'

The door closed. Levi poured his tea and took his lemon. 'That brings me onto another matter,' he said. 'Exactly what are you doing here?'

'Lady Carol Sylverton is my fiancée. Then the boys will become my stepsons.'

'A Countess? You're marrying a Countess?'

'I am.'

Levi laughed and shook his head. 'You're joining the nobility, who would have thought it ... And what do you take from this?'

'Not a cent.'

'But why?'

'He's the younger twin. Martin is the Earl; the estate is his. Any income that Graeme can earn will perhaps help to restore some balance.'

'He'll do well.'

'Let's hope so. Fancy a look round?'

'12.5%.'

Bard put his fingers to his lips. 'Shh. Don't give away secrets.'

Graeme grinned and clapped both hands over his mouth.

Levi looked from one to the other his eyes narrowed. 'Have you set me up?'

'Not at all. What do you estimate your first print run will be?'

'Fifty thousand.'

'That's a lot.'

'Yes Graeme, it is. But Mr Steiner deals in dollars and not pounds and at the present exchange rate $2000 is about £800. And we don't know the price that will be charged in the United States.

'Bard?' Graeme had the broadest smile. 'Am I going to be rich?'

Standing face-to-face in Carol's suite. Bard's hands clasped loosely behind her hips. Her hands behind his neck.

'And Graeme asked that?'

'He did. And Levi paid 12.5%. His grandfather will splash this across the US TV networks. They're all commercial, nothing like the BBC. It will be a good Christmas and New Year.'

'So, Graeme is going to be wealthy?'

'I wouldn't bet against it.'

'I do love you,' she said and pulled him towards her waiting lips.

She sighed as they parted. Looked at him and smiled. 'You know I promised you children you could claim as your own?'

'Of course,' he paused as she broke into a broad smile. 'You are?' she nodded. 'When?'

'Seven months.'

Seventy-One

Parking in York is never easy and today was no exception. The sun was blazing. It was 09:50 when we parked. Lucy, carrying Claire, and I joined the short queue entering the Register Office Marriage Room for the wedding between Martin Beck and Lady Carol Frances Elizabeth Sylverton. Inside it was almost full.

'Will there be room?'

'I hope so,' I replied. 'We do have an invite. We can squeeze in at the back.'

I handed the card to Givens. 'Ah, Mr and Mrs Blake, thank you.' He turned and handed the card to Christopher.

He glanced at the card and smiled. 'Mr and Mrs Blake, this way please.'

'But,' said Lucy as we walked passed the rear seats.

Two rows from the front Christipher stopped and ushered us into the remaining empty seats. He smiled, handed me the card and returned to the door.

I pointed at the occupants of the front row from right to left as we sat and whispered. 'Duke, Duchess, Duke, Duchess and their four daughters.'

Alicia looked over her right shoulder. 'Brian,' she said and smiled. 'And this must be your wife, Lucy and daughter, Claire.' The four girls turned in their seats smiled and waved at Claire who waved back.

'Yes, it is.'

'Lucy, this is ...'

'Alicia and Bertie,' she interjected.

Bertie shuffled round in his seat. 'Both hands free now, Brian,' he said displaying his bandage-free hands and held his right hand out. 'I can shake hands.' I took his hand. 'Jessica is still talking about your fairy magic.' He laughed. 'Wants to know why I can't do it. You've got some explaining to do. You're going to the house?'

I grimaced. 'Yes, we are.'

The registrar walked to the centre of the room.

'In that case we can continue at Oldeney.'

Carol's parents turned inwards. 'Mr and Mrs Blake, we will see you at the House.'

I grimaced. 'Yes, your Grace, Duchess.'

He nodded and turned to the front as a wheelchair containing Martin propelled by Graeme emerged from the opposite side of the aisle.

Claire pointed, waved and gurgled. They waved back.

'We've seen your racing cars,' said an excited Martin in a stage whisper that had those nearby laughing.

'They're exciting,' said Graeme.

'Yes, I know,' I put my finger to my lips as a smiling Lady Carol Frances Elizabeth Sylverton, accompanied by Martin Graeme Beck sauntered passed.

THE END

Bibliography

✶ [1] Danger in Deep Space by Casey Rockwell (1953)

*[2] The Offences Against the Persons Act 1861 Section 56

Child-stealing.

Whosoever shall unlawfully, either by Force or Fraud, lead or take away, or decoy or entice away or detain, any Child under the Age of Fourteen Years, with Intent to deprive any Parent, Guardian, or other Person, having the lawful Care or Charge of such Child or the Possession of such Child, or with Intent to steal any Article upon or about the Person of such Child, to whomsoever such Article may belong, and whosoever shall, with any such Intent, receive or harbour any such Child, knowing the same to have been, by Force or Fraud, led, taken, decoyed, enticed away, or detained as in this Section before mentioned, shall be guilty of Felony, and being convicted thereof shall be liable, at the Discretion of the Court, to be kept in Penal Servitude for any Term not exceeding Seven Years and not less than Three Years,—or to be imprisoned for any Term not exceeding Two Years, with or without Hard Labour, and, if a Male under the Age of Sixteen Years, with or without Whipping: Provided that no Person who shall have claimed any Bight to the Possession of such Child, or shall be the Mother or shall have claimed to be the Father of an illegitimate Child, shall be liable to be prosecuted by virtue hereof on account of the getting Possession of such Child, or taking such Child out of the Possession of any Person having the lawful Charge thereof.

Don't miss out!

Visit the website below and you can sign up to receive emails whenever Jon Mason publishes a new book. There's no charge and no obligation.

https://books2read.com/r/B-A-ZRTW-IBNID

BOOKS 2 READ

Connecting independent readers to independent writers.

Also by Jon Mason

Blake Detective Series
Dance With the Devil
The Blooding of Brian Blake
Nemesis
Counting The Dead
Death in The Slushpile

Watch for more at www.jonmasonbooks.com.

About the Author

JON was born into post WW2 Yorkshire in England. His brother Stuart was born in 1938. His father, demobbed from the RAF where he had been a Dispatch Rider, returned to the tailoring industry. His mother had spent the war years x-raying wheels for battle tanks.

They lived in a small, inner two-bedroomed terrace house. There was no damp-proof course, double glazing, central heating or hot water on tap. The tin bath hung from a nail under the stairs and the lavatory was across the back yard..

Leaving school in 1962 he joined the West Riding Constabulary as a Cadet and as a Constable in 1965. His initial training carried out at No3 District Police Training Centre, Pannal Ash, Harrogate, in the then North Riding of Yorkshire.

Over the next three decades he gained experience across much of what the police service has to offer. 1965-70 on uniform beat patrol. From 1970-75 in the Road Traffic Division as an advanced driver and also where he was firearms trained. From 1975-77 Force Control where he learned his radio and computer skills before being promoted to the Western Area Control Room in January of 1977, Twelve months later he was seconded to the fledgling Computer

Development Unit working with Ferranti International in the development of Stage 4 of a resource handling and incident recording system known as Command and Control (Not big Brother) and the setting up of the Communications Training Wing at the West Yorkshire Police training school. December 1983 saw him transferred to an inner city sub-division where he spent the last 10 years of his service as uniform patrol sergeant where he also worked closely with the Air Support Unit, Custody Officer and the last four years as the Station Sergeant.

In May of 1967 Jon and his fiancee married. A marriage which so far has lasted for over 56 years. They had two children, tragically Andrew, the elder, died of a heart attack in January 2018 - he was 48. Their daughter is still going strong.

Prior to retirement Jon qualified as a fitness instructor and subsequently head-hunted to work in a new community based cardiac rehab programme where he had the opportunity to study cardiology at Leeds University Medical School and exercise physiology at Carnegie. He also studied bio-mechanics.

All that knowledge and experience Jon brings to his books.

Read more at www.jonmasonbooks.com.

www.ingramcontent.com/pod-product-compliance
Ingram Content Group UK Ltd.
Pitfield, Milton Keynes, MK11 3LW, UK
UKHW040854171025
464041UK00001B/4

9 781916 757110